GOING FAST

Also by Elaine McCluskey

The Watermelon Social

Elaine McCluskey

GOING FAST
a novel

GOOSE LANE EDITIONS

Edited by Bethany Gibson.
Cover illustrations: boxers copyright © 2008 www.ronandjoe.com;
boxing glove copyright © 2008 Lawrence Manning/Corbis.
Cover and interior page design by Julie Scriver.
Printed in Canada on 100% PCW paper.
10 9 8 7 6 5 4 3 2 1

Library and Archives Canada Cataloguing in Publication

McCluskey, Elaine, 1955-
Going fast / Elaine McCluskey.

ISBN 978-0-86492-525-1

I. Title.
PS8625.C59G63 2009   C813'.6   C2008-907190-5

In the writing of this novel, the author recognizes the support of the Canada Council
for the Arts and the Nova Scotia Department of Tourism, Culture, and Heritage.

Goose Lane Editions acknowledges the financial support of the Canada Council for
the Arts, the Government of Canada through the Book Publishing Industry
Development Program (BPIDP), and the New Brunswick Department of Wellness,
Culture, and Sport for its publishing activities.

Goose Lane Editions
Suite 330, 500 Beaverbrook Court
Fredericton, New Brunswick
CANADA E3B 5X4
www.gooselane.com

To Tom, for his knowledge and humour

Johnny LeBlanc climbed two flights of creaking stairs. He leaned into a door. Tootsy's Gym had one yawning room with a sixteen-by-sixteen ring, a water cooler, and the disembodied air of a monastery or a fat farm.

Johnny ambled across the worn hardwood floor, a kit bag in his hand. An old-timer in a Legion blazer was leaning on the discoloured ring ropes, taking bets on a phantom fight, hair slicked, shoes buffed, waiting for a parade to form. CHAMP OR CHUMP? a poster over his shoulder asked and then replied with conviction: THE DIFFERENCE IS U.

"How are things, Barney?" Johnny asked, voice lilting.

"Superb."

Sun streamed through Tootsy's bare windowpanes, casting crosses on the scuffed floor. The air was still except for the short puffs of wind that marked each blow to a stained heavy bag — *pah pah pah* — and the *rat-a-tat-tat* of the shuddering speed bag. A fighter, a kid who looked about twelve, was skipping a leather rope, spraying sweat through the air like a Gardena Sprinkler. His name was Ricky. He lived in a housing project the colour of Love Hearts, a bunker of dope and dysfunction, and he lied about his age.

Johnny nodded at Ricky and settled into a metal chair. Barney turned his head expectantly as though he had heard someone call his name and then headed for the door without speaking. The back of his neck was criss-crossed, Johnny noted, like the imprinted lines on a supermarket turkey freed from a plastic net. He smelled of cologne. Johnny sniffled, wondering when Ownie would arrive. His stitches had dissolved, he noticed in a mirror, leaving a light scar that gave him an edginess, a touch of danger that he liked. The mark — on his right cheekbone — was shaped like a boomerang.

Tootsy's smelled musty, he decided, as though it was shaking off dust and depression. Mousetraps sat on the floor below laminated newspaper clippings tacked to the wall and curling around the edges. A fluorescent light dangled from two rusty chains like an empty trapeze. Out back, Tootsy's had a shower, ten rusty lockers, and more inspirational posters.

THE FIGHTER'S EQUATION

DISCIPLINE + DETERMINATION + DESIRE = A CHAMP

Tootsy's was in downtown Dartmouth, which the wise guys called Darkness. Johnny lived a couple of kilometres away in the north end in a cheap apartment over Video Madness, a store that specialized in X-rated movies and Martin Sheen epics. Open twenty-four hours a day, Madness also offered well-priced milk, Lotto tickets, and an excuse to leave home at midnight.

Johnny stole another look at himself in a floor-length mirror and smiled.

Last week, he had collected four stitches and two hundred bucks for going six rounds in a New Brunswick rink that smelled of stale beer and soggy plywood. It was the usual crowd: stews, old-timers, and rows of Annie Oakleys. September 20, 1992 — he had recorded the date in his head. A plastered bar owner sat ringside, his face twisted into a grotesque smile, teeth exposed, straining so hard that sweat rolled down his fleshy face. Why, Johnny wondered, would a man with dough look so lame?

It had been Johnny's first fight in eight months, and he'd busted a gut to make 145, running six miles a day in a Glad jogging suit, and then climbing into a sauna. Ownie, his trainer, had him cut down to birdfeed in the final weeks, which had been cruel but necessary.

"C'mon." A stocky man named Louie Fader appeared before him. "Let's work the ball 'til Ownie gets here. Make the most of our time."

"Awww." Johnny shrugged ambivalence and then struggled to his feet. Slowly, he removed his red jacket, which had the name of a brewery on the chest and *LeBlanc* on the sleeve. Johnny was handsome, born with the kind of looks that established the psyches of working-class stiffs, who became angry wife-beaters or genial charmers who fumbled for your name. Johnny was smooth.

"They asked me to show up at one of their events as a celebrity and I told them I'd need some grease," explained Johnny, pointing to the jacket. "They said there was nothing in the pot, but they gave me this. I figure it's worth a C-note."

"At least," Louie allowed. "It looks waterproof."

"It's good P.R. too." Johnny nodded. "It could lead to an opportunity down the road. Them brewery reps, they make serious dough, drive company wheels, don't take too many shots to the head."

They both laughed.

Thump. Johnny caught the medicine ball and threw it back. Johnny wondered why he was training so soon after his fight. He should be taking it easy, he decided, enjoying some downtime. On the wall, he noticed a Caesar's Palace poster with head shots of Leonard and Hagler, the personification of good and evil. The poster listed the undercards like an eye chart, the letters shrinking along with the purse.

Thump. Louie returned the ball with force.

Unlike Johnny, who was 12-4-3, Louie had never had a

fight. Since he'd started coming to Tootsy's three months ago, he had collected every fight book and video he could find: *Great Grudge Matches. Tyson's Best. One-Punch Knockouts.* With an endearing earnestness, he called himself a student of the game. "He's got the time and money," Johnny had explained to Ownie. "He's a fireman."

A former bodybuilder, Louie looked determined in his tie-dye sweats and a Pit Bull Gym singlet he'd purchased from Stripped and Ripped, which also sold leather do-rags, XXX Amino Liver Extract, and huge jars of a mystifying substance called Protein Plus, thirty-four ounces for $29.95. Louie swore he was off the gorilla juice since Kevin, a powerlifting buddy, had gone to London, Ontario, for a seven-hour heart transplant that ended with him having a donor heart grafted to his ravaged body and his breastbone secured with steel wire.

Louie caught the fifteen-pound cowhide sphere as though it were a beach ball. About five-six, he was runner-up in Mister Nova Scotia 1991 Short Class, an honour he was quick to mention to the ladies. Louie's pad was filled with tapes from his bodybuilding career, including one in which he stormed off the stage, waving his hand dismissively at the judges as though he had been robbed.

"You know my brother, Marcel?" asked Johnny, already bored with the ball.

Louie nodded. He'd met Marcel, one of those guys who lived in the margins of life with hot plates and shopping carts and flammable winter jackets.

"I saw him yesterday outside the liquor store and he says to me, 'Hey, Johnny, I'm a counsellor now.' And I said, 'Okay, sounds cool,' since he's been on the disability for about ten years. 'Who are you counselling?'"

Louie returned the ball with too much force.

"And he said, 'People who have lost their pets.' It turns out he's a grief counsellor at the animal shelter, which sounds all right." Johnny nodded his head in approval, suggesting, it seemed, that Marcel's new vocation was a sign of good things to come.

"What's that involve?" blinked Louie, who appeared unsettled by the mention of Marcel, who reminded him of people and circumstances he would rather forget. Louie had protruding eyes that he blinked constantly and brows that peaked in an inverted V, giving his face a quizzical look.

"He does most of his work by phone at the shelter. But sometimes he'll go with people if they are having a funeral and they need someone to fill up the place. He said they had a dandy send-off for a Maine coon cat named Jackie. There wasn't a dry eye in the room. It's working out good for him."

"Right on."

Printed signs laid out Tootsy's rules in inch-high letters: DON'T SPIT ON THE FLOOR. PAY YOUR DUES EVERY FRIDAY. FILL WATER BOTTLES BEFORE LEAVING. A log sheet had been posted to record roadwork and sparring minutes. The handwritten entries were smeared by sweat.

To keep the business viable, Tootsy, a taxi driver who was rarely at the gym, had started admitting civilians: cross-trainers, women, ninety-pound weaklings plotting revenge. With the fight game at a low, it was hard for the absentee owner to make ends meet.

"Hey, Ownie." Johnny spotted the trainer easing through the door in a heavy sweater, pockets filled with unknown objects. The old man lifted his head, and Johnny, smelling work, wished that he had stayed home.

"What?"

"I was talking to Dylan Atwood."

"Yeah?"

"He was up in Moncton for my fight the other night."

"I hope he paid for his ticket this time," snapped Ownie. "Cheap bastard."

"He says I should've taken the fight to Cormier, that I wasn't aggressive enough."

"Yeaaah." Ownie zipped open his kit bag. "Spectators don't get hit much."

Ownie had a slow, droll way of talking, a way of taking something serious and giving it a jab into the absurd. Sometimes, he telegraphed his intent with a shift in tone; other times he caught people cold. It reminded Johnny of an artist he'd seen at the mall. The guy started off drawing something that Johnny thought was a clown, and then, at the last minute, he added a line and Johnny found himself looking at a bull elephant, which made him laugh.

Ownie pulled out a piece of wood with padding attached. "I've been in this business fifty years, and no one's had the sense to come up with a decent taping device." He paused, admiring his apparatus. "Of course, most guys I know are brain-damaged.

2

Ownie opened his morning newspaper, the *Standard*. He spread it flat on his dining room table, ignoring news on the Charlottetown Accord, and flipping to the obituaries. Retired, he reminded himself, he had time for this.

Ownie picked up his pen at the sight of a name that he liked: Orestes MacNeil, 91. Orestes was uncommon, he decided, writing it down in a spiral notebook. Last week, among the Johns and Peters, he had spotted a Silvanus and a Holgar, both as rare as hen's teeth. The old names, disappearing from the local landscape like train tracks and lighthouses, were for his daughter, Millie, a schoolteacher who collected curiosities. Millie, who had the good luck to resemble her mother, had her own odd ways that neither he nor Hildred truly understood.

Corrilda, he noted. Kelton.

Ownie thought about the Moncton fight and wondered whether there would be talk of a rematch with Hansel Sparks, Johnny's nemesis. Sparks could be trouble, Ownie acknowledged — more trouble than Johnny, a walking smorgasbord, could handle at this point. The day after the fight, Ownie had received a call from a sports reporter at the *Standard,* a guy named Scott, who had been in Moncton.

"What kind of a future do you see for LeBlanc?" asked the reporter, who seemed, to Ownie, unsure of himself.

"Very bright," lied Ownie. "He's only twenty-two, and he's talented."

The reporter then asked Ownie if he could foresee resurgence in the sport. Ownie had only a vague idea of what the reporter was after, but he gave his standard response.

"Anything is possible," said Ownie. "I've seen the highs and I've seen the lows."

The sport, which once had packed the Metro Centre with nine thousand fans, which once had a Maritime circuit that included Charlottetown, Sydney, New Glasgow, and Moncton, was pulling in crowds of five hundred or less. Boxing needed a draw, it seemed, a hometown favourite to bring in the hockey fans, the college students, the vainglorious politicians wanting to be seen, the people who might never have followed boxing. That was the reporter's angle.

LeBlanc was a decent kid, Ownie believed, just lazy and content to take life's easy path.

Louie, who, like most firemen, had time to burn, had driven Ownie and Johnny back from Moncton three days ago. It had been raining. Halfway home, they had driven by an illuminated sign — PREPARE TO MEET YOUR SAVIOUR — erected in front of a wanton farmhouse where nobody farmed. At the end of a muddy driveway, the farm had a Dodge pickup, scrub firs, and an unshakeable feeling of doom. Parts of the province seemed so senseless, Ownie noted, houses plopped along the highway like boulders left from the ice age, biodegradable lives slowly breaking down. There were no stores, no discernible jobs, nothing to slow the decay, just two lanes of asphalt, some all-terrain tracks, and a twelve-dollar bus ride to town.

"Can you imagine living out here?" asked Johnny, reading Ownie's thoughts.

"Not really," conceded the trainer.

"I'd rather be in the cooler. At least in the cooler, you got company and cable." Louie kept his eyes on the rain-slicked road as Johnny added quickly, "Not that I ever been in myself."

Ownie returned to the obituaries, deliberately putting Johnny and Hansel Sparks out of his mind. Years ago, when the game was hot and the town was full of rough tough guys who'd been overseas, when promoters would jam the Armouries with yokels reeking of aftershave and El Producto cigars, Ownie had trained Sparks's uncle Thirsty, who was a bit of a clown but far more likeable than Hansel.

Audley, he wrote down, as a good one caught his eye. Vina.

Millie's kitchen was filled with wooden chairs, all painted in brilliant colours that would have made Thirsty, who loved anything comical, grin. She'd found the chairs, then beige and white, in a fisherman's shed. On her kitchen floor, she had a hand-hooked wool rug with rabbits soaking laundry in a washtub. The rabbits were wearing dresses.

One day, to help with Millie's hobby, Ownie had picked up a St. John's, Newfoundland, paper filled with rambling grey stories and obituaries for dearly departeds named Gonzo, Aloysius, and Horatio. The name Horatio reminded him of a strange summer's night when he and Hildred had driven to the Valley for apples.

On the outskirts of a town, a mélange of simple homes and sea captains' mansions, they saw cars parked by a field and people traipsing over tangles of clover, armed with binoculars. Ownie and Hildred joined the crowd at the edge of the field, which overlooked the bay. All around them, people waited, oddly calm, unfettered by time or need. A baby whimpered. Two chubby girls kept saying "ain't." As the sun dropped, a fisherman named Horatio filled the silence by announcing in a reverential tone: "He is following the herring right now. He can stay underwater for forty-five minutes."

Men nodded and a boy nonsensically asked, "Did the whale

eat all the raccoons?" Then it happened. A humpback whale, thirty tons of dorsal fins and flippers, leapt into the air, spinning, lobtailing, waving.

"Ahhh, there he is." Fingers poked the air and binoculars dropped. The whale vanished and then surfaced, an arc of black and white, thirty metres ahead, and then he was gone, like the Loch Ness monster or a penny dropped in a well.

Ownie thought about that whale, about how he had stilled an entire town, erasing urgency with his God-given magnificence. He thought, both then and later, about the power that some creatures, larger and more mystical than others, had to turn people's lives.

Ownie jotted down today's disappearing names, along with the hometowns of their owners: Azade, Volney. Unlike the ghouls who attacked the notices like vultures, sucking the bones for sorrow, Ownie got no satisfaction from the daily toll.

Clyke, Henry James, 88, born in Weymouth Falls. Ownie laid down his pen for a moment's remembrance. A member of First Light Baptist Church, Henry is survived by his loving wife, Sophie, seven sons, and three daughters.

"Hildred," he called to the kitchen. "Hildred."

"What?" she shouted back.

"Bobcat's gone."

By the time that Ownie met Bobcat Clyke back in the 1950s, he was a tired old fighter who sauntered into the ring like a mangy bear. He had a taste for the hooch so he ran hot and cold. Bobcat was married to a fire plug just over four feet tall, a despot with a kewpie-doll face and the iron will of a claims adjuster. The Little General, they called her. Any time a promoter wanted Bobcat, they had to go through her. "There were days," moaned Bobcat, a mere foot soldier in the General's army, "that I'd be down in the cellar with a keg and the devil and she'd be upstairs with the Lord and I'd know to stay put."

Once, Ownie recalled, Harry Fitzgerald was putting on a fight in Glace Bay with Bobcat as his headliner. Before the fight, Fitzgerald went looking for Bobcat but found only the Little General. "Bobcat is not coming out," she announced. "Bobcat does what I tell him and he is not going to fight."

Fitzgerald was screwed because this was Cape Breton and a pissed-off crowd could tire-iron him, so he pleaded, "What would it take to get the Bobcat out?"

"Another fifty bucks," replied the General, and that was that. Bobcat, Ownie realized, was just like him: a sucker for a pretty face, which, in the long run, wasn't so bad. "Okay, Bobcat," ordered the Little General, who had the biggest eyes Ownie had ever seen. "Get in that ring!"

Bobcat climbed in, Ownie recalled, barely moving. In the third round, he went down like the *Lusitania*. The ref — it was Gil Doucette, and he only had one eye — knew there'd be a riot if the fight ended early, so he started counting slowly. Gil stopped at eight and pleaded under his breath, "Come on, Bobcat, *please* get up."

The crowd, mostly miners and steelworkers, was ready to rip apart both Gil and Fitzgerald if they didn't get more. Another eight. "Get up, Bobcat," Gil begged, fearing for his good eye. "Pleeease, I know you can do it." On the third eight, Bobcat growled, "What wrong with you, man, you got no schoolin'? That's your third eight."

Thinking about Bobcat and the Little General made Ownie sad, and he wondered if the best had passed, if he was doomed, despite his skill, to spend his days reliving history, enjoying the glory days with dead men. Was this it?

Ownie was jolted out of his thoughts.

Hildred had appeared in the dining room, wearing an

apron over a cotton turtleneck decorated with snowflakes. On the apron, in silver letters, were the words *Sweet Dreams*, the name of the cake-decorating business that she ran from their kitchen.

"Did you use one of my bowls for the dog?" she demanded.

"Naaahhh." Ownie was indignant. "Don't be so foolish."

"If the health department ever found out..." Hildred snapped.

"G'won."

Hildred couldn't stand to see him relaxing, Ownie decided, but at least she still was pretty. There was something to be said for that. He thought about poor Tootsy's wife, who had a big rubber belly that hung down to her knees. She wore Tootsy's old T-shirts and sweatpants stained with grease, but she had a kind nature, according to Tootsy. Last year, he had told Ownie with more than a touch of pride, she rescued a baby robin and nursed it back to health, feeding it with an eye-dropper.

Ownie heard Hildred shout something, which he ignored. It was no wonder, he decided, that after he'd retired from the dockyard he'd returned to the gym full-time. Undisturbed, he could pass his time at Tootsy's, helping with a few up-and-comers and dreaming, as only an old man could, of having one real fighter.

Being a top trainer without a *real* fighter was like being a jockey without a mount. How could he ever prove, Ownie pondered, in the time he had left, how great he really was?

Getting on his feet, Ownie opened the door to the backyard and muttered, "C'mon in. I'm the only one around here who looks after you," as a dog scampered in. Ownie patted the comely mongrel with a copper coat and a wounded heart worn on one sleeve. Arguello, Ownie had named the dog, after the handsome Nicaraguan with the shattering right and three world titles, a five-ten feather with class. Like Alexis, who'd been born into poverty and war, the dog had had a rough start in life, beaten and abandoned on the side of a road.

Before long, Ownie realized that the dog was, in fact, female, but he kept the name because it was foreign and none of the morons he associated with would know the difference. Jumpy, with the bad nerves of a hard beginning, Arguello had chewed up Ownie's false teeth when he left them on a table. Ownie fixed the teeth with Krazy Glue but, like most things in life broken or bruised by carelessness, they never felt quite right.

Arguello hid under a chair as Ownie stared at one of Hildred's knick-knacks, a leggy ballerina with a blonde chignon. The ballerina smiled an empathetic smile as though she'd known him when the game was different, when Halifax was pumped up from the war, full of troopships and Russian brown squirrel stoles, crazy with the hope that life could start again. Back when Ownie had A Fighter with a capital *A*, a prince named Tommy Coogan.

Louie, the mole, had informed him that Johnny wasn't doing his roadwork as ordered. "Keep the reports coming," Ownie urged the fireman. "I'll like you better that way." LeBlanc's career was going nowhere, Ownie believed, and guys like Louie were nothing but tourists, helping Tootsy keep the gym lights on.

Maybe you get *that* kind of chance only once, in that extra-ordinary time and place, Ownie thought. Maybe, that's *it*.

Arguello whimpered as the phone rang, and Hildred shouted, louder this time: "It's for you. Some man sounding businesslike."

Ownie patted the dog's back as he shuffled to the kitchen. "It's all right," he assured her, pleased that he had kept the name Arguello, a classy name that sounded as strong and fearless as the photogenic champ, a warrior who had KO'd Boom Boom Mancini in the fourteenth round. "It's all right."

3

Sports had five phones and six computer terminals in the back of the *Standard*'s newsroom, which sprawled open and endless like a gymnasium. The newsroom was on the second floor of a nondescript building in an industrial park.

Scott MacDonald was on the phone conducting an interview, one ear plugged to block out the invading noise. Scott, who had worked at the *Standard* for fifteen years, was back reporting after a decade on the desk. Three weeks earlier, he had driven to Moncton for the four-fight Maritime Extravaganza, his first road trip in years, prompted by the presence of one local, Johnny LeBlanc.

Scott liked LeBlanc, who didn't look like a punk, a hood, or a two-bit pimp. At five-nine, Scott decided, Johnny could pass for a junior hockey player, intact, with only the rumour of scar tissue, only a sniff of desperation. When Johnny walked into a bar, he carried himself erect like a ballroom dancer in pressed jeans and a crisp T-shirt. He greeted the doorman, shook hands with the barkeep, and nodded charitably to patrons who had no idea who he was.

Johnny was smaller than Scott, who in his day had been a sprint kayak paddler. Not just any paddler, he liked to remind himself, but a good one: a 185-pound paddling machine, a cardiovascular genius with a resting pulse rate of thirty-eight.

It was noon, and Smithers, the hockey reporter, was jogging on the spot near Scott's desk, refusing to stop despite glares in his direction. Smithers then announced, as though anyone believed him, that his new and much-younger girlfriend was a dancer.

"A table dancer?" Warshick, the sports agate editor, took the bait.

"Postmodern, you idiot, like that dude, Mark Morris. They have a studio, performance events, *muscle control!*" Leering, Smithers lapped the sports desk, straining the tights he had squeezed into for his lunchtime jog. "It's called mixed media, and it's very cutting edge."

A phone rang, and Warshick, who was fat, sloppy, and pleased about it, answered.

With Warshick occupied, Smithers trotted by an older man hunkered over an Underwood typewriter. Buzz Bailey had heart palpitations, high blood pressure, and diverticulitis, but he kept his troubles under his hat. Buzz, who had been given the title senior sports columnist, wrote about goalies and shortstops from the 1940s, nonentities called Curly, Muckle, and Gee Gee. Talking to Buzz about sports was like visiting the twilight zone, Scott thought, a parallel universe of postwar euphoria and yesterday's youth, icons who could never be matched.

"Don't let her sell you any lessons," Buzz barked at Smithers.

"What?" Smithers stopped mid-*pointe*, cheeks ripe.

"You heard me. Don't let her sell you any lessons." Buzz adjusted a straw hat topped with a green fairway. "I had a friend in Red Deer who started going out with a dancer. She sold him four hundred dollars' worth of lessons at Arthur Murray, and he never learned a step."

"That's different," said Smithers, who looked like a pornographic cherub, round and lascivious. "This is very avant-garde."

Buzz was unmoved, knowing that Smithers's avant-garde

world revolved around hockey and cartoons. When he wasn't chasing underage hockey groupies or bar waitresses, he refereed hockey games and collected pucks from the OHL, NHL, AHL, CHL, IHL, along with arcane leagues from glacial towns. The pucks were indexed and mounted on his bedroom wall. He still lived at home.

"That's what my friend said." Buzz was back in the debate. "The poor sap took out a three-hundred-dollar loan — two hundred for the Big Apple, an extra C for the Turkey Trot. That's all those dancers are after, some big stiff to sell their lessons to." As Smithers grumbled, Buzz tapped his straw hat and lobbed a parting shot. "He couldn't Turkey Trot worth spit."

Smithers peeled off his jacket, revealing a T-shirt that the dancer had sold him: CULTURAL CARNIVORE printed over an image of four Japanese hanging from ropes, upside down, like tuna. Outside, a truck backfired and Buzz jumped.

On the advice of a productivity consultant, everything in the newsroom, from phones to filing cabinets, had been dipped in green. Gem Newspapers had moved the *Standard* from its original location in downtown Halifax near the courts, cops, and lawmakers to an industrial mall in Dartmouth, kilometres from anything that smelled like news. It was easier, the new owner explained, for the trucks that left at 1 a.m. for Port Mouton or Necum Teuch bearing papers stuffed with flyers. And the rent was cheap. The industrial park was filled with warehouses and banished workers who toiled without the comfort of chip wagons, without architecture or trees, leaving the sterile grid on weekends to driver-ed cars and biker hit men.

Smithers touched his leg. To protest Sports' location at the back of the newsroom, he had taken to wearing a pedometer, which he used to track his daily mileage to the lunchroom and the can. "At this rate, Buzz will need a hip replacement by

Christmas," he liked to say. Scott frowned. He could barely hear his interview over Smithers and the clatter of trucks.

"You know, Doughboy," Buzz growled at Smithers, "ever since you took that puck to the head . . ." One year earlier, Smithers had been hit by a puck he had dropped for a faceoff, a freak accident that shattered two teeth and left him with caps, which made him sound like he had ice cubes in his mouth.

Hating the sight of the hockey reporter in his tights, Scott kept his head down, refusing to acknowledge Smithers' indignant response to Buzz. Sometimes, Scott envied people like Smithers, who had never really competed, people who believed that a brisk walk was as good as a run, people who could dabble in tennis or golf, happy to let their bodies move through unobstructed, never needing the pain. People who had never been to the emptiest, cruellest point of existence, knowing through hurt and triumph that there is no such place as a comfort zone.

Abruptly abandoning Buzz and their argument over dance lessons, Smithers shouted at Scott, "Hey MacDonald, are you expecting some friends from church?"

"Huhhh?" Scott finished his phone call.

"There!" Smithers gestured across the newsroom. Scott lifted his head.

At a table in front of the elevator door, Ownie was signing the visitors' book with his left hand, forming each letter slowly, earnestly, like a man whose signature still meant something. Scott studied the trainer, confused, like the time he had seen his dentist in a bar and could not, for the life of him, place the genial stranger outside the whirl of drills.

It's him, he decided, Ownie Flanagan, but why is he here? And why does he look so small? Maybe it's the tweed jacket he's wearing, Scott reasoned, or the fact that here, outside Tootsy's, in this green terrarium of flickering lights and murky people, he's no longer in charge. Or maybe it's an optical illusion, like water running uphill or two lines joined in an upside-down T. Although they're the same length, the vertical seems longer. Maybe it's something like that, Scott reasoned, an illusion created by the giant to Ownie's left.

Tall, dark, and overshadowing, the giant was wearing a no-name grey sweatsuit filled with boulders. Stretched across his back, which flared like muscle-bound wings, was his calling card: TURMOIL DAVIES, HEAVYWEIGHT.

The heavyweight kept his hands folded like a coiled chain while Ownie finished signing in. As they started to move, light-footed as cats on crusty snow, Scott was again struck by the disparity in their size. The giant could have picked up Ownie, tucked him under one arm, and carried him. Only their walks were alike: straight, upright, stretching for the beam of success. The giant was ramrod, unlike many tall men who went through life slouched down and apologetic, straining for the dialogue of man. Ownie had the perpendicular gait of the Short Man, the heliotrope reaching for the sun.

"Must be Sports," someone mumbled as the pair passed. Across the room, Scott saw Garth MacKenzie, the paper's managing editor, staring as though he was not sure what he was seeing.

"This is Turmoil Davies, a heavyweight prospect." Ownie introduced the giant to Scott. "We brought the story to you first because we figure he's going places."

Scott took a reflex step back as the giant approached, his size and energy sucking up the space around him. Looking up, Scott felt eclipsed, shaken, as though the visitor had single-handedly shifted the bell curve of men so that he, Scott MacDonald, was in with the middling masses. Scott extended a hand, which the giant absorbed. "Pleased to meet you," Scott offered.

The reporter looked for something to disqualify the giant

from the curve: a freak-like flaw or hints of an unnatural aid, like the fertility drugs that led to outbreaks of quadruplets. A buried tumour, a gargantuan head, the mythical tail of a dragon. Like a basketball trainer in a marsh of slam-dunking storks, Scott checked for Marfan's syndrome: spidery fingers, a deformed chest, weak double-joints, and a flawed heart that would fail by fifty. At a loss, he asked, "Is Turmoil your ring name?"

"Iss the name mah mooma give me." The voice was surprisingly high and melodious. "When ah was born, there was much trouble in the eye-lands. She say 'Ah will call you Turmoil and there will come a day when ebbyt'ing will be quiet but you.'"

Scott had never seen a tall man so solid and perfectly proportioned. Turmoil Davies had bowling-ball biceps, a GI Joe waist, and hands as wide as family Bibles. As Scott fumbled his pen, he surreptitiously sniffed the air for steroids, for the constipated bulk and angry skin of a juicer. No, the giant was smooth and symmetrical.

"Ahhh." Scott nodded like it made sense. It had to be natural and inherited, he decided. Louis Cyr, the famed strongman, had lifted five hundred pounds with one finger. Writers said his mother could climb a barn ladder with a one-hundred-pound sack on each shoulder. It had to be something like that.

The giant, Ownie explained, was from Trinidad and had heard about Halifax at a pre-Olympic tourney. "They made it sound like a good place to live." Ownie was going to train him. "This got sprung on me pretty sudden." A group of businessmen had drawn up a two-year contract and, in return for exclusive services, Champion Management would provide an apartment and living expenses.

"He's six-foot-five and weighs two-forty," boasted Ownie. "And he's fast as a cheetah. He can press three-sixty and run six miles in twenty-nine minutes. He's got power and speed. It's worth twenty bucks just to watch him walk in the ring."

As Turmoil nodded, his face radiated from a hidden spotlight while everyone else looked algae green, shot without the fluorescent filter. Scott felt excited about the story, sensing that Turmoil Davies was, indeed, different.

"He's Ben Johnson, Magic Johnson, and Jackie Chan all rolled into one," said Ownie, the newsroom surprisingly still. "This man is a natural wonder; you don't get to see this type of athlete very often. Take a very good look."

In his frugal kitchen, Scott MacDonald buried the remains of a frozen dinner and tried not to think about work. He tried not to dwell on the giant who had invaded his psyche and would, it seemed, be impossible to ignore.

Scott flipped through the manual of the Sony CD player he had just bought. He liked the machine. Easy to operate, it held six discs at a time. It was only the second stereo he had owned. He hadn't bought his first until he was twenty-five. He was thirty before he had attended a rock concert, thirty-five before he'd bought an album by the Stones. Scott MacDonald may have been the only man his age who had never played air guitar or mouthed the words to "I'm Eighteen."

At forty-two, he was a baby boomer. A member of the rock 'n' roll generation.

Woodstock.

Moody Blues.

Procol Harum.

Bill Clinton hunkered over a sax on *Arsenio Hall*, wearing Blues Brothers shades like a 1960s service badge, reaching out to millions of balding, pot-bellied flower· children who had almost forgotten he was theirs.

Power to the people, Mr. President.

Rock on.

It all left Scott unmoved, as distant as the Fug.

Had the 1960s really touched down in Hope, Arkansas, with enough force to change the course of America, but missed

Dartmouth, Nova Scotia? Or had Scott MacDonald, the Kayak King, been out for a paddle?

Earlier that day, before Turmoil Davies had affected his equilibrium, Scott had bought Eric Clapton's *Unplugged* and then picked up a *Rolling Stone* with the icon on the cover. Inside, Clapton talked about "Layla," heroin, booze, and the death of his four-year-old son. To Scott, it was like reading about Scott and Zelda Fitzgerald or watching Lena Wertmüller movies. If Clapton was the Guitar God, who were his disciples? What was his spiritual legacy?

The only old song implanted in Scott's brain was one that his former training partner, Taylor, used to sing about a guy named Patches. No, there was another one about Timothy and cannibals, and Taylor liked it because his name was Tim. Tim Taylor was a thick, power-driven beast who thundered down the lake in his canoe like he was caught in the path of a forest fire, reaching, driving, lurching with every stroke, fighting for his life. He wore an Afro that bobbed like an impermeable mass of cotton candy, never melting in the rain. A demented road warrior made from salvaged parts, he had teeth divided by a thumb-sized space, one finger bent at forty-five degrees, one ear mangled by a dog.

Scott had a picture of him grinning at the camera one year at Nationals. Under Taylor's arm was the head of René Cartier, a kayak paddler from Montreal who wore wooden clogs and drove a TR6. Cartier seemed stunned by the headlock, Taylor delighted.

Scott plugged in a laptop with failing power. He felt like he was running through shallow water, fighting the undertow of ennui. Fatigued, he stared in a mirror for signs of cancer. He had deep hazel eyes, a straight nose, and a mouth that hung loose, expectant like a volleyball player waiting for the spike. When Scott smiled, one tooth hid behind the other.

He'd grown a moustache once, but it looked ridiculous, as though he'd soon start smoking a pipe or wearing a cravat.

Scott thought about Turmoil, who fit his theme of a boxing resurgence. He felt good, he decided, that Ownie had come to him first, especially since he had been off the street for so long. After the interview, Scott had, in a show of faith, found a *Standard* photographer who had taken Turmoil to the studio and shot him in front of a sky-blue backdrop.

Scott stared at the empty wall, ignoring his ringing phone.

Last week, his mother had called and told him with a curious blend of horror and exhilaration that she had seen Tim Taylor driving a bingo bus. "He pulled out in front of a Chevette and nearly caused a horrible crash. I was so upset when I saw it was him and the bus was full of seniors."

Taylor only had one speed: full-out. While others glided to the wharf for a flawless side-on landing, Taylor charged until the last spectacular second, breaking the impact with one leg lifted like a dog. Never bothering with a warm-up, he left the wharf pumped. "Give me fifty metres," he would shout, trying to erase the advantage that a kayak naturally had. It was never enough, not with Scott in the sleek, winged kayak and Taylor fighting the wind in a rudderless C-boat that rode through the water on the point of a V. Taylor called kayaks "women's boats"; Scott called him Joe Freak. One side of Taylor's torso was larger than the other, pumped from the uneven motion of paddling C-1, steering the diamond-shaped boat with his paddle, teetering on one knee, straining his hamstring until it snapped like an old rubber band.

After practice, while Taylor's knee was still white and dented as cottage cheese, they would stop at a corner store to refuel. Without fail, Scott bought a dark Vachon cake, the Joe Louis, while Taylor asked for the "the half lune moon." Scott tried to tell him that *lune* was French for "*moon*" and he didn't need to say it, but Taylor wouldn't listen. He liked the sound of "half lune moon."

Scott's apartment was sparsely furnished, the walls bare.

On a side table, Scott had a square photo of himself as a paddler, drenched and boyish after a downpour. His hair was blond, his shoulders endless. Wearing a red Canada singlet, he was holding a wooden Liminat paddle upright like the iconic pitchfork in *American Gothic*. If he looked closely, he could see veins that resembled earthworms extending from his bicep all the way to his hand, clutching a medal. In the picture, he had skin that you expected to smell like Scandinavian furniture and feel like the back of a horse, powerful, yet vulnerable and exposed.

He lay on the couch with the stereo playing, an archaeologist combing the cultural ruins, picking through the broken pottery and cave drawings of the 1960s. He'd picked up *Rolling Stone* but couldn't focus on a college fashion layout. Was this the counterculture?

In the winter, they used to run and lift heavy weights. They did chin-ups and circuit training, abs. In the spring, at the hint of thaw, they dragged an aluminum pleasure canoe onto the ice and hacked out a path with an axe. Taylor couldn't swim, so they had a deal in the event that Taylor tipped: if he wore a lifejacket on one ankle, Scott would try to reach him before he drowned. If he didn't . . . well . . . fuck it.

When you're eighteen, there are no consequences, just endless possibilities and dreams you have to dream. On the water at five-thirty, back before supper, sleep racing by ten. If he tried, he could see himself in sweats and a Maple Leafs toque hauling open the boat bay door, flooding his Cave of Wonders with early-morning light, filling his soul with longing and dread. He could smell the mouldy towels and feel the cold cement floor stinging his feet.

He had to reach up to touch it: twenty-seven pounds of cracker-thin wood, as finely crafted as a violin, as smooth as a dolphin. His magic carpet, his ride to the stars.

Scott could see mist rising from the lake in a mass resurrection as he lowered her into the water, fixed the footboard with pins, placed a towel on the seat, heightening the excitement, prolonging the work. He took off his shoes, and when he eased into the cockpit, gently, like a mother laying down an infant, he shivered from the touch of wood.

He took a tentative stroke on the right, then the left, pushing off into another world of pain, hope, and nirvana. Swish. Swish . . . swish . . . swish . . . . Set the rhythm from the start.

5

Champion Management had not placed Turmoil in an apartment as promised, but in a musty Halifax rooming house with a shared bath and crackheads.

After Ownie had seen it, he had invited Turmoil for dinner, and now, with the meal over, he was waiting for an opportune time. His grandson, Millie's boy, had given him a list of phrases in Turmoil's ancestral language. "Show him that you're interested in his culture," Jacob had urged. "Display some linguistic latitude. Make it clear you're a man with international scope."

Ownie had listened to the teenager, who was, according to his mother, an honours student and a computer genius. Privately, he had his doubts about Jacob, who was also, according to Millie, going to become rich from his extensive comic book collection, which they had stored in a vault and insured for two thousand dollars. Jacob was always, if you listened to Millie, making some amazing deal that collectors around the world would envy. He was the only person who appreciated the potential value of Prince Namor, the Sub-Mariner, she said, and was hoarding books based on the Marvel character. Jacob had one friend, a *Star Trek* fanatic, who claimed to be a world-class computer hacker.

"Eyd toer d'eyd kotore." Ownie read the first phrase from Jacob's list.

Turmoil stared back blankly.

"Eyd to-er d'eyd ko-tore," Ownie spoke slowly, overmodulating like a hockey announcer with a Czech roster full of consonants. "Kooooo-tore." A noncommittal shrug from Turmoil. "Don't you know what I'm saying?" asked the trainer.

"No, mon." Turmoil tilted his neatly trimmed head sideways as though a better view might help him navigate through the linguistic dilemma. "No, ah dohn." His knee beat a self-conscious *rat-a-tat-tat* on the underside of Ownie's dining room table.

"It means, 'Are you well?'" Ownie was starting to feel foolish, like that time he had approached an Eaton's mannequin and asked for help finding ties, thinking it was a clerk. Leave it to Jacob, he figured, to get him in a mess. "In *your* language, your ancestral language."

Ownie handed Turmoil the list of phrases and pretended to admire the view from his window, which overlooked the duck pond. *Rat-a-tat-tat.* The knee tapped faster. Give the man time, thought Ownie, as he focused past the impasse and the off-white sheers, listening to the muted voice of night.

Ownie had lived in the same house for thirty years, a two-storey with three bedrooms and a bay window. It was modest compared to the ambitious labyrinths that filled the suburbs, mazes with swimming pools and basketball nets, but it had a rose garden and a shed, and the walls were made of plaster and the doors real wood. Nearby houses were of similar construction. A few had succumbed to siding or flats; others had been gentrified by yuppies who painted them with period colours. Real estate agents, foreseeing a downtown revival, cruised the streets armed with condo flyers.

Turmoil cleared his throat as water splashed under the tires of a rumbling bus. Ownie tried to stay calm, but suddenly, adding to his discomfort, he felt smothered by the room's knick-knacks: Russian dancers and fat-faced Hummels, squirrels and merry mandolins, gifts from the kids, Pat and

Millie. All this junk, Ownie cursed, and Hildred had made him throw out forty years of hand tapes, archival records of every fight he'd worked. Jesus. Jesus. Lord, forgive me for swearing.

"Take your time," Hildred told Turmoil as she cleared the remains of dessert. "My goodness, he was hungry," she whispered in Ownie's ear.

Ownie heard a goose honk. The pond, an undulating oval, was home to ducks, geese, and four pairs of whistling swans, which mated for life. It had been dredged in the 1800s during construction of a canal that would stretch from Halifax Harbour through lakes and rivers to the Bay of Fundy. Only the ruins of the canal remained, but the pond had endured, with a bandstand, an island, and a totem pole donated by West Coast natives. In the spring, the city planted flowers, forming a backdrop for wedding parties and graduation photos. Middle-aged men launched remote-control aircraft carriers that occasionally, to everyone's amusement, escaped.

"This is going to be heavy sledding," Ownie whispered back.

"Shhh!" Hildred said to him as she smiled awkwardly at Turmoil. "It's not important."

"Maybe he ant-kay eed-ray," said Ownie, this time too loud.

Ownie had known guys who couldn't read, guys who got robbed on percentages and ripped off on gates. They approached strangers in the grocery store, pretending they'd forgotten their glasses, and asked for the price on a can of beans. They waited for hours at night under signs that said No Bus Service after 4:00 p.m., and after a while it made them angry, hiding a secret that big.

"Cesa ge apeg." He tried a different phrase from the list.

Ownie's uncle Dew Drop could read, but only barely. Every few months, Dew Drop would set off like a prehistoric beast, lumbering down a red Island road, rubber boots stuffed with paper, carrying a coat and a towel and soap. Dew Drop knew how to pace himself — some people would start off fast, then burn out, but not Dew Drop. When night came, he'd find a haystack, pull out his towel, and wake up fresh and covered with dew. On one trip, he made it as far as the Great White Hope fight-off in Madison Square Garden, where he fought three times in one night with six-ounce leather gloves stuffed with horsehair that turned sodden and as heavy as death.

"Forget it," Ownie said as rain dribbled down the double-paned windows. "It don't matter."

"This a nice howse." Turmoil smiled relief.

He's wearing that same no-name sweatsuit, Ownie observed, and those vinyl sneakers that give you a rash. I can't believe they'd send an Olympian up here with nothing, Ownie thought, no shoes, no foul cup, no headgear. On his first day at Tootsy's Gym, Turmoil had pulled out a cheap plastic mouthpiece that was so new it didn't have a tooth mark. Ownie took Turmoil to a dentist and got him fitted properly.

"Mah mooma live in the same howse all her life."

You can tell he's never had a *really* tough fight, Ownie figured, as the linguistic standoff came to a merciful end. Nothing is patched up or pieced together; everything is from the original dye lot. Some guys were so ugly that you did them a favour when you got them scrambled, mangy dogs with missing brows and pitted skin. With Turmoil, everything was smooth, his face so clean that he hadn't started dropping his head to hide the damage. He had the prim hair of a Baptist preacher.

He was big though, Ownie reminded himself, and still young for a heavyweight. "The whole world loves to see the heavies," Ownie had told Scott, the reporter. "They are the kings, the top of the food chain. If they are any good at all, there is money to be made." Ownie had thought about money

— he didn't have much — when Champion Management had phoned him at home.

"Are you interested?" the lawyer had asked.

"I'll give it some thought," Ownie said, feigning misgivings.

Ownie called the lawyer back that night. They negotiated a percentage, they talked about dates, and three weeks later, the heavyweight arrived, as big and young as promised. He could probably, Ownie decided, after sizing up his frame, carry another ten pounds. Ownie could feel the possibilities, vast and heady, but he tried to mute his excitement, believing, in the dark way of his Irish ancestors, that too much joy — childish, unbridled joy — is ripped from your heart by tragedy. Keep it quiet, keep it under the radar, and maybe, his fatalism had taught him, you can slip through unpunished.

"You said it was in the country, didn't you?" Hildred asked.

"Oh yes, it hef a big v'r'ndah where you cahn eat or play cards. Mah mooma mek dresses to sell off our v'r'ndah. One day she sell three dresses to the same wummin, all diffr'nt colour."

Ownie stared past Turmoil's head at a mounted Pope plate. So what if Tumoil couldn't read? Why the hell should he care? Ownie had a friend named Squid who was street-smart and cagey as hell. Squid drove a bus for challenged kids, and they loved him because he joked with them and made faces behind their teachers' backs until one day some biddy told the boss that Squid couldn't read. He got fired, the kids cried, and Squid, exposed and unemployed, moved to Toronto, where he ended up boosting rings from the Eaton Centre.

"Turmoil's got no problem with his weight," Ownie told Hildred in an attempt to shift to a comfortable subject and put the language issue behind them. "His body fat is just 10 per cent. Some heavies run as high as 22 per cent."

The Pope smiled a wise smile with his eyes. He had been hanging on the wall since 1984, the year that he had come to town, blessing everything that moved. In Ownie's mind's eye, he could still see a mother shoving a dying boy through a break in the frenzied crowd, eyes closed, hoping that one holy touch from the Polish Pope would cure him. Every time Ownie looked at that plate, he could feel the pain of that mother and her poor little boy; he could feel it in his gut like an ulcer.

"Ah used to play soccer," Turmoil explained, ending the meal on an upbeat note. "Ebbyone in Trinidad play soccer."

6

The dinner, Ownie decided, had been a moderate success, so two days later he invited Turmoil back to watch a title fight on TV. Johnny and Louie were in the downstairs rec room when Ownie heard a knock at the door.

When he first met Turmoil in the Champion office, his mood was tempered by the unfamiliar: the lilt in Turmoil's voice, the way he moved his head and his hands, the strange words he used. Words like *basa basa*, *chupid*, and *pesh*. Turmoil was unlike any of the local fighters he had trained. Ownie had no reference point, and Jacob's linguistic exercise had only widened the cultural chasm.

Who cares? Ownie abruptly decided as he opened the door. He was a trainer, not the Welcome Wagon. Besides, something terrible had happened on the street last night; one of those bastard geese from the duck pond had killed his neighbour O'Riley's cat, and *that* was a problem.

"Come on in. See those damn geese over there?" Ownie gestured at the pond through an opaque curtain of fog and drizzle. "One of those bastards killed a cat, a nice one too."

"Really?" Turmoil squinted. "They dohn look so bad."

"Baaad?" Ownie scoffed. "They're like rattlesnakes; they're pit bulls with wings. I saw them swarm a kid with a bread bag last week with the mother standing right there. That kid let out a scream that I ain't heard since the war."

Turmoil threw back his head and laughed.

As they headed to the rec room, Ownie thought about the

drizzle, about the eternal damp that ran through life like a virus, rotting underpads and warping young souls. Ownie couldn't decide what he hated more: the dampness or the attack geese. One night, in a dream that he tried to relive for days, the roof of his house peeled back like a sardine can. Overhead, someone had set up a giant grow lamp that the dopers used for weed. Ownie turned the switch to high and baked everything dry, zapping dust mites, futility, and mould. When he sank into his armchair, it felt as warm as a hug, and then Hildred came home and found yellow roses growing in the bedroom.

Turmoil picked an armchair next to Johnny. Ownie sat beside Louie on the couch, thinking about the geese.

"I'm worried about my dog," Ownie told the fireman. "You see, them geese, they're not so waddly as the ducks, they've got better balance. The legs are farther forward on their bodies so they can get up speed. One of those bastards comes after me, and I'll deck him, goose or no goose, but Arguello, she is timid."

"I noticed that," said Louie, who sensed that Ownie, after years in the ring, was just waiting for a reason, even half a reason, to deck someone, anyone, even a goose.

The TV fight was not on for an hour, so they had time to kill. They talked about the geese, they discussed the weather, chilly for late October. Before long, Johnny steered the conversation to his favourite topic, his one fight in New York City, which seemed to symbolize Broadway, Times Square, and a sweat-soaked cathedral named Stillman's Gym.

In the fight, he had beaten a guy named Lopez, whom Ownie had described as "a horizontal fighter, a million-dollar hitter with a ten-cent chin."

"I've got the tape with me," he told Ownie, who shrugged. "I'll put it on."

Unlike Ownie, Johnny lived life unguarded, celebrating

everything that gave him pleasure, never fearing it would be snatched, unfamiliar, it seemed, with suffering and penance. Johnny popped the tape in the VCR and smiled as the ring announcer introduced him in a dramatic crescendo.

"First, in the red corneeer in the black trunks with red trim." Voice building. "He weeeighs in at one-hundred-and-sixxxty-pounds. This young man has twelllve wins with seeeven KOs, and he hails alll the way from Daaartmouth, Nova Scotia. Ladies and gentlemen, let's welcome to the Biiig Apple, Johhhnee LeeeBlooong."

On the screen, Johnny lifted his hands and then threw air punches. In the other corner, Lopez was rocking his head like he was trying to remove water from his ears.

"With LeBlong, we'll have to see how well he trah-vills." The commentator's accent placed him squarely in the Bronx. "It's his first faght out of Kan-a-da. Some faghters get stah-struck, tight when they're on the road."

The camera panned from the ring to the front row, zooming in on a man with a handlebar moustache and a sketch pad. Turmoil, who had been quiet up to this point, bolted upright and shouted at the TV: "Thass the mon. Thass the mon. Some day I hab him do mah picture."

"That's Newman," Ownie offered. "No, Neiman," correcting himself. "Neiman." He repeated the name to make sure he had it right. "He was at the Ali fights. He's a very famous artist."

Turmoil nodded his agreement. The camera zoomed in on Lopez, showing the back of his head, which had been carved up like a jack-o'-lantern.

"I he-ah that LeBlong's a country singa," the announcer continued.

"They have them up there in Kan-a-da?" asked his colour man.

"Oh yeah, they got country singas in Sweden."

"I'm writing a country song now," Johnny informed Turmoil, who looked unsure of how he should respond. "It's called 'The Earth Moved but You Were on Mars.'" Johnny looked at Ownie for approval, but the trainer ignored him. On the TV, round four had started with Lopez hanging on like a marathon dancer, a dehydrated zombie with rubber legs.

"A good fighter, he comes out and sets the pace," Ownie whispered to Louie. "You've got to truck and pretty soon, if you can't keep up, he knows he's got ya. He lands two jabs, you land one, he gets a hook and you don't. Pretty soon, if you don't do something special, you're on Queer Street."

Ownie could call Johnny's fight in his sleep: a six-round decision that was about as special as a wedding suit from Sears. The real champs were the guys who went for broke, the guys who put it all on the line, like Tommy Coogan.

The Kid had been a beautiful little boxer, a slam-banging welterweight who came from nothing and almost had it all. Tommy was raised by his grandmother, who worked as a cleaning woman. A lifelong resident of the North End, Vera had lost an eye in the Halifax Explosion. She was gone by the time Tommy fought the world champion in South Africa, fifteen brutal rounds that ended with a split decision in an open-air stadium full of rich, misguided Afrikaners. Maybe if it hadn't been for the head butts in the fourth round, it could have been Tommy's fight, Ownie told himself, before admitting, with an honesty that hurt, maybe not. The South African could fight like hell.

"Okay," Johnny urged. "Watch this!"

The fight was over. On the screen, Johnny was standing mid-ring draped in a white towel, which Ownie removed as the announcer read the judges' numbers: 80-78 . . . rubbing Johnny like a race horse . . . 82-76 . . . 84-74. Thrilled with the win, Johnny hugged Ownie and kissed him. Ownie whispered instructions in his ear, and Johnny leaned in to the camera, so that his handsome face was distorted. Sweat dripping into his eyes, he smiled a convex smile — "Yee-haw" — and strummed the air guitar of a country singer.

"That was genius, the guitar," Johnny laughed. He looked at Ownie, who smiled.

After a couple of moments, Louie, who was always eager to ingratiate himself with Ownie, turned the conversation back to the geese and Ownie's neighbour. "I know O'Riley," he volunteered. "He was a cop, right?"

"That's him," said Ownie. "He did thirty years on the force."

"Was he big in the church?"

"Yeah, the whole family was into it heavy. The sons were altar boys, and the wife played the organ. O'Riley used to read the gospel and carry around the collection plate."

"All right," Louie blinked.

"I'll tell you a little story," Ownie offered, and Louie blinked again.

"O'Riley had a brother named Frankie, who was a couple of quarts low. Frankie hung around the church too. He'd shovel the driveway and take out the garbage. Every year they'd have a St. Patrick's Day show in the church basement. They'd put on these worn-out skits, sing 'Danny Boy,' and sell fudge. O'Riley was always the emcee. Anyway, one year they put Frankie in a skit; they made him a leprechaun on accounta him being so short. Someone made him a green suit, and he grew whiskers. Everybody thought it was swell."

Louie, who usually didn't like short jokes, smiled.

"A week after the show, he was still wearing the suit. Another week went by, still in the suit. Finally, it dawned on them there might be a problem, so O'Riley goes up to him and says, 'Now, Frankie,' and Frankie cuts him off right sharp. 'Don't call me Frankie no more. I'm Larry the Leprechaun.' He had a little poem to go with it: 'He has lots of secrets I'm told, he even has hidden a fine pot of gold.'"

"When was this?" Louie asked.

"Ten years ago."

"Is he still a leprechaun?"

"Yeah, you see him downtown all the time. The suit's shabby and full of holes. O'Riley said the doctor figures it was a combination of things. First, the fact that it took place in a church gave Frankie idea that it was God's plan. Also, it got him attention, and then, the doctor said, deep down Frankie might've been getting back at his brother for being a cop *and* so prominent in the church."

"That right?"

"For a while, O'Riley couldn't bring himself to go to church because Frankie, or Larry, would be there in his old green suit. So when O'Riley didn't show up a few times, Larry got his job taking around the collection plate."

"No shit."

"That hit O'Riley as hard as a death, but Larry had the time," Ownie shrugged. "He could do the morning mass as well as the weekends. He and the priest got pretty tight."

By the time Ownie had finished, Johnny was telling Turmoil a story about New York, about how they couldn't find the gym when they first arrived, and how Ownie had pulled the mattress off the hotel bed and said, "There's your heavy bag. Go to it." Johnny laughed, and Turmoil looked confused.

Hours after the TV fight, after Louie had driven both Johnny and Turmoil home, Hildred awoke Ownie in the rec room. She had a book in her hand. In his half-sleep, Ownie remembered the first time he'd met Hildred, a tall blonde in a belted green dress, with natural curls and a saucy demeanour. Hildred was with her sister, Pearl. Pearl, who wasn't bad-looking herself, was one year younger than Hildred. Pearl and Hildred were boarding at a minister's house when they met Ownie outside the five-and-dime. One of the Dartmouth Arrows, a handsome first-baseman from Boston, was sweet on

Pearl, but in a tiff, she left him and married Harold, a night manager at a hotel, and one of the most annoying human beings Ownie knew.

"Look at this." Hildred shoved the book in his face. "Page 97."

"I can't see nothin' without my glasses."

"The language of the Tagature," she read, sounding as important as O'Riley when he used to deliver the gospel in church before he was upstaged by Frankie. "The Tagature, who lived in the far mountains of Tagaran, last colonists of the First Empire, used a fiery dialect that betrayed their blood-soaked past."

She handed him his glasses. "Do you see?"

Ownie stared, trying to figure it out. Hildred flipped to page 101, and Ownie squinted at the strangely familiar words, the same ones that Jacob, the boy genius, the comic book mogul, had given him for Turmoil.

"Eyd toer d'eyd kotore." The curse of the Earthshaker.

"D'evl eyd onno ga klo?" Does the day find you well?

"Cesa ge apeg." I am deeply moved.

He looked at the cover: *The Tongue of the Tagature: An Illustrated Encyclopedia of the Greatest Alien World Ever Imagined, Toas Publishing science fiction/reference.* Jesus. Millie's boy had set him up; he had him talking to Turmoil in an alien language, mumbo-jumbo made up by a science fiction writer.

"Honestly," Hildred sighed as Ownie laughed. "I wouldn't laugh if I were you," she warned Ownie, whose eyes were filling with tears. "If Turmoil finds out, he'll think you're crazy."

"Maybe, I am," choked Ownie. "Maybe I am."

7

Garth MacKenzie, the *Standard*'s managing editor, pushed the elevator button and nodded at the two cleaners sharing the space. The hefty one was juggling a stand-up vacuum, a Coke can, and a bag of all-dressed nachos. In her twenties, she had skin stretched so tight she looked like she was smothered with Saran Wrap.

"I like your hair, Doris." She nudged a broomstick of a woman with a spray bottle strapped to her belt gunslinger-style. "Didya change it?"

"Gotta perm the other day." Doris patted the frizz.

"Looks good." The fat one spoke with authority. The bones in her face had vanished like twigs in a pit of human quicksand. "Not too tight."

"Corkscrew. I weren't too fussy about it at first," Doris admitted, chewing on a nail. "Takes a while to loosen up, you know, with them perms."

The fat one smiled girlishly as if she was about to let Doris in on an amazing secret, like how to lose weight by eating french fries and sausages. Leaning closer, she rocked her deboned head, shook her hair until it moved, and whispered, "*I* wouldn't know."

"What?" Doris feigned surprise and then stared at the head like it was a spaceship. The short curls appeared hot-glued to the scalp with unsettling patches of pink showing through. "That's natural?"

"Uh-huh," the fat one giggled, then flicked her head. "Sure is."

MacKenzie, who was bald, stared straight ahead, deeming the conversation beneath him. In his sixties, he had a basketball-shaped stomach under his short-sleeved shirt, and the washed-out colouring of someone whose hair had once been red.

"Well, you're some friggin' lucky."

She smiled, eyes closed, head rocking with the zonked-out bliss of a zealot. "I know. My mother had curly hair." She opened her eyes for a top up of Coke. "I'm the only one in the family that gots it, and it drives my sister crazy."

The elevator door opened, and MacKenzie stepped out. He flinched as a flushed reporter slid by with a kit bag. "Out for a jog, Smithers?" He stopped the man.

"Ahhh yeah." Smithers fumbled his response. "I like to get my five miles in before it gets too busy. I make it up at the end of the day," he added nervously.

"I know what you mean." MacKenzie tried to suck in his stomach. There was something about Smithers, he decided, that he did *not* like. "It keeps the mind alert. I do stairs myself. Uh-huh, good aerobic workout, stairs."

The new publisher, Garnet Boomer, a numbers man from Advertising, was always talking about fitness, knocking booze and junk food, Garth reminded himself. Boomer was so relentless that Garth had resorted to club soda at lunch, Coke at the office Christmas party. Keep on top of Sports, Garth had advised himself after one of Boomer's speeches on fitness; let it be known that you have a solid understanding of what they are doing. Also, find out what those two characters were doing in the newsroom. The old one, he decided, looked suspicious, like a wise guy.

Smithers nodded tentatively as though he had been caught in a *Candid Camera* gag. Stairs? MacKenzie weighed about

260 pounds, Smithers estimated, and was shaped like a seagull with an undersized head, a thick torso, and stick legs. Prone to lower-back problems, he looked like a man with varicose veins.

Garth walked across the newsroom, unsure whether he had mentioned stairs to Carla, his secretary and a valuable conduit of office news. If not, he should.

Garth stared in the direction of Smithers's empty desk. Through an oversight or an act of malice, Sports had been located near an Entertainment writer named Blaise, who had Caesar hair and wary eyes. Fearful of invasion, Blaise had erected a blue partition decorated with an autographed picture of Karen Kain. He kept his files locked in a drawer and his stories separated into two distinct piles: "Before" and "After," a reminder to editors that he was keeping track of changes. Fond of grand stage gestures, he'd played Brick in a Tennessee Williams tribute. Today, there was a lily on his desk. Garth nodded at Blaise, who, if Carla's intelligence was correct, hated Smithers.

Garth settled into his chair and stared at a wall covered with portraits of past managing editors, a decades-old collection of humourless men in suits, all except for Dee Hardcastle, 1941-45. Hardcastle was an anomaly, an editorial Frankenstein created, out of necessity, by German U-boats, Nazi storm troopers, and sixteen-year-old farm boys led to war. Hardcastle's rein lasted for four years, during which she ran the newsroom like a general, until the war ended, the men returned, and she was demoted, bitter and broken, to the ranks, where she seethed like an angry ex-wife.

Garth thought about exercise. He'd done a sit-up once, but it had wrecked his back. He'd thought about walking, but who had time when you were in bed by eight-thirty and at work by seven?

Hey diddle diddle, the cat and the fiddle. Garth smiled,

comforted by the line he found himself repeating like a mantra. When he mouthed the words, his mood shifted as though he had emerged from a car wash into daylight, his mental windshield cleaned. *Hey diddle diddle.* Most of those walkers were nuts, Garth reckoned, *volksmarchers* with forced grins and chirpy track suits, chased by demons. One of the night editors got off work at five in the morning, walked the streets until ten, and then went home and cried.

Garth lifted a snapshot from his desk: an election-night photo of him and the boys back when his hair was red and everyone called him Sparky. Why should he, Sparky MacKenzie, let some number cruncher dictate his lifestyle with talk about fitness and the evils of drink? It was just a knee-jerk reaction to Gem's medical insurer, which had threatened to raise premiums after a carpal tunnel outbreak. There was a time, Garth recalled, when drinking was as much a part of the business as hot type. Frank Mobley was the best newspaper man he'd ever seen, and he drank a case of Keith's before lunch and never missed a deadline. Garth could see Mobley bursting in, throwing down his notepad, and telling the desk to Hold the Presses, Hold the Presses, back when newspapers actually did it. Frank had a hot one that day. Someone had been shot on the waterfront . . . Garth reminisced, or was it the Commons?

Sure, Frank had his bad days, but the warning signs were as bright as Vegas: the dirty brown Stetson and the Hank Williams songs. Frank was singing "Why Don't You Love Me?" when he took a poke at Gillespie just because Gillespie, the day editor, told him to put on a shirt. Luckily, Gillespie was a fat son-of-a-bitch and Frank could run. Garth smiled at the memory.

Next to Frank, Garth was never considered that much of a drinker. Now, he wouldn't mind a drink, with all of the pressure brought on by the new publisher, community advisory groups, downsizing, graphics, pagination, electronic picture desks, reader surveys, email, Internet, the need to be innovative, pro-active, reflective, and still cover the news. Gem had blueprints of how a newspaper should be structured, templates for every city of a particular size. On top of that, the chain was under pressure to promote more women into management and to "better reflect Canada's cultural and racial diversity in its staff."

On Garth's desk was a memo from Boomer, the publisher:

MEMO TO STAFF:
(Please post on bulletin board) 11/01/92

Katherine Redgrave has been appointed city editor of the *Halifax Standard* effective Feb. 1. Ms. Redgrave, 36, comes to the *Standard* from Ottawa, where she served as Hill editor for Gem. Prior to that, she was a correspondent in Washington and London. She is the co-author of a book on health policy and the winner of a National Newspaper Award for feature writing. Ms. Redgrave started her career at the *Toronto Star.* She is a graduate of the master's program in journalism at Columbia.

G.C. Boomer, Publisher.

8

"My father saw Jack Johnson in a honky-tonk in New York," Ownie recalled. "He was sitting on a stage fieldin' questions for a buck. He was wearing crocodile shoes and smoking a cigar through a holder. My old man paid his money and asked, 'Mr. Johnson, who was the greatest fighter ever?' Jack flashed his gold teeth and said, right saucylike: 'You're lookin' at him, boy; you're lookin' at him.'" The audacity tickled Ownie. "See what I mean?"

"Uh-huh," muttered Scott, taking notes.

"Not only was he a great fighter, but he was bigger than life and all the rules that hold the rest of us down like gravity. He was Genghis Khan and Chuck Yeager, cracking sound barriers with a jab. He showed up for one fight in pink pyjamas; he married white women when it weren't done. When he beat Jeffries, there were riots from California to North Carolina."

Nodding, Scott let his eyes roam Tootsy's in search of colour. "Spartan," he wrote in his notepad, with three heavy bags, five speed bags, and a grab bag of weights. The ring's off-white canvas was stained with dirt and the rusty red of dried blood. Scott spotted a truck tire lashed to a pole.

"Does Halifax need someone colourful?" he asked.

"Halifax needs a top fighter with crowd appeal."

Full-length mirrors, apparently salvaged from a defunct five-and-dime store, still warned: SHOPLIFTING IS A CRIME. Functional, Scott decided kindly. The gym had one whitewashed brick wall, a wood ceiling, and bits of shag carpet that seemed to have crawled from a 1970s rec room. "Grubby," Scott wrote, and then amended for the kinder "traditional."

"Right now, we have one Canadian champion in Halifax," said Ownie. "Hansel Sparks. He fought my boy, Johnny LeBlanc, a while back, but for some reason the people didn't take a fancy to Sparks. He's a good enough fighter, but he didn't catch on."

"Why is that?" asked Scott, soaking up the room.

He liked the spare feeling of the gym, its single-mindedness, its utilitarian decor, the anonymity it granted, the curtain it hung on the outside world. In a place like this, no one was divorced, unemployed, bankrupt, environmentally ill, married to a Holy Roller, or anguished over a rebellious child. It was a refuge from life, an escape from a world that had become as unreal as the circus funhouse, a world you grew up believing that other people lived in.

"God knows." Ownie picked up a 7-Up water bottle. "Maybe he's been around too long, maybe they don't think he's going anywhere," Ownie looked up, making his meaning clear. "I'm not knockin' Sparks. I know the family."

"Uh-huh?"

"They're nice people. I hear Hansel and his mother, Girlie, are thinkin' of openin' a bed and breakfast."

Scott let it pass, reflexes slowed by desk rust. "What about Turmoil?' he asked. "Could he have the crowd appeal?"

"He's raw, but he has the physical ingredients." Ownie took a deep breath. "He's a heavy, and he's personable, but he's not from here. We'll have to see what happens."

The gym was on the second floor of a wooden building that sagged like an old sofa bed full of crumbs. Downstairs was a wedding shop named White Lace and Promises. Across the street was a strip club run by bikers, brutes with shattered psyches numb to the violence that defined them, men with spiderwebs tattooed on their elbows, crosses on their cheeks.

From Tootsy's second-floor window, Ownie could see Halifax and the harbour where convoys once queued, forming a lifeline to Britain. He could, if he tried, smell the uncertainty of young boys besieged by fear, and bombs that exploded like solar flares on the surface of the sun.

The trainer taped a ball. He had careful movements and a time-worn code that had got him this far.

1. Watch out for smiley-faced guys.

2. Never wear a dead man's clothes.

3. Never train a fighter under the thumb of his father.

4. Don't hunger for revenge; it ain't always sweet.

"See this guy." Ownie pointed at a pug-nosed fighter doing rapid-fire sit-ups. "He can hit, he can take it, and he ain't too smart. They call them guys dogs. They're good for nothing, really."

As the Dog grunted, a pair of hungry eyes and jagged cheekbones loped up the stairs, a college distance runner trying to build strength by punching the bag. He was part of Tootsy's outreach program. Scott watched him shed his backpack, his face a hollow homage to the Cult of Serious Training, a cult that owned his body and shunned non-believers. His arms were as thin as broomsticks.

When Scott had trained at Dalhousie University during the school year, the outdoor track was full of cross-country runners who seemed cold and wet, bloodless wraiths who came up behind you like a ghost ship, then vanished.

As Ownie waved at the Runner, Scott studied the trainer's hands, which had two dented knuckles and age spots. Feeling Scott's gaze, Ownie held up a big mitt for inspection.

"When I was a boy, my father thought I was going to be a giant. He saw my hands and feet and he kept waiting for me to grow into them. But I never did," he snorted. "Five-foot-seven with triple-E feet." He laughed at the ridiculousness of it. "Practically a dwarf."

"I read once that everyone is born with a three-inch height range," said Scott, an inch over six feet himself. "Whether you reach five-six or five-nine depends on what you eat. If you grew up in the 1930s, maybe the nutrition . . ."

"Nutrition?" Ownie laughed. "You'd sell your soul for a turnip."

Age had shrunk the fabric of Ownie's face, leaving an oversized Irish nose and ears under an HMCS *Prince Rupert* ballcap. Ownie's blue eyes were fixed on the Dog, who was lying face down on the floor until, with a slight grunt, he executed a prone push-up.

"The best athletes are either extremely smart or extremely stupid." Ownie pointed at the Dog. "They'll put their bodies through the worst punishment and they'll repeat it over and over without ever getting bored." He looked at Scott. "The smart ones are seeing something new each time, a fine point the others miss. The dumb ones are just too dumb to get bored."

Scott wrestled with the theory and all its implications.

After years of being a reporter, Scott had learned to be unreadable, to keep his judgments to himself. He wanted, for reasons he did not totally understand, to be free to come and go at Tootsy's, a place he found both soothing and uplifting. He wanted to see how this all would end. It had been years since Trevor Berbick had fought in the city, years since Clyde Gray had brought in fans. Could the drought be ending?

Scott watched Ownie draw chalk targets on the heavy bag. As a favour to Tootsy, Ownie had stretched out the Runner — "Man, you're as inflexible as the Pope" — then laced his gloves.

"Every punch has a number," he was explaining to him: "1: left hook to the ribs, 2: right to the jaw; 3: right to the body. Sometimes, we order a combo to make it interesting."

"What's the hardest punch to learn?" asked the Runner,

showing greedy teeth, calcium gluttons that had starved his birdlike bones. His hair was orange, and his entire face, even his brows and lashes, were covered with a yellow-orange wash that made his eyes seem naked.

"The left jab. It should be the easiest, but for some reason it's not." Ownie shrugged. "It's a punch that you'll need if you're going to go anywhere. The left jab isn't used as a club, it's used as a whip. If you know how to use the left jab properly, that means you can box, and that keeps you in a fight."

The Runner, Scott noticed, had been wearing a black Adidas jacket. Scott's first real sweatsuit was a red zip-top Adidas, back in '71, before the world of sportswear was fast and slick and ruled by Nike. The baggy jacket crawled up Scott's back, the stirrup pants were uncomfortably short. The suit was made of a material that seemed impervious to rain, sweat, or dog bites, a cold, clammy fabric that never wrinkled and smelled like the backseat of a taxicab. He'd checked the label once before washing: Made in Yugoslavia. 45% cotton. 55% Helanca, the Greek goddess of synthetics.

At a time when everyone looked like rejects from the East German track team, Tim Taylor was a fashion insurgent in two-stripe North Stars and cut-off jeans that hung below his navel, cinched with a belt. His furry torso, two sizes too big for his legs, burst out of a chewed-up singlet. At the time, Scott thought Taylor was the only man in paddling with a hairy chest; everyone else had smooth, sculpted pecs that tanned to almond. One day, Taylor finished practice, changed, and got married, a life-altering move Scott heard about one month later.

Ownie had finished with the Runner, who slipped back into his jacket. He must be one of those slow-twitch muscle types, Scott decided, the kind of athlete who could run thirty miles but needed help with a twist top. His hands were about three fingers wide.

The door opened and in walked Turmoil and a mesomorph who was insulated from the world by black shades, earphones, and a French Foreign Legion head scarf. The two men weren't speaking.

"Ahm gohn teach Donnie how to box." Turmoil patted the mesomorph's back, laughing even though nothing seemed funny. Donnie's muscles tensed, straining the seams of a hot-pink T-shirt and leopard-print sweats. Behind the glasses, his unyielding eyes roamed the room like radar, slipping contact. "All Donnie know how to do is beat up white boys."

"Donnie's here to spar three rounds." Ownie cut the small talk. "He knows the drill."

Eyes inaccessible, Donnie unbuckled a Grizzly weightlifter's belt, then stripped to a singlet and Lycra shorts. *Bam. Bam. Bam.* Punching counter-clockwise, an arc-shaped blur of muscle. While Donnie was warming up, a woman in a Raiders jacket crept through the door and found a spot in the corner. Her hair was pulled up tight in the fashion of a synchronized swimmer. She anxiously chewed her lip.

The door opened again and Johnny trotted in, smiling as though everyone had been waiting for him. He pulled up a chair next to Scott, ready for the show. He nodded at the woman. "Theresa met Donnie when he was doing community service. He got one hundred hours."

Scott looked at Theresa and then at Donnie, who was following his chest into the ring. His head seemed to be attached to an invisible string coming from the ceiling.

"He okay now?" Scott asked.

"Oh yeah," Johnny smirked. "He's an expert on the spin cycle."

Turmoil stripped to a white cotton T-shirt from Champion Management.

"Champion Management," Johnny chuckled. "I heard that

they're a bunch of chisellers. I know a waitress who hooked up with their lawyer, Douglas. She says he's cheap as hell."

Ownie set the timer and the two men moved slowly in the ring, shuffling, touching gloves. Turmoil was half a head taller, but Donnie was, in Ownie's words, "wrapped tighter than a Christmas surprise." It was well known that Donnie had a weakness for women *and* a nasty disposition. When he had sparred with one of Tootsy's former fighters, he had punched the guy's lights out and then *insulted* him. "You couldn't do nothin' with me," Donnie had scoffed. "And I had sex twice before I came in here today."

"Turmoil should be able to handle him easy," predicted Johnny. "Donnie's only a blown-up cruiser."

Turmoil raced out, throwing punches.

"Hey, man," Ownie shouted. "Pace yourself. It's not amateur hour, you're not training for three rounds."

"Man," Ownie muttered, trying to process Turmoil's performance in the ring. "You've got amateur written all over you, and not even that good of an amateur. You're not getting the power because you're not delivering right."

Pop! Donnie's jab struck Turmoil like a snake. Johnny shrugged surprise while Turmoil shook his head and moved forward.

Pop! Donnie got through again.

An old man was sitting ringside in a wooden chair. He laughed uproariously, like this was funnier than Fibber McGee and Molly, better than vaudevillian braggarts and blowhards. He slapped his leg and stomped a white leather shoe. He needed no introduction. In his prime, before his hair was as white as his shoes, before Fibber met Throckmorton Gildersleeve, Suey Simms had racked up one hundred and thirty fights, starting as a feather and working his way up to welterweight. He had fourteen bouts in Madison Square Garden, the mecca of boxing, the amphitheatre for gladiators such as

Joe Louis, Ali, and Duran. "Suey Simms was in the ring for twenty-five years," he liked to say. "Long enough to get an indexed government pension."

"Ice!" Suey hissed each time Donnie's jab connected. "Iiiiice."

The old man, who was wearing a red scarf and a plaid tam, continued to cackle. Johnny nudged Scott, and Theresa freed her lip, relieved. Turmoil looked at the dirty canvas, eyes wide and disbelieving, as Suey doubled over in a fit of coughing, stomping one leather shoe until he caught his breath and hissed again, "Iiiiice."

Three minutes ended with a buzz.

Ownie climbed into the ring, showed Turmoil something with his hands, and then climbed out. Puzzled, Turmoil stared at the canvas again. The corners of Donnie's mouth curled into a smirk, like a flower opening to the sun. No one was paying his board, lining up fights, or hiring a trainer, no one was promising him a four-by-four; he was just a local fighter, as common as clay.

"It's all right," Ownie said to no one in particular, convincing himself. He turned to Scott, who pretended not to notice Donnie's smirk. "It's nothing we can't fix," Ownie told the reporter. "You see, some fighters soak everything up; they just want to learn, learn, learn. They're hungry for direction, just wanting to be getting better."

Turmoil blocked a jab and fired off a right.

Suey flashed the patented grin of the Tumblebug, the nickname he'd earned by celebrating each win with a handspring and a spectacular flip across the ring. "Suey Simms fought them all, black, white, yellow, and red," he'd claim without provocation. "In all them fights, he never kissed the canvas."

"Others haven't got the self-confidence to admit they don't know it all," continued Ownie to Scott. "They got to tell themselves they're great or they can't fight. With them, you've got to *make* them see what they don't know, make them see the hard way. Let them take a few shots to the head." His voice dropped, and he added improbably, "So this could be good." Turmoil blocked his first jab and sighed.

9

Turmoil needed spending money, and Louie had a plan. Driving his Jeep Cherokee through the old streets of Halifax, he looked confident. Johnny was riding shotgun, and Scott, the reporter, was along for the ride.

Louie turned a corner. A garbage bag blew up the narrow street like a tumbleweed, flipping over and over until it snagged on the guts of a discarded couch. The street was empty except for an Orange Crush can, an air of hopelessness, and two boys batting rocks in the air. *Ping. Ping.* Joe Carter in the cage.

One rock bounced off a three-quarter Georgian cottage tastefully restored in slate blue. The asymmetrical house, circa 1809, had grey trim, a maroon door, and the painful look of someone who had overdressed for a party. *Ping.* Another rock hit the vain little house, bouncing off a rose trellis. *Ping.* Hitting a doorknocker shaped like a fox's head. *Ping.* Ricocheting off the urban renaissance that had not, to everyone's dismay, yet arrived.

"I've got a new book with a section on ring names," announced Louie, the self-described student of the game. "See if you know who this guy was." He pulled a printed page from his pocket and read: "Walker Smith?"

"That's Sugar Ray Robinson," snorted Johnny.

"Okay." Louie brought his Jeep to a near-stop while the boys, slowly and deliberately, shuffled off the street. A mutt ambled by with a ham bone in its mouth and then stopped at a row house with one half sided in green. In the back seat, Scott stared out the window and wondered exactly where Turmoil lived.

"Okay," Louie said. "How about Archibald Lee Wright?"

In the shadow of Citadel Hill, the neighbourhood had once looked like a developer's dream, a downtown core ready for revival, a motherlode of history, proximity, and urban chic. For a while, there was talk of heritage properties, rare Georgian designs, and the historical footsteps of Adèle Hugo, Victor's tragic daughter, hopelessly pursuing a British military man.

"The first name's a giveaway: Archie the Mongoose Moore."

They passed a silver Quonset hut harbouring an auto body shop. Leaning against one wall was a mattress plugged with bullet holes and a sign: No LOITERING. Plastic geraniums sprouted in the cracked window of a house that advertised ROOM FOR RENT, SEE DEPARTMENT OF SOCIAL SERVICES.

Scott stared at a double Queen Anne who had let herself go, shabby, melancholy, comforted by a lava lamp and a stuffed cat with glass eyes. A man was sitting on the front step, smoking a cigar. Why, Scott wondered, would you stuff a dead cat?

The buildings, all soggy wood and vinyl, were attached to each other, or separated by mouldy space. Some had boarded-up windows, others the allure of a root cellar, with no front yards, no trees, no room for anything but regrets. Inside, Scott could imagine a soil floor, 90 per cent humidity and ethylene gas. The dark streets reminded Scott of the city's origins: a garrison town founded two centuries ago by the British, a sinister place full of roaming press gangs, a cold grey port you couldn't turn your back on.

"When we were in New York, we went into this joint in Little Italy," Johnny recalled, escaping the dreary surroundings. "The owner had fight pictures on the walls. I looked at them, and the fighter seemed real familiar, so I said 'Is that him? Is that really Tony Danza?'"

"Was it?" asked Louie.

"Yeah," Johnny nodded. "The owner said his brother used to train Tony before he got into acting. They were pretty puffed about it."

"Right on," Louie responded, like it made perfect sense.

Scott watched a man lurch down the street, sinking under the weight of an enormous backpack. His eyeglasses were strapped to his head with an elastic, and the ankles of his pants were sealed shut with duct tape. Sticking out of the backpack was the head of a chihuahua with round eyes and a sharp nose.

"I think that's Marcel," Johnny noted.

"Yeah?" Louie blinked, and looked unnerved.

Before Johnny could get a better view, Marcel, who had a room somewhere, vanished around a corner and Louie parked outside a three-storey building shaped like a cereal box. The fireman hopped out, leaving Scott and Johnny in the Jeep.

Turmoil's rooming house had a decaying porch and layers of bumpy paint, archaeological evidence of time and changing owners. Wind whipped through windows that had been covered with plastic that could not obscure the view of a drug-dealing corner two blocks away.

Louie mounted the steps muttering, "What a dump."

DOBERMAN BITES, warned the adjoining house, which had cardboard boxes stacked to the windows, the unclaimed assets of tenants who had returned to the street like runoff. RODNEY SNOOKS HAS MOVED DOWN THE STREET. HE DON'T LIVE HERE NO MORE.

Louie knocked and then dropped to the sidewalk, looking up. The porch window, covered with red nylon curtains, was filled with a chain gang of baby teddy bears, hanging from their necks in a mass lynching. Eight altogether, one with red hearts on his feet pads, another in a jaunty Christmas cap, victims of a pagan ritual or Druid sacrifice. No wonder Rodney Snooks had moved.

Louie opened the door and mould assaulted his nose like smelling salts. Before he could go any farther, he heard footsteps. When Turmoil appeared, too bright, too formidable for his shabby surroundings, he looked like he'd been asleep. After a few words with Louie, he followed the firefighter to the sidewalk. As he cimbed in the back of the Jeep where Scott was sitting, Turmoil rubbed his eyes and pointed to a library book clutched in one hand. "Ah been readin bout the Eskimos, how they keep wahm."

Two blocks later, Louie stopped the Jeep for a daycare crossing the street single file. The children were walking in the same controlled fashion as the Soviet seamen who marched the streets during port calls, mute, drab men trailed by an omnipresent keeper. They all seemed depressed.

"Now, the secret is to start off slow. Don't expect too much from yourself off the start," Louie cautioned Turmoil. "I been doing this for, ahhh," he said, checking his mental datebook, "ten months."

"Okay, mon." Turmoil nodded.

"I can give you some direction after we line things up with Merle. He and I are tight."

In the front seat, Johnny had fallen asleep. Three nights a week, he worked at a bar named the Dory Shop, a marshalling yard for faded women and wayward men. It had an oyster bar made from a buff wooden dory. LITTLE SISTER, the sign said, for the benefit of tourists, who were then informed that this was the smallest dory the old shops made, ninety-five pounds of pine and oak. Johnny filled in for Ken, the regular barkeep. Ken was a pro. He'd worked in Seattle and on a cruise ship. "A good bartender is hard to find," waxed Ken. "Too green

and you can't cut it, too seasoned and you are probably a thief."
Johnny figured that Ken stole, just not enough to get caught.

"Now, the pay's decent, seventy-five to one hundred bucks depending on the gig," Louie informed Turmoil. "You don't have to report it, which would be perfect since you're not allowed to work anyway."

"Ah could use the money, since ah'm been freezin to death."

Through the window, Scott noticed a comatose bum still clutching a bread bag and a can of lilac air freshener. His coat was open.

"I told Merle that I had a friend," Louie added, "someone who looked after himself, a boxer. He was *very* interested."

"Where do they have these things?" Johnny asked, struggling up the stairs of a low-rent office tower, home to a cleaning service and a telemarketer.

"Generally at someone's house or an office," said Louie, attacking the stairs with his usual vigour. "It's mainly showers, going-away parties."

Scott saw Turmoil shiver in a leather car coat purchased for ten dollars at Gussy's, a used clothing emporium with a pipeline to New England. Gussy had generously described the coat as a "garment for all seasons with slash pockets and a zip-out Orlon pile lining." The lining was missing.

"You get feelers?" Johnny asked.

"Naaah," Louie scoffed. "It's entertainment."

From the doorway, Scott studied Merle, whose jacket sleeves hung over his stumpy fingers. That's a popular look with fat guys, Scott noted: buy a huge jacket to cover the corpulence and then never get it shortened. Merle shifted sideways in a swivel chair that creaked in protest. CLASSY MALE ENTERTAINERS, said the sign over his desk, SUITABLE FOR ALL OCCASIONS.

Merle pretended not to notice the four men filling his doorway, continuing with his phone conversation. "Well, darlin'," he drawled. "I'll be there soon enough. You tell Marie to put on one of her lovvvellly boiled dinners and, for God's sake, save me some triple-yolked eggs."

Louie knocked, but Merle kept gushing. "I had ten the last time I was down home, cooked up lovvvellly, with a little bit of juicy ham, sawwwsidge, a hint of home fries, not too greasy, mind you, and" — his voice was as euphoric as a 1-900 sex line worker — "melt-in-your-mouth oatcakes."

He gulped, thick with consumptive foreplay, while the caller squeezed in advice. "Ha ha ha." Mock indignation. "You don't need to worry about me, m'dear, I'll live forever. Ha ha ha. My great-grandfather, Dan Alex MacLean, lived to be one hundred and four, the oldest man in Cape Breton. They erected a granite monument to him, they did. Dan Alex kept his meat in a fifteen-metre well all winter long."

Glancing up, he finally mouthed to Louie, "Come in."

"When he was ninety years old, he could hoist up a whole side of lamb and swing a maul hammer like a child's toy, and evvvery morning for breakfast, what do you think he had?" He paused, waiting for the inevitable. "That's right, a plate of triple-yolked eggs!"

All four visitors found metal chairs. In the cramped, windowless room, Merle's skin smelled like saturated fat. He hung up his phone.

"How are you, Louie, my son?"

Merle's capped teeth were too small for his bloated head and stupendous appetite.

"Good, Merle."

"How did the last one work out?"

"They seemed to like it." Louie shrugged modestly. "I wore the leopard posing suit, the one I was telling you about, with the wet look. And the name worked well, the Arabian Knight. I think it's better than the last one."

"Plus, the novelty of something new." Merle nodded.

"I'm probably going to get the tear-away pants," Louie added.

"You don't have those yet?" Merle sounded surprised.

"No, but I will.".

"Good, son, good."

The owner wore his kinky hair straight back, smothered with gel. Under the jacket was a crushed-velour jersey that looked like the hide of an elephant. Merle had been eating like an elephant since he was written up in the *Strait Standard* as the county's biggest newborn forty years ago. He had been eleven pounds, twelve ounces, born during an extended visit from Cape Breton to the mainland.

"Did I ever tell you about Billy Campbell from down home?" Merle asked as he stealthily slid a hand across his desk. Maintaining eye contract, he reeled in a yellow flyer. LADIES ILLIMINATE THE STRESS AND FRUSTRATIONS OF LIFE WITH A RELAXING FOOT PEDICURE BY BRENT. DONE IN THE COMFORT OF YOUR OWN HOME. "Well, Billy used to hang around the Legion day and night. He never drew a sober breath."

Merle tucked the incriminating flyer in a drawer.

"They didn't mind him there during the week to play a little darts or tarbish, but they didn't want him at the top-drawer functions, the weddings and such. So, do you know what they did?"

Louie shrugged.

"They put a sign up: NO RUBBER BOOTS ON WEEKENDS, and that kept Billy out."

As Merle laughed a shifty laugh that bared his undersized teeth, Scott felt disgusted. He hated Merle, he decided at that moment, in the same way that he hated the soft and imperious Smithers.

"So you're a boxer?" Merle turned to Scott as though he had sensors, the acute antennae of the grotesque, finely tuned to slights. "I've seen lots of good fighters down in Cape Breton, all as hard and rugged as Lingan coal."

"Actually," Scott muttered, "I'm a reporter."

"It doesn't matter, my son, it doesn't matter. I had a doctor work for me once, a neurosurgeon." He paused in the lie, twisting a sapphire ring to unleash his oral powers. "He just liked to get out a bit. He was in demand all right, as popular as Amphora pipe tobacco."

Louie cut in, blinking. "No, it's not him. It's him." He pointed at Turmoil, who was nervously rubbing the leg of his knit pants patterned in a subtle check. Behind Turmoil was a poster of step-dancers in curly bobs and plaid, airborne.

Merle stared and then smiled lamely. "Ah, yes, I'm afraid I can't use him."

"You said you needed someone," Louie protested.

"Yes, my son. But I can't use *him*."

"Why not?"

"I'm going to be honest with you, Louie. I've always been an honest man. Mention the MacLeans any place, any time, and people say, 'Damn honest buggers all of them. As honest as a Sally Ann matron with a Christmas kettle.' "

"Okay."

"I'll tell you."

"Uh-huh."

"He'd scare the women. He's too big."

"He looks great." Louie's voice rose an outraged octave. "This man was in the Olympics." Turmoil nodded confirmation.

"I don't care if he was in the Ice Capades, my son, he's too big." Merle caught his breath. "And he's too bloody . . ."

"What did you say?" demanded Louie.

Scott dropped his head.

"I said, Try coming back. Maybe if he gets smaller."

10

Katherine Redgrave nodded at a forty-ish woman with dreary hair and the pinched face of a disillusioned nun, an aging ascetic who shopped for day-old bread and walked her blind little terrier in rainstorms.

The woman stopped to collect herself as she entered Katherine's office at the end of the newsroom. Her faded paisley blouse was buttoned to the collar, drooping on birdlike shoulders, and then tucked into a wool skirt with front pockets. Oddly enough, for someone who appeared unaccustomed to any self-indulgence, she was smoking.

"How are things going, Glenda?" Katherine asked.

Katherine had been cautious since she'd arrived at the *Standard*, sensing that it had cliques and customs and unwritten rules. Land mines. Glenda drew and exhaled nervously on her cigarette, each puff etching a line in her smocked mouth. The wrinkles reminded Katherine of the cushions her mother used to make as Christmas gifts, pleated accessories in corduroy or velvet, occasionally red, but usually the yellow of sunflowers. Mother made the cushions, bright and hopeful, until the time that everything changed, until their lives were irreversibly altered by a darkness they could not stop.

Glenda was the type of person who could disappear off the face of the Earth without a trace, Katherine thought with a pang of regret, a person you would describe in a feature story as "unremarkable." As she looked at Glenda, she had the uneasy feeling that Glenda knew exactly what she was thinking.

"Fine, Katherine."

"How is the series on cellphones?"

In her career, Katherine had been happiest as a feature writer, describing people and places, issues and lives more complicated than they appeared on the surface. But Gem had needed to meet its self-set quota of female bosses, and Katherine, had seemed like a safe choice. First came the editor's job on the Hill, and then, after a curious interview in Toronto with two other female candidates, the transfer to Halifax, a foggy city full of strangers. Katherine knew she was an interloper at the *Standard*, a paper with habit and history; until proven otherwise, she was a suspicious agent from Gem.

Glenda's face relaxed as they talked about projects in Lifestyles, which was staffed by three middle-aged women with modest ambitions. Glenda studied Katherine's short black hair and European nose, features that Glenda's co-workers had, on a generous day, compared to those of Isabella Rossellini.

"Anything else new?" Katherine asked.

Glenda froze like she was about to be struck, girding herself with prayer and the vows of poverty, chastity, and obedience. "Nooo." Glenda looked at Katherine and seemed to weigh the risks. It was a look Katherine was familiar with: the glare of women who expected her to waive the rules of the workplace and rise to the call of sisterhood.

"Well, I'm engaged," blurted Glenda.

"Congratulations."

Glenda looked at Katherine defensively. Glenda knew she belonged to another species, a family of hunched women in flat shoes and hats with chin straps, women whose faces had been reshaped by disappointment. None resembled Rossellini or her glamorous mother. Few were, like Katherine, six feet tall.

Katherine was silent. While Glenda stared, daring Katherine to judge her, the editor was, unbeknownst to Glenda, engaged in her own internal struggle, one that the bosses at Gem could hardly imagine. Katherine was writing letters to people who had ill-treated her in the past, in an attempt to address the most grievous wrongs against her and thus remove their impact from her soul. Since moving to Halifax, she had written four. Her plan was to neutralize each outstanding trauma, each act of cruelty, and then move on with life unencumbered. The fourth one, composed the night before, she had sent to her grade three teacher.

Dear Mrs. Carew:

I was in your class at Rocky Brook School, a tall girl with curly hair and glasses. One day, you made me stand in the corner while my class performed a square-dancing display. I was not allowed to participate because, according to you, my skirt did not meet your specifications. Mine had unauthorized poodles near the hem, embroidered by my mother.

"What is wrong with your mother?" you demanded. "Why couldn't she make it the way I asked?"

Your attack set off weeks of taunting on the playground, a refrain of "What's wrong with your mother?" It was relentless, and you encouraged it. At the time, I attributed your cruelty to the fact that your husband was having an affair with Mrs. Uxbridge, the gym teacher. Often, I saw them leaving the Holiday Inn bar, then parking by Grand Lake.

Now, I realize that was no excuse. You were simply a bad person with an evil heart.

Katherine Redgrave

Glenda's stare turned petulant. "We're working on the arrangements now," she told Katherine. "It's complicated."

"Okay."

"I may have to take some vacation." *You don't believe me, do you?* Glenda's look bore the rage of involuntary spinsterdom. *You think that only women like you find men.*

Katherine sighed, knowing that Ottawa had been full of thirty-ish career women who had dated too many men from too small a circle. Katherine had seen them walking home in Mad Bomber hats, chi-chi glasses, and jogging shoes. Some decided to surrender, to immerse themselves in work and a close circle of friends who met for Sunday brunch, Gatineau weekends, and skating parties for the lonely. Some turned to booze, ultra-marathons, or the sanctum of fringe feminism. Some carried on hopeless affairs with hopelessly married men; others married the first man who asked them and, to everyone's surprise, blossomed into motherhood with such brilliance that others found them painful to be around.

"You don't see any problems?" Katherine asked.

"No." Glenda's eyes were as hard as a strap.

"We are not attempting to interfere in your personal life, Glenda, but the *Standard* is a concerned about how this reflects on us, on our being objective in our news coverage. It is not a normal situation."

Glenda's face froze at the word "normal" and her jaw jutted with defiance. "I am well within my rights. All my personal affairs are being conducted on my own time."

"I am just pointing out how the personal lives of journalists are sometimes hampered by their professional obligations. It's like running for a political party or being involved in —"

"My lawyer is prepared to make a Charter case out of this."

11

For thirty minutes there had been a stream of visitors into Turmoil's dressing room. Fight night brought out the has-beens, the wannabes, and the distant relations, the kind of people who drifted to funerals and testimonials for folks they barely knew.

Ownie saw an ex-champ named Darren make his way across the room. Darren grabbed the arm of his friend, a pony-tailed goliath with feet too small for his body. "Hey, Ownie, this is my buddy Zach," Darren shouted in a voice like a broken muffler. "Ownie here had me for twelve fights. He wrote the master plan when I took the Canadian title off Losier in Montreal."

Ownie nodded. "Losier quit after that and took up window dressing."

Darren laughed. His body was so tumid, Ownie noticed, that he could have been wearing a padded suit. His face was irregular, as though it had been patched with fibreglass and then painted flesh-tone. He had a fibreglass patch on one brow, another on his cheek. On his head, which looked like it was covered with bee stings, was a blue seafarer's hat.

"Darren." Ownie pulled the ex-champ close. "You know me, man." Ownie paused and Darren nodded his rebuilt head. "You know I always give it to you straight."

"Never steered me wrong." Darren looked anxious.

"You look great," Ownie declared. "Tops!"

"Yeah?" Darren blew out relief. "I'm feeling healthy, Ownie. I'm feelin' good."

"You're comin' on, man, you're comin' on. I can tell."

Darren eased away, and Zach followed, teetering on an invisible balance beam. Johnny moved in to fill Darren's space.

"Christ!" Johnny watched Darren exit, lumpy and scarred. "Darren looks gruesome. Did he get hit that much?"

"Naaah." Ownie dismissed the suggestion as absurd. "He's all puffed up from them steroids. When he finished boxing, he said he wanted to see how big he could get, just like a Howard Dill pumpkin. I touched his arm and it was like granite, so he must be shooting everything."

"Yeah?" Johnny had seen busted noses and cheekbones, but Darren's face was smudged and out of focus. "He looks like a monster."

Ownie shrugged. "That seafarer's hat don't do nothin' for me."

It will soon be time for everyone to leave, Ownie told himself, looking over his shoulder at Turmoil, sitting on a bench with Tootsy.

A thick, older man entered the room and stood, face frozen into a mask of grumpiness. He had a scar shaped like a half-moon on one cheek, and his chin stuck out like he'd been insulted. He walked toward Ownie, over the skate scars and electrical tape left by a hockey team, making it clear that no one was going to rush him.

"This is my brother Butch," Ownie told Johnny, who smiled while Butch grunted ambiguously. Taller than Ownie, Butch had the same big ears covered by a salt-and-pepper cap. His nose was smashed too flat to determine its original shape, his eyes were hematoma slits acquired in 120 pro fights. He had fought all over the United States and down as far as Aruba: 80-30-10.

"He was the first fighter I ever had." Ownie was playing with Butch, taking the parts they'd assumed fifty years ago. "Take a look at him now." A two-beat pause. "He's a mess." Butch grunted again. "I didn't know what I was doing back then. As I went along I got better at it; the guys didn't get beat up so bad, they ended up less ugly than this."

Butch acted like the banter was beneath him, then barked in a voice as threatening as a summons: "Is this guy you got worth looking at or are you pissing away my time?" Johnny's eyes widened as Butch continued. "He looks too tall, like some goddamn freak. I hear he's got no power, that he stinks."

"He's got power, and he's not that tall."

"Some goddamn Gil Anderson circus freak."

The big crowd was gone now, the dressing room quiet. Johnny, Tootsy, and Suey were permitted to stay while Ownie readied Turmoil. Round and round Ownie wrapped the surgical gauze and tape, pleased with his new taping device. "My God, I'm a smart man," he said.

"Huh?" Turmoil looked up.

"I'm a regular Einstein."

That's all Ownie wanted: a peek at Turmoil's eyes, an instant readout on blood distribution, heart rate, pupillary constriction, and electrical activity in the skin. Before a fight, some fighters asked strange, unrelated things, like, "Who cleans the rink?" "How did you meet your wife?" They would spit, garble words, but their eyes were the key, because eyes show fear. Nerves you can work with, Ownie believed, you can can 'em like shaving lotion, but fear is fatal.

Ownie had seen a quarter-pounder shrink like an inflatable doll on his way to meet Tyson in the ring. By the time he hit the ropes, he was a mass of empty rubber punctured by fear. Before a fight, Ownie had never needed to check on Tommy.

He was as cool as Aqua Velva. Tommy Coogan was a man with a job to do every time he climbed in the ring, and Ownie never had to deal with fear or doubts so deep they could destroy you.

"Ah dohn want him here." Turmoil pointed at Suey Simms sitting on a bench, still wearing his plaid tam and white shoes.

"I had me a stroke," Suey had been telling Johnny. "Monday, no Tuesday, over at the Woolco."

"Was it bad?" asked Johnny, surprised.

"Hmmm, hmmm, I knew somethin' was happenin', so I went to that clinic. I had one of them foreign doctors check me out. When he finish, I say, 'Thank you very much, doc. I gotta get goin' cuz it's Dollar Forty-Four Day.'"

As Suey chortled at his own joke, Ownie thought about all the eyes he'd looked into. Just once, he'd like to see eyes like Tyson's, cool, unchecked, free of guilt or anyone's expectations, the eyes of a man who would walk through a plate glass window just out of spite. Of course, you'd never admit that, so you kept it private, like the fact that you couldn't do fractions or had once been to court.

The Tumblebug banished, Turmoil started to shadowbox. *Rat-a-tat-tat* like a jackhammer. Reggae music, supplied by a tape deck, bounced off the concrete walls and a photo of a hockey team in black-and-gold jerseys.

"Le-le-le-lettts ga-ga-go, killer," urged Tootsy. Ownie let the gym owner, who suffered from a stutter, be the second. The trainer put a silver robe around Turmoil, who was helpless now that his gloves were taped on. Ownie tightened the satin belt.

"I seen Sanchez," said Johnny. "He's got the cold creeps, all right."

Turmoil nodded and stared at something beyond the OUT OF ORDER urinal. Bending on one knee, he closed his eyes to pray. When the prayer ended, Ownie put a hand on Turmoil's neck and rubbed out the tightness. Tootsy picked up his bucket and towels, and Ownie, like a death row guard, announced it was time. "Let's go. We got a job to do."

The tiny entourage rounded a corner.

"Le-le-le-lettts ga-ga-go," urged Tootsy.

They passed a hot dog vendor and a rent-a-cop talking to a bald man in a yellow sweater. The egghead looks familiar, Ownie thought. Polite applause and Tex-Mex music drifted downstairs as Sanchez entered the ring, a migrant worker in a red bandana and boots with bells. Then a boo and laughter from the crowd.

Listed as thirty-two, Sanchez was older, Ownie figured, a faceless trial horse with an expedient past that changed like a story passed through a bar. As part of the fraud, he shaved his head to hide the grey; he hoisted his trunks up high to cover a gut; and he wore black leggings over broken veins the colour of grapes.

"S-s-s-sounds like a like a g-g-g-good ca-ca-crowd," said Tootsy, hopeful.

Turmoil looked distracted, touching his ten-ounce Everlast gloves together, shaking his legs out, biting his lower lip gently like he was trying to put a name to a face. What was he thinking, Ownie wondered before moving ahead.

Turmoil ducked under an insulated water pipe as Ownie checked his gear: adrenalin, Vaseline, cotton swabs, dry towels, all tidy, and just the way he liked it. Ownie did not think that Sanchez would last long. The old fighter had arrived in town with just a kit bag for company; Champion had hired a local to work his corner. "It don't matter," Sanchez had mumbled to the promoters. "I just need some sleep."

"Oh-oh-oh-nee," Tootsy sputtered. "Oooh."

"What?" Ownie turned, impatient. "What?"

"T-t-t-tur," Tootsy sputtered, and Ownie saw the second pointing at Turmoil, who had stopped under a Christmas decoration.

"Are your boots okay?" Ownie asked the fighter. "Are your gloves all right?" This was nothing new in the fight book, Ownie told himself. Riddick Bowe held up a bout once for twenty minutes, fussing, for no good reason, over gloves. *C'mon.* Ownie pushed Turmoil's back, but the big machine was frozen. "What's wrong?"

Ownie waved off Tootsy to give them room. Just then, the men's room door swung open and an old-timer in suspenders hobbled out, smelling stale and medicinal. Ignoring him, Ownie rewound fifty years of mental tapes shot in bingo halls and morgue-like rinks, stadiums and casinos, looking for the answer. Over the years, Ownie had seen battle royals, deaf-mutes, bears, and midgets. He'd seen guys walk out after round one, fall down drunk mounting the steps, throw up, find God in the ring, but he'd never seen a fighter go cold in the hallway.

"Ownie." The old-timer was chasing after him.

"Ah cahn fight," Turmoil muttered, staring at the concrete floor. "Ah cahn fight." Is this it, Ownie asked himself: the punchline?

"We're having a merchant marine reunion." The old-timer was hobbling toward them on legs as stiff as stilts, unstoppable it seemed. "Now that we've got benefits."

"Why?" Ownie tried to catch Turmoil's eyes, which were darting from side to side, chasing imaginary fireworks in the sky. Everything around them seemed to vanish: signs, overhead pipes, broken hockey sticks. Jesus, Ownie thought, if he can't handle Sanchez, if he's freaked by this, we are done, because this is routine, man, this is as predictable as death.

"Iss that mon," Turmoil moaned.

"Who? Sanchez?"

"The mon we juss saw in the suit."

"Can you tell me how to get in touch with your brother Butch?" the old-timer shouted before Tootsy pulled him aside.

Oh, *that* man, Ownie realized, the guy dressed in a V-neck sweater and slacks as though he was auditioning for a role in a Disney movie.

"What about him?" Ownie had seen the man in the office of a hockey team that had reportedly used his services as a hypnotherapist. How would Turmoil know anything about him?

"He put a spell on me," Turmoil claimed.

"Whaaaaat?" Holy Mary Mother of God, thought Ownie. What kind of trip was this? It was as crazy as the time that George Foreman convinced himself there had been a plot to pump poisonous gas into his dressing room, or the night that Boom Boom Vachon accused Snowball Dooley of sleeping with his wife, and the poor wife was so ugly she'd have made Snowball melt. Ownie weighed his options.

"It's okay. It's all okay."

"Noooo." Turmoil hugged his chest like he was in shock, like someone emerging from a car crash with glass shards stuck in his forehead. "He put a spell on me."

"He can't put a spell on ya, walkin' down the hall."

"Yesss."

"A big man like you?" Ownie laughed a desperate laugh.

Turmoil stared at the floor, a quivering hulk of power and nerves. Up above, the crowd was strangely still, as though someone was planning a surprise party with horns and streamers. What, Ownie wondered, was Sanchez doing to pass the time?

"Okay, maybe he did," Ownie conceded.

Turmoil nodded and folded his body in two. Ownie didn't think that Turmoil really believed the man had put a spell on him. It was nerves, he told himself. No, it was *fear* looking for a way to stall. Whatever it was, he would play along.

"I never told you this, but I studied that stuff too. I learned it when I was with Tommy Coogan over in South Africa. Some of the Zulus taught me." Turmoil looked at Ownie's face for hope. "They had bareknuckle boxing goin' on behind a wall of elephants, and I was helping. So, the long and the short of it is: I know what spell he put on you and I can take it off."

"Ah you shur?"

"Man, I never been so sure of anything in my life. I don't like to do this, because you could handle Sanchez if you were in a coma . . ." Ownie closed his eyes. "But here it goes. Watch my hand." He put his mitt in Turmoil's face, a blur of age spots and dented bone. "You are in my power, you will do as I say. When you awake, you will win the fight in round six."

"Is that it?"

"Yeah, man, we're back in business."

"Finally, ladies and gentlemen, Turmoil Davies."

Instead of Islands music, Turmoil had selected "Farewell to Nova Scotia" to court local fans. Three piss tanks waved beer bottles in the air as Turmoil climbed through the ropes, grim and detached, and Ownie entered introduced as "Ownie Flanagan, the man who brings champions to life."

"Who are you? Frankenstein?" a hoochhead yelled.

Ownie blocked out the noise.

12

Two office workers sat at the Athena's counter fixing their lips in the glass of a revolving pie case. "When we were kids, we found a hoary bat in our cottage, tangled in the curtains." One woman's teeth were stained with Jungle Berry, which gave her a carnivorous look.

"I hate bats."

The first woman was undeterred. "My sister's boyfriend, Hector, was an amateur taxidermist. He killed the bat and mounted it on an album cover."

"Can you be an *amateu*r taxidermist?" asked her co-worker.

"I think so. It's not like a mortician, is it? Anyway, I think the cover was Jethro Tull." She squinted, trying to visualize the cover. "Or, uh, Led Zeppelin. I know I wouldn't give them my James Taylor because he was too cute."

Scott looked across the Athena Restaurant's counter and wondered with the detached interest of an eavesdropper, Who is Jethro Tull? He checked the time on the sunburst clock with rickety arms that stuck on twelve. A collection of handwritten ads, taped to the front window, blocked his view of the street.

VEGAS ELVIS, INCLUDES FLASHING LIGHT AND SOUNDSTAGE. ELVIS HAS JUMPSUIT, GOLD-PLATED RING, BELT BUCKEL, SILK SCARF, AND MICKROPHONE. PLAYS FULL VERSION OF HOUND DOG. PAID $340, CAN SELL FOR $150. CALL BERNICE.

Scott wasn't interested, he decided, in calling Bernice, but he was glad that the Athena was located on the same block as Tootsy's, kilometres from the industrial park and the managers of Gem. Scott had persuaded Sports to resurrect the boxing beat by predicting a resurgence in the sport. Without warning or explanation, MacKenzie had decided that Sports was a priority and could hire two part-timers, freeing Scott to come and go as he pleased.

Scott liked the Athena's red vinyl booths, cloth carnations, and faded posters of blinding Greek beaches. He liked the rundown clientele. More than anything, he liked to escape. Escaping meant less time around Smithers and Warshick, less time under the capricious eye of MacKenzie. But deep down, Scott knew it was more than that. He was witnessing something singular, he believed, an athlete with the tools, the physiological wiring to perform the magical, the magnificent, something he had seen before, and that he needed, for reasons he could not explain, to observe once again.

Scott recognized a quality in boxers, individual athletes who had chosen a solitary course. The boxers, the swimmers, the paddlers, the runners, all lined up alone and exposed. There was no hiding in a crowd, no substitution. Individual athletes wanted to control their destiny, but, in some, the drive went deeper; they needed, at the core of their being, to beat *everyone,* and that ego rejected team sports.

TWIN CITIES DOG SHOW. PRIZE FOR OWNER AND DOG WHO LOOK MOST ALIKE.

A jogger, bundled up against the wind, shuffled by at a laconic nine-minute pace. Scott had recently read that Edwin Moses, the great Olympic hurdler, the winner of 107 consecutive races, had run with Bill Clinton. Afterwards, Moses, a biomechanical miracle, a genetic mutation, a track god unbeaten for ten straight years, was quoted as saying that he had trouble with the president's seven-forty pace. "He's in surprisingly good shape," Moses purportedly said. The story and all of its ramifications ate away at Scott like acid and he pleaded, Don't do it, Edwin, remember who you are!

Scott felt no bond with the aerobics followers and softball duffers at work, the spandexed masses of untested flesh. There was no common ground, no spiritual communion. He was like a junkie who had given up smack and found himself surrounded by weekend tokers. Training, like dope, was not something to be trifled with. It was a power unto itself, it was delirium. It was stumbling out of bed at 5 a.m. in a howling wind, freezing his fingers until they turned white and hard. It was pushing his body until his mind entered an afterlife of soft lights and silence; it was the only thing that mattered, and in the end, it was too cruel to care.

Maybe Moses was joking and the reporter was too dumb to know, Scott thought, as the waitress delivered a coffee and Danish. The analytical athlete, who made winning look too easy, was often misread by the public and press. "This should be good," the waitress said quickly. "It's just out of the oven."

Scott's face flushed, his personal space invaded. He believed in a professional covenant that covered specific relationships: lawyer/client, priest/sinner, clerk/customer, a covenant that precluded comment on his food as well as his behaviour.

"Thanks." He acknowledged the gawky redhead in the non-mutilating ear cuff. Scott bit into his Danish as a stripper wobbled to the counter for smokes. Under her coat, she wore a T-shirt that announced: RIPE WHEN SQUEEZED. The waitress handed the stripper cigarettes and then, to Scott's annoyance, turned back to him. "Why does everyone have something written on their chest, some emotional shorthand that says who you are, where you've been, what you believe in?" she asked rhetorically.

Scott looked at her closely. She was only about twenty, he

figured, thin, in loose black pants and a T-shirt. She had an order pad tucked in a black apron next to a pack of Trident.

"It's human interaction without the humans," she argued, making her case. "It's faxes, Internet, phone machines, pagers, talking T-shirts, all devices to keep us from talking, to keep us safe, sterile, and remotely untouched."

Ambushed, Scott nodded dumbly and wondered why she cared. Focusing for the first time, he saw green eyes, a snub nose, and a wide mouth that hiked across her face until it could glance up and see the outer corners of her eyes. The face of a red-headed duck.

"I think we're going to keep going until our vocal chords disappear, shrivel up like that extra toe we used for climbing." She raised her eyebrows like it made sense. "We will evolve into mutes."

"Maybe."

"My name is Sasha." The delivery was rapid-fire with no time for inflection.

"Is that Russian?" Small talk stuck in Scott's mouth.

"Ah ha, it is the familiar form of Alexandra, which, of course, was the name of the tragic *tsaritsa* whose execution in that horrible half-cellar in Yekaterinburg is too monstrous to envision." She stopped briefly before plunging forward. "I changed my name, actually. It used to be Darlene, which is Old French for 'little darling.'" She laughed. "I liked Sasha better."

Scott shrugged. "Yeah, sure, my name is Scott. Maybe I should change that."

"Scott is a good name, Old English." She seemed confident. "Scott Glenn, Scott Fitzgerald, Scott Baio."

When she laughed, Scott was relieved to see good teeth and a sense of humour. Since he had started frequenting the Athena, Scott had often seen her coming to work, dragging a tapestry bag containing her past, her future, and her pecca-dilloes. She stuffed them under the counter with the industrial-size vats of ketchup. I wonder if she's one of those women who totes around a favourite book, he thought, like his sister, who'd been consumed in her teens by *Marjorie Morningstar.*

Sasha checked the six-burner Bunn-o-Matic. She sprayed disinfectant on the milkshake machine with the satisfied movements of a kid playing dress-up.

"Just don't call yourself Scotty." Sasha was back. "That has some strange connotations for me."

"How come?"

Inside the coat rack by the door, Scott noticed a forlorn sweater with a metal hanger poking through the knit. Underneath was one winter boot.

"When I was growing up, we had a squirrel monkey named Scotty." Her voice was guileless. "He used to sit in the kitchen all day, eating orange slices and pears like a sultan from the movies." She glanced to see if he was listening. "One day he bolted out the back door when Mom was hanging out the laundry. He ran across the clothesline — *Whooooosh!* — like he had suction cups on his feet. From the clothesline, he leapt to a tree infested with caterpillars. Then he started peeling off the caterpillars' skins and popping the bodies into his mouth. It took us two hours to get him back inside with bribery and negotiations."

"How did you ever get a monkey?"

"My uncle phoned one Christmas Eve and I was the one who answered. I was about six. He said, 'How would you like something cute and furry for Christmas?' and I said: 'Yeeeaaah, great,' thinking, I dunno, a stuffed bear. The next day he showed up with a monkey. My uncle had been to Indonesia on an oil rig; I think he won Scotty in a card game."

"Was he a good pet?"

"He was duplicitous. My grandmother lived with us. When she and Scotty were home alone during the day, he was friendly, but only because he needed her. When other people were around, he would pull her support stockings when she walked by him and pinch her legs with his fingers, which were as sharp as tweezers."

"I guess he had it in for her."

"He knew she was vulnerable. He knew she had little power in the household. He had established the hierarchy." With that, she smiled a toothy smile and walked away with the straight, controlled walk of someone who had studied dance. "I gotta go."

"Where's the shop steward?" Scott heard Smithers shout across the newsroom. "I've got proof that it's two kilometres a day to the can and the staff room."

Smithers craned his neck to see whether Blaise had heard him, but the Entertainment writer was on the phone, juggling two prescription bottles and a host of neuroses.

"The walk will do you good," sniped Warshick, who was wearing his favourite T-shirt, the one with the warning on the chest: DANGER, EXPLOSIVE GAS IN REAR. While Warshick tossed out insults, he used one hand to open an electric cooler that he kept by his desk stocked with frozen Revellos.

It was a good time to pick on Smithers. The reporter had become visibly agitated since the hockey season had started and he'd discovered that, when refereeing, he had a personal heckler. Francis Lundrigan was forty-five years old, short, and partial to Moe Howard haircuts. Two years ago, the junior team had made Francis an honorary stickboy. Then, cementing his celebrity status, he had appeared on The Christmas Hope Telethon, singing "I'm a Little Teapot Short and Stout." Every time Smithers reffed, Francis was there, three rows back, clamorous and relentless. "Hey, forty-four," he would say, pointing at Smithers's number, "is that your IQ?"

And the crowd would laugh. "That's Francis," they'd chuckle, a one-name persona like Cher or Sting, a celebrity in wool hats and mukluks. "Remember he was on Christmas Hope."

"Knucklehead." That always got Francis rows of laughs. "Smithers, you are a bum head, an oofus. Dummy, dummy, dummy." More laughs.

The *Standard*'s book page editor, who was as small and angry looking as Squeaky Fromme, walked by, gave Smithers a deadly look, and muttered something that sounded to Scott like *cockroach*. Squeaky's desk faced a corner and a faded tall ships poster that she bowed to each morning. It was her shrine to ten heady days of brigadoons and puffy sails that had billowed and creaked over the skyline like a canopy bed, a cocoon of romance and laughter. A rare streak of sunshine had heightened the abandon and the exotic tans of sailors, and for a while, as though the dashing visitors and their swashbuckling ships would never leave, the whole city had smiled.

Months after the tall ships had sailed and the smiles had faded, a photographer had found Smithers and Squeaky in the darkroom sprawled over the enlarger. Smithers swore that he'd passed out from the Christmas punch and that she'd undressed him against his will. "They could use her at Baker's Funeral Parlour. For her size, she's surprisingly strong when lifting bodies."

"Squirrel monkeys are very small."

"Uh-huh." In under an hour, Scott had found his way back to the Athena and a counter seat. Some days he hated Smithers with an intensity that surprised him.

Sasha continued. "We weighed Scotty on a Weight Watchers' scale, and he was two and a half pounds exactly!"

Scott watched Sasha unload a tray of metal teapots that

leaked when you poured them. From his counter position, Scott could read an antique brass plate that said, MEMBER OF THE INTERNATIONAL ASSOCIATION OF FINE RESTAURANTS. He tried to imagine a monkey on a food scale.

"Squirrel monkeys are New World monkeys. They come from South or Central America and have wide noses and nostrils that are far apart. Scotty had a tiny face with a white Lone Ranger mask, like a raccoon in reverse. And his eyes . . ." Sasha stopped, seeking the exact description. "His eyes were very dark and superficial."

"What happened to Scotty?" The name was surprisingly easy to say.

Sasha wiped the specials board clean of the vegetarian lasagna. "He died in my sister's arms. We think it was a heart attack, but we're not sure. We just know that he let out a shrill scream and toppled over."

"Maybe the caterpillars killed him."

"We buried him in a coffin made from a Buster Brown shoe box lined with a pink facecloth. Even though he was mean to my grandmother, she insisted. We dug a grave under the caterpillar tree and sang 'Jesus Loves Me.' I don't know why we chose that song. I think we must have heard it in a movie. It seems so American, don't you think?"

13

Louie picked up Johnny outside Video Madness.

They passed an electric-blue house so loud it echoed. The neighbourhood had once been homogenous: rows of prefabs built with wartime rations, three rooms on bottom, two on top, as simple as a Monopoly house. With the 1980s came a mid-life crisis and a need to make a statement with vinyl siding and hallucinogenic paint. Some of the houses had grown a storey or sprouted an incongruous deck. Others had added the artifice of brick.

Johnny was writing a song, he informed Louie as they headed to Tootsy's. "Here's the chorus," he announced. "Tell me what you think."

> Take my heart and break it,
> Take my day and make it
> Take my picture off your drawers,
> Leave that cat, he ain't yours.

"Good," shrugged Louie, not really a fan of country music.

"I think it's got potential," offered Johnny, who had been inspired by a TV program on Carol Conway, an old doll from the sticks who had made it big in Nashville. Carol had grown up in a tarpaper shack without plumbing but now had enough cash to buy every abandoned lighthouse and destitute fish shack in her former county.

Kitty, kitty kitty, don't go away.
Kitty, kitty kitty, you got to stay
Kitty, kitty, kitty I'm on the ropes
Kitty, kitty kitty, you're my only hope.

"It's for a contest," Johnny explained. "The top prize is an all-expenses-paid trip to Nashville."

"If it doesn't interfere with your training, what do you have to lose?"

"Eight months of winter." Johnny could already smell the dogwood and the hairspray of Tennessee. George Jones was singing a welcome song in his head.

"If you live down south, man, you could be fat, dumb, and happy for life." Johnny sighed. "I wonder if they have subways in Nashville. If I'm in a city with subways, I feel like I'm going somewhere." He paused. "And Italians. I like a place big enough to have Italians."

"Listen." Johnny sobered as they arrived at Tootsy's and circled for a parking spot. "If Ownie asks, tell him I already ran."

"Yeah, yeah." Louie, the mole, blinked nervously.

"I will," Johnny added lamely, "ah, when I get a chance." And then: "My Achilles has been a bitch."

Louie made another circle of the block. The strip club was swarming with bikers. Led by a cracker in an overcoat, they had gathered around a Neanderthal whose butt spilled over the seat of his Harley like saddlebags. Joe Diffie. The name popped into Johnny's head and he smiled, proud of this talent. Not everyone had the ability to look at an ordinary person and spot his celebrity twin. There was Danny Glover changing oil at Ultramar, Tanya Tucker cashing cheques at the Royal Bank.

"The cops told me he offed a kid last year." Louie pointed at Big Butt. "He shot him in the head over four Cs. The fixer there" — he pointed to the overcoat, a lawyer who had run in the provincial election — "got him off when the main witness disappeared on a Rhodes Scholarship or something."

The lawyer's eyes looked like prunes in folds of uncooked pie dough. He squinted across the street at two undercover cops who were drinking coffee and dialling Big Butt's pager every ten minutes for entertainment.

A hophead in a beanie helmet climbed on Big Butt's Harley. On her back was a crest that said, PROPERTY OF JAKE (THE SNAKE) PORTER. She had skin the colour of plum sauce and a fetal-alcohol face with flattened cheekbones, small eyes, and smooth skin under her nose. *Vrrrmmm*.

"My days of ugly women are over," Louie vowed. "A man should always go with a woman who is better-looking than he is. If he's a five, she should be a seven. If he's a seven, she should be a nine. Otherwise, guaranteed, it cannot last. It's all about the balance of power, man. It's science."

"I don't think I could find someone better-looking than me." Johnny laughed.

"They're out there, man, they're out there."

More bikes arrived. They had teardrop gas tanks and forked front ends, five-hundred-pound outlaw hogs with rebuilt bodies and unknown origins. Some of the riders were carrying stuffed animals, which puzzled Louie until he saw the sign: BIKERS' TEDDY BEAR RIDE FOR SICK KIDS.

"See that guy." Louie pointed to a gorilla with a noose tattooed around his neck. "He's the sergeant-at-arms. He grew up next to me in Low Rental, one of those fat, change-of-life kids with old parents. He had a sister in my class, Doreen, who decided to join the Brownies. The third week in, the pack leader told Doreen that she couldn't come back until she had the full uniform. Doreen quit but wouldn't tell her parents why. When Sarge found out, he went to the pack leader's house and torched her shed."

"Kerosene?"

"Probably." Louie pulled in to park. "You know how they started, don't you?"

"Who?"

"The Brownies. They were a paramilitary group like the Hitler Youth or the Red Brigade. Just on principle, I never buy their cookies."

"Well, that's easy for you, man, since you don't eat sweets."

Johnny shuffled into Tootsy's trying to look like a man who had pulled six hard miles, a man ready to rumble with Hansel Sparks.

"How's Turmoil doing?" he asked Ownie.

Ownie took his time responding. Unlike Johnny, Turmoil did the labour. Every morning, in rain, fog, or snow, he ran his six miles. He arrived at the gym at 2 p.m. and he worked the speed bag, the heavy bag, and the medicine ball. He did push-ups, chin-ups, and he skipped until he left a pool of sweat, slick and symbolic.

Ownie was old school, so they didn't lift heavy weights, which he believed would tighten up Turmoil and bind him like Louie. "He needs to be mobile." It was the same template that Ownie had used with Tommy, only more intense, because Turmoil's large body could handle more. Turmoil ate the right food, Ownie had noticed with approval, and the fighter believed — from the moment he arrived at Tootsy's Gym — that he was destined for greatness.

"I had him spar three rounds with Donnie blindfolded," Ownie said.

"How did that go?"

"Pretty good," Ownie decided. "I think they're engaged."

Ownie watched Turmoil lift an aluminum bat, weigh it in his hands, and position himself before a Motomaster tire strapped to a pole. *Whammm.* The chop rattled the steel-belted radial. *Whammmm.* His arms reverberated, shock running up his triceps like a chill.

"The man's problem is concentration," Ownie continued. "He loses it and he loses the rhythm of the fight. He starts thinking about what he's going to have for dinner and pretty soon he's done. So blindfolded, he has to concentrate. He has to feel what's happening."

Louie trotted over, harbouring his report on Johnny's delinquent roadwork.

"I was reading a story with Hagler's trainer." The fireman was stalling, hoping that Johnny would duck out, as he often did, to the convenience store, and he could squeal to Ownie. "He said some doctors think the chin gets weaker if you get your wisdom teeth out."

"Yeah?" Ownie shrugged noncommittally, keeping an eye on Turmoil, who had teeth like Chiclets. Whammmmm. Another chop of the Louisville Pro.

Turmoil had scored a TKO over Sanchez, who, after earning his pay, had stretched out in the sixth round and refused to get up. Sanchez had hit Turmoil more than Ownie would have liked. "He is still raw," Ownie told Scott. "I call him the *steak tartar* of boxing." Turmoil had to be taught how to slip and slide, how to avoid being hit by someone more substantial than Sanchez. The plan was to build him up with a few soft fights — maybe four in the first year — and then, as his name became known and as his skill increased, take on tougher men. While Ownie handled the gym work, Champion controlled the matchmaking and promotion.

"What do you think?" Louie persisted. "About the teeth?"

"I think I'm a bad one to ask, since I've had fighters with no teeth at all. When Hungry Hannaford fought Rocco James, he looked like he was ready for the glue factory."

"That why they call him Hungry?" Louie asked, with Johnny still within earshot.

"Naturally."

14

Garth found a seat in the fast-food restaurant. He tried not to look at a woman who was hunkered over a chrome table, face hidden by hair and a greasy mask of shame. Beside her, a pale boy, probably her son, was picking at french fries. Their feast, which consisted of the fries, chicken fingers, nachos, and Hawaiian pizza, had been unwrapped and laid out for sharing.

"You should eat, Justin," the woman panted, justifying the spread. "You *said* you were hungry."

Her chair was pushed in tight to the table's edge, like the armless woman Garth had seen at the library, turning pages with her mouth. Russian history seemed to be the woman's area of interest: Peter the Great, Ivan the Terrible, anything to do with barbarism. To get to World War II, Garth's desired field, he had to pass her table, and every time he neared the Reformation, he prayed she wouldn't be there.

Have Carla check phone bills. Trying to ignore the glutton and her insipid boy, Garth was logging reminders in a book that he carried close to his heart, like a hidden wire.

Pick up #124 Red. Garth smiled, thinking about his passion. The red paint was going to be for a splendid WWII formation of model airplanes on his bedroom windowsill: a Flying Fortress, a P-51 Mustang, a P-38 Lightning, and, up front, where the sun would strike it first each morning, the spunky Spitfire. *Get waxed paper.*

Numbly, the woman reached for a chicken finger, the sleeve

of her ball jacket embroidered with her nickname, Powerhouse. Her lips quivered and her eyes rolled.

Check the lunchroom. Garth added an annoyed asterisk. Last week, Boomer, the publisher, had confronted him about a Queer Nation sticker plastered over the mouth of the softball mascot. "Where did it come from?" Boomer had demanded. "I wouldn't worry," Garth had assured him. "Monarchists are generally a low-key group except for that problem with the Girl Guides and the oath." Christ, it was these bifocals: *Queen, Queer,* they looked the same.

Garth glanced up as an ancient man with translucent skin pulled himself from a plastic seat. He looked like a crooked Q-tip with a cotton-ball head. He was wearing a plaid shirt buttoned to his thin neck and wool pants. The man's bones cracked as he lurched to a wrestler's crouch, bracing himself on a chair back.

Look at Cullen's expenses. Garth underlined the notation, angry at the unsettling man. First the library, now here. Was there no place you could sit in peace, where you didn't have to be reminded of other people's afflictions?

He figured that Cullen, the legislature reporter, was robbing them blind. Someone was skimming petty cash too. Three years ago, the publisher caught Hart in Advertising selling long-distance calls to outsiders, routing them through the paper as conference calls.

Get very fine sandpaper. The old man took a step. Why can't he wait until his friends return? Garth wondered, as the man stumbled to another chair back.

Come up with good story idea for Sports. Where Are They Now?

What is Smithers up to? What happened to those two characters?

Garth thought about his planes. They had their own room now that Garth and his wife, Jean, had moved into her dream house, a two-storey in the South End, a society bunker sealed off from the hoi polloi and the guilt of scorned relations. "An address," Jean had sighed. "I finally have an address."

Jean had written the listing in her dreams:

> Stately, tree-lined south-end boulevard, area of some of Halifax's finest homes. Well-appointed. 4,200 square feet. Hardwood. Three baths, four bedrooms. Built-in china cabinet, leaded glass. Walk-up attic. Very few properties come up on this street.

To Jean, the front hall of the house smelled of grandfather clocks and acceptance. Honorary consuls, the Halifax Club, the Waeg, and Neptune Theatre. Upstairs, it was Junior League, kermesse, ladies auxiliary, and aerobics at the Y. "Ahhh," Garth could hear the voices dripping with a disappointment that Jean would just have to ignore, "so you're not related to the judge." Unfortunately, Jean's family had only appeared in court as defendants. He thought about how happy Jean was with her heated bathroom floor and a built-in scale. All of this for a girl who'd grown up in a trailer court eating bologna.

Garth's mood darkened when he looked up. Powerhouse was emptying her tray like a murderer disposing of a body. Garth felt angry at the old man teetering in the aisle, as though he was imperilling them all. She's going to mow him down; she's going to hit him. Garth watched Powerhouse waddle down the aisle, rolling on the sides of her shoes past the warning: DO NOT BRING SHOPPING CARTS INSIDE. Oh God. She'll crush him like a steamroller, leaving a geriatric mess for the rest of us to look at.

Adding to the peril, a horde of teens arrived. "Hey, lend me a buck," one shouted at another, who replied, "Screw off."

Oh Christ! Garth muttered. The old man's arms were

trembling; his colourless flesh hanging from his skull. Why doesn't he stay put?

Powerhouse closed in, and the man, unaware, lurched again. Just as Powerhouse and the teens reached the decrepit man, a woman carrying food appeared and, with the speed of a pickpocket, grabbed his arm. Relief flooded his face as she lowered him into a chair, where he steadied his glasses. Then he lifted one blue-veined hand, as flimsy as onion paper, and pointed to the table he had felt compelled, at any cost, to leave. "No smoking," he rasped. "No smoking."

15

Ownie and Turmoil had decided to walk from Tootsy's to the Champion office in Halifax. They were nearing the entrance to the harbour bridge when they met an elderly man in a Cossack hat and matching car coat.

"How you doin, Slugger?" asked Ownie.

"Well, not too bad." Slugger's replies were punctuated by the pauses of a censor delay. During the war, Slugger had served in the navy and boxed. "For a dinosaur." A five-second pause. "I'm eighty-four, you know."

"This man's eighty-four." Ownie nudged Turmoil. "Look at what good shape he's in."

Slugger *did* look trim, even to Turmoil. His nose had a slight dip courtesy of an air force sergeant named Powalski, and he walked with the nimble, hot-footed step of a log-roller. "I still like rough weather," Slugger would muse when the wind screamed and the sea convulsed like a wringer washer. "When it was calm out there, I could never sleep. That's when it happened, you know, that's when you got the business."

"You look good, mon," Turmoil allowed. "You muss eat rite."

Slugger acknowledged the compliment with a nod and then looked up at Turmoil and concluded with a swallow: "You're a *big* fella."

Turmoil nodded back. Slugger paused as a tiny jogger scurried by. Spring will have to be here soon, Ownie told himself, ending the impossible gloom that encircled life like a hospital bed curtain. The bad weather was a drag, Ownie decided, because he did a lot of his travelling by bicycle. Hildred used the family car for business, and he hadn't had a licence in decades.

"I swim, that's what I do." Slugger adjusted a shoulder bag from a travel company. "In the winter, I swim at the YMCA every day." Pause. "I still do a mile, sixty-four laps. With flip turns."

"I know *kids* who can't swim a mile," said Ownie.

Slugger touched Ownie's arm, then looked at his face, searching like he'd once searched the sea on a still night when the city was rimmed by lights and alive with the *clickety-clack* of troopships and the buzz of planes, when the war was so new that American tourists came north to gape at convoys.

"I've had a few problems, though. You see, these old women — I call them old, even though they're younger than me — complained to the manager at the Y that I splashed them when I dove in, that I got their hair wet."

Ownie pulled Slugger into a huddle. "So what happened?" Sometimes, when the sky was this grey, Ownie felt that life was like a dirty blackboard, and nothing it recorded was ever sharp and clear.

"The manager said I couldn't dive when they were there because of the complaints, you know." Slugger wiped the corners of his bloodless lips. "I was ready to live with it, but then, a week later, they went to the manager again. They said they could see through the back of my new bathing suit." Slugger looked at Ownie to see whether he understood the magnitude of the charge.

"I felt terrible." Slugger's brow was twisted into a plea for understanding, underscored by the fear that maybe, somehow, he had done something wrong. Ownie silently cursed Slugger's accusers and others like them, getting old people so confused they didn't know themselves, projecting their own hang-ups onto others.

"So I took the suit back to The Bay and I asked the lady, 'Can you see through this?' And she said, 'Of course not,' but she was nice and she gave me a new one." He wiped his mouth as though he was wiping away the last traces of shame.

"They just hate to see a man like you doing somethin'," Ownie reassured him.

Ownie noticed Turmoil stomping his feet, so he tapped Slugger's arm as a sign that he was about to leave. The heavyweight had trouble adjusting to the weather, Ownie noted. The rooming house was freezing, Turmoil had complained, and, to make matters worse, someone had found a dead man in the front hall. Turmoil was also fed up with a wild-eyed bum who, after months of threatening silence, had jumped from a nearby doorway while Turmoil was out running and screamed, "Put some clothes on or I'll shoot you with a rocket launcher." He'd had enough of him.

"Where are you going now?" Ownie asked.

"I'm going to the bank. My son's having some problems with his business, and I'm going to lend him some money, five grand."

"What'll they do, write you a counter cheque?"

"Naaah," Slugger scoffed at the idea. "I don't like to bother with that stuff. I'll get the cash." He tapped the shoulder bag.

"Do you think that's a good idea with all the robberies?"

"They're not going to bother with someone like me. They're looking for an easy mark, somebody old and weak."

"Right on."

Ownie saw a couple approaching on the mile-long bridge, eyes aglaze with post-coital bliss. The man was a wearing a Sure Shot camera, the woman a white sailor's hat and dreams of moving to Charleston, South Carolina. The wind caught the man's words and laughter as he whispered in a voice as sweet and southern as pecan pie: "Y'know, honey, if you lost thirty pounds, you could be a model."

She giggled, holding his white hat and all her silly hopes with one hand.

"I'm serious, honey, you're beautiful."

It was a lie as old as the city, Ownie decided. He peeked over the railing at a US aircraft carrier looming over pint-sized destroyers. It would be a busy week downtown. Anticipating the influx of four thousand sailors, businesses had responded in the usual manner by stockpiling Montreal escorts and Cuban cigars that filled the air with a pungent smell.

Ownie pointed up the harbour past a red Coast Guard ship. "During the war, they put an underwater net out there for the German subs," he shouted. "It was made from steel cable. The outer part had grommets, round pieces of steel that would keep a torpedo from going through."

Looking down, he could still see the convoys, dozens of disparate ships, hastily armed with young boys, ready to be sprung onto the North Atlantic like pinballs, zigzagging past the death traps, blind and erratic, hoping God would take them through. Boys like him and Slugger and his best friend, Teddy.

The wind picked up, swaying the suspension bridge nearly two hundred feet above the water. Ownie braced against the nameless forces, the ones that lured the jumpers and shoved luckless workers to their deaths. Up this high, it felt surreal, post-apocalyptic, with all rules suspended, like some maniac could come along and toss you over or you could lose your faculties for one split second, just long enough to jump. Ownie tried to take his mind off the height.

In the distance, a dilapidated bum was fighting the wind. He was wearing a Scout's hat and wheeling a bicycle decorated with a tiger's tail.

"Look, look!" Turmoil pointed at the bum's bike. Mounted on the handlebars was a milk crate and a sign that said, QUEEN OF THE JUNGLE. Inside the crate, was a cat wearing a bow.

"I always heard that white cats are deaf," Ownie noted. "I had one once, but it was the most awful excuse for a cat. It had missing fur and rheumy eyes that were always sore."

"Mah sister had a beautiful cal'co cat," Turmoil shouted over the wind. "And then she loss it. She wuz so sad, she just mope aroun till one day ah comin home from school and ah see the cat. Ah pick it up and put it under mah shirt. Well this cat, he fight me like a tiger; he just abou tear me apart cuz he been spooked. When ah get home, mah sister open up my shirt, take one look at that cat, and nearly faint. 'That not mah cat,' she say."

They laughed into the cold. It was one of those raw days when the wind sliced through your clothes and brought tears to your eyes, the kind of raw that settled in your bones and bred arthritis, and for a moment, Ownie decided that Turmoil was, despite any reservations he might have had, okay company.

"I heard that all calicos are female," said Ownie.

"Ah dohn know nothin 'bo that. Ah dohn know much 'bo cats at all."

They passed a green support tower with blotches of red primer paint. Ownie followed the blotches up to a maintenance worker, dangling from a belt, and then steadied himself. "It's an awful height."

Turmoil stopped and turned as though he couldn't believe what he had heard. Then he bounced on his toes like he was waiting to return a tennis serve. "No, mon, it not high."

"Not high?"

"No, if ah had mah bathin suit, ah dive right off here." Turmoil bounced again from a hidden trampoline, higher and higher, until his hips kissed the railing.

"You'd dive off here?" In a moment that he would later replay in his head, Ownie felt the mood change as though someone had cut the background music at a party or turned the lights on too soon. He stood still to make sure he had heard correctly.

"Oh yes, mon, ah would."

"You'd be broken into a dozen pieces if you dove off here."

"No, mon." Turmoil laughed like Ownie was crazy, speaking in Tagature language or claiming that all white cats are deaf. "Ah dive off higher places than this back home."

"I've got my doubts about that." Ownie looked in his eyes, but he couldn't find the laughter, he couldn't see the joke.

"Oh yesss."

16

"I wuz in a seniors' home for a spell," Suey confessed.

"How was it?" Ownie was sitting on a bench at Tootsy's.

"I might as well been in the hoosegow," Suey snorted in disgust. "They seen me comin' inta my room one day with a big blonde lady and they start chewing: 'Suey Simms this, Suey Simms that.' I said, 'What Suey Simms does is *his* bidness; you bess get that straight.'"

"Right on." Ownie laced a glove.

"She was a nice lady too, 'bout forty, forty-five."

"Ahhh, some people can't let nothin' be."

"There was a time when Suey Simms had three wimmin. Three wimmin. You rememba that, doncha?"

"Sure."

"All good wimmin too. I loved them all. Yeah, I loved them all."

Suey spit into a handkerchief and stared at a speed bag.

"I didden care if they wuz big and fat."

"Right on."

"I loved them all."

"Why not?"

"I hear Girlie been after LeBlanc about fighting her boy, Hansel."

"Yeah." Ownie shrugged. "She and Hansel been around, trying to rattle his cage."

"You know Girlie, doncha?"

"I trained her brother."

"Which one?"

"Thirsty."

"Oooh, he's baaaaad."

"Years ago, we were down in New Glasgow for a fight." Ownie chuckled. "Girlie and her friends were there, all doozied up, watching Thirsty go through the motions. Anyway, Butch was on the same card, fightin' a six-rounder, and the old man showed up with a teddy of shine in him. Ever since Butch was a little boy, the old man called him Kitty. Everyone else knew him as Butch. So the old man starts screamin' 'Come on, Kitty, for Jesus' sakes, do somethin', you no good bastard.' His voice was like a stepmother's breath, the way it would go right through ya. 'Come on Kittttty!' he said again. Girlie and her friends were lookin' back and forth, rumbling like a volcano. I thought, Christ, there's going to be trouble; they're going to blow. Finally, Girlie spins and says, 'Man, I don't know what you been drinkin', but there's no kitty cat in that ring, just two sorry white boys.'"

They laughed, and Suey spit. "Your boy gonna fight her boy?"

"I dunno." Ownie stopped laughing, sobered by the suggestion. "Hansel's been after LeBlanc ever since they had that fight two years ago. The two of them, Girlie and Hansel, came into the bar where LeBlanc works and tried to run him down, trash talking in front of the customers."

"Yeah?"

"They caused quite a ruckus. Girlie yelled right loud: 'My boy, Hansel, is gonna whip you just like your momma did when you was five years old and she caught you choking that chicken.'"

"Girlie has got a mean mouth onta her."

"Hansel had the big title belt on," said Ownie. "He let

Girlie do the slammin', and he just stood there in the crouch, fingerin' the belt."

"He's a big mama's boy," Suey spat, disgusted. "He used to stool on his old man, get him in hot with Girlie, tell her when Delbert had hooch or a little whoop-de-do on the side. Finally Delbert couldn't take it no more, so he split."

"Don't blame him."

Ownie picked up a newspaper and skipped to the obits. Alfaretta Kingsley, 92, of Upper Rawdon. Survived by sisters Lorinda, Eldora, and Annora.

Ownie had heard a few stories about Suey's brief stay in the seniors' home, which had a radio show hosted by volunteers. The volunteers, when not announcing bingo or crib games, played Charley Pride, Burl Ives, and the odd piece by Marty Robbins. On Mondays, a retired nurse named Marguerite took requests. Marguerite tried to make the show personal, Ownie had heard, by dropping in notes about seniors from the home and offering newsy updates.

"Velma Pace is home from the hospital," Marguerite informed listeners after the ever-popular "Cape Breton Rose." "It's good to have you back, Velma. You still have lots of tests, and they may not all turn out the way you hope, but it's still great to have you back. Welcome."

"Congratulations go out to Wilma DeWolfe and Suey Simms, who are engaged to be married this summer. We understand that Wilma no longer needs her walker. Your children may not be happy, mainly because of Suey's finances and his past history with the ladies, but *still*, congratulations. Best of luck to you both!"

"Didn't your boy beat Hansel?" Suey sat up straight as if he had just remembered.

"Yeah, but Sparks is twice as good now. My fighter's got no left, he throws the occasional overhand right about once a month; he can duck a bit, slip some punches, but then he doesn't counter. He goes to sleep, narcolepsy in the ring. Plus, he thinks he's a singer now, Johnny Cash."

Suey nodded. "He can't infight."

Ownie wondered if he'd heard right. "Who?"

"Girlie's boy. I been watching him over at the amateur gym. He's got no power inside at all. He needs to stand back and crank one in at you. I tole him, and his trainer tellin' him, but he won't listen."

"I thought he had it all by now."

"No, he can't infight worth spit."

"Jesus." Ownie blew out a lungful of pressure.

"Imagine turning in your old man juss because he wuz friendly with some ladies, juss because they liked him. Delbert didn't go lookin' for ladies; they juss came to *him*."

"Maybe we got a prayer. I could stick LeBlanc in his face all night just like smog and smother him."

"Delbert never had to look for a woman in his life! They come to him like bees to honey."

After a couple of minutes' silence, Suey spit in a hanky and cleared his throat. Suey knew the score, he'd been around the block and back. When Suey fought at the Garden, Ownie recalled, he trained at Stillman's, where you could, on a good day, see Sandy Saddler, Willie Pep, or Ray Robinson, who was more electric than the movie stars who ventured in. Butch had been there once, getting ready for a fight.

"That Turmoil, he's a dilly."

"You've got that right," Ownie agreed. "Between me and you, there are times when he looks good, and then there's other times he looks so bad I can't believe it, like he don't know nothin'. On those days, I gotta ask myself, 'What am I doing wrong?'"

Years ago, in a gym, Ownie had met his idol, the famed

Charley Goldman, the man who had taken Marciano into the stratosphere, the genius with the derby hat and the cigar. Goldman, whose gnarled hands were reminders of his own fight career, had watched Ownie working with Tommy Coogan. When Goldman was on his way out of town, a reporter asked him what he thought about Ownie's skills.

"He looks pretty good," offered Goldman, who usually had a smart quip for the press. "I'd say he knows what he's doing." Those words stayed with Ownie over the years, through the bums and hopefuls, through the dry spells and the bursts of action, and now he felt himself gripped by the same fear that had plagued some fighters. If this didn't work, if Turmoil did not become something, Ownie would be blamed by people who did not have the knowledge of Charley Goldman, people who could not see the obstacles he faced.

"You ain't the only one noticin' thangs 'bout that cat."

"Yeah?" Ownie put down his paper.

"Like maybe he ain't all right upstairs."

"Whadya mean?"

"I was in the hood after my little stay in the seniors' home, and I decided to go up and see his pad. It's no problem, everybody know Suey Simms, the Tumblebug; I fought them all, black, white, red, so on and so forth. Anyway, I knock on his door. He comes out and he's wearing a bathrobe like he's at the Playboy mansion. I say, 'Hello, brother,' and he just look at me for a five-count and then he floor me with the right!"

"Jesus Christ!"

"I never even seen it comin'."

"Yeah?"

"Pole-axed."

"The dirty bastard."

"I went down like a guillotine. When I come to, he's standing there and he whispers 'Iiiiiice,' juss so I know where he's coming from. And then, like nothing ever happened, like he hadn't just sucker-punched Suey Simms, a living legend, he smiles right cute-like and says, 'Hi, Suey, c'mon in.'"

"What'd you do?"

"I went in." Suey shrugged. "What could I do? I didn't have no gun on me."

17

Through her office door, Katherine saw Scott MacDonald push the elevator button. He had his head down to avoid being noticed; he had a notepad in his hand.

Katherine liked Scott's looks. She liked his balanced body and his straight nose. She liked the way he walked, as though he had a place to be, as though he had not realized he was the same age as the shufflers in trench coats and fedoras. She liked the fact that he wasn't part of anything: the potlucks, the card games, the cheese club. He didn't partake in lunchroom gossip, and he didn't, as far as she could tell, care about changes at the paper.

Cullen, the legislature reporter, lived for office rumours. MacKenzie was convinced that Cullen had broken into his office at night and copied a personnel file. Sometimes, while pretending to be working, Cullen and the Ports reporter sat at their desks, on opposite sides of the newsroom, and gossiped with each other on their phones.

A practitioner of *l'humoir noire*, Cullen floated about on a cushion of bad puns and clever bon mots. He had dubbed the massacre of three people in a Sydney River McDonald's the McMurders, he was first with the bad Waco jokes. Cullen and his wife were a yuppie power couple. For his birthday, Cullen told the lunchroom, she had bought him a '62 Fender Strato-caster, pre-CBS, fiesta red with a tweed case.

"I've been working on the licks, trying to find where the crazy stuff lives," said Cullen, wearing a Django Reinhardt

T-shirt. Django had a smoke dangling from his lips and a thin moustache shaped like a child's drawing of a cat's mouth. "You can get some strange articulation."

Katherine had the impression that Scott MacDonald couldn't pick Django out of a police lineup and didn't think that Waco was funny.

The elevator arrived and Scott escaped. MacKenzie, Katherine noticed, had taken a new interest in Sports and the boxing beat, hoping, it seemed, to prove he was still relevant. Katherine doubted that Boomer, obsessed with ad revenue and the rationalization of staff, had noticed.

Katherine had an hour before a meeting with Boomer. She opened a computer file and, in an exercise that had become both crucial and familiar, closed her eyes in composition. She was addressing the past, she reminded herself, laying ghosts to rests. If she didn't, she told herself . . . This letter was addressed to Deryk, her former fiancé, now living in Toronto. Katherine believed that the letters were ridding her body of toxins that had accumulated in the form of old hurts and injustices. When purged, the toxins left as caliginous clouds of poison, but if left unchecked, they could destroy her as they had her mother.

> *Dear Deryk:*
> *When I went to London to see you, I was wearing the pearl ring you had given me for my birthday. It was my talisman.*
> *It had been a long trip, but I was thrilled to know that you were working on the movie set as we had long imagined. When you came through the door to meet me, you seemed subdued, and then you looked across the table and gushed as though something marvellous had happened.*

"Well, I've got news." I smiled, intrigued. You stuck out your hand and said, "I got married."

Since you had only been gone three months and we had never broken up, I was speechless. What could I possibly say? Before my mind could clear, an assistant whisked you back to your set, where you remained, ending our meeting and a chapter of my life with an expeditious wave of the hand. You were a coward, Deryk, and a duplicitous person.

> *Sincerely,*
> *Katherine Redgrave*

Katherine entered the publisher's office, its walls decorated with a Dale Carnegie certificate and plaques of appreciation from community groups. The air was cold. On Boomer's desk was the largest nameplate Katherine had ever seen: twelve inches of brass, gaudy and polished as the decor of a fern bar. G. K. BOOMER, PUBLISHER, relocated so often (fourteen times in ten years, to be exact) that he left the name of the paper blank.

Boomer bustled in, a short, shoulderless creature drawn by the playful pen of Dr. Seuss. His body was dominated by a tremendous forehead that left his eyes pale and shrunken. His bushy hair was parted but stood straight up, a triumphant weed that had found the sun.

Garth was supposed to be at the meeting, but Boomer started without him.

"What are you going to do about Webberly from Business?" Boomer dumped problems on people abruptly, a tactic he had adopted to take control.

"I talked to him," Katherine reported. "I told him he can't wear his volunteer firefighter's uniform in the office."

"Make sure it's in writing, a formal letter on his file."

Katherine nodded and decided not to mention Webberly's belt buckle, which was engraved with shooting flames.

"Half of those volunteer firefighters are pyromaniacs," Boomer added.

Garth shuffled in late. Clearing his throat, he settled in a chair. He pulled out a pen and a notebook, mumbling out of range. There was a terse discussion about overtime and early retirement, and Garth muttered something under his breath about Sports. Boomer ignored him and asked about pagination.

Garth had three stock facial expressions, Katherine had noted: the tense, pursed lipped face of disapproval that he wore when employees were summoned to his office; the fist-pumped, let's-go-get-em look of a ball-busting newsman; and the look of total confusion, as blank as a TV that had just lost cable — a look that appeared, without his knowledge, whenever the topic became too complicated.

Noting the blank look, Boomer shot Garth a glare.

Katherine wondered whether Boomer was still angry at MacKenzie over the Bentley funeral debacle. Richard Bentley had sold the *Standard*, a family newspaper, to Gem and died three months later at his country estate. Garth had been one of four people asked to speak at Bentley's funeral; he was the working press, followed by a senator, a horse breeder, and a nephew.

The church was tiny, with wide pine floors and scarred pews marked with heather and a single mauve ribbon. MacKenzie was wearing a white shirt and his good blue suit.

"Richard Bentley was ahead of his time," he boldly declared. MacKenzie looked out at the crowd, hoping to convey the proper image: forceful, reflective, but humbled by the occasion, a mere employee of the great man. Bentley's father and grandfather had run the *Standard* before him, operating on the time-tested principle of noblesse oblige.

"He told reporters to use their eyes and ears."

A woman in an Eva Gabor wig breathed heavily as MacKenzie extolled the dead publisher for his integrity, his foresight, and his contribution to modern journalism."I always remember Richard Bentley telling us: 'Go further. Give the readers more.'" His voice rose. "'Let them feel, smell, and hear the places you're writing about. Let them know what makes a person tick. You're journalists, *journalists*, not some damn recording secretary like Albert Conrad from the *Cumberland County Bugle.*'"

Garth's eyes panned the crowd, past a chic woman in a leopard-print suit and cat's-eye glasses, past a teen in a yachting blazer.

He ignored a photographer kneeling up front, and he glanced at Boomer for reaction. MacKenzie panned until his gaze came to rest on a pot-bellied man in a threadbare suit. The man had the same stunned look of a woman he had once seen on a Cancun beach, pummelled by a wave and knocked to the swirling bottom, groping through sand and confusion. When she had stood up, blood dripping from her nose, the top of her suit had been pulled to her waist, exposing flaccid breasts.

The man was Albert Conrad, Garth realized far too late, and no, he was not dead.

Boomer now stood up from his desk and rocked on his toes, gaining two inches of precious height. Up. Back down. Uuup. Boomer had risen beyond his dreams and his natural place in the order of man, Katherine realized, passing taller, smarter, more genetically gifted humans. He had tasted success, sweet and surprisingly bitter, and he was not about to let it go.

It had not been lost on Boomer that Conrad and Garth

were the same age. Both had started in the business as copy boys, although Garth had insisted, for days after the funeral, that they "had nothing in common."

"Now, this business with who's it from Lifestyles," Boomer said.

"Glenda?" volunteered Katherine.

"Is she still visiting that murderer in Dorchester?" Boomer asked.

"Yes. I talked to her. I explained the paper's position."

"Did she mention his press releases?"

"No, although it's pretty clear she's writing them . . . And . . . ah . . . " Katherine was reluctant. "She says they're getting married."

"Happy honeymoon. She gets one more warning."

"She says she has a lawyer."

"Good. He can find her a job. When we fire her, she'll be blackballed from Heart's Content to Squamish. Make sure she understands that." He shook his gigantic head in disbelief. "How did these people ever get hired?" he asked, apparently not expecting an answer. He ended the meeting before Garth could speak. "That's all."

18

The shabby grocery store reeked of indifference. Located four blocks from Tootsy's, it had eternal lines, dented cans, and registers that broke down just as your exhausted lettuce landed in range. The meat section was stocked with overpriced bologna, produce with deformed turnips.

Marj, the head cashier, was talking to a couple paying for their order with a welfare cheque. "No, you have to spend it all. We aren't allowed to give you change." The woman grumbled as Marj patiently explained: "You can't get cigarettes."

Marj had been at the same cash for twenty years, working split shifts and weekends for minimum wage, a pro in tinted glasses and freshly set hair. She looked at the man, who was ominous in a grey Confederate hat and pile-lined vest, and she sympathized. "It's not right, is it?"

Scott thumbed a *Time* magazine with Bill Clinton, the new president, on the cover. Unlike Clinton, who rose from modest beginnings, these were the people who would never escape, Scott thought, the people who looked out of place at beaches, skin too pallid, hair too long. Clad in cut-off jeans, the men churned up the water in furious imitations of the overhead crawl, pulled up exhausted, then performed raucous dives, the kind that led to spinal injuries. Scott always felt uneasy around them, convinced one of them would drown in a feat of aqua-machismo.

He had gone to the store with Johnny and Louie to pick up water for the gym. He was feeling good. He had been given two weeks to research a series of boxing flashbacks ordered by MacKenzie, who said that Boomer had commended his interest in the Sports section.

"Did you hear about Edwin Moses running with Clinton?" Scott asked Johnny.

"Ah no," admitted the fighter, puzzled.

They had left Louie in the express lane holding two jugs of sparkling water. A crone in red sneakers had eased in beside him. Staring into space and holding a mackerel and a six-pack of bingo markers, she had positioned herself at Louie's elbow, moving forward every time he took a step, her breath on his neck.

"Well, you see, Moses ran with Clinton, and then some magazine quoted him as saying he had trouble keeping up," Scott explained.

"Maybe he got paid." Johnny shrugged.

Louie and the woman stepped over a broken jam jar. Her breathing sounded like the short, startled gasps of a bicycle pump. Trying to ignore her, Louie blinked at Scott and joined the conversation. "That reminds me of when they had Joe Louis refereeing rasslin' or Jesse Owens racing a horse in Cuba," he said. "Personally, I don't think it's right."

"I read a book about Jesse Owens," said Scott. "A teammate said he was the most coordinated person he had ever seen. When he ran, it was like water flowing downhill."

Louie shuffled forward, the woman clinging to his arm. It was clear that she was not going to give in. He gestured for her to go ahead. "Thanks." She smiled a gummy smile of mock surprise and then yelled louder than expected: "Sadie, just put those there."

Sadie, who seemed in no hurry, ambled past Louie and dropped two bags of sour-cream chips, dip, and a mini magazine offering 100 Easy Ways to Lose Weight on the counter. An angora cat the colour of peach ice cream coyly but unconvincingly purred from Sadie's sweatshirt: I'M NOT FAT, I'M FLUFFY.

The express cash had frozen.

Johnny and Scott left Louie and walked to an outside wall lined with boxes soliciting grocery tapes for homeless cats and bowel disease. Nearby were two mechanical rides: a blue elephant and a race car. A distraught toddler was sitting on the elephant, which had one chipped ear, and he was crying.

"Let me try again." The boy's mother kicked the elephant's coin box and rattled the wall plug to no avail. The elephant was dead.

Johnny reached into his pocket and produced a folded sheet of looseleaf, which he handed to Scott. "I'm thinking of running this ad in the newspaper."

Scott read:

> Wanted: Investors and Manager for unique singer/songwriter/sports personality to finance high-quality recording for recording career. Have over 24 original songs with more coming. All investors will realize excellent return within one year. Don't miss this opportunity. Phone J. L.

"Whaddya think it would cost?" Johnny asked.

"Leave it with me. I'll find out."

Scott had always believed that the athletes he interviewed, the hockey players in blazers, the point guards in sweatbands, could not see that he had once been one of them, an elite athlete. And then one day at Tootsy's, Ownie told him to put on the gloves and try the speed bag. On another day, he asked him to go a round with Johnny, who, he reassured him, was "only a welter and won't do any damage to a man your size."

Scott left the ring in a semi-euphoric haze. Anxious, protective, and thrilled by the simple knowledge it was there, Scott harboured the feeling in his chest, buried where no one could touch it. What motivated Ownie, Scott did not know, but after a while, it didn't matter because it made him feel alive, it made him feel, for the second time in his life, part of a self-contained world with its own language, values, and worth. He could probably, he decided, get Johnny a deal on the ad.

Scott saw a woman in a white pantsuit stop at the broken-down elephant. He had seen her in line with two porterhouse steaks and a Camembert clutched to her chest like they might be snatched from her. The woman stared at the mother and the tow-headed boy, apparently about to speak. Why would she talk to them, after ignoring Marj, who had wished her a good day?

"Do you do anything to his hair?" she demanded.

"Huh?" responded the mother, confused.

"His hair. Do you do anything?"

"Here." The mother handed the boy a box of Nerds, hoping to stop the sobs that were heaving through a shirt that said, MY DAD IS IN THE PERSIAN GULF.

"Do you dye it?"

"No!"

Johnny poked Scott and with misplaced confidence named the woman's celebrity lookalike: "Angie Dickinson." Scott could see a faint resemblance, but the real Angie, TV's *Police Woman*, immortalized in reruns, had a much better figure.

"He's only two," the mother added, but Angie was no longer listening. She was teetering through the exit on purple pumps, clutching her cheese and her overpriced steaks. Out-side, she climbed into a Mercury driven by a man whose face graced bus stop benches across the city, a man in a pumpkin blazer and a name tag. Harvey Rich, a member of the Platinum Club and a Registered Relocation Specialist, had twenty years of award-winning sales experience. As Harvey pulled away, leaving the shabby shoppers to their predestined futures, Scott realized where he had seen the woman. In MacKenzie's office. It was Jean, the wife.

19

Ruff. Ruff. The barking startled Ownie, because Arguello was usually as quiet as a blindman's snow, the soft spring cover that could, according to Island folklore, cure cataracts. *Ruff. Ruff.* Ownie crept down the stairs and peered into his rec room. Good God! Tanner, the promoter, was on his knees staring at the little dog.

"Meow." Tanner mimicked a cat.

Ruff. Arguello arched her back.

"Meeeooow." The crazy bastard was tormenting Arguello. *Ruff. Ruff. Ruff.*

"Ow-nee," Tanner yelled innocently over his shoulder. "Thayres somethin' wrong with your dowg. She's a bit of a flutterbug, you."

Tanner had slicked-back hair and a South Shore accent that seemed stuck at sixteen rpms. Ten years ago, the promoter claimed that someone — he didn't know who — had drugged him, and that he'd walked sixty miles to Truro before landing in a greenbelt and taking off all his clothes.

Ownie waited until Tanner was on his feet before he rounded the corner and stated, "There's nothin' wrong with my dog!" Imagine this fool teasing Arguello after all she'd been through!

"How's Louie's weight?" Tanner asked in a false voice. "They'll be some savage if there's problems there."

"His weight is A-1," Ownie snapped, holding a notepad crammed with coded names, weights, and records.

"Good, I don't want no trouble, you."

Tanner was putting on a rinky-dink card and had agreed to give Louie his ring debut. As a favour to Louie, Ownie had arranged for the fireman to meet Tanner at his house, where he could keep a critical eye on the promoter. Ownie was surprised that Louie, who had been pulling down a twelve-hour shift at the fire station, had not arrived by now.

Ownie could only take so much of Tanner. The promoter had grown up on Big Tancook, a South Shore island adrift between Then and Now, an eerie oblong roamed by hybrid cars and the odd birdwatcher. Once a car made the fifteen-minute boat ride to Tancook, it never looked back. It lived out its days without insurance or plates, free of service stations and streetlights. Ownie had taken the ferry to Tancook once after the glory days of schooners and fish, when a special trip for the doctor was five bucks, for the undertaker, ten. In the general store, he had met a skinny kid named Percy, who told him that he had made contact with a church that recruited members on the radio and was planning his break any day.

"We got a lot of money tied up in phone calls," Tanner claimed.

"Yeah, you and Donald Trump."

Relieved, Ownie could hear Louie upstairs talking to Hildred, who had been in the kitchen with a client. "Rocky Marciano is my idol," he was telling her. "He was only five-eleven, you know. When he fought Joe Louis, he had a sixty-eight-inch reach, while Louis was seventy-six." Hildred, Ownie knew, had no interest in anything he was saying.

And why would she? Ownie asked himself. Louie wasn't even one of Ownie's fighters. Louie hung around Tootsy's and paid his weekly dues. And in return for drives and other favours, Ownie helped him when he could, knowing nothing serious would ever come of it.

Louie trotted down the stairs and held out his hand. "How

are ya, Tan?" Ownie winced, refusing to call the promoter — whose full name was Tan Norman Tanner — by his redundant first name.

"Finest kind." Tanner's eyes had raccoon circles.

The promoter laid out the terms of the contract, squeezing his lips as though they were chapped. "I'll be looking for you to get weighed three days before the fight. Three pounds either way. At the last card, some boy from Shediac ended up in hospital dried up like a Digby chick," said Tanner. "He waited until the day of the weigh-in to lose eight pounds."

Louie frowned, evidence, he hoped, that he would never do anything so foolish.

"Don't tell me his trainer was payin' heed. Now the commission's right owly with me."

Ownie knew that the real reason the commission was owly was that Tanner had staged a tough guys' fight-off that ended when a kick-boxer beat the bejesus out of a long-haul trucker in a new definition of tough.

"He wants his pay up front," Ownie said.

"No problem." Solemnly, Tanner pulled the contract from his attaché, his bony hand drooping under the weight of a sapphire ring. He handed Louie a gold pen, engraved, not surprisingly, with his initials, TNT.

To save Louie money, Tanner had arranged, he said, to get his brother, who'd been in corners before, to do the job for free. "He's rock steady," Tanner said. "His name is Verne."

With Tanner gone, Ownie and Louie settled into the rec room chairs. Ownie liked to tell old stories, he admitted to himself, and Louie, who was in need of something, liked to listen. Louie was an emotional orphan, Ownie concluded, in search of a surrogate family. He had joined the fire department, Amway, the gym — he had even done a stint with the Jehovah's Witnesses — seeking the familial bond that he lacked.

"Years ago, whenever we fought in New Glasgow, half the

town would show up for the weigh-in," Ownie told the fireman. "I remember once, it was so crowded that you couldn't breathe. I had Thirsty — Girlie's brother — fighting, and he was worse than LeBlanc in terms of laziness."

Louie, the mole, laughed with him.

"When Thirsty got on the scale, I stood behind him and slipped my hand in the waist of his trunks. Butch started a little noise across the room: 'Your guy's a yokel,' that kind of bullshit, just enough to get everybody watching, hoping for a brawl, while I held up Thirsty until he made weight."

They chuckled.

Ownie could hear voices upstairs, which meant that Hildred's client was being escorted to the door. Hildred's cake designs were becoming more intricate, he noticed, requiring blueprints and a calculator. Sometimes Hildred reminded Ownie of a diamond cutter, the way she handled the fine detail, hunkered over a Byzantine plan of colour-coded blocks.

"When the bad weather hit, the fights shut down around here, so we'd head stateside," Ownie told Louie. "I was up in New York one winter and fought thirteen fights: Park Arena, St. Nicholas Arena. Madison Square Garden was a big feather in your hat, the same as Boston Gardens."

"Man," Louie gushed. "I'd love to fight the Garden."

"Butch was in Toronto for a bit, and he'd drift across the border like acid rain. They were gypsies, those guys; they never had a steady job, a good education, or a trade. A fight would net them a couple hundred bucks and hold them over till the next one. There was no pogey or nothing."

"Did you know that Marciano had a KO percentage of 0.880?" Louie asked.

Ownie stopped to ponder Louie's fascination with giants from the past. Did he understand his place? Did he know his limitations?

"They said that if you hurt the Rock, all he knew how to do was attack," Louie continued. "He wouldn't try to protect himself, he would instinctively attack."

"That's what made him so great," Ownie allowed, "but that was Marciano, not *you*."

Louie paused and then lifted his eyes like a man who had just seen the future. "I dunno, but I think I've got that in me."

20

It was fight night and Verne was in Louie's corner. He looked like a House of Hu waiter, in a black corner man's jacket with short sleeves, a V-neck, and a red zipper-front. He'd had his name stitched over the heart by a local seamstress, but she'd left out one *N*.

"I was right disappointed," he admitted to Louie, "but what could you do? She was as sweet as a honeydew melon."

Louie nodded, unsure of Verne's abilities. Tanner's brother lived in the sticks surrounded by hosers with beaters on their front lawns and starved dogs out back. They started grease fires at night, they drove into clotheslines on snowmobiles. Given that milieu, Verne was thrilled to be in town.

"Holy chain lightnin'!" Verne squawked after he accidentally tipped the water. And then to himself: "Be careful, you!"

Tanner had managed to pull in a small crowd for the event, which was being held in a bingo hall. The promoter was walking around the room, skeletal in a white dress shirt and undershirt. On one calf, hidden by dress pants, was a long-legged pinup, circa 1950. He nodded at Ownie, sitting ringside with Johnny and Turmoil.

When the three men had arrived, Turmoil had boldly strutted past everyone in the lineup to the front, where Tanner was wielding a gigantic stamp that he used to mark paid spectators' hands. Turmoil was in the habit, Ownie had noted, of going wherever he pleased, of strolling into banks, office

125

buildings, and newspapers, bypassing receptionists and guards. Who, Ownie wondered, was going to stop him?

"Okay, let's settle 'er down." Verne steadied himself. "It's the old dog for the hard road." Verne checked his ears for cut sticks and then told himself: "Why even think about the jacket when half these fellas can't spell?"

"He's yours if you want him." Verne tapped Louie's shoulder and pointed across the ring at the opponent. "He's just sittin' there like a big, bald-headed cabbage."

Louie nodded, slipping into the lethal form of the Manassa Mauler, loaded and aimed at Jess Willard. Rotating his neck, he recalled Ownie's instructions as he studied his opponent. "Don't go doin' nothin' stupid. Take your time. See if you can feel him out. You're in no rush."

Louie decided to ignore them, knowing his destiny lay elsewhere. Drawing from boxing lore, Louie recalled that it took Dempsey just three rounds to punish Willard so badly that he couldn't get off his stool. A twenty-punch combination immortalized in a mural on his Broadway restaurant. Dempsey gave Willard a broken jaw, six busted ribs, and missing teeth by taking the fight to him. He could do the same.

Louie smiled at the ring girl, who was smoking a cigar. Coyly, she waved a gloved hand. He thought that maybe she knew his old girlfriend, Sandra, or perhaps she recognized him from the firemen's beefcake calendar, a fundraiser saucily named *Hot Stuff*.

"Here they go, ladies and gents, four rounds of first-rate fistiana." The cable TV announcer was a community college student, his colour man a former ring judge who spoke only in 1940s slang and generously estimated the crowd at 250. "We've already seen a couple of clever ring generals."

Louie was wearing white, twelve-inch-high, leather boxing boots with a St. Christopher medal taped inside the laces. Johnny had offered to lend him gear, but Louie had declined.

"The first fight's special. I've paid a guy to videotape it, and it's going in my collection next to *One-Punch Knockouts, Mike Tyson's Greatest Hits*, and *Legendary Champs*."

Louie left the corner flat-footed and parked himself in front of his opponent, who was as tall and as impossibly thin as a barefoot Kenyan who could run highland trails for eight hours straight. His name was Kyte. "Don't be fooled," Ownie had warned. "Some of them tall guys are made of wire. Tommy Hearns had feet that hardly touched the canvas and a right cross that could send you to the moon."

Louie let loose with a haymaker. "Height don't mean squat," Verne shouted. "It's the empty vessel looms largest."

When Dempsey fought Luis Firpo, there were eleven knockdowns in two rounds, Louie recalled. Firpo was down nine times, Dempsey twice, once clean through the ropes into the laps of the pressmen. Man, that was tough with a capital T.

Verne nodded with excitement when Louie attacked.

"That was a dandy," noted the announcer. "Lots of spirit in there tonight."

"Back in the 1930s, there was Panama Al Brown," Ownie had cautioned Louie, who was now flying solo. "Almost six foot and one-hundred-sixteen pounds, destroying guys nine inches shorter. He was a character; they said he knew Hemingway and could speak seven languages."

Kyte hit Louie with two shots to the breadbasket. Louie shook his head. "No, man," he muttered. "Iron abs, Mr. Nova Scotia, you can't hurt me." Verne nodded; the crowd laughed appreciatively, forcing the ring girl to smile.

Then Louie decided to do the Ali shuffle, to lean away at the last possible moment. He loved it when Ali circled Liston, taunting the Big Ugly Bear, slipping and sliding like a shell game. After he fought the champ, Henry Cooper said Ali could judge the distance of a punch to a quarter-inch just like radar. The Arabian Knight, a favourite of the ladies, would show them all some steps. Ha. Ha. Louie lowered his arms and stuck out his chin. He felt so good, so confident that he winked.

Pow. Kyte connected. Bull's eye.

"That's it!" The colour man thumped his desk. "That's the flattener!"

The crowd let out a collective groan and Ownie shook his head. Johnny tried to remain expressionless. Turmoil, who had just returned from a fight in Toronto, a unanimous decision in his favour, laughed out loud. He laughed, Ownie noticed, until tears formed in his eyes.

Louie didn't feel the punch, but he sensed his mouthpiece flying through the air as he toppled backwards. He hit the ropes, mouth open, legs spread, dropping to the canvas. It was a curious sensation that later he could only compare to the time he'd had his wisdom teeth removed and, coming to, sensed bodies nearby, vague and indistinguishable. The ref sent Kyte to his corner and the ring girl covered her face.

"He's gone down the blackout highway and it's a one-way trip."

"What a way to end your first fight: one minute and twenty-two seconds."

"A bitter lesson in the sweet science of pugilism."

Kyte lifted his arms triumphantly and waved to the crowd, flashing metal teeth. His trainer patted his back and handed him his robe, a Quality Inn bath towel with a hole cut out for the head. The fight was over.

"Sweet humpbacked Jesus," Verne cursed and then started to move across the ring. Verne ran like a cat, legs swinging inward toward his body, perfect for navigating railings but awkward in a human. He went back for his towel and started to run again. Every two years, the *Standard* would carry a story of some rural man, who, while visiting friends at a camp in the woods, decided, in minus-twenty-degree weather, to walk across a frozen lake but, since it was 3 a.m. and he was completely drunk, became lost and may now lose all his toes. One year, that man was Verne. Louie was still dangling from the ropes as Verne wailed: "Jesus, I hope he ain't dead. I don't care for dead people."

Verne raced past the ring doctor and the ref and across the canvas to the media pit, where Scott was sitting. "Here you! In here!" He motioned to a photographer, who looked around to make sure Verne meant him. "In here. It's a dandy." Verne parted the ropes as the kid scrambled through. "Look at him!" Verne pointed as they reached Louie. "Look, he's colder than a whore's heart!"

The photographer got off a flurry of shots, kneeling for a close-up, then changing his lens. The ring doctor peered into Louie's eyes with a pen flashlight, one, then the other. The photographer turned the camera horizontal. Click. Click. Then vertical. Satisfied, he nodded thanks and scurried off.

Louie squinted as his stretcher slid into the ambulance. "Thanks," Louie muttered as Verne clambered up to join him. "I'm flattened and you're telling a photographer to get in close."

Verne's face split in two as he leaned down and whispered, as though he had a right to be indignant. "I couldn't do nothin' for you, he'd already darkened your lights. I thought maybe this would be the kid's break, that maybe the picture would make him famous or something."

Louie tried to shake his head but couldn't.

"Yooou," Verne said accusingly. "Yooou'd a been paht of it too!"

21

Scott watched the girl turn around, a moving Monet of white hair, pink cheeks, and pastel flowers. She had blueberry eyes and hair so clean you could smell it.

"Would you like an ice cream?" asked her mother at the Athena counter.

"Can Barney have one too?" the girl inquired coyly.

"Dinosaurs don't like ice cream." The fat mother shared a manic smile with Scott, convinced he was as enchanted as she was. The mother was wearing a grease-stained anorak and sweats. She belonged to a sect of middle-aged women who had sacrificed themselves on the altar of Motherhood, laid down their youth and sex in a heap, hacked off their hair, stuffed their flaccid thighs into Northern Nights sweatsuits, and grown unplucked whiskers. Why? Scott wondered. So the gods would be good to their children?

A three-foot urchin with Billy Ray Cyrus hair approached the girl, bouncing in rubber boots, keeping time to something in his head. Behind him, a big man had ordered takeout fries with gravy.

"Say hi to the little boy." The mother's eyes were commas, typed deep into the pages of her swollen face. *Bounce. Bounce.* "Her name is Logan." The mother beamed. "She is named after the highest mountain in Canada, fifty-seven hundred metres, in Kluane National Park."

As Logan opened her rosebud mouth, the boy kicked a rubber boot into the air in a modified martial arts manoeuvre copied from TV. "Ohhh Ohhh Poweeer Raaangers," he chanted, spinning in a circle, leg extended. "Do do do do Mighty Morphin . . ." head bobbing trancelike, arm reaching for Barney.

"Waaah," Logan yelped as he snatched the dinosaur from her hand. "Waaaaah."

"Jordan!" A bored voice drifted across the Athena past an ancient wooden highchair. "Give it back." A woman wearing eyeliner and a Mixed Dart League jacket had one hand on her hip. Jordan ignored her. "Hey, bud." She smiled a what-can-you-do smile. "I said, give it back." Then she cackled to Scott, "He's tough as nails," as a regular named Bert took a counter seat and ordered the Big Breakfast. "He's only four, but he ain't afraid of nothin'."

Don't Let Someone You Love Fall Off Their Chair and Crush Themselves. Buy This Mint Condition Geriatric Chair. $30 obo. Phone Gavin.

"Kids are under so much pressure today," Sasha decided after the two families left. "I was in a school and the walls were plastered with warnings against the evils of the Earth: Halloween, fur, perfume, rap music, chocolate, bicycles, unwashed fruit, Barbie, and pogs. It's as though the yuppies, the peace-love-and-pot generation, had their fun and now they want to put their kids in a sensory deprivation tank, to never smell, feel, or touch, to never challenge what they had."

Scott nodded, wondering what a pog was.

He watched a squat man trudge down the street pigeon-toed. He had a blue duffel bag on one shoulder and a purposeful look on his bearded face. He was heading somewhere — a place that must have been worth walking to — in full goalie gear.

"My friend Pru worked as a nanny for a couple with four kids. The mother was a doctor who ran marathons, the father a stockbroker. Do you know the type of people I'm talking about, the ones who mail in updates of themselves to *Alumni News* to make sure they're real?"

Patrick Roy. Scott read the signature on the guy's hockey helmet. The man had an orange metal net slung on his shoulder, and Scott, to his own surprise, felt an urge to follow him wherever he was going. The hockey net made him think of Smithers, whom he rarely saw, since he was spending most of his time out of the office. Scott had a laptop in his apartment and a list of stories to complete.

Last week, Ownie had let him spar two rounds with Johnny. It had been going well, Scott recalled, until Turmoil stormed into the gym and changed the mood by demanding to know why Ownie had not phoned him about something inconsequential, something he didn't even care about. There were days when the giant could invigorate the gym, Scott noticed, days when the other fighters could feed off his size and booming laugh. On those days, he raised the collective bar. And then there were days when Turmoil was menacing and sullen, and everyone felt small.

"The whole neighbourhood was creepy," Sasha continued. "All of the adults were working and the kids were in daycare, so when you went outside, it was like you were in the Nevada desert during nuclear testing."

Scott nodded. He wasn't a part of *it* now any more than he had been twenty-five years ago. Pre-schools, time-shares, and rotating gourmet dinner parties. Montessori. Jerry Garcia neckties and Fender Stratocasters. Scott was on the outside looking in, a time traveller, stumbling over the footprints of his generation, numb to the culture that bound them, deaf to their music, blind to their signposts. He was a man who had never dropped acid or attended a drive-in movie.

Scott was never going to be part of his own self-worshipping generation, but he could, he decided, talking to Sasha at a chipped booth in the Athena Restaurant, be part of society.

"Do you ever read *Runners World*?" Scott asked. "They had a story recently on Bill Clinton . . . ah . . . he's a yuppie." He struggled to justify his segue.

"All right."

"The man weighs well over two hundred pounds, and he lumbers along like a big, goofy dog. I give him credit for being active but don't go writing about him like he's a real runner."

Scott hoped he could get to his point, the one that haunted him for reasons he was trying to explain. "He ran with Edwin Moses a while ago. You know who Edwin Moses is, don't you, the greatest hurdler ever, one of those genetically gifted people? He had over one hundred consecutive wins and two Olympic medals."

She nodded vaguely.

"And then Clinton ran with the winners of the Boston Marathon. The Boston Marathon! I don't know." Scott thought about it as Bert shuffled to the cash. "There's something indecent about that, something disrespectful."

Sasha looked at him seriously, weighing the point.

"I don't think it should be allowed. I mean, the Americans have laws protecting the flag, you can't desecrate it." Sasha nodded in understanding. "Laws against betting on your sport. Look what they did to Pete Rose, banned from the Hall of Fame. Laws protecting historic buildings, eagle feathers, and endangered frogs."

"That's true."

"Why not a law protecting the dignity of people like Edwin Moses? How do we know he wasn't coerced into running? That maybe the CIA or some nefarious government agency wasn't involved? I'm sorry." Scott felt embarrassed by his uncharacteristic outburst. "Is it really beyond the realm of possibility?"

Scott located his sandwich in the lunchroom fridge of the *Standard* behind a tub of three-bean salad. He moved a block of old cheddar bound with shipping tape and labelled PROPERTY OF MARCIA G. SMITH, proof that the coveted Cheese Club orders had arrived, a highly anticipated event in the newsroom.

He returned to his desk, where Smithers was searching for news on a top draft pick, a centre from the Peterborough Petes. The hockey reporter was in a foul mood. After he had been dumped by the dancer, the junior hockey team had given Francis its Most Devoted Fan Award, ensuring months of continued torment.

"You know what I heard about the centre?" asked Warshick, sensing that Smithers was down, vulnerable to attack. "From a buddy of mine who covered the training camp?"

"What?" Smithers snapped.

"I heard that when little kids come up and ask for an autograph, he takes the card with his picture and signs it. Then he deliberately crumples it in his hand before he hands it back. That way it's worth less."

"Bullshit!"

"It's true, and he smiles when he does it."

Smithers saw Carla heading toward Sports, cause for alarm. The *Standard* had always been a place of closed doors and whispers, of drastic decisions that no one ever saw coming. A call to the ME's office could be trouble. For a short while, Cullen, whose desk was outside MacKenzie's office, had been able to predict some of the layoffs, transfers, and management coups by eavesdropping but then Maintenance installed a soundproof door, and everyone went back to guessing.

Carla hadn't been looking for Smithers, he was lucky this

time. Her target was Scott, who had made the mistake of visiting the *Standard* during daylight.

Now sitting in MacKenzie's office, Scott looked at the walls, which were covered with photos of biplanes, triplanes, and supersonic jets, some in flight, some with labels in the margin of the shot.

"I see that you've been doing a few stories on this Davies fighter, the big heavy," MacKenzie said.

"Uh-huh." Scott nodded from a chair. "That's right. I went to Montreal."

The same consultant who had ordered the newsroom dipped in green had advised Gem to increase its coverage of visible minorities, and MacKenzie, seeking approbation, had thought about Turmoil.

"He reminds me of a slugger named School Boy Langille, who was built along the same lines. Langille fought out of Glace Bay for most of his career, but he had some super bouts down in New England. A real corker."

Scott wondered when he had last heard "super" and "corker" in the same sentence.

"The best fight I ever saw was between Langille and a southpaw named Gunboat Callaghan. They packed the Halifax Forum tighter than a sardine can. Gunboat knocked School Boy to the canvas three times." MacKenzie had slipped into storyteller mode, mental gears greased by the memory of School Boy, a Cape Breton brawler with twenty-two wins, twelve losses, and a draw with obscurity. When he shot Scott a glance, white hairs bristled under his chin like the hairs on a pig's belly.

A week ago, a big story had broken and the newsroom was mobilized. Reporters were dispatched, photographers summoned, phones manned, and Garth had stood in the centre of the storm, unable, it seemed, to remember what to do. The ME looked stricken, Scott had noticed, as though he *knew* he was lost.

"Hey diddle diddle," MacKenzie muttered incongruously, and then stared at Scott through glasses smeared with grease and dandruff. Scott froze, pretending he hadn't heard, determined not to speak. Phobic about interruptions, MacKenzie had once fired a features editor, a woman named Sally, who had dared to finish his sentence.

There were no female editors in Sports. Scott doubted that any woman could stand being that close to Smithers and Warshick, who took up too much real estate. Scott thought about the new city editor, Katherine. She must be six feet tall. With her height, he decided, she could have been a rower. Didn't Silken Laumann, the iron Viking with battle scars, call rowing a haven for big, awkward girls? Size counted, especially in a headwind.

Scott thought about the summer when two girls had started rowing on his lake, leaving a parallel wharf at six each morning like a train with a schedule to keep. Some days, it was just him and them on the water, and Scott felt a kinship, a bond.

They were part of the ecosystem, like the lilies, the errant eels, and the white sand dumped on a beach each spring, where it languished until the first good storm. The girls had appeared with the crocuses, swinging their oars like long-legged bugs so awkward they seemed wounded, catching, crabbing. By summer's end, they were muscular seabirds that had learned to fly.

One morning, the sky was hidden by a slate ceiling streaked with danger, and Scott felt special, removed from the sleeping masses. By the time Scott had paddled to an overhead bridge, hungry waves were lapping the sides of his boat. The wind shifted to a crafty cross, nudging like someone gradually taking over a bed. Hit properly, keep your paddle down where the wind can't grab it. And then, without warning, a gust attacked, twisting the paddle in his grip. Wind flooded his mouth, flapping his cheeks like a jib, freeze-drying his teeth.

It felt cleansing, the harsh air sucking grease and spent cells from his body. An icy wave goosed him, and then it started: sheets of hysterical rain that felt like BBs, bouncing off the lake, blinding, driving so hard that the world vanished and the waters stilled. Monsoonlike rain. "Oh my God!" the girls shrieked, the most uncensored laughter he had ever heard. Whooping, they turned to shore, water filling their fragile boat. They shouted something as they passed him, but he couldn't make it out.

The managing editor tilted back in his chair. And then abruptly, as though he had been hit by School Boy, MacKenzie pulled out a notepad and said, "I think it's time for a . . ." In his head, Scott finished the sentence before MacKenzie could spit out the dreaded words: Where Are They Now?

What had started as a simple experiment, a look at old newsmakers who had vanished from the public eye, had spread like an outbreak of chinch bugs. MacKenzie's problem was supply. After four months, he had used up his store of worthy subjects from the past and what remained were the School Boys, the Gunboats, the woman who may or may not have met the Duke of Windsor in the Bahamas, the man whose great-uncle had perished on the *Titanic*, the perfectly ordinary people whose perfectly ordinary lives were drawing to a close.

Scott stared at MacKenzie's shamrock cardigan.

"I don't know where he is, but I'll tell you how you can get a lead. Call Wimpy MacPherson down in Glace Bay; he used to manage School Boy. He was an outstanding senior hockey player and could skate like hell. Super guy to talk to."

MacKenzie stood up and turned toward his door, giving Scott a clear look at the back of his cardigan. Hunt Club. XL. Yes, he realized, it was inside out.

22

To Ownie, the new rink felt like an airtight shipping container on the waterfront. When a puck hit the boards, it made a hollow pop, echoed by row after row of empty bleachers. There was a sense of timelessness in the windowless fabricated enclosure; it could have been noon or three in the morning, Ecum Secum or Istanbul.

Ownie glanced at the sheet he'd been given by the team.

Weight	213	210
% fat	13.8	11
VO$_2$ Max	53.7	+55
Training HR (low)	138-143	140-145
(high)	156-161	160-165
Sprint Test (Peak)	12.4	+13
Mean	57.3	+60
Bench Press	200	245
Chin-Ups	4	25
Dips	10	+25
Sit-Ups	N/A	+60

It didn't matter, he decided, stuffing the printed sheet into his pocket. They only cared about one thing. "Okay, Jonathon," Ownie shouted, knowing exactly what that was. "Come here."

Jonathon glided over the blue line, drawn by an invisible magnet under the ice, a towering automaton who stood six-four on his Bauer Supreme stainless steel blades, a Van Halen disciple with a partial plate. The rink was empty; he and Ownie had the ice to themselves.

"Let's get down to business," Ownie ordered.

Jonathon nodded inside a plastic shield. Through the shield, Ownie could see *it*: a scar that masqueraded as a harelip until you got up close and saw the irreversible damage: twenty-four stitches, a fractured skull, and a million-dollar contract hanging by a suture.

"When we finish here, you're gonna feel like George Foreman," Ownie announced. Jonathon smiled a mechanical smile that opened from the middle like an elevator door, showed a flash of teeth, then shut, a smile devoid of warmth or humour. "Only not so old."

When Ownie first saw Jonathon a couple of years ago, the boy walked with a swagger. You almost expected him to hoist up his pants and spit. He had Elvis sideburns, a scowl, and a mean grimace on his boyish face. Ownie knew what that was for: it was a cover, a way to pretend that everything wasn't perfect, that he wasn't really blessed, so that ordinary mortals wouldn't realize what an awesome life he had and try to take it from him. Now the swagger and scowl were gone. Jonathon's mouth was frozen in shock, like a skier looking into the face of an avalanche.

Ownie was holding up a pad, which Jonathon was punching with his right hand, the left hand extended as though he was holding onto an opponent's sweater in a fight. "You wanna get in three or four quick, straight punches, and then an upper cut, all while keeping your balance," Ownie explained. "You can't get knocked off your feet. If you go down, you lose."

Still boyish, Jonathon's shoulders were like coat hangers, metal edges that time would pad. From the corner of his eye, Ownie saw a jogger wired to a Walkman chugging around the top of the rink. The jogger veered around something that was low and out of sight, probably, Ownie concluded, a kid salvaging errant pucks.

"That's beautiful. Now work on your balance, stay centred," Ownie yelled. "Keep your legs spread, your ass down. You'll have it made."

Ownie didn't know if Jonathon would make it. He'd give him his best shot: teach him how to fight, build up his confidence, and arm him for the next round of goons. That's all he could do. On his next lap, the jogger veered again, Ownie noticed.

"Ray Robinson had phenomenal balance; he was smooth and graceful with everything he did," Ownie explained. "He was a dancer in Paris for a while."

Jonathon had never been to Paris; he was a first-round draft pick: a power forward in the Ontario Hockey League who scored twenty-one goals and forty-three points in his rookie NHL season before he was taken out by a goon, a no-talent thug who fought his way up from East Coast league hockey, a scalp-collector who earned his bounty by knocking off kids.

"It's all balance and rhythm."

Ownie checked the Pepsi clock with the puck-shaped puncture. When he did, he saw something flash behind row M, near the jogger's detour.

He'd been working with Jonathon for a week, a recurring sideline that started when the AHL came to town. The team called him a trainer and kept his real role secret, which was fine with him but gave Butch something to bitch about. "What are you, a leper?" demanded Butch, who tried to take the good out of everything. Ownie got his satisfaction not from recognition, but from resurrecting guys like Bryan McSweeney, another casualty who'd come to him shell-shocked. For an entire month after he'd arrived, McSweeney picked the skin off every finger on his hands, trying to get to the root of his fears. They worked on strength and fighting until, convinced he was invincible, McSweeney skated circles around the dressing room, shredding the rubber mat, and yelling, "He's mine, man, he's mine."

The jogger veered again.

Last week, Ownie had seen McSweeney on TV scoring two goals. He'd rather think about that, he decided, than Butch's bullshit.

Uuup. Ownie saw a flash of something above the seats. Holy Mary, Mother of God. Dooown. It was Turmoil. What the hell was he doing here?

Ownie packed his gear and headed outside the rink, confused. He banged the side window of a Delta 88, a beater with a sunshade stuck in the windshield, despite the fact that it was snowing. "Take that thing down, will you!" Ownie pointed to the sunshade, which was decorated with toothy squirrels lounging on lawn chairs and sipping margaritas. "Are you nuts? People will think you're a dope dealer or somethin'."

From the driver's seat, Turmoil grabbed the squirrels and stuffed them into the backseat, rattling the rigid cardboard, jamming it past the headrest as though he was acting under protest. Ownie climbed inside, where the two men sat in sullen silence. Heavy flakes were falling, the kind that filled the Emergency Room with frantic wives and chest pains.

"Why you foolin round with them ole hockey players?" Turmoil demanded.

"Pardon me?"

"Them ole hockey players. You shudden have nothin to do with them."

Ownie stared at the snow, insulted. First of all, he didn't like anybody telling him what to do. Secondly, he happened to like hockey, which would have been his sport if he had been any good, if he'd had speed, and a pair of hockey boots and skates that fit, shin pads instead of Eaton's catalogues.

"You should be lookin after *me!*" Turmoil banged the pile steering wheel for emphasis.

"Yooou?" Ownie stretched the word into disbelief.

"Ahm the one who got a fight comin up in two months." Turmoil hit the wheel again. "Ahm the one you s'pose to be training."

"I spend plenty of time with you." Ownie was impatient. "You get three hours at the gym every single day. What more do you want?" Christ, Ownie muttered to himself, he never had to deal with any of this shit with Tommy. He was family, and nothing ever changed; he was the same person every day of the week.

Turmoil mulled it over, staring ahead and then sideways; he fiddled with the dials on his radio, trying to escape the static and Ownie's stare. "Ahll drive you home."

Even Turmoil had legroom in the outsized car he had recently purchased, noted Ownie, who was used to Louie's Jeep. Through the window, Ownie saw a Cougar in summer tires fishtailing up a hill, stopping, starting, then sliding back with a growl. "Gear down, will ya," Ownie urged. "It's slick."

"Do they make good money?" asked Turmoil as Ownie shifted in his seat, which was covered with acrylamb. "Them ole hockey players?"

"Yeah, not bad, depending on what kind of contract they have, who owns them, that stuff. You take a star like Lindros, a showstopper, he signed for three-point-six million."

"Three million dollahs!" Turmoil spun his head sideways. "How come you nebber tole *me* bout this?"

"Why would I tell you?" Ownie asked as the Cougar slid into a lamp pole.

"*Ah* play hockey."

"You do?"

"Yeah, mon."

Ownie pursed his lips for a full twenty seconds. "Hockey?"

"*Ye-aaa-sss!*" As Turmoil extended the word to three ex-cruciating syllables, Ownie shifted, suddenly feeling trapped. The side windows had been tinted by the snow, and the interior of the car felt as dark as a hearse.

"Well, with your size, they'd make a policeman out of you. You've got the horses to do it. You'd make big money."

"Oh, mon, me a poleesemon." Turmoil started to laugh, thin, frozen notes cracking in the air. "In the eye-lands, the poleesemon, they shoot you. You dohn do wha they wahn. *Bang!* In your howse, at the horse races, in the mahket. Oh, ·mon."

"Well, you wouldn't get no gun."

"You show me how we get one of them contracks."

23

It was a clear, starched day, the kind of day that emptied houses of kids and sledders. For a fleeting moment, before the slush and the grease arrived, winter was, Ownie decided with unusual largesse, both white and inviting.

"How big is Lindro?" Turmoil asked, driving.

"Lindros?" Ownie blew out air while crunching numbers in his head. "Ummm, he's big, almost the biggest man in the league. He'd run about two-thirty, I'd say, but pure power. He drives you into the boards right, he'll separate your shoulder or break your collarbone. He don't care."

"Ah cahn handle him."

Ownie shrugged, making sure Turmoil didn't get his hopes up too high. "You could handle him in a *fight*."

"Yeah, yeah, that's wot ah mean."

They were two blocks from Ownie's house, nearing the lake, in a neighbourhood of single family homes with rec rooms and pets. They drove by a clothesline of frozen underwear and T-shirts. A snowman.

"When ah live in Trinidad, ah haf a pet duck," Turmoil said as the car rattled on chains. "His name was Bob." Turmoil smiled at the memory. "He use to follow me ebbywhere. One day he follow me to the rink, where his feet got stuck right to the ice." Turmoil started to laugh. "Just like glue. Ah had to cut him out."

"How were his feet after that?"

"Oh fine." Still laughing. "Jus little bit sore."

Two teenagers whizzed by, bodies low to the ice, licorice legs churning. Hellbent, they chased their hockey sticks like greyhounds pursuing a rabbit. *Zwish. Zwish. Zwish.* The boys raced by Ownie and Turmoil, braiding their legs as they turned in a blur of speed honed at power-skating camp.

Ownie looked up the lake. Enthusiasts had already shovelled several rinks for skating. "We won't bother with any plays," he announced.

"Ah know lots of plays."

"Well, that's not our concern at this point. What they're interested in is your size, your power, not your play-making ability. As I said before, they'd want you as an enforcer, a policeman."

Turmoil nodded as a boy chased a loose puck, then jammed on the brakes, spraying powdered ice. "Okay, ah mek a good poleesemon."

Ownie sat down, savouring the Christmas-card lake in the heart of the city. It was the first thing he'd seen when he'd come to Dartmouth, and the best thing left. It was one of twenty-three lakes, an outdoor sports facility with a twelve-month membership. Swimming and boating in the summer, skating in the winter.

"Whadya got on your hands?" Ownie asked.

"Gloves."

"I can see that. What kinda gloves?"

"They run by batteries." Turmoil opened a pouch on the wrist gauntlet, exposing a D-cell. "Keep mah hands nice and wahm. Ah bought them at C'nadian Tire."

"I thought maybe you were the Bionic Man."

Two women stared at Turmoil, who was dressed all in white. Sometimes, when Ownie walked through town with

Turmoil, he felt heads turning. At times, the heavyweight was so expansive, so full of life, Ownie noted, that people were drawn to him, his vast smile, his open-mouthed laugh, and the way that he touched your arm as though he was bestowing a blessing.

Ownie pulled out a pair of black CCM Ultra Tacks, borrowed from his son, Pat. For a man his size, Turmoil had unremarkable feet, size thirteen. Nostrils tingling, Ownie listened to the clicking of blades around him, cutting into the ice, mixing with the clack of sticks. *Click. Clack. Click. Clack.*

"Are these like the ones you used to wear?"

"Lemme see them." Turmoil studied the Tacks closely, turning them upside down, touching the blades, squeezing the DuraTex lining. Trying to show he knows quality, Ownie figured, stretching the full inspection to sixty seconds. "Yeah, only mine were nicer colour. Blue."

Ownie thought about Turmoil's comment and then decided to let it pass. He bent down to lace his own skates, toe scuffs covered with tape. "I never had a pair of skates fit me right in my life." He shook his head at the injustice. "My feet are too wide, they're webbed, so I can't get nothin' to fit around here. Maybe if I went to Montreal or Boston or someplace that carried more than one size, some place with better shopping than Moscow, I'd have some luck."

"Your feet webbed?" Turmoil asked. "Cahn you swim?"

"Like a duck."

Turmoil laughed. Two girls were trying to skate backwards, wiggling their behinds and hoping their skates would follow. A man zipped by, towing a red-cheeked baby in a sled that was moving at a frightening speed.

"Okay, show me what you can do," Ownie said, standing up.

"Ah wish you had a camera to take a picture of me," Turmoil

beamed. "Mah mooma would be so happy to see me back on skates."

"Yeah, well, let's see what you can do," repeated Ownie, who didn't know what to expect. If Turmoil could just skate and check, he could learn the rest.

Not everyone was like Jonathon, a commodity bred for hockey and shipped at age fourteen, already signed and packaged by a fast-talking agent, to a stark town that only spoke French. Turmoil could pick up the plays that Jonathon had mastered. He could learn when to fake, when to deke, when to drop the gloves and teach some meathead the meaning of respect. If he just had the basics, God, in all his mystery, had given him the rest.

"Okay, let's go." Ownie squinted as Turmoil pushed off.

In his mind, Ownie could see two giants, one black, one white, stripped to pads and skates, as the crowd screamed for blood. In the picture, Ownie was in the good seats, next to a man in a sheepskin coat. "I figured he could handle Lindros," Ownie told the man, who may have been a doctor. "I'm his trainer, you know."

Turmoil took two half-steps, then slid forward, feet together, arms out like he was surfing a wave. What's he doing? Ownie wondered, as the women whizzed by, giggling. Turmoil lifted an arm to wave, and his feet shot out.

"Ah dohn like these skates," Turmoil protested as Ownie hauled him up from the ice. "Ah think they dull."

"There's nothing wrong with them skates." Ownie strained under the huge man's weight, wincing as his bad shoulder creaked. It was the one he'd frigged up decades earlier when he swiped a two-hundred-pound buck from the roof of a Studebaker parked downtown. He made it four blocks with the buck on his back before he slipped on loose roofing shingles and lay there, pinned. "Give it another try."

Ownie pushed and the shoulder screamed in pain. He had only taken the deer because it was jacked; because Benny Burgess was driving around town like he'd been on a safari instead of out in the woods with lights.

Moving Turmoil was like trying to stand a strip of rolled-out clay on its end. He managed to shove the fighter upright. On skates, the big man looked as pitiful as a newborn calf whose spindly legs could not yet support him. Turmoil lifted one foot, fast and high, as though he was warming up for a sprint. Then another fast high step, bending the knee to his chest, and collapsing on the third precarious step.

"Ah dohn like them skates," he said, rubbing his head with a battery-operated glove, nursing what would soon become an egg-sized bump.

"C'mon, let's get out of here." Ownie couldn't believe he'd been so stupid, a man his age. He felt like one of those dotty seniors who mails in five hundred bucks to a scam artist after being told that he's won a car.

"Ah tole you mine were blue," Turmoil shouted. "Blue skates. Thas what everyone uses in Trinidad."

"You are wasting my time, you goddamn liar. You've never been on skates in your life."

24

At Video Madness, two cops were dragging out a man who was hanging motionless. He looked like Gandhi, if Gandhi wore a buttonless Naugahyde jacket cinched with a belt and lace-free sneakers. Another cop was talking to an agitated store clerk named Robert.

The store was run by a Lebanese family, short, unshockable men who worked for eight months and then, without explanation, disappeared. Flexible, they waived late charges to regulars; they slipped free candy to Dickensian waifs. There was no damage deposit on the upstairs apartments, and working girls got one call a night on the CUSTOMERS ONLY payphone.

"He looks like he could fight a bit." From Louie's parked Jeep, Ownie nodded at Robert with approval. "Just crazy enough."

"You think?" asked Louie.

The Jeep door opened and Johnny hopped in. The houses on the street looked like accident victims, Ownie thought as they pulled away. The original shingles had been replaced by foot-high boards that skewered the symmetry; big wooden windows had yielded to squinty-eyed metal ones that made the downtown's demise easier to observe.

They drove by an old woman propelling a wheelchair with her legs, a cigarette dangling from her lips. Hanging from the back of her chair was a liquor store bag.

Ownie glanced at the window of Tony's Hairstyling, which was covered with faded models in 1950s hairdos, swarthy men with strong jaws and open collars. Inside, Ownie could see Tony, dressed completely in white, finishing a cut. With his powdered brush, Tony whisked the customer's neck, ta-da, the same cut for thirty years. One day, Tony had beckoned Ownie into the corner of the shop where he stored his towels and pet food. Tony always kept his dog, a teacup poodle named Bambino, with him during the day, placing the dog in the empty chair between clients. "When I worked in New York, some wise guys wanted to set me up," he whispered to Ownie while Bambino dozed.

"Yeah?" asked Ownie, who thought wise guys were more stylish.

"Oh yeah," said Tony with an ominous tone. "I had to leave. You can't say no to wise guys."

Louie had parked the Jeep around the corner from Tootsy's. Johnny ambled up the gym's stairs followed by a greaseball named Damien, whom he'd found lurking outside the building.

"How's your brother?" Johnny asked as he unlocked the gym door.

Damien did a quick shadowbox, then feigned a shot to Johnny's stomach, a sign he was feeling good, sprung after sixty cool days for possession. "He was in for the autopsy." Damien tried to sound knowledgeable. "He's just waitin' now."

"Yeah?" Johnny fiddled with the lock, wondering what was keeping Ownie and Louie, who had told him to go ahead.

"They should have the results in ten days."

"That long, eh?"

"Yeah, them doctors, they don't know nothin'."

Pleased with his appraisal of the medical profession,

Damien puffed out his chest and strolled into the gym, which was still empty. IF YOU THINK I'M UGLY YOU SHOULD SEE WHAT I WOKE UP TO, his T-shirt warned. On his shaved, pinched head was a leather do-rag.

"I'm waiting for Godzilla," Damien explained.

"He should be here soon."

Godzilla was Turmoil's latest sparring partner. Another Great White Dope, Ownie called him behind his back, a mucklehead who made it one Olympic round before he fractured his elbow. His real name was Dylan Atwood.

Atwood arrived at the same time as Louie and Ownie, who greeted him with a curt nod. "This guy had it handed to him on a silver platter," Ownie explained to Louie when they moved across the room. "There hasn't been a white heavy-weight champ since Ingemar Johannson back in 1959, so whenever a good white guy appears, it's as exciting as an albino ape. The handlers were so thrilled about Willie DeWitt that they took out kidnap insurance."

Out of earshot, Atwood was changing. He was two hundred and forty pounds of pig-headed arrogance with the mindless superiority complex that started in the reinforced crib of a thirteen-pound baby. A maple leaf tattoo adorned a bicep with stretch marks. After his Olympic fizzle, Ownie remembered, after he'd worn his Canada tracksuit to every rum room in town, after he'd been introduced at city hall and the legislature, Atwood turned pro. In the third round of his debut fight, when a banger from Chicago was playing "Wipeout" on his head, Atwood's mother started screaming, "Stop it, stop it," like Atwood didn't regularly hurl drunks down stairs, like she wasn't an old grease bag with a grey rat-tail. Before Ownie could intervene, she threw a towel into the ring. "You'd have stayed in that ring all night before I'd have stopped it," Ownie told Atwood. "Things were just getting good."

Champion Management paid for Atwood's services, and, for the most part, left Turmoil's training to Ownie. Champion's lawyer, Douglas, did, in a nod to modern science, arrange to have the heavyweight tested by a sports physiologist at one of the universities, a dour little man named Attilla. Over two days, Attilla attached Turmoil to wires, he pinched his skin with calipers, he sat him on a bicycle ergometer and made him breathe through a mouthpiece while wearing a nose clip. He did blood lactate tests, anthropometric testing, and a flexibility assessment, and concluded, to no one's surprise, that Turmoil was an extraordinary athlete. "I have only had one athlete, a powerlifter, score higher on the strength tests," Attilla reported back. "And Turmoil's VO_2 max was astounding."

In the ring, Turmoil swatted the red spittoon. "Ah met girls who hit harder than that," he shouted at Atwood.

"Shut up and go to work," Ownie ordered. "You couldn't do nothin' with the man last month."

Atwood nodded and wiggled a tooth, checking for firmness. On most nights, Atwood worked as a bouncer at Kissin' Cousins, a dive with watered-down beer and line dancing. When bored, Atwood used to hurl drunks down the stairs, fracturing two skulls before someone sweetened the tank of his Monte Carlo.

"Okay, mix it up a bit," Ownie shouted. Atwood was useful, but everyone knew Ownie didn't like him, not since he had ruined a lovely little middleweight from New Glasgow. The kid's coach was a moron who put him in the ring with Atwood, and the fathead punched him out of his boots.

Turmoil charged, his punches moving Atwood backwards, stealing his counterpunches. *Boom. Boom. Boom.* Atwood took two pokes, but the blows slid off Turmoil's chest like a sparrow hitting a plate-glass window.

"Okay, take it easy," Ownie ordered.

Atwood's bulky torso was dotted with the pink patches, like oversized flea bites. *Boom. Boom. Boom. Boom. Boom.* Turmoil pummelled the bouncer with a five-punch volley and then charged again. Atwood's legs were moving in the wrong direction, as though he was trying to balance on a unicycle. Turmoil connected low and Atwood screamed "Aaah!"

The sparring was over. Ownie knew that beating up Atwood was progress.

After Sanchez, Turmoil had picked up three wins, two at home and one in Montreal. The second fight was the only setback, a strategic error, a loss to Art Moore in Montreal, six months too soon. Now, Ownie decided, they were back on track.

The trainer nodded at Scott, who had slipped in during the sparring and sat on a bench. Ownie then headed across the gym to talk to Louie, who he suspected was back on the juice. Ownie heard Turmoil following him.

"Ah got a good idea, Ownie." Turmoil beamed. "Ahm gonna buy you a pair of gloves."

"Don't get into it." Just when things were going well. Ownie cursed.

The trainer braced himself for another mental arm-wrestle in a power struggle Turmoil seemed determined to win. Ownie thought they'd established something during glove work when Turmoil, in a test of dominance, let loose a thundering hook and the old man stayed as fixed as a tackling block.

"I told you before," Ownie growled. "I'm not rubbing you down."

Turmoil stormed across the room, took a drink from the water cooler, and announced his return with one high-pitched syllable: "Why?"

"I don't need to explain myself no more."

"What am ah s'posed to do?"

"Go see Benny Bishop over at the Ocean Boxing Club. He's a lovely man, always nice to the sailors on the weekend. He takes them in and never charges a dime."

Atwood, recovered from his beating, snickered as Turmoil's face scrunched in pain. "Ah muss be the only fighta in the worl' who cahnt git a rubdown. Ah godda sore neck and mah own trainah wohn do nuthin 'bout it." Turmoil touched his neck theatrically; Scott lowered his eyes.

"I told you before, I'm no masseuse." Ownie felt the irritation creeping up his neck while Atwood poked Damien's ribs. "That's not my thing."

"Ah juss say ah godda sore neck! That dohn mean it godda be mah thing."

"I've heard more about those rubdowns than the troubles in Ireland." Ownie turned a page and the air tightened. "I don't want to hear it no more!"

"You thin Michael Moorer, he can' get rubdown?" Turmoil waved his arms, summoning Moorer as an expert witness. "You thin he beggin his trainah cuz he got a sore neck? Ah dohn think so."

Ownie pointed a finger. "No more, you hear?"

Ownie glanced at Scott and wondered whether the reporter understood the thing that worried him, the unacknowledged but unavoidable mental *if*. Scott lowered his eyes and pretended that nothing had passed. But, on Turmoil's face, Scott had seen not just petulance, but desperation, a sense that maybe there were moments when he was not in control, moments that scared him. Scott saw how the fighter, even when battling Ownie, when testing and pushing, understood the old trainer's stability, which he envied, resented, and, at times, found more calming than anything he knew.

Turmoil charged across the room, grabbed the door, and lobbed a parting shot. "You shun even call you'self a trainah."

This Store Sold a $100,000 Winner.

Turmoil opened the glass door, which was heavy with Lotto stickers and the hope that lightning could strike twice. Inside, a faded photo of the winner presided over a case of hot pepperoni. The lone cashier was engrossed in a *True Romance* magazine and a smoke.

Briiing. Briiing. A bell on the door announced a ravaged man with Irish moss hair and a beard. His Mary Maxim sweater, once a lively duck-hunting tableau, looked shot full of holes. The man shuffled to the counter and thrust out a crumpled two-dollar bill.

"Yes?" asked the clerk. Holding out his money, the man stared past the clerk, his glasses sagging with electrical tape. Unencumbered by shoes, his feet were swaddled in layers of work socks, coarse and grey as his beard. The clerk tried again. "What would you like?"

"I'd like to be a Lipizzaner stallion!" he decided abruptly and turned his eyes skyward as though his wish might be heard by a higher being. "I'd like to enter this world dark, drab, and awkward and metamorphise into a spectacular white acrobat."

Standing in an aisle, Turmoil moved up, drawn by the man's performance. "The prima ballerina of the horse world performing caprioles and pirouettes." The man did a spin, Irish moss hair afloat. "I'd like to become more brilliant each year instead of fading and rotting like human garbage. That's what I'd like." He kicked a shoeless foot.

The cashier shrugged, poured a coffee, and dropped a doughnut in a bag. "Whatever," she muttered, as the man reverted to his catatonic state. "Have a nice day."

Through the window, Turmoil watched the man reclaim

his shopping cart on the sidewalk. With a flick of indignation, as though he was used to better surroundings, Turmoil dumped his sunflower seeds on the counter. "You gedda lotta crazy peeple in here?" He nodded at the ringing door. The clerk looked at him suspiciously, at the bare arms, at the Everlast helmet, at the ten-inch-high boots, then handed him his change. It was clear she didn't like the question.

"Why?" She blew a puff of smoke in his direction. "You plannin' to start a club?"

The wind was an icy needle, tattooing misery on his skin. "This place," Turmoil grumbled outside the store. "Ah shun' never come here. This cole is killin me. If ah be back home, ah could be sittin outsahde in mah shorts."

A pickup truck with a Polaris snowmobile in the back rattled over frozen speedbumps, catching Turmoil's eye. He stared at the Polaris, a deluxe model with heated handlebars, a headlight cover, and carbide runners. As he stared uncomprehendingly, everything surreal and confusing, a bus painted like a beer can slushed him. "Ah-yah-yai," he moaned.

25

It had taken them an hour to reach the movie set of a town, a tasteful backdrop built on rum and cod. On the drowsy main street were widow's walks and gingerbread trim, period colours and dormers that drained the tension from Katherine's body.

Meandering down the coast past fishing sheds and pilings, Katherine and Dmitry had taken the back road from Halifax, arriving around 7 p.m. They stood outside a restaurant, where a fisherman was arguing with the owner, a man in a red chambray suit.

The fisherman's voice floated through the brackish air, joining a veiled chorus of rocking boats and buoy bells. Under the restaurant's porch light, his jacket looked as damp and rubbery as a shark. The owner was trying to guide him down the steps while mumbling something about an out-of-order phone.

"Ya lyin' dog," roared the fisherman, whose name was Lester. "You're not fit for gull's bait."

The owner winced. He was part of a wave of Americans who had migrated north in the 1970s, looking for something different, determined to make everything the same. They descended on tax sales, scooping up whole islands for ten thousand dollars; they transformed rundown Cape Cods into *Country Living* makeovers with herb gardens, horses, and sheep; they salvaged wooden boats, raised long-haired kids, and waxed, when anyone was within earshot, about Groton and Smith.

Lester kicked the door, rattling a weather vane shaped like a pig. The owner shot Katherine and Dmitry a can-you-believe-this look, while Lester shifted his duffel bag and took an anxious puff of his make-em.

"Hey, Lester." Dmitry waved a thick hand in the air. "Come here."

Lester shuffled down the steps with the lead-footed walk of the shift worker. Up close, he looked like a shirt washed too many times. A side tooth was missing, one finger on his left hand ended at the knuckle, the pockets of his pants stuck straight out.

Dmitry ran a hand through coarse, greying hair. He was a big man, with the body of a worn-out catcher with square fingers. Dmitry had knees ravaged from the weight of the silver boxes he travelled with, magician's trunks. He pulled out a cellphone. "These are the 1990s, you know."

Lester puffed out air, tension leaking from his sleep-deprived body. "I juss wants to make a phone call," Lester apologized, making it clear he was not unreasonable. "Them boats leave roight on time. You miss 'r, they got someone ta take yur place roight off there. I can't afford ta miss a trip to Georges this time a year as the scallaping's too rich."

While Dmitry showed Lester how to use the phone, Katherine scanned a posted menu illuminated by a lamppost. Kippered herring, finnan haddie, and hodgepodge. Part of a sea captain's mansion, the eatery was named Tongues and Sounds for the crispy dish with salt pork and onions.

Inside the restaurant, with Lester safely dispatched, Dmitry leaned back and studied Katherine across the table. With one finger, he stopped the drippings of a candle that smelled like vanilla.

"How's Dan?" she asked of a mutual friend.

"I saw him in Bosnia and he kept saying 'Ciao.'" Dmitry looked tired. "Every time he did, I thought it was time to eat."

Katherine laughed. "I heard he was getting married."

Dmitry held up four square fingers.

"Number four?" she asked in disbelief.

"Uh-huh, and every time it's the last. It's love, it's passion, it's Mount Vesuvius for six months." He shook his head. "Dan's the supernova of love; he burns out fast."

Katherine took a bite of her scallops smothered in a creamy tarragon and pink peppercorn sauce that tweaked her senses. She chewed the fish slowly and let herself taste it.

"Those guys, they all want to be Sean Flynn but stay alive."

The food was arranged on antique china plates of mixed patterns, roses and checks brought together by a theme of apricot. The same colour was picked up in the cotton curtains and the pads of the cleverly mismatched wooden chairs, the overall effect serendipitous.

"You look great," he said, as though he was seeing her clearly for the first time, as though apricot became her. "What have you done: changed your hair, lost some weight?"

She sipped her Beaujolais and nodded.

"I thought so. You know, when I met you, I thought: fantastic woman, great smile, impossible legs, but a bit of baby fat." He smiled a bashful smile that came from somewhere in his past, a trick smile that made you look beyond the puffy lids and the broken nose. Katherine wondered whether the smile was real or contrived, if he thought about when and where to use it.

"That's because I was a baby, remember?"

Dmitry broke into a full grin, more persuasive than the smile. The first time she saw it, she had felt like she was in Vegas buying the whole counterfeit vista. "Don't lose too much. They've proven that people who like food like sex. You have to keep the pleasure channels open."

Mmm. Now and then, an audible phrase rose from

surrounding diners and drifted over antique pine tables up to a painted tin ceiling, playing to a whimsical audience of long-lashed oxen and cows hung on the walls.

"Look at this." Dmitry leaned close, pressing his face near hers, so that she could see the scar on his brow. She feigned nonchalance, teeth chattering. "I got it playing pick-up hockey in Prague." The top button on his shirt pulled open, showing a chest so hard that it made her ache. The chest reminded her of a beautiful boy she had met her freshman year in college, a boy as tall and lean as a sapling, with long hair that turned up around his ears and crinkly green eyes. He wore a pendant around his neck on a string of leather, and when he drew her close, she felt the pendant and his heart beating beneath his skin. They were destined, she decided, after two weeks of secrets and naked poems, and then she went to his room and found someone else pressed against the pendant.

"Did I tell you I met Nelson Mandela?"

After the fettuccine with smoked salmon and leeks, Dmitry had tackled a rack of lamb with honey hazelnut crust.

"What was he like?"

"Well, he had it, that presence, that aura you can't define. All the big people have it, the Pope, Bono, Castro. The clarity, the definition; they are always in focus. It's as though they're being shot with a Hasselblad while the rest of the world is on Polaroid."

She picked at a white chocolate and strawberry ice cream torte. The owner, the man who had rebuffed Lester, hovered over the table like he was ready to close. Dmitry whispered something and the red chambray shirt vanished. Katherine relaxed, knowing Dmitry was in control, able to handle anything.

"The more you do, the more they want. They always give you the feeling that there's someone ready to do your job, but there isn't." Dmitry looked hard to make sure she understood. "Not everyone can do it."

There was something absolute about the eyes, something that said, Don't cross me. Maybe you needed eyes like that to work in war zones, to pay your way through college diving for cadavers in Massachusetts river bottoms.

"I almost didn't get sent to Bosnia. They wanted to send one of the new bucks just to try him out. Now they're glad they didn't." Dmitry finished his wine. "They offered me a desk job in New York; I couldn't handle a desk job." He flexed the catcher's hands, stretching out stiffness. "The agency had a going away party for Gallagher. The boss's wife was there, tarted up, looking for someone to . . . ah . . . talk to. Within twenty seconds, she tells me she's lonely, she's depressed, that her husband doesn't do it any more." Dmitry frowned. "Now this guy's my boss."

"How old is he?"

"Forty. So I sympathize. Who wouldn't?"

Once at an airport, Katherine had seen a flushed woman dash across the floor, gasping, "My God, Dmitry!" and for a strange heightened moment, Dmitry and the stranger were part of something glorious, something he could not, for the life of him, recall.

"She tells me that it's the agency's fault; it's keeping him from her and the kids, killing his libido with stress." Dmitry pushed aside his mud pie. "Anyway, she half believes it — or she wants to. So I tell her she should do something for herself, like take a course. So then she says, 'Yes, that's a great idea,' that she always wanted to be an actress, that people had told her for years she was the spitting image of Sissy Spacek. Of course I had been thinking along the lines of computer programming."

"Hmmm."

"So I told her I'd take some pictures for her sometime." He winced in shame. "It was the best I could think of at the time, honey. It made her feel better."

"I bet."

"I'm never in New York anyway."

Walking to the bed and breakfast, they lingered at store fronts. The town teemed with craft shops and art galleries that proffered everything from majestic oils of schooners to purple pigs with polka dots. Unchanged over the years were the established merchants that had provided socks and sweaters to generations. A jewellery store displayed dusty fiftieth-anniversary plates and silver-plated cases that said, OUR WEDDING CERTIFICATE. Next door was a ladies shop that sold knitwear and mother-of-the-bride dresses. At the General Supply Store run by Wick's Trawlers was an endless supply of work shirts, coveralls, and rubber boots.

"I hate those pictures of people covered with bees," Katherine laughed, sloshed after a languid dinner topped with Grand Marnier. "Please tell me you've never taken one of those."

"No."

"Why do they keep moving them? Every few months, I see one on the wire, a guy with a bee beard, a bee body suit. They're gross . . ." She leaned back and closed her eyes. "Why stop at bees? Why not go for rats or cockroaches?"

Katherine caught a glimpse of herself in the gilt mirror on one wall, so relaxed that her body had dissolved like bubbles. There was no need to fear the future, no reason to lament the past. "Who are you living with now?" she whispered.

"No one."

"Really?" She uttered the word like a prayer.

"No." His voice was hoarse. "Does it matter?"

26

Turmoil was being readied for a TV appearance. Parked in a hydraulic chair, the heavyweight's clothes were covered by an apron decorated with a galaxy of shimmering stars. An elflike man with cropped hair and taut cheeks was working on his face.

"Mek me beaut'ful now," Turmoil urged him.

"Don't worry, dear." The makeup man slashed on highlighter and then tapped him scoldingly. "I'd give my entire collection of Alan Ladd movies for bones like these."

Moving behind Turmoil, the man tilted the boxer's head on its axis. MALCOLM GREY, MASTER ESTHETICIAN, THEATRE MAKEUP. His card was tucked in the corner of a mirror, near an Arthur Kent (the Scud Stud) press pass and the inky pawprint of a dog named Shane. Turmoil admired himself while Malcolm rotated his head, examining his canvas from every angle. Malcolm's iguana tongue shot out, licking his upper lip. The wall behind him was a heavenly blue. A tree strung with miniature lights twinkled in the corner.

"Thass a nice bowtie," Turmoil said, and Malcolm reflexively touched his Nova Scotia tartan, a garish plaid that flourished in airport gift shops. Underneath was a starched white shirt. "Sum people dohn dress rite for the jawb," Turmoil complained. "Ah t'ink it's importan to dress rite. Ah tell mah trainah that all the time."

Malcolm scrunched his nose for an impetuous I-can't-help-myself-look, then whispered like an unrepentant sinner seeking absolution: "It's a bit camp."

"No, mon, dohn go talkin like that."

"Well."

"Ah know all 'bout clothes." Turmoil checked the windowless makeup room for an audience, accustomed, by now, to the notoriety that had grown with each triumphant fight, the celebrity that had somehow eluded Hansel Sparks.

In his second year in Halifax, Turmoil had racked up three straight wins. Champion had negotiated a rematch against Art Moore, the man who had handed Turmoil his only loss, and Turmoil had won. There had been names at the Montreal bout: actors, big-time fighters, and mobsters who controlled the local action. Turmoil posed for pictures with the fighting Turner triplets, Lloyd, Floyd, and Boyd, who handed out business cards with three identical headshots. Feeling good after the win, Ownie had got a laugh from the burly Texans when he studied their cards closely and quipped: "I thought maybe you were the McGuire sisters."

"Mah sister, she a fashion d'signer in New York," Turmoil announced.

"Really? I love New York. I have a friend who worked on Jerome Robbins's musical *Broadway*. That show had over one hundred wigs and four hundred costumes. How long has she been there?"

"Three-four year. She wahnt me go live with her but ah say, no, ah go to Canada. Some ver-ver importan men got a contrack for me. They be waitin for me to arrive."

A TV jock appeared in the doorway, smelling of hairspray. "Everything okay in here, big guy?" he asked Turmoil.

"We're fine." Malcolm made a machinating motion with his mouth as though he had gum hidden inside, then he stroked Turmoil's hair with a star-studded brush that matched the apron. "It's the Andromeda Galaxy, the object farthest from Earth visible with the naked eye," he liked to explain. "I like things, honey, that are far out."

"You shud get this mon to do you," Turmoil told the jock. "You might end up lookin as good as me."

"Don't get my hopes up, big guy," laughed the jock, who believed he was already handsome.

"You want miracles, go to Lourdes," Malcolm muttered as the jock disappeared from the doorway. "Aristotle believed we share the traits of whatever animal we most resemble." He met Turmoil's eyes in the mirror. "Is it my imagination or does that man look like a sloth?"

Turmoil laughed and the autographed picture of Roch Voisine joined in.

"I *love* your name!" Malcolm announced abruptly, as though he had decided to unburden himself of a wicked secret and now couldn't stop. "When I heard you were coming here today, I looked something up." He paused. "If you don't like it, don't worry about my feelings. Underneath this meek exterior beats the heart of a Roman gladiator." Malcolm cleared his throat and closed his eyes.

"'And from this chasm, with ceaseless turmoil seething.'" The words were shooting stars that left a trail of wonder.

> As if this earth in fast thick pants were breathing,
> A mighty fountain momently was forced.

Opening his eyes, he pulled off the Andromeda Galaxy apron. "That's from 'Kubla Khan.'"

Turmoil nodded, admiring his unlined blazer in the mirror, lifting one hand for a glimpse of a ring that glimmered like something celestial. "Ah like that. It sounds ver-ver pow'ful, like myself."

"Yes, yes, that's what I thought."

Turmoil adjusted his wool jacket. He shopped on Spring Garden Road now instead of Gussy's, a trendy downtown strip filled with shops, bars, and eateries. On any given day, you could see ordinary folks and poseurs, primped and coiffed to fit the role: aspiring artiste, passé punk, moneyed matron, powerbroker. Panhandlers and slow-moving tourists filled the corners of the open-air stage like potted plants.

"Ahm a very han'some mon, wohn you say?" He had bought his Italian pants from a store that promised to phone when the next extra longs arrived. "You'll be the first to know," swore the owner, who carried his schnauzer in a Snugli.

"You know ah get a call from a man in Hollywood." Turmoil didn't wait for Malcolm's reply, which would have been effusive. "He said he wahnt me to be in the movies like Ahnol Schwarzneg. Ah say: 'G'won, ah dohn have time for that ole movie stuff.' And he say, 'No mon, you're much mo' han'some than Ahnol.'"

Malcolm chewed the invisible gum.

"What d'you think? You think ahm moh han'some than Ahnol?"

Malcolm leaned down impulsively and whispered in the powdered ear: "Muuuch."

Turmoil laughed hard enough to rock the miniature lights. He felt generous. "You know, you got nice hair too."

Malcolm leaned so close that his mouth almost touched Turmoil's ear: "It's a weeeeaaave. We aren't all blessed."

A middle-aged woman appeared at the door wearing lemon-shaped glasses and a belted girls' school tunic. She had been sent to pick up Turmoil and deposit a frumpy woman who had been promised anonymity in a piece on welfare fraud and needed to be disguised.

"You done a good job," Turmoil told Malcolm.

"My pleasure, dear." Malcolm swiped his lips with strawberry balm and stroked his apron. And then, as if to stall the welfare woman and her vulgar story, he gave Turmoil a parting tap of powder. "I don't want you getting shiny!"

Ownie found himself in a university runoff of slim Victorian houses with cramped gardens and gauzy curtains. Some had stained-glass windows and ornate trim; others bore the temporary indignity of flats. He could overhear two students chatting at a bus stop.

"I'm thinking of switching my major to psych," revealed the boy.

"Did you know that doctors once thought that you could tell a crazy person by his smell?" asked the girl, who was wearing a nose ring. "They also believed in physiology, that certain body types were predisposed to certain ailments. They made plaster casts of faces and measured people's skulls."

The boy wobbled under the weight of so much information. "I'm still drunk," he confessed, and the girl shrugged.

Ownie stood on the front step of a tan two-storey and admired the paint job. The trim on the windows and panels was darker tan and the accents plum. You had to do these old places right or they looked like hell, he thought. Scrape them down, soak them with linseed oil. Ownie concluded that the whole block had shopped at the same Colonial paint store, picking complementary shades of Comfrey Green and Empire Grey, accents of Tansy Button and Elderberry. Skewering the effect was a turquoise infidel, inhabited by a fraternity of beer-guzzling party animals and shunned by the neighbours.

When the door opened, Ownie felt like he had entered a

tropical fruit factory, lush and ripe. In contrast to the muted facade, which resembled the dried flowers of the dead, the interior walls of the house were cantaloupe, the floor pimento red. Everything throbbed with colour.

He noticed two paintings hung over a white piano. So alive, the paintings tugged at Ownie's senses like the smell from a bakery. Come closer, they invited, and he took a step toward them. They seemed to be depicting someplace hot, a place with orange tigers slinking through grass under a sky of feathers. A market bustling with vendors and dogs, a busload of shoppers, faces pressed to the windows. Ownie looked harder, sensing something different, like the time Hildred dyed her hair red and it took him a week to figure it out. That's it: everyone was black, from the bus driver to the vendors.

"They're by a Haitian artist." The voice came from a woman with airbrushed skin and pulled-back hair.

"Nice," Ownie observed. "They're full of life."

The woman's chin tilted up slightly so that the light caught the broad planes of her cheeks. Her brows arched in a look that seemed to say: So? Her look drew you in, and then shut you out, a curious mix of warmth and inaccessibility. She was about thirty, Ownie figured, and stood around five-six. Her eyes were topaz.

"It's amazing that a country so poor and troubled produces such wonderful art," she said. "It's an escape from the insanity, I guess, an insistence on doing something life affirming."

"They are nice."

The woman offered him coffee.

"Ah, sure," Ownie said. "If it's not too much trouble."

"Not at all. Sugar?"

"Just one." Ownie could feel the energy of the room; he could hear people laughing on the walls, eating fresh fruit, soaking up sun, and swimming in waters as blue and clean as mouthwash. He thought about his elusive dream with the gro-lamp and the yellow roses. He thought about being happy and warm.

"You shunn eat that junk." Turmoil was lolling on a plump lemon couch, TV remote in one hand, an apple in the other. "Sugah is the devil food. It will kill you like it kill all mah peeple."

"Uh-huh."

"When they bring mah peeple ovah from Africa, they put them to work on the sugah plahntayshins." Turmoil raised a hand. "They dohn let them live with their famlies, they dohn feed them right, they work them to death. By the time they finish, more than half is dead!" He lowered the hand in a curse: "Sugah!"

"I hear ya." Ownie nodded thanks for the coffee he was handed. "I've got the same bad feeling about potatoes."

Ownie cleared a space for his cup, nudging a stack of texts and papers. *Toward an Africadian Renaissance*. He tried to read a cover upside down: *How to Encourage the Rejuvenation of Nova Scotia's Black Neighbourhoods*, written by Lorraine Waters. Could that, he wondered, be her?

Where is he meeting all of these people? People I've never met in fifty years. Ownie stared at Turmoil for an answer. The week before, Ownie recalled, Turmoil had come into Tootsy's with a tall Mi'kmaq in wire-rimmed glasses. The stranger's skin was smooth and even as if he'd been under a sun lamp. Next to the blanched locals, sun-deprived and spotty, covered with zits and angry patches, he looked like he was wearing body makeup. He looked like natives would have looked, before the white man poisoned their blood with booze and reservations. The man — Ownie had forgotten his name — was wearing a singlet. On one shoulder was a tattoo the size of a kiwi, a pawprint of something: a badger or a bobcat? It looked meaningful, left by an animal spirit or a native god, not by a cheap tattoo artist who branded bikers. Turmoil said the man was a professor.

The fighter finished his apple and threw the core on the pimento floor.

"What did you do that for?" Ownie snapped. "Don't you have no manners?" Ownie checked to see whether the handsome woman had seen. "Keep that up and you'll be back living in that dump, that boarding house."

Stretching his legs, Turmoil yawned dismissively. "When ah was fourteen year old a spir't come to mah house in Trinidad."

Ownie tapped the arm of a flowered chair and asked, despite himself, "What kind of spirit?"

"Ohhh it was a bad spir't. It could put curse on your famly or on your howse."

"Yeah?"

"Yeah. The spir't try to get me. Ah be in my room. It try pull me out a window. It say 'Come wid me, boy.' But ah too strong. Ah held on to both sides till my fingers sore. Ah wudden let it tek me 'way."

"What was this spirit going to do?"

"It could keep you in the jungle for a long-long time. It might let you go, it might nevva let you go. It ver-ver searyus bisnis."

As they were leaving, the woman, all fine skin and searching eyes, pecked Turmoil's cheek goodbye.

"She's a smart woman, Ownie," Turmoil said as the bevelled glass door closed behind her. "She a politishun."

"That right?"

"You shud know who she is: the first black wummin in the Nova Scotia guv'men. You shud know her name if you payin attenshun at all."

28

The phone awoke Katherine with the fear that something big was breaking. On top of the daily logistics of news gathering, there were labour issues at the paper. Scott MacDonald was probably the only staffer who had been given less work, the unsuspecting beneficiary of MacKenzie's misguided interest in Sports.

A consultant had recommended surveillance cameras. Unbeknownst to workers, Gem was planning a "rationalization of staff," and Katherine had been called as a witness in Glenda's unfair-dismissal suit. During the day, moving from crisis to crisis, Katherine was tight, controlled, never stopping to reflect. At night, she felt adrift and in pain, fearful of what could happen.

Earlier that evening, Katherine had been standing outside the paper, waiting for a cab, when a black Camaro approached slowly, unsure of its surroundings. In the still night air, the gravel driveway crunched. The Camaro stopped and the driver wound down a window.

"Is this the newspaper?" asked a slight man with a diamond stud in one ear.

Before Katherine could reply, she smelled the heady scent of musk oil and felt a rotund woman with red hair and boysenberry lips sashay past her. *Swish swish swish*, the woman headed for the car, swinging her hips with rhythm. *Swish swish swish*. She placed her pointy-toed boots with tantalizing precision.

"Helooo, sweetie," she greeted the driver, breathy. The woman's lips parted, forming a slight line in a face as pale as a porcelain doll. She patted her munificent chest, making her words vibrate.

Katherine recognized the temptress as Billy DeVan, a clerk from Accounting. She had heard (but had never truly believed) the stories about Billy, who reportedly thrived on sailors, raw, interchangeable, barely in their twenties, all named Pierre or Mario. Most were submariners, whose squadron had the motto WE COME UNSEEN. Their returns from sea, from a claustrophobic cell of oil and sweat, were celebrated with food, drink, and sex. One celebrant brought Billy a silver spur, it had been whispered, another a copper ring that she wore on a matching chain around her neck, bouncing off her ample buxom, and suggesting something daring and indecent.

Who, Katherine wondered, after seeing Billy's seductive greeting, had given her a licence to be so free?

"Oh, hi," Katherine answered her phone.

"I was thinking of you," said the caller.

"Ummm," Katherine muttered.

"It's November 25, St. Catherine's Day, patron saint of spinsters."

Katherine laughed. "Thanks."

"I'm looking at a picture of you from that bed and breakfast, and I am feeling the loneliness. Pack a bag; I'll meet you in the morning."

"Where are you?" she asked.

"Geneva, and the weather reminds me of you. The phones are shitty, but the weather is beautiful."

"Geneva?"

"Yeah."

"Not tonight."

"C'mon, I'm celebrating. *The Times* has a new guy here,

and he can't get his pictures out. He thought he had the world by the nuts, but he can't move a thing."

"Isn't he the guy who won a Pulitzer?"

"Yeah, but it was like Moses and the Ten Commandments. He has no idea how he did it or where it came from. For once in his life, he was shooting with the finger of God."

"And you're enjoying it?"

"Not really. I'm a comrade, so I said, 'Dynamite stuff, Cal, maybe you can mail them home to your mother for a retrospective.'"

"I can't come."

"Remember how much fun we had in Amsterdam, hanging out in the brown cafés, sneaking into dirty shows. Remember that dancer, the Korean girl, who tried to get you on stage, and that little hotel in Leiden? Well, this is way better."

"Give me your number and I'll call you in the morning."

"Okay, gorgeous, sleep on it."

29

Scott stood in the airport with his parents, one eye on the baggage carousel. "I hear that Heather's class is trying." His mother's voice sounded strained, as though she was forcing her words through a filter of sadness. "I heard," she offered, "that one boy keeps, ah, keeps setting fires in the washroom."

Scott shrugged a noncommittal shrug. He was watching a gangly teen with a surfboard lope across the lobby to retrieve his dog, still in a travel cage. Terrified, the collie had foam on its lips. The teen clapped his hands in greeting, and the dog yapped, relieved.

"A US airline cooked a dog," Scott's father announced.

"Why would you tell a story like that, Rusty?" his mother demanded.

"It's true!" Rusty was indignant. "When the case went to court, they said the temperature in the hold of the plane went up to one hundred and forty degrees Celsius."

Scott watched the boy free his dog, which celebrated by chasing its tail. The surfer then hugged his mother, a tall woman straddling the line between gaunt and glorious. Time had erased the softness from her face, leaving it chiselled and angular, her teeth and nose larger, her smile more feral, more like the boy and his dog. They seemed at ease in the world, he decided, still open to adventures.

"Is Heather at school today?" his mother asked.

"I dunno, Mom. She's gone."

His mother swallowed. "What do you mean?"

"I mean, she's gone."

His mother looked distressed. She liked Heather, who was attractive and good with children. But she knew better than to press Scott. When it came to women, Scott was like a man walking through a sandstorm, she decided, the wind filling in each step as soon as it was formed, so when Heather left, she was gone, his mother realized, just gone.

Scott darted forward as his mother's suitcase rolled down the belt. When he returned, his mother asked, in lieu of anything important: "Did she take the Wyeth print?" Scott shrugged a yes.

Raindrops were hitting the windshield, spreading like poached eggs, fat, clear circles of unpredictable size. Scott was driving his parents home.

"How was Cora's funeral?" he finally asked.

"Oh, it was fine." His mother sighed. "It was a long trip. . . . That's all."

"I'd give it a four," snapped Rusty. "A two for artistic impression."

In the rear-view mirror, Scott saw his mother staring at the white-grey sky, which had, on this day, no clouds or gradation in colour. It was a flat, finite sky, without mystery or joy. It had been years since Scott had seen Aunt Cora, a widow who had moved to Florida. Once there, Cora joined an order of Wallis wannabes, older women who fashioned themselves after the late duchess. Anorexic, they chain-smoked Camels and lived in discount loungewear. Liberated from family by death or design, they drank heavily and made a point of boasting that they dressed for dinner.

For a moment, Scott was tempted to tell his parents about Tootsy's, about Turmoil Davies. He was tempted to tell them he had sparred with Johnny LeBlanc, an actual fighter with thirteen wins. He was tempted to tell them about Ownie. And then he decided against it, remembering how his parents had lived for his paddling, and how he'd crushed them when he quit. If he told them about the gym, they would latch on to it, they would make too much of it, trying to reclaim the relationship between parents and athlete, the exhilaration and the hope. They would try too hard.

"It was the headstone," said Rusty. "It started off okay. It said, 'Cora Henneberry, wife of Bernie.' And then it said, 'You Reap What You Sow.'"

"It was Cousin Bryce," his mother whispered. "Cora had wanted angels."

"He got into drugs when he was a teenager," Rusty offered for his wife's sake. "It wasn't anyone's fault."

They arrived in Dartmouth. Smithers called the city Darkness, but he and Scott were not talking about the same place. Dartmouth wasn't a high-rise, a shopping mall, or an industrial park. That was the extraneous backdrop, but that wasn't it. Dartmouth was water, one pivotal piece in the jigsaw of life. That's all Scott saw when he crossed the bridge from Halifax; that's all that mattered.

"Oh, I saw Timmy." Rusty was hoping to salvage the outing. "He was driving the bus to bingo."

The lakes, the essence of Dartmouth, were a gift from the ice age, left by glaciers on their slow retreat, twelve-thousand-year-old craters filled with meltwater and purpose. Dartmouth had two dozen lakes, but Scott only cared about one, the world's greatest flatwater course. Scott called it the Lake, but there were really two, connected at a narrow point, and part of a longer, broken chain. The course, with lanes for one thousand metres, was on the lower lake, but paddlers trained on both. Rowers shared the space.

Historians waxed about the beauty of a pristine waterway in the heart of a city, they described the thrill of seeing an otter or a crane, the joy of passing under a stream of commuters while communing with secrets of the past. When alone, you could imagine porcupines in hemlock stands, bears in bogs. Scott never thought about deer or birchbark canoes, but he knew how many strokes it was from the overpass to a scraggly spruce. He knew which lane got wash.

"Tim always liked to drive," Rusty added. "Remember he used to drive the boats up to nationals?"

"I went with him once," Scott reminded Rusty.

His mother attempted a conciliatory smile, drawn from happier times. Going to Nationals had been a ritual, like putting up Christmas lights, a ritual that peaked on a summer night when the boats departed. Anything, it was understood, could happen after that.

"Do you remember when he slept under the boat trailer outside Montreal with a Swiss Army knife?" Rusty asked.

"The Quebéc police wanted to arrest him," his mother added.

Taylor was a safe subject. If Scott's parents were not allowed to talk about paddling, a sport that had once consumed the family, they could, they had discovered over time, still talk about Tim. Tim was raw and rough with a deformed finger and a mangled ear. He was outrageous. Charging down the course, Tim exemplified fearlessness and ferocity. Scott's parents had loved to watch Tim race, and in their minds, that's all there had been: the glorious, death-defying drive. They had not seen the setbacks, the heartache and pain, and Scott had, in some form of kindness, allowed them that much. After Scott quit paddling, Taylor stayed in the sport, reaching, driving, lurching, with every step forward fighting for his life. That's all, Scott believed, that he knew how to do.

"I remember he wore that T-shirt: SECOND PLACE IS THE FIRST LOSER." Rusty chuckled. "And the other one: REAL MEN PADDLE C-BOATS."

Scott's mother smiled. Scott laughed and everyone, it seemed, felt better.

A drained woman in support hose and a Burger Dog visor sank into the Athena's number-three booth, sucking in nicotine, blowing out rings of despair.

"Awww, who's gonna know?" She shrugged to a man in a quilted vest sitting across from her, who was hunkered over a job application, inventing, through creative details, a potential Employee of the Month.

Scott heard the woman's legs creak as she eased them onto the Naugahyde seat and blew an empty ring. "If he thinks he can pinch my ass for four bucks an hour..." Her trailing voice carried across the near empty restaurant. "I told him . . ." She seemed too tired to finish. "I told him I'd make a deal: he keeps his paws to himself and I keep my old man from crushing his nuts with a ball-peen hammer." She tilted back her head and blew.

CINDERELLA WEDDING DRESS. SIZE 17. SHORT PUFFED SLEEVES WITH BOWS. LOW NECKLINE. TWO-LAYERED BOTTOM. TOP LAYER LOOPED WITH BOWS. VALUED AT $1,200. WILL NEGOTIATE. NEVER WORN. DON'T ASK.

Scott looked out the window past the posters. He saw a couple pushing a shopping cart stuffed with shabby toddlers, arms tangled, faces pressed against the cold metal squares. As the parents exchanged a smoke in an effortless handoff, a fourth child clung to the side of the cart. The family was so close now that he could see the mother's swollen belly, the father's tic-tac-toe tattoo. He could spot open seams in the overworked clothes and count, in his mind, the previous owners.

MOOSE HEAD SHOULDER MOUNT WITH PLAQUE. 48" SPREAD. 8 PTS. MOOSE DIED OF NATURAL CAUSES. WAS NEVER SHOT. ASK FOR SHERMAN.

After Scott had arrived at his parents' house, his father had announced that he was going to paint the guest room. Whenever Scott slept in the room, during holidays or breakups, he awoke from habit at 5 a.m., ear cocked to the wind, reading the signals that told him whether the lake was calm or choppy, flat or bristling.

Scott watched a gull raid a garbage dumpster, tearing open bags. One day, he had told Sasha about the lake and his training, and now, as though she had read his mind, she lobbed him a challenge. "Wasn't it ever just fun?" she asked. "Paddling?" He looked at her face, framed by frizzy tendrils. "You know, fun?"

"Well, yeah." He remembered, with satisfaction, sitting on the rough wharf with Taylor, eyes closed, senses channelled to the perfect mental race. Down the thousand-metre course they paddled, every stroke precise.

"Yeah, what?"

When everything was exact, the blade sliced the water cleanly, leaving no ragged edges or fray. With each sublime cut, Scott felt a tingle that started in his arms and moved to his gut: the thrill of the ultimate backhand, the delight of driving a metal shovel into a mound of glutinous snow.

"I remember my first big trip, when I made the Canadian team racing in the North Americans. We took a bus from Cleveland to a town in Ohio."

It had been a freakishly hot summer scented with Bain de Soleil and the sweat from Taylor's torso. Scott remembered dipping one hand in the water and feeling the tug, tug, tug as his boat drifted forward, as he formed a cup with his fingers.

One day, an invasion of flying ants, a biblical pestilence, lasted eight hours, leaving a grotesque blanket on the water. Whenever Scott took a stroke, his curved blade flung their corpses through the air.

"They put us up in a YMCA in Ohio. There were cots set up in the gym, with a divider — sheets hung over a badminton net — separating the guys from the girls. At bedtime, people started carrying on, throwing pillows, tipping cots." It had been years since he'd thought about this. "That went on for a while, and then everyone settled down. There were two Hungarians on our team who'd been stars in the old country. By then, they were past their peak. Well, first thing, they climbed the ropes — you know the ones they have in a gym — and swung over the net like Tarzan. The girls looked up and screamed. They were both naked."

During the bus trip, a blonde girl from Toronto had climbed on his lap, smelling like baby oil.

"How did you like Ohio?"

"Ohio?" Scott was thinking about the girl, who paddled for Mississauga, or was it Balmy Beach? That night, back at the Y, he saw her in a babydoll nightie, clutching her heart in horror and waiting for him to come to her rescue.

"Hmmm, I dunno. I remember we all played water polo in the Y pool. Some of the Quebec guys knew how to play. Taylor, my training partner, couldn't swim, so he borrowed a life jacket. He jumped in and nearly drowned a paddler named Picard."

Gwen. That's it. She brushed up against him in the pool and said she wanted him to be on Scott's team. He told her it was full.

"I don't understand how you just quit everything." Sasha bit a breaded zucchini. "If it was that much a part of you, it must be painful not to even watch."

This part Scott could not explain. There was a time when

everything seemed simple, when working stiffs triumphed over right-wing bullies, when Locke stomped Hobbes, before life had a chance to kick the shit out of your idealism. Sasha was too young to understand the vagaries of life, and in a way, that was good.

It had been twenty years since Scott had picked up a paddle, twenty years since he'd gone a day without a drink. After years of living the abstemious life of an athlete, of honing his body for one narrow purpose, he had decided to party. At first, he drank with strangers, soaking up the sights he had missed in college: fern bars, pubs, and piano players. Pretty soon, he tired of people and set his own routine. He slept all day, worked the night desk, and came home to drink.

One night, before the late scores were in, Smithers had stormed into the *Standard* and demanded that Scott join him on a bar crawl. Scott couldn't leave before the scores were in, and Smithers was already pissed. Smithers locked him in a bear hug from behind. Scott remembered trying to unlock Smithers's fingers and shake him loose. He remembered it all like a slide show: one bright, disconnected moment after the other: being hoisted from his chair, feet losing contact. Scott had no idea how he had landed with enough force to drive the desk spike through his wrist, or how an innocuous office implement stacked with memos could have entered his flesh and surfaced like an armour-piercing bullet. At that moment, his breath stopped like someone had pulled the hose from a central vac, breaking the electrical connection.

Sasha was talking about something, but he wasn't listening.

31

Stripped of its paisley curtain and matching towels, it looked like a bus station men's room, a threadbare pit stop on the way to someplace better. Gone were the superfluous flowers and Gustav Klimt prints. After Heather left, the bathroom was cold and cruel. Scott liked the feel.

"And now for twenty minutes of uninterrupted Gooolden Oldies."

Scott flipped the toilet lid open with a plunger. He always checked, ever since Heather had locked eyes with a twelve-inch sewer rat, a pin-headed beast with pipe-cutting teeth and thalidomide legs, swimming, hissing, bent on escape.

"We've got Paul McCartney and Wings and Aretha Franklin, but first . . ." Another Golden Oldie aimed at the fading synapses of middle-aged brains.

Scott had poisoned the invader with Javex, but he always suspected there were more, an army of reserve rodents dog-paddling to the surface, fanatics who multiplied five times a year in litters of fourteen, coarse-coated outlaws who preyed on cats and chickens and carried typhus fever or plague. Flushing the toilet, he slammed the lid closed. Weren't rats in the toilet an urban myth? Like alligators in the sewer and WELCOME TO THE WORLD OF AIDS on the motel mirror?

Heather used to have a cleaner come in on Fridays, an older woman with a flowered apron and emphysema that stopped her in her tracks. Scott was supposed to tell her about the rat but forgot. "An Iowa scientist has worked out a formula," Heather had explained. "If you see one rat during daylight, it means there are one to five hundred." One more sin that no longer mattered. Scott had been surprised that Heather had Javex in the apartment, since she seemed intent on creating as small of an impact on the ecosystem as possible. She used tiny plates at dinner, and instead of turning up the heat, she took a hot water bottle to bed. Scott ate off paper plates and opened the windows whenever he pleased.

Scott adjusted the bathroom scale, moving the gauge from the minus zone to zero. One-eighty-five, unchanged since 1971. After the age of thirty, most people gained weight, one insidious pound a year that appeared from nowhere like dust, but Scott didn't need to worry, rarely eating a solid meal at home.

"Just read David Cassidy's book, *C'mon, Get Happy*," the radio announcer reported. "Verrry interesting. There is a juicy section involving *L.A. Law*'s Susan Dey. Dave says he and Susan tried to get it on, but she wasn't cheap enough for him." The announcer stuck his tongue in his cheek. "Oookay, Dave."

Scott stood in front of a full-length mirror with a hairline crack down the middle of his face, separating his good and evil selves. His dirty blond hair had receded but not enough to affect the aesthetics of his face, which had sunspots he feared would turn to melanoma and cheeks that had started to droop like icing in the heat.

"How many of you knew that Dave's nickname is Dong?" The announcer cracked up. "Seriously," he laughed. "It's right here and we're not talking Avon Lady."

Ding, Dong. Scott unbuttoned his twill shirt and unzipped his thirty-four chinos as though he was preparing for a medical exam. He peeled off his navy jockeys and socks. Naked, he sucked in his stomach and puffed out his hairless chest.

He had been in the ring half a dozen times by now. He was

learning to hit the speed bag. Maybe, he told himself, he would cut back on his drinking and eat better food. He had been an athlete, he reminded himself, every bit as dedicated as Turmoil Davies, every bit as tough. Maybe, he decided, he would run.

Mercilessly, Scott stared at his reflection for the first time in years, moving past the hazel eyes, conventional nose, and loose, expectant mouth. He stared with the mercenary eye of a horse breeder, with the dehumanizing gaze of a casting agent, and he stepped back in shock. Part of him was gone! How could a layer of flesh have melted like ice: cells, neurons, and blood vessels dripping into a gutter of idleness? How could his eighteen-inch biceps, his tumescent shoulders, his rippling back, have dissolved? Where were the shadows, the definition?

Scott turned sideways, then back to his shrunken self. The overhead light was glaring on his triceps, which seemed as empty as a depleted udder. What had happened to his granite abs, his swollen pecs, his substance? There was a time when every ounce of his body was tuned and purposeful, with no waste or confusion. How could he have lost it all and not even noticed? He could hear Turmoil laughing.

Killing the radio, Scott headed for the bedroom. At one time he enjoyed walking; with every step, he felt a taut muscle flex. Picking up a book, raking the lawn, every fibre was relevant and connected, while now he felt nothing. His brain was moving his limbs like a puppetmaster, right, left, right, left.

Scott felt a stab of neuropathic pain. The impotent body in the mirror couldn't be his. It belonged to a middle-aged loser who had never tasted greatness, to an endomorph like Smithers. It was too undersized, too insignificant. Scott MacDonald was big, goddamn it, he was mighty; he was a fucking powerhouse. That couldn't change, that's who he was!

He finished his beer and crawled into his closet. Panic was moving his arms, the disorienting fear that follows a nightmare when reality and horror merge. He needed reassurance, he needed something more substantial than his shadowy memory.

Scott opened a scrapbook with a rocketship on the cover. *Scott MacDonald. Shubenacadie Canoe Club* printed in inch-high letters. There! The time he won Juvenile K-1, a euphoric teen with shaggy hair and a smile. He turned the page gently, protecting the faded clippings held in place with dried tape. He stared at six young men in Canada Games uniforms, a Lawrence Welk chorus in blue blazers, open shirts, and white bell-bottoms.

A plane ticket from his first international trip. A training log for 1971. Junior K-1. First place. Canadian championships. One thousand metres in 4:14.1. A crest: NATIONAL RACES CANOE KAYAK CHAMPIONSHIP SALT FORK STATE LAKE.

A receipt for green Gazelles.

A quote by running guru Dr. George Sheehan: "Racing is the lovemaking of the runner. It is an excitement in the blood. There is the same agitation, the same stirring of the pulse, the same feeling in the chest, the same delightful apprehension you feel when nearing the one you love."

He thought about the two-hour workouts, about the time Taylor blacked out and sank, sucking in weeds and water, about the day he ruptured a disc. Water so cold that his hands ached for days, wind so mean it ripped his skin like a grater, blisters that bled and healed, then bled again. Fartlek training and wind sprints uphill. Brewer's yeast, a shell slicing a K-4 in two. He remembered standing in his boat for balance, paddling the perimeter of the lake on one side to even his stroke, the first time he broke four minutes, and the time he paddled at midnight with a light on his bow.

He remembered pushing so hard that everything went

black except for a white-gold horizontal line, a floating chin-up bar, from which his body hung, arms, legs, and soul. It was all so complete.

He opened another beer and looked at a quote from Roger Bannister describing his historic mile. "I felt the moment of a lifetime had come. There was no pain, only a great unity of movement and aim. The world seemed to stand still, or did not exist."

He closed his eyes.

A judge's boat roared up the course, whipping up wash. Scott steered his frail boat into the surf, alone and adrift as an ancient burial fifty feet from shore.

"Three minutes to start!"

He laid his blade on the water surface, sucked in air, and stared down lane five, a vertiginous shaft of swirling buoys, hot pain, and otherworldly doubts. Fear stared back and Scott felt a hand on his back.

"Mr. Starter, you have the race!"

Think about the perfect one thousand, he told himself, shrugging off the hand, steadying his boat, as fine as pecan shells, seamlessly joined and gleaming. Follow the blueprint in your brain. With mental acupuncture, he blocked out the waves, the roaring freeway, and the shrill jabs of a jackhammer on shore.

Focus. Focus. The course was cold and dispassionate: a man-made canal of ten lanes, each nine metres wide, a sterile trench in the gut of a concrete city that owed him nothing. Unlike his lake, this course had no trees, no gently sloping beaches to soften the landscape. It was, by design and fate, an aquatic bowling alley with the ambience of a shooting range, and, Christ, it looked so long.

"Okay, gentlemen, bring your boats up. Let's not have a misstart."

During warm-up, Scott had noted the landmarks: wooden

bleachers at the five-hundred-metre mark, a navy blue tent at the seven-fifty. He picked out joggers, he fiddled with his taped grip, he watched boys on bicycles race beside the course like thieves. After twenty minutes, his consciousness shifted, his body lightened, his eyes focused on that narrow point in space: the point where the 3-D picture takes shape and everything around it disappears. He entered the anaesthetized state that told him to go, to push, push, push into the danger zone, past the warning pains, past lucidity and reason.

"Slow now," warned the starter. "There's a tailwind . . . evvverybody mooove forward."

He had to hit that point before a race. He had to know the feeling and where to find it; he couldn't be searching, he had to know.

"Move up, now."

Scott spotted Nash, a kamikaze blond with azure eyes and a print bandana on his head. The American was in lane four, but he stood apart, longer and leaner than the prototypical paddler. Scott stared ahead, timing his approach, while Nash hung back twenty metres, where Scott could feel him.

He had a clean face with white brows, spare, angular features, and the chlorine-ravaged hair of a competitive swimmer, frizz-dried under the bandana in spiky tufts. Nash looked like a man who had seen more, done more, heard more of life's conflicting secrets. He came from a country that put men on the moon, a land of two hundred million people filled with bold boasts and cold-beer stores with pretzels.

He probably owned a VW van and a dog named Biff, played the flute, visited Morocco, and hiked through Spain. He probably had a girlfriend who looked like Cher and a cousin named Bo who had been to Vietnam.

"Stay back, gentlemen."

He was Dwight Stone and Jackson Brown, brash and brazen, sensitive and disarming, more audacious and alive than anyone Scott knew, as foreign as burritos, as exotic as a weekend in New York City.

"Back, number three!"

But was he fast?

"Back it up, four!"

That's all that mattered.

Scott held his boat on the line, bow on, not over.

You are strong, you are omnipotent. When you pull through that water, you could move a train, a bus, a shopping mall.

He heard someone shout "good luck," and then the wind stopped, as if a door had slammed. Everything was still: the water, the flags, a canvas tent on the right side of the course, filled with food, clothes, and essential boat parts.

Block out everything and listen, he told himself. Listen. It takes a hundred and twenty thousandths of a second to respond to sound.

"Back, seven."

The rapid-fire commands sent shockwaves through his body.

"Over, five."

Jesus, that's me! He took a sideways stroke.

Scott blew out the tension that clung to the walls of his chest like blackened creosote. Remember, it's four short hard ones, then twenty fast, then break. Hit top speed, lengthen it out, move into your race, stay with the rhythm, hope to hell you're in the lead.

"Up, three." He's going to do it.

"Paddles ready." Okay, baby.

BANG!

Go! Off the line 1-2-3-4. Quick!

The water flew from an invisible blender, a paroxysm of noise and confusion. The start was an arm wrestle, a dead lift, a crude test of brute strength that picked the boat off the line and thrust it into motion. Alll righhht, Scott thought, we're moving.

Forty strokes out, he could feel his position. It was just him and Nash, head tilted forward like a sniper taking aim at an invisible target. They had open water, and the pack was fading like fireworks in a black night.

Pump with the legs. Pull with the lats.

At seventy metres, he hit maximum speed.

Scott could feel the oxygen-charged blood rushing to his screaming arms, racing through arteries that had opened like the mouth of a trout, arteries as big and elastic as a wind tunnel. Pump. Pump. Pump. Tearing past stop signs, driven by a turbo-charged heart the size of a cantaloupe.

This is what you trained for, Scotty, this is all you want.

Scott heard the noise five strokes before he reached the seven-hundred-and-fifty line. One of the Americans on shore had a cowbell, another had a bongo drum, tracking Nash, clamouring, beating when he passed. The cheers were fading by the time Scott hit them, pulling with his teeth, his ears, every muscle in his corded neck, pulling so hard he forgot to breathe.

"Move it, Scotty!" Taylor barked in a hoarse voice that confirmed his every fear. "Don't save nothin'!"

Hit your groove. Make it move.

Scott glanced to his right and saw Nash surge.

He's got to break, Scott thought.

He can't keep it up. He's got to lengthen out.

Relax, relax.

Race your own race.

He caught a glimpse of the American's back as it twisted and pulled, his blade working the water like cogs. *Swish. Swish. Swish.* Down the course like a phantom he soared, passing the five hundred on a cushion of air, just starting to move.

Scott began to choke up. His boat wobbled. He took a bad stroke.

"C'mon, Scotty!" Taylor shouted, his voice cracking. "Go with him, or it's too fucking late."

Scott's arms were seizing, shortening his stroke, his body taken over by an insidious form of rigor mortis he could not control. *Slap, slap.* The strokes were too shallow, too short. His knees trembled, and his boat shook uncontrollably; his two-hundred-centimetre-long paddle was an unwieldy lead bar.

Unable to get the reach, his blade was missing the good water, the water that counted. He was Frankenstein's monster, arms frozen in front, flailing at the water, lurching forward in a macabre dance, a herky-jerky motion while Nash got smoother.

The oxygen gone, Scott's lungs were bursting; he could feel the lactic acid poisoning his muscles like sugar in a gas tank. His heart was ready to explode.

Scott knew the race was lost, and the longer it lasted, the more hideous it became. Nash picked it up and the crowd shouted as he shifted gears. Scott could feel Nash's speed as he crossed the two-hundred-and-fifty-metre buoys, he could hear the cheers as lane four surged forward, invincible.

The cowbells were mocking him now. Taylor's voice had faded.

Scott could feel the eyes at the finish; he could see the podium and empty trailers. He could spot people trading T-shirts and looking at fibreglass gear; he could read Nash's name on the Harry "Pop" Knight Trophy, and he could visualize the time.

His hand hit the gunwale, stinging like the truth. He's better, Scott admitted in an epiphany of pain. He's that much better. No matter how hard I try, no matter how badly I want it, I will never be that fast.

Scott wanted to take a freak stroke, to miss the water and

topple in, to sink into the mean black canal and vanish like Jimmy Hoffa.

It would be easier than this.

Taylor was standing on the wharf, arms akimbo, when Scott crashed the dock, too numb to stop. Together, like pallbearers, they carried the boat to a grassy bank, where Scott lay down, silent and spent, praying he was dead. Closing his eyes, he hid the tears.

Suddenly, he was embarrassed by his dreams, ashamed of holding himself up to the brilliance.

3:49. The time drifted through the crowd like the smell of lilacs, and then it started to rain.

Scott closed the scrapbook. He was shocked by the vividness of the memory, having been unable, in the past, to recall the race. Subconsciously, he had blocked it, buried it with the decision to quit paddling. It was the turning point of his life, the moment he swore off sports, the moment he decided he'd been ripped off by God, a capricious God who, on his own, determined greatness. God alone picked a select few, people like Nash and Turmoil Davies. After that, Scott MacDonald hung up his blade and settled into a life of mediocrity, vowing never to expose himself again. The wonder was gone, the promise. Scott MacDonald entered the real world as a disillusioned man, a man who liked to drink.

32

A legislative page stood in the doorway and yawned. The room, which had a lofty ceiling and velvet chairs, was damp, as though the heating system had been installed by the eighteenth-century despots who graced the walls. Sniffling, Turmoil searched the crowd for Lorraine.

A woman handed the page an empty teacup, which he placed on a table.

"Look out, Junior." A grizzled man in a torn jogging suit pushed by, wearing a Bruins toque and mittens secured to his jacket by safety pins. The page appeared startled by the force of the arm, which looked as frail as a balsa wood airplane.

The jogger ran four steps in a Kip Keino victory jog and then loaded a Best Buy bag with sandwiches. The page could smell the cold in the man's bleached beard, in his tattered Reeboks, and deep in his balsa wood bones. Surprised, Turmoil watched the old man lift an egg sandwich, sniff it, and return it to the tray.

"That old man is snatching all of the food," noted a woman in a choir robe.

"Is nobody going to stop him?" asked another.

The page took an assertive step forward and then reconsidered. Pages were the lowest form of legislature life, a social amoeba that spent its days fetching water, delivering Hansard, and ducking the passes of higher life forms. Threatened and bored, they sought refuge in the basement, a dark pool of reefer madness, and avoided confrontations.

Ownie had no idea why he was attending the reception with Turmoil, who had been ignoring him since they arrived. Turmoil, who was making no effort to ingratiate himself with anyone at the gathering. On good days, the big man could win over a room as soon as he entered; on bad ones, he was so arrogant and dismissive that it was almost sinful.

Like most occupants of the room, the choir members were African Canadian, men and women in suits, robes, and vivid African clothes made from *kente* or *shedda*. Ownie recognized a legal aid lawyer and a pastor with a gift for inspirational sermons. The gathering had a strange mood, he decided. Most of the guests, while proud of their accomplishments, kept their emotions in check, doubting, it seemed, the sincerity of their hosts, mindful, still, of the segregated schools of the 1960s, the not-so-distant movie theatres with Negro sections.

BLACK HISTORY MONTH. ERACISM, announced a poster.

His bag full, the jogger bounced on his toes as though he was waiting for a light to change. He sipped on a coffee. The steam melted the ice crystals on his beard. A local character, as well known as the drifter who dressed like Pavarotti, he lived in a men's shelter and called himself, with an odd mix of madness and bravado, the Running Joke.

"How long is this going to last?" a politician in a white wig asked a colleague. Alex Francis MacDougall was shaped like the Fruit of the Loom apple character, with stick legs protruding from a round torso. Unlike the singing apple who sometimes chirped about loving your underwear, MacDougall was pompous and a bore. He had a minor portfolio.

"Who knows?" replied his cabinet colleague.

Stepping forward, MacDougall squeezed a woman's hand as though he was testing a melon. The hand belonged to Lavinia Crawford, an elderly artist who had been featured in an NFB documentary on basket weaving. Her intricate maple designs were now in galleries, exhibits, and the National

Museum in Ottawa. Lavinia told the filmmaker that the craft had been passed on by ancestors, former slaves who had walked to Halifax from Preston selling baskets, blueberries, and mayflowers. "The talent was a gift from the Lord." With talk of an imminent Order of Canada, there was a mad rush among the in crowd for Lavinia baskets, a rush fuelled by the Maud Lewis craze and the buzz: What if Lavinia was the next folk art genius?

Ownie studied a poster of a map shaped like Nova Scotia.

BLACK FIRSTS IN NOVA SCOTIA:
LAWYER JAMES ROBERTSON JOHNSTON 1895.
POLICE PERSON ROSE FORTUNE CIRCA 1885.
VICTORIA CROSS WINNER WILLIAM HALL 1859.

"I'm Alex Francis MacDougall from Pick-tou Cen-ter." Done with Lavinia, the politician sidled up to Turmoil. "Highest majority in the province. And who are you?"

"Ebbyone know me." Turmoil took a piece of pineapple from a tray.

"Oh?" MacDougall scoffed.

"Ahm the mon they all wahn to meet." Turmoil looked over MacDougall's head as though he was trying to locate someone important. He saw a government photographer snapping Lavinia, posed with one politician after another.

"Who?" MacDougall challenged him.

"Ebbyone." Then, after a moment's silence the fighter added, "Ahm Turmoil Davies."

"I see," MacDougall smirked.

Turmoil kept searching the room, skimming the tops of heads like a lighthouse beacon, ignoring Ownie, who, used to fending for himself, was now having a pleasant conversation with two of the choir women.

"When you leabe here, you be tellin your little ole wife you met me," Turmoil told MacDougall.

"Oh?"

"You'll say, 'Wife, you wohn believe wha happen to me today. Ah met Turmoil Davies, the next heavyweight champeen of the world.' And she will say: 'G'won, dohn go foolin me.'"

"So you're a pugilist?"

"No mon, ahm the next heavyweight champeen of the world. Ahm the mon ebbyone here to see."

"My wife isn't much of a boxing fan." MacDougall rolled his eyes.

"That wha you think, mon."

"I think I can safely say —"

"Wha she goin tell a little ole fat mon like you?" Turmoil cut him off. "With a white wig on your head." He shook his head in amusement. "Little fat belly and ahms like a baby girl. She goin tell you she wohn to meet a big mon like me?" Turmoil laughed loud enough to turn heads.

"Excuse me." MacDougall bolted. "I have some urgent government business."

Once across the room, MacDougall draped his arm around Ducky Blades, a country boy who had just been elected by the good people of Lower East Pubnico and was now skipping down the Road to Ruin like Pinocchio on Pleasure Island. "We're cutting a deal, now," MacDougall told the new backbencher, making it sound important. "Make sure you're there for the vote."

"Uh-huh." Ducky nodded. In Halifax, far from home during the legislative session, boys like Ducky could play pool, smoke cigars, and stay up late. There were no rules, no nagging wives, no Jiminy Cricket to tell them they were turning into donkeys, just crooked old men like Alex Francis MacDougall.

"It's that damn NDP," MacDougall confided. "Fruit merchants, you know."

MacDougall summoned the page with a flick of the finger. Pages hated MacDougall, who lunched at the Thirsty Beaver and returned to the house a drunken windmill, waving for water, sending obscene notes across the floor. What did he want now?

"Ahm thinkin of goin into politics myself." Turmoil was back at MacDougall's side. "The peeple wuhd love me."

"Oh really?" This was an affront.

The people had elected Alex Francis MacDougall in four straight elections because he delivered at the same predictable rate: fifty bucks for a worker's compensation form, one hundred for a veteran's disability hearing. A letter of reference cost twenty-five dollars, free if you worked on Alex Francis's campaign.

"Oh yes, the smart peeple." Then Turmoil dismissed the red room with a wave. "Some these peeple, they jes chupid." Turmoil reached for a pineapple chunk. "They dohn know nothin 'bou nothin; they nebba been nowhere."

And then, Turmoil gave MacDougall a wide-eyed warning: "You bes be careful; ah might get your jawb."

Ownie saw Lorraine talking to the director of the choir. Emmett Grouse had started piano at the age of five and had attended Berklee College of Music. In addition to directing the choir and playing the organ at church, he produced radio programs and volunteered with youth groups. The choir women had told Ownie about the director and he, in turn, had given them the lowdown on Hildred's cake business.

Ducky, the backbencher, was cornered by a zealot who regularly crashed legislature events. Alasdair MacIsaac, a wild-eyed crusader for Gaelic rights, was resplendent in a grey ponytail and plaid vest, and he was waving a stack of papers, all related, he claimed, to "systemic racism."

"It's the same ethnocide." He painted the room with an ink-stained hand. "Denying people disclosure of the lineage of a significant cultural progenitor. The oppression must cease."

Ducky nodded, suddenly feeling oppressed himself. As Alasdair placed a hand on his shoulder, Ducky visualized his table back home at the Legion. If he closed his eyes, he was smelt fishing. How long, he wondered, would the session last?

As Ducky pulled away from Alasdair, Turmoil spotted Lorraine in a CBC circle. She was a newsroom favourite: young, a visible minority, left, a quotable female, who had worked with the Jesse Jackson Rainbow Coalition and volunteered in Zimbabwe under Canadian Crossroads International.

A bloated reporter inched closer to Lorraine, feet seemingly not moving. Last month, Natalie Marr had filed a grievance against a sports announcer who had sworn in the newsroom. For re-education, the announcer was sent to a sensitivity seminar run by an actor in a Big Bird costume who asked, in a session on gender stereotyping: "Am I a male or a female, and does it matter?"

"I bought a wonderful book at Kwanzaa," said Natalie. "It's by a Jamaican author who writes all of her work in Creole, very powerful."

"Oh." Lorraine tried to look interested. "Do you know Creole?"

"Ah, no." Natalie's teeth stuck to her lips.

MacDougall eyed the exit, which was now blocked by Alasdair, a man with a back injury, and the non-custodial father, all chronic crashers to be avoided at all costs.

"How long do we have to stay?"

"God knows," said his colleague.

"None of these people are from my riding." MacDougall frowned, still avoiding Alasdair, whom he had hated ever since the crasher had criticized a Pictou pipe and drum band. In an unpardonable act, Alasdair had appeared in the Gaelic press denouncing "pipe and drum music born from British military tradition. It is time we return to our traditions, to the older strathspeys and reels that speak to the Gaelic heart."

"Tell Ducky he has to stay."

Ducky was staring at his feet, left numb by Alasdair's monologue. How could he argue with Alasdair, who had such a keen interest in the supernatural and the bochdan, along with his gift of the second sight?

"This is Turmoil Davies," Lorraine said.

"Ah." Natalie winced as though she had been knifed.

"Someone tole me the premier was lookin foh me," Turmoil said, ignoring the introduction. "Ah can' stay aroun here all day. If he show up, you tell him to give me a call." And then he gestured at Ownie, still talking to the choir ladies. "Iss time to go."

33

Garth MacKenzie's wife was parked on a chair outside his office, rooting through her purse. She pulled out a receipt, stared through tethered glasses, and sighed a lung-clearing sigh. "I wish he would hurry up."

Carla, the secretary, dropped a letter in her in-out box and smiled. "This time of day he's always busy."

"I don't care what time of day it is. My lovely house is going to be ruined."

"Your house?" asked Carla while admiring the tole-painted box on her desk. On the "in" side, she had painted a plump raccoon in Ray-Ban shades, bike shorts, and Nikes. On "out" was his double in a belted lime-green leisure suit. One of the interns, that tall boy who carried a bodhran on his bicycle, said she had it backwards, that the leisure suit was wicked. She thought he was funny.

"Didn't he tell you?" Jean, the wife, demanded.

"Ah?" Carla didn't know what the safe answer was.

"When we were in St. Pete's last month, some, some" — her voice climbed a ladder of exasperation — "horrible smelly rummy started feeding pigeons on our lawn. By the time we got back, they had moved in — hundreds of them, mothers, babies — and now we can't get rid of them. They're on the roof and in the trees. You know what they call pigeons, don't you?" She fixed her stare on Carla and teetered.

"Ah, no."

"Flying rats. My beautiful house is infested with rats!"

"Have you tried scaring them off?"

"We've tried everything. It is horrible, with droppings all over my lovely deck, my blue lawn swing, my —"

"That's too bad."

"Then this morning, I caught him red-handed. When I came home from Tone and Trim, he was there, the vagrant, feeding them. I told Garth that he'd been doing it all along. That's why they won't leave. Garth has to take care of this."

Carla typed a letter while Webberly from Business stopped to admire Jean's purple pantsuit, telling her, "You look younger every time I see you. Ha. Ha. How do you do it?" It was true, Carla noticed grudgingly, Jean did seem younger.

As the wife had grown tauter, something eerie had happened to MacKenzie, Carla observed. Slowly but surely, his physiology had changed. His cheeks had become soft and rosy, his beard so faint it had nearly disappeared. MacKenzie had turned into a Russian stacking doll, pear-shaped, with shrunken shoulders, broad hips, and babushkas.

"He's almost through," Carla noted.

As Jean walked to Carla's desk, the secretary decided that she must have noticed the mailbox, since everyone loved it. "You should have a booth at the Christmas Craft Show," people told her. "You're so eclectic." Carla smiled, keeping her pride in its place, and the wife stared back.

"Your hair really *is* red, isn't it?"

"Uh." Carla flushed as MacKenzie shuffled out, wearing his green sweater.

"You can never wear pink lipstick." The wife stared pointedly, waiting for a response, then demanded, "Can you?"

MacKenzie couldn't go home, he told his wife in a low voice, he had a meeting with Boomer, the publisher. Furious, Jean tossed two envelopes containing bills on Carla's desk for mailing. Carla stamped the envelopes, one to Uptown Furs, the other to Mary Kay Cosmetics, hesitated, then put them face down in "out," so they couldn't see the lime-green leisure suit with the comical lines, so they couldn't for a minute pretend they belonged.

Craving a beer, Garth looked around the black-and-white restaurant decorated with tiny photos of Chinese peasants. Boomer and Katherine were across the table. What kind of a place was this, anyway? Garth wondered. No one seemed to be drinking. For years, he'd been able to nurse a beer at work by pouring it into a Tim Hortons coffee mug and sipping it during the day, but now with Boomer and his bloody safety nurse, he couldn't take a chance.

Garth studied the menu: olive fettuccine with gorgonzola and ricotta, curried corn bisque, calamari with garlic mayonnaise, raspberry fool in phyllo tulips. With those peasants on the wall, you'd think there'd be sweet and sour or Bo Bo balls, thought Garth, who enjoyed a good bowl of won ton soup.

At the next table, three career women were gabbing. One, according to their conversation, was married to a doctor.

"Kevin said they had a lesbian couple in maternity; one gave birth and the other nursed the baby."

"Do you have to take hormones or is it a symbiotic thing?"

"I don't know."

"What did Kevin say?"

"He didn't have a clue."

"He's a doctor!"

The woman leaned across the table and hissed: "He's a pecker checker."

Boomer pulled a notebook from his tan, single-breasted

overcoat, a Sears standard for decades. Underneath was a tweed jacket and striped shirt with solid collar. Somewhere along the way, in a pit stop in Northern Ontario or rural Manitoba, he had picked up the affectation of suspenders, his trademark.

"Head office is preparing for a mid-year review." The publisher kept the overcoat on, a warning that he was all business, too driven to care what anyone thought about his head, his hair, or his pale, shrunken eyes. "Social trends. How are we faring in that department?"

While Katherine replied, Garth gazed out the window, thinking about pecker checkers and disappointed with his lunch: cold potatoes in mustard dressing dumped on lettuce. The restaurant was one of those places that never seemed clean, he decided, where your table had one leg that was too short, where the profits, according to the menu, went to a weird religion.

An ancient woman stood on the curb, bowlegged in a knee-length mink cut like a housecoat. A pillbox hat sagged over her face, which had been painted for a silent movie. She was teetering in calf-length, spike-heeled boots from the 1970s. Cocktail boots, they used to call them, with a perky tassel on each foot. She gathered herself up slowly to cross the street, looked one way, then stepped off the curb, waving her arms wildly like she was trying to fly. Startled, Garth turned back.

Years ago, they'd hired a guy for trends, Garth recalled, but Bentley fired him for hitting on a copy boy. "No more funny fellows," Bentley had ordered. Garth suspected the odd one slipped in now and then through the cracks. He certainly had his doubts about Blaise.

"Any inroads into beefing up numbers in Yarmouth County?"

"We're working on it," Katherine explained. "I've hired a new stringer."

The women picked up their briefcases, as stoic as miners returning to the pit. "I'd be a lesbian," said Kevin's wife, weighing her options, "but I couldn't stand the drama. With men, if you're having a bad day, you can tell them to piss off, and they know that they deserve it."

And then, before Garth could explain in elaborate detail all of the stories that Sports had written and all of the flashbacks he had suggested, Boomer reached for the bill and said, "Prepare for some restructuring."

34

"How you doin'?"

"Good," Suey allowed. "I'm gonna be in a movie. That movie man, he's makin' a picture 'bout Sam Langford. Me and Sam related way back."

"That right?" Ownie asked.

"My mother from down them parts. Weymouth."

"I thought all Sam's people were gone."

"Maybe, the close-close relations."

"Oh."

"My mother had pictures of Sam, some took before he fought Jack Johnson." Suey paused to let Sam catch up, to amble past the battle royals, the Great White Hopes, and colour-coded crowns. He let the great man linger on the gay streets of France. "Sam, he weren't much taller than me. All my mother's side is squat. Sam was broad, though, and his arms was long."

For the uninformed, it was all in the *Coles Notes on Boxing*: how Sam, who moved to Boston at age fourteen, gave up six inches and thirty pounds to Johnson; how the Boston Tar Baby, the greatest fighter never given a world title shot, was mugged by a time and a place.

"I did a visitation on Sam when I was fighting down in Beantown," Suey said. "He was blind by then. The books give him four hundred pro fights and one hundred KOs, but Sam said no one knowed for sure. He fought all over, Down Under, Mexico, every coupla weeks. He seen more rings than a Times

Square fence. Since they wouldn't let him fight the white boys, he had to keep at the same black guys over and over, they travelled together; some dude called it the chitlin trail. Sam fought Harry Wills twenty-five times, Sam McVea fifteen. He said he got so sicka lookin' at Harry's face, they might as well been married."

Ownie laughed and finished taping a split glove.

"Once," Suey recalled, "Sam said Joe Jeanette and McVea knocked each other down thirty-eight times in one fight. He said he didn't know what those boys was doin' wrong that night."

"Who won?"

"I ast Sam, and he said, 'Who cares? After thirty-eight knockdowns, you bess forget about the whole thing. You bess forget it ever happened.'"

"Sam was in our house in Charlottetown once. He was travellin' around, fighting exhibitions. He came looking for the old man, since he needed someone to come in the ring with him. The old man wasn't home, just my mother. She looked at his ear. It was all puffed up. She'd never seen a cauliflower ear before, so she said, 'Mr. Langford, what happened to your ear?' Sam, who talked with a lisp, said, 'I forgot to duck.' He had a real good sense of humour."

"Yeah," said Suey. "He did."

"Not everybody knows that."

"Sam was all that and a box of Moirs chocolates." Suey eased his bones off the bench. "See you 'round."

"Let me know when your movie comes out."

Suey nodded, then turned back slowly as though he'd forgotten something. "I seen that ole sidewinder. You know that ole guy —"

"Slugger?"

"Yeah." Suey coughed and spit. "He was playing crib at the seniors' complex. He says some wise guy in his forties come in, a real John Wayne. Slugger says this man starts using filthy language. Slugger don't abide by that with wimmin there, so he tole the man: 'Out, out, you go. You're not welcome here!'" Suey laughed. "Oh yeeeaaah." The thought amused him. "Slugger wanted to put the run onto him. Well, Wayne, he turn to Slugger and says, 'Come outside, we'll settle this.'"

"The rotten bastard," Ownie swore. "The man's eighty-four."

"Slugger said he wudden go outside becuz he knowed Wayne was a dirty fighter. If they went outside, he'd go straight to the boots. Slugger could have ended up in the body shop, so Slugger tole him: 'No, man, I fight you here but not outside.'"

"Slugger's no fool."

"So then Slugger, he look at me, and he say, 'Suey, I was in a no-win situation. Since I use to be a pro-feshnul boxer, I coulda been charged if I hit the man.'" Suey laughed. "I said 'yeah, we ole guys got it tough.'"

"You ever see this dude, this Wayne?"

"No, but I tole Slugger, if he go jammin' you, come round me up. I go down there sometimes to visit some of the ladies, you know. If Wayne get too bad for us, I'll get a couple of the brothers to come by."

"Owww, you could handle him," Ownie scoffed. "Drop a slider in on him."

"I know." Suey pulled a blackjack from his jacket and bounced it in his palm. "I carry insurance these days."

"Way to travel, brother."

By the time Suey left, Ownie was in an unsettled mood. Listening to Suey talk about Sam, the epitome of class, had made the trainer angry with LeBlanc, who, at this point, shouldn't even call himself a fighter. Ownie was too old, he decided, to be made a fool of by LeBlanc who, according to Louie, hadn't run in weeks.

The welterweight had taken an easy fight a few months back. LeBlanc was so fat he had to cut weight for a week, dehydrating with pills, garbage bags, and a sauna. At the weigh-in, Johnny stepped on the scale and held his breath until his weight popped up. And then, in a moment that still made Ownie livid, Johnny collapsed unconscious in the old trainer's arms, eyes closed, wearing only a pair of black bikini underwear. The ignominious moment, captured by a *Standard* photographer, was proof, Ownie believed, of how ridiculous the fighter had become.

Ownie summoned Johnny across the room and squared a scale on the hardwood floor. According to Suey, the photo was posted at Hansel's gym along with insulting comments. "Get on," Ownie ordered. "Let's see if you're even close to fighting Sparks."

"Oh, maaan." Johnny tried to look betrayed. For support, he glanced around the gym but saw only the Dog doing push-ups and Louie, hiding the guilty face of a mole. "I just ate."

"You give me a time, a particular hour, when you haven't just ate." Ownie was getting crankier the more that Johnny protested. "I said, get on!"

Slowly, looking for time and a way to drop five pounds, Johnny peeled off his red jacket and his Ironman watch. He hawked into a spittoon and stepped on the scale, claiming, "These cheap ones aren't that reliable." His eyes widened like Charlie Chaplin as the needle raced past one-fifty, then one fifty-five, every notch an indictment, every pound a lie.

"Ouch," Johnny winced as the scale stopped at one sixty-five, twenty pounds over weight. He pulled a disbelieving face that reminded Ownie of a woman he'd seen at customs after officers hauled a two-foot Polish sausage from her suitcase. "I don't know," she had stammered, pulling the same counterfeit face. "I don't know how."

"Look at that," Ownie ordered. "Twenty pounds of blubber. You are as fat as a lactating seal."

"Aw, I can get it off. I'm in the grind now."

"Bullshit!"

Johnny's face was making Ownie as sick as that sausage woman, who had mugged with her mouth open, incredulous, as though the sausages had climbed in by themselves. Hearing the commotion, the Runner and little Ricky wandered across the room.

"You can get it off, but what'll you have left?" Ownie barked.

"There's a lot of muscle."

"You'll have an empty tank. You should be ready to rock and roll for ten rounds, ready to drop the Fancy Dan, ready to charge in and tear Sparks's head off. That man's case-hardened by now; he been fighting world-ranked fighters Stateside while you've been hanging around like an old washerwoman eating jelly doughnuts."

"But —"

"You are flabby, your reflexes are slow, and you're out of shape. You make me look like a bigger fool than I already am." While Ownie paused for breath, Johnny gave the scale a hateful look. "You've got no bounce, no spring. Forget it, man, you are done."

"I gotta fight him." Johnny lowered his brows, shifting from shock to determination. "I gotta bad hate on for him, that gasbag, I gotta get it outta my system."

"You hate him that bad, you fight him on the street. But don't go draggin' me in there to watch you get your head beat off."

"I gotta, man. He's so much talk, him and that mother, Girlie. I *hate* her."

Ownie could understand why Johnny didn't care for Hansel, who trash-talked non-stop, most of it for show. Hansel liked to keep busy, and LeBlanc, with his weight problem, would make an easy tune-up. Hansel's handlers weren't stupid; they weren't like the idiots who took fighters to hotbeds like Philadelphia to train and got them punched to pieces in the gym, every session more damaging than a real fight. They weren't that dumb.

Disgusted, Ownie walked across the room while Johnny mumbled something about cheap bathroom scales from China that could never be trusted.

Ownie stared out the window at a taxi stand. Tootsy worked there sometimes, but he preferred the airport route, which was safer. The drivers at this stand looked like truckers, middle-aged men in failing health. Except for a midget and a grandmother whose licence plate said *Hot Mama*, they were interchangeable.

A month ago, two new guys showed up, both with long, bleached hair like that band, Nelson. Somehow, they managed to park together as though they were planning a gig, even though the line was supposed to be random. One day, while heading to the gym, Ownie glanced through one of their windows and saw instead of a sweet-faced teen a fifty-year-old man with a pitted face, Charles Bronson in a blond wig, which is how you deceive yourself, Ownie figured, how you end up in a mess like this.

Johnny was surprised to see the trainer back before him. But then again, Johnny figured, they were too tight to end things this way.

"Okay, up to now, we've been working on the honour system," Ownie said, and Johnny sucked pounds from his cheeks. "That doesn't seem to be getting us anywhere, right?"

"Right." Johnny was prepared to agree with anything.

"Now, if we're going to go through with this, if we're

actually going to fight Sparks, we're going to have to do things my way."

Johnny nodded willingness.

"This gentleman here" — Ownie pointed to the Runner, who was hovering in black tights and a long-sleeved jersey, a resistance-free mass of hollow bones and weightless muscle — "he is going to help us out. From now on, you'll be running with him."

"But I . . ." Johnny stared at the Runner, a helium-filled fanatic with grasshopper legs. The Runner sniffed his orange nose, and Johnny thought he looked anemic or like someone in chemotherapy, with his eyes too large, his face too drawn. The Runner's body always seemed to be in a state of recovery, rebuilding cells and replenishing glycogen.

The man is so crazy, Johnny wanted to tell Ownie, that he would rather run than watch the Stanley Cup on TV, he would rather run than have sex with two women. Johnny looked at the greedy teeth, the narrows hands shaped like claws, and he wanted to set Ownie straight.

"You two start tomorrow," Ownie ordered. "I'll be expectin' reports, because this man" — he pointed again at the Runner, who seemed more surprised than anyone — "this man is an intelligent man. This man wants to make something of his life. This man is not a big, fat, good-for-nothin' washerwoman."

In the back of the Press Club, under a cover of ferns, Scott could hear a couple flirting. "I met my boyfriend at sculpting class." The woman laughed an airy laugh that sounded forced. "We had to do each other's heads."

"Ahhh, that sounds romantic." The man feigned enchantment.

"It was, but now whenever we move we have to cart these big plaster heads." Another laugh, which added a tinkle of whimsy. "Monstrosities that weigh ten pounds."

"Ahhh, love." As the man sighed, Scott stole a glance at the couple. The man was Michel Coté, a national newspaper correspondent from Montreal, banished to the boondocks, where women and intermittent marine disasters were his only solace. Short and dark, Michel had a habit of running a hand up his forehead, brushing back his hair and, with it, the problems of the world.

"Mine doesn't even look like me," the woman complained, and Michel rewarded her with a sympathetic pout.

The door buzzer sounded and a TV anchorwoman in orange makeup trotted in, two discreet steps ahead of the married producer she was dating. An old flack draped over the bar managed to lift one arm in a wave that she ignored. "I had her!" the scorned man then told the room. "She was nothing special."

"Did I ever tell you my first marriage ended when my wife caught me having an affair with her best friend?" Michel raised his forlorn Raúl Juliá eyes. Partial to oversized trench coats and thin Italian loafers, he had already confessed his disappointment with the lack of improv theatre and Thai restaurants in Halifax. "The three of us enrolled in a gourmet cooking class. My wife noticed that we were spending too much time shopping for fresh basil." Scott sensed a *je-ne-sais-quoi* shrug. "It isn't that hard to find, you know."

Scott stole a look, trying to see the woman, who, to his surprise, turned out to be Squeaky, the Books editor, the same woman who had wrestled with Smithers in the darkroom and now hated his guts.

"I am not myself today," Michel moaned, stroking his hair. "My girlfriend has me tired out. She always wants to stay up and talk after sex, while me, I just want to sleep."

Michel's girlfriend was a twenty-two-year-old nymph who sold art supplies. "But I am in love." She wore bowling shirts and cut her hair like Edith Piaf. "I have decided the woman should always be at least ten years younger than the man; it is more natural that way."

A blast of frigid air shocked the room as the door opened. Hmmm. Recognizing the *hmmm*, Scott shrunk in his seat. Ever since he'd been ordered to profile School Boy, he'd been avoiding MacKenzie, who now cleared his throat and headed for a smoker with a beer. MacKenzie seemed blind to his surroundings, Scott noticed, his vision narrowed to a one-foot corridor. Scott kept his head down where all he could hear was Michel and Squeaky, two sensitive souls afloat in a sea of White Russians.

"Why did you leave the wire?" she asked.

Michel pushed back his hair and, with it, the philistines who had once signed his cheques. "I did not fit their colour scheme. They want to paint everything brown, while me, I see more colour in life."

"I know what you mean. Some of the morons I work with."

MacKenzie's voice was suddenly clear. "Hi, Dick. How's the lodge?"

"Comin' along, comin'." The chain-smoker was wearing vinyl shoes and false teeth that rattled in his mouth. "I had a little problem with them raccoons, but I took care of them."

"That's good."

"They can be buggers if they get into the roof."

"Terrible nuisance."

"Not any more!" Dick's sadistic smile signalled a grisly end for the creatures.

"Doing any hunting?" Garth asked.

"I got my name in for the moose lottery," said Dick with a conspiratorial wink. "I got pretty good connections, you know."

Dick had oily skin with pores that looked like they had been created by an HB pencil poked in clay. He had ingrown whiskers that festered and black, subversive brows that filled in as quickly as a dredged channel. Dick's face was well known in his small town, where he ran a weekly paper with nine employees and a circulation of one thousand, a shoestring operation kept afloat by printing circulars. Reporters used their own cars and cameras, and Dick kept a meticulous log of long-distance calls, ensuring staffers did not exceed their quota.

"I seen Corky Bungay last week." Dick looked up from his beer.

"Best damn baseball player ever to play on Canadian soil."

Garth sounded like a poll had been taken and Corky had been named the indisputable winner.

Dick kept the editorial operation as simple as his outlook on life. Whenever he received a press release, he pencilled out the date, inserted (STAFF) after the placeline, and sent it to composing. He ran speeches from the local politicians verbatim; he filled pages with social notes and free submissions.

"I seen him when they won the Maritime title."

"With the Liverpool Larrupers."

"That's right, that's right." Dick was excited.

"Hell of a team."

Scott flinched, wondering if MacKenzie would think about the unfinished Where Are They Now?

The mention of Corky seemed comforting to Dick, who was burdened by rumours that his paper was about to be sold. With a grade eight education and no real skills, he was as vulnerable as the raccoons, so Dick, a survivor, had staked his future on a fishing lodge, a ten-cabin spread on a river.

"Corky was in for the knee replacement."

Michel and Squeaky wobbled to the door, unseen by Garth, who had met Dick thirty years ago at a mine cave-in. While Garth's politics had evolved since then, Dick's had congealed in the 1960s, forming a wall against the forces that were, in his mind, oppressing him: women, minorities, and unions. Dick's loyalties rested with the town's biggest employer, a pulp mill that sponsored the paper's softball team. Last year, in a show of allegiance that the mill rewarded with new uniforms, Garth wrote a spirited editorial after the CBC did a story on asthmatics allegedly dying from airborne pollutants.

Seething from the anchor's snub, the smelly flack, who claimed he had once been a figure skater, was yelling at the bartender: "I had so many women when I was with the Ice Capades that I actually got sick of them."

"I bet," said the barkeep, who had trouble reconciling platter lifts with the bloated mess before him.

"You wanna believe it!" The flack wobbled, eyes closed under glasses that skimmed the tip of his nose. "I was the only straight guy in the whole chorus, I was like a kid on Easter morning surrounded by chocolate bunnies." Scott kept his head down, trying to hear MacKenzie over the flack. "Those little skaters are horny too, with legs like a vise."

Scott could catch snatches, something about an investigative piece by Cullen, the legislature reporter, the MLA Alex Francis MacDougall, mill money, and safety violations. MacDougall was Dick's partner in the fishing lodge, it appeared, guaranteeing all of the necessary grants. MacKenzie said Katherine Redgrave had sent Cullen's story to the *Standard*'s lawyers, where it was being X-rayed for libel. Garth slid an envelope across the table, past a pile of dead smokes and all moral qualms. "Alex Francis might want to see this so he can head them off at the pass." At least, Scott decided, it had nothing to do with him.

In a crisis, MacKenzie always went to his greatest strength: moral ambivalence. It presented him with myriad opportunities that would never have arisen for a fussier man.

"I'll see that Alex Francis gets it."

"It should help."

"Don't worry about nothin'," Dick assured him. "Them lawyers of yours, they get a lot of government business. One call from Alex Francis and this story will have more holes than a block of Swiss cheese. If I'm not mistaken, one of them partners is hoping to make judge. He ain't gonna do nothin' to piss off people in high places."

An hour later, Garth parked at a brick low-rise with a wheelchair ramp and a sterile entrance. Two nurses were wrestling with a stretcher. Inside, the blue hall smelled like Lysol. Dust formed a shroud over dried flowers that reeked of death. God, Garth hated it here, with TVs blaring and orderlies bustling past dry mouths and vacant stares.

He had every right, he figured, to blindside Cullen and that Redgrave broad, since he knew damn well why Gem was promoting her. It was only because she was so bloody tall. Garth had heard about the interviews in Toronto, how the mucky-mucks had marched the four finalists for city editor into the boardroom like prize steers. "Her!" said Gem's CEO, dismissing the others on sight. "That way we get our money's worth. If we are going to promote women, let's go for get the most bang for the buck." A features writer, Garth swore, a goddamn sob sister.

TODAY'S BIRTHDAYS
MARY KNOCK IS 87.
WINSTON MACKENZIE IS 82.

A gerontologist walked by, bored by the predictability of it all. Garth hadn't seen a doctor in five years, even though his ankles were yellow and as springy as a water balloon. Jean went every week, but that was different, since the change had made her so irritable that she couldn't stand him in the same room.

WINSTON'S ROOM, announced bright block letters. Garth knocked and entered a stale square with pulled shades. He saw a nurse.

TODAY IS MONDAY.

A skeletal man was sitting in a rocker, his stubbly chin wet.

He had a blanket on his lap. Without the infrastructure of teeth, his cheeks had collapsed.

"I haven't seen you since his last birthday," scolded the nurse.

"No." Garth cleared his throat. "I've been busy."

The drawers had been labelled since his last visit: CANDY, UNDERWEAR. Garth moved a pair of plaid slippers off the bed and adjusted the man's blanket, the nurse watching with the proprietorial air of a store owner who had brought out a tray of rings for his inspection.

"How is he?"

"The same," she said, staying close, as though Garth couldn't be trusted with his own father. "He's never any trouble."

36

Johnny was standing in Ownie's basement, in the space off the
rec room. In a stack of memorabilia, next to an Etch A Sketch
and a Jon Gnagy art kit, he found a fight program that had
yellowed like a chain-smoker's fingers.

MONCTON STADIUM. SEPT. 8, 1954.
10 cents.
Sponsored by Sportsmans Club. If You Don't
Participate in Sports, Be a Sport.
Door Prize: 1st prize $10 cash;
2nd prize, a Presto lighter.
MAIN BOUT
10 rounds

Floyd Patterson   vs.   Chief Alvin Williams
Brooklyn, NY   Oklahoma City, Okla.
171 pounds   175 pounds

Ownie pointed to the small print, the Presto footnotes.
"See, I had Schmeisser on the undercard." Ownie paused.
"Cheapest bastard who ever lived. He had his wife work the
corner once to save money."

"Isn't that Schmeisser?" Johnny pointed to a photo on the
basement wall. In the midst of a black-and-white cluster was
a grainy blow-up of a flattened fighter, toes pointed at the
camera. Shot up, from ringside, it made his boots look enormous.

"Yeah," said Ownie, "that's him. I put it up as a reminder."

They laughed and Ownie touched an empty ceiling hook, all that remained of the heavy bag he punched until Hildred made him remove it, claiming the vibrations cracked the upstairs plaster. What a goddamn shame, he thought, taking down that bag. Ownie believed in collective powers, that the stronger he was, the stronger his fighter became. When he had trained Tommy, he ran ten miles a day in army boots, he went eight rounds on the heavy bag, and then, because he could, he lifted Tommy into the air when the little fighter won.

Johnny crossed the basement, drawn by more photos. There was Ownie with Yvon Durelle, Ownie meeting Ali, Ownie hugging a dark-haired fighter with a cartilage-free nose and a lantern jaw. "My brother Butch, wanted to be a big ten-round fighter." Johnny looked at the youth, cut-up and swollen in an Eliot Ness overcoat. "He wore the double-breasted serge suit and Bulova watch and never gave me a cent for working the corner. I had to live through that."

Johnny chuckled and leaned toward Butch, who looked like he had golf balls growing under his skin.

"So, how's the roadwork?" They had moved into the rec room.

"Ah. . . ." Johnny paused. "Good, good."

Understanding that Johnny's fight days were probably numbered, Ownie relaxed and pulled out his *Ring Record Book*, eight hundred pages of life stories compressed into half-page columns. Joy, triumph, death, and destruction sanitized and condensed into the colourless *Win/Loss/Draw*.

Ownie marked a page in his book, which was dog-eared with pencil marks next to unknowns from Brooklyn or Kalamazoo who may, or may not, have made worthy opponents. Picking a match was like ordering a suit from the Sears catalogue; they might, if you were lucky, send something that corresponded with the description.

"It's just that this guy is very intense," Johnny blurted. "I mean, we're barely moving and he's talking junk miles, oxidative damages, high-glycemic foods." Johnny's protest drifted across the rec room. "He's serious about what he's doing," said Ownie.

Ownie still had time for Johnny because he liked him, but they both knew that Turmoil was on a different track; they both knew that people, years later, might talk about Turmoil with jealousy or awe but always with the understanding that "He meant something." They knew that.

"See," Johnny plunged in, "he's got this time he's got to beat. So he never forgets it, he's got it as his bank code, taped to the ceiling over his bed, and written on his watch strap."

"By race time, he'll come apart like a cheap pair of polyester pants, splitting at the seams."

Johnny laughed, relieved. Ownie opened his book and copied down numbers. In the front were the World Ratings, the ultimate honour roll, a sign that you had left the masses and moved to a greater place, an elite world inhabited by giants, freaks, and legends. Over the years, Ownie had three fighters in the Top Ten. The Kid was number two in 1948, when there was one world champ per division and eight weight classes, when being heavyweight king was like being president of the United States, a guarantee that your name would stand forever.

Arguello settled at Ownie's feet, which made him think about the dog's Nicaraguan namesake, who was making a comeback at forty-two despite a heart condition. The little dog jumped, startled by a thunderous laugh that bounced off the low basement ceiling and rounded the corner into the rec room. Arching her back, Arguello whimpered.

Turmoil was in the doorway, arms akimbo, shaking his head, with Louie behind him. Why, Ownie wondered, protective of the dog, does he have to be so loud?

"What's so funny?" Ownie demanded.

"She wahn to put me on contrack."

"Who?" asked Ownie.

"Lorraine. We talkin 'bout gettin marrieeed and she say ah have to sign some contrack. Ah tole her ah already hab one."

"That's a prenuptial agreement," Ownie said.

"Ah ain' signin no contrack with nobody."

"Well," Ownie shrugged. "That will be the end of you."

Turmoil threw back his head and laughed loud enough to frighten Arguello. He laughed and laughed when nothing was funny. Ownie frowned, thinking about the bridge and the evil spirits. He knew what happened to people who'd been diagnosed and branded. Back in the bad old days, families could sign you into the nuthouse, where they'd dope you up, then run currents through your head like they did to poor Cec DeWolfe when his wife took up with a taxi driver and wanted him gone. "I'm afraid he'll turn violent," she told the authorities. "He's taken too many punches. I just can't trust him." That's all it took, and Cec was a ghost.

Louie started up the VCR, loading the tape that Ownie had ordered from a guy in England, who charged him a hundred bucks. "This is our key, boys, our decoding device."

When Ownie and Tommy had prepared for a fight, there was no need for strategy, no need for tapes. Ownie could turn Tommy loose and he would fight his own fight; he was all guts and heart. It was different with Turmoil. In a fight between two men of his size and power, you couldn't take chances; you couldn't let it just play out.

"What she want me to sign a contrack for?" Turmoil asked.

"So you won't get her money," Louie explained.

"Ahm goin to be so rich, ah wohn need nobody's money."

"Shut up, will ya." Ownie squinted as two fighters left their

222

corners on the TV screen and circled like tomcats. "You've got to get through this fight first."

Ownie was taking notes from the TV, focusing on one of the fighters. Ownie had heard that Calvin Mackey, the man who would stop or start Turmoil's career, had been a gang-banger, a mean bastard with hate for a heart. Love and hate complicated everything, Ownie figured, even in the fight game. The people loved Joe Louis so much they never forgave poor Ezzard Charles for beating the Brown Bomber. What was Charles supposed to do: lie down and die? He'd already killed Sammy Baroudi in the ring, and he had to live with that. Ezzard Charles was an unlucky man, born at the wrong time, sharing the ring with Louis, damned to die bitter.

"I heard Barry McGuigan wants to start a union so fighters won't end up broke," Louie said.

"Ah wohn have no trubble like that," Turmoil announced. "Ahll get me a smaht lawyer and make investments with real estate and race horses."

Edgy, Ownie was trying to concentrate, seeking knowledge he just had to have. Watch the tempo, he reminded himself. Every fighter has his own rhythm, and you have to get inside that. If you break it, some fighters get messed up. *Everyone* has a weakness: some fighters can't handle tall guys, some have trouble with southpaws, some can't deal with awkward-ness. You just have to figure it out. One. Two. One. Two. Like dancing.

"Now watch here." He pointed at the tape. "Watch what Mackey's doing! *That's* his flaw, right there."

37

Ownie couldn't remember the man's name, just the eyes, cobalt blue with the longest, curliest lashes he had ever seen. It was as though someone had stuck the fringed eyes on the mashed face as a practical joke, then forgotten to take them off.

"What you up to these days?" Ownie asked the visitor.

The eyes, Ownie remembered, always looked uneasy, as though they knew that people were struck by the incongruity. On the wrong day, a day of low horizons and drought-stunted dreams, it could make a man anxious enough to pop someone. *Boom!*

"Cooking," the visitor replied, twisting a MedicAlert bracelet as though he was cracking open a jar of gravy. "I'm in the kitchen at Lucky Lou's. Right?"

"Uh-huh." Bambi, that's what they called him, Ownie recalled. Once, Archie Diggs, who was a bad bugger, started a rumour that Bambi wore false eyelashes, that he'd seen him buying them in a beauty salon on Gottingen Street. "What were you doin' in a beauty salon?" someone asked, poking holes in Archie's report.

"I was in to talk bidness with the manager," Archie said, his voice rising with each exorbitant detail. "My wife wasn't satisfied with the quality of the previous work, which burnt her head up like a marshmallow. Them beauty salons are like transmission shops; they'll double-shuffle you silly if don't have no man behind ya. You know that, doncha?"

Bambi and a guy named Dooley had a running act for a bit. They fought each other on seven undercards, the high points being two knockdowns and a TKO. They were best buddies outside of the ring, mortal enemies inside, according to the storyline, so it made for good press.

"My specialty is egg rolls, because I have a fine touch." Bambi gently folded an imaginary roll, and when he looked up, the cobalt eyes reminded Ownie of a cheap bottle of aftershave. "I'm very precise."

"Well, you're good with your hands." Ownie nodded like it made sense.

"We had a screwball working with us for a while. He said he was an ex-army tough guy and a trained assassin, soldier of fortune. He was always leaning on the helpers when it was busy, threatening to take them out if they got in his way, especially the slow learners. He kept it up until I had to ice him. One shot. *Boom!*"

"The world's full of crazy bastards, ain't it?"

"Tell me about it. I hear Dooley's taking a fight up in Moncton." Bambi sounded anxious at the thought of Dooley, half of his ring identity, entering a bout without him.

"Ahhh," groaned Ownie, who had last seen Dooley with the midway, running the machine-gun marksman sideshow. "Wave a few bucks in front of those guys and they'll fight from a wheelchair. Dooley had his chance when he fought Turcot in Montreal, and he didn't do nothin'."

Ownie paused as Tootsy's door opened for a middle-aged woman with a halo of hair.

"Didya hear what happened when we fought down in Sydney?" Bambi's tone lightened. "When Tan Tanner was promotin' the card?"

The woman was struggling, Ownie noticed, with a carpet bag and a tape recorder that seemed to be alive. Nothing involving Tanner would surprise him.

"Well, they didn't get much of a draw. Right?" Bambi continued.

"No fault of yours," Ownie allowed.

"No way, man. We could bring 'em in, me and Dooley, not like that Archie Dibbs, he couldn't draw peanuts. His mother wouldn't pay to see him. Afterwards, Tanner gives all the fighters their pay envelopes. Right? He says, 'Don't look until you get it home.' Me and Dooley figure there's a little extra for us and he didn't want the other guys to know. Right?"

"Right on."

"I got home and mine's half-empty. I called Dooley, and his was too."

Ownie watched the woman wander across the gym, her flowered dress skimming the floor like a stage curtain. "Tan Tanner is nothin' but a small-time thief. He'd steal your long underwear, you still in them."

She was probably that woman who'd phoned him, Ownie figured as Bambi left, a freelance writer doing a piece for a magazine. She had given him her name and the name of the magazine, but he had forgotten them both. "How come you can name every fighter Joe Louis fought in twenty-five title defenses but can't get your son-in-law's name straight?" Hildred once scolded him. "I'll tell you why: you don't try."

The woman was chatting with the old-timer named Barney, who stopped in from time to time in his Legion blazer and medals. Barney, a compulsive liar, always looked polished enough to appear at a veteran's appeal board. Sometimes he left without saying a word, other times he would talk your ear off.

That's her, Ownie decided, when he heard her British accent. Scott said that she was married to a surgeon, so she didn't need the money, just something to do. The woman strolled the gym, her mike raised like a Geiger counter, sticking it near the ring, where Turmoil was sparring with a lanky man with a Zorro moustache. "Keep the hand up," Zorro ordered Turmoil. "Double it up, throw combinations side to side, watch what you're doing, and work like a champ."

The man was wirier than Turmoil but three inches shorter; he looked like a pro baseball player with a trickster smile. "Billy Dee Williams," said Johnny. Louie, who was tired of the game, blinked *maybe*. They were sitting by the window, taking in the show.

Ownie made the introduction. "This is Fred Green. We brought him in from Chicago."

Leaning forward, the woman peered at the sparring partner as if she were studying an abstract painting, a non-objective canvas of colour and composition, an enigmatic blur. "I'm Constance Stanhope. I'm doing a magazine piece."

"Pleased to meet you." The trickster extended a gracious glove.

"This man is crucial to what we're trying to do," declared Ownie like a pitchman. "He's worth his weight in gold."

"Ah," said Constance, stepping into a shaft of light, where, exposed, her pale skin seemed to redden, then melt like a plastic spoon.

"This man is ring-wise, experienced. He knows how to get the best out of Turmoil. He's tough and comes back at you, and he's exactly what we need."

"I consider myself a professional sparring partner," said Fred, taking his cue. He pulled off his helmet, showing a receding hairline. "I've been doing it since I spent seven weeks with Tyson to get him ready for his fight against Michael Spinks. Working with Tyson should have made my career, but there was a newspaper strike on at the time."

"Uh-huh."

"Now I'm hoping to hook up with Lewis or Bowe." He paused and pointed at Constance's recorder. "I don't think it's working."

Gold bangles clanked as she fiddled with the dials. "What is Turmoil learning from you?" she asked, making a quick recovery.

"I like to change my style as I go along." Fred shifted his shoulders, slipping undetectable punches. "Sometimes I'll stalk him like Joe Frazier, while at other times I'll use my speed, like Spinks. I like to think that while working with me he'll learn all the different types of opponents he'll face in the ring."

Constance snorted. "How does he look to you at this stage?"

"I've been boxing fifteen years — I got a quadruple left hook — and he has no difficulty staying with me. It's amazing what he's accomplished this soon."

"Sparring is essential," Ownie explained to Constance. "Getting a guy ready for a ten rounder, I start with four rounds, then work it up to six. Finally, two weeks before a fight, I put the sparring up to ten every second day to see how he carries ten."

"Can Turmoil stay here and be a success?" Constance read from her notebook, her skin back to its raw, freckled state.

"Certainly," said Ownie.

"What is the hardest thing to teach a fighter?"

"You have to be a psychiatrist; you have to get inside their heads, to make them really believe they have a chance. You never want your fighter to think the other guy is better, because with that thought, no matter how much you train him, ten to one he will lose."

After Ownie excused himself, Barney approached Constance, humming a distant song that may have been the "Siegfried Line." Constance muttered almost to herself: "He's a very well-built man, isn't he?" She pointed across the room at Turmoil who was practising a jab on his sparring partner.

"Very true, madam," agreed Barney. Constance, Barney noticed, had a horizontal line across her nose from years of pushing up the end, the result of nervousness or allergies. "Kind of like a young Ali, don't you think?"

"Ah, yes." Two quick snorts showed that Constance liked the comparison.

"Very perceptive of you to see the parallels."

"Why thank you," she said demurely.

Barney took a liver-spotted hand and rubbed his face back and forth as if to clear his thoughts, and then he took the hand, the same one that had fired a Browning .303, and placed it solemnly on Constance's arm. "Not everyone would pick that up."

"I'm shrewd with faces," she replied quickly. "It's my arts background; I studied photography with Sherman Hines *and* I paint watercolours."

After flattering Constance, who was desperate to prove her worth as a boxing reporter and a student of humanity, Barney swallowed hard, his Adam's apple bobbing in the folds of his loose turkey neck. He had a thin, wooden mouth and the hinged jaw of a ventriloquist's dummy. "Did you ever see Ali fight?"

"Ah no," she allowed, afraid to admit too much.

"You're probably too young."

Constance blushed, convinced that her look was working: bohemian, but not too bold, a touch of earth mother and earnest truth-seeker along the lines of Joyce Carol Oates.

"I did. And every time I watch this man it sends shivers down my spine."

Constance stared at Barney's medals, trying to read the inscription with her near-sighted eyes. Then she looked up, seeking clarity. "Oh?"

Barney pointed at Turmoil, as the fighter moved across the

ring, focused on Fred. "The genetic fingerprints are as clear as day. Now, they fight differently, granted, but that's because Ali was probably the fastest heavyweight ever."

"I'm sorry," Constance apologized. "I know I seem knowledgeable, but I usually don't cover boxing. As I mentioned, I have an arts background."

"Well, you are obviously a versatile woman."

"Thank you." Turmoil and Fred were talking to Ownie, the trickster's eyes intent but unreadable, like a pitcher taking signals from the plate: thumb in for screwball, four fingers for a curve.

"Perhaps I was being a bit obtuse," Barney apologized, "discretion being the better part of valour. There has always been speculation that Ali had a missing son."

"Really?"

"Now, I'm not saying . . . I would never be so bold or presumptuous — but I'm going to let that thought sit with you." Constance's head flicked with two rapid snorts and Barney, giving her a quick appraisal, muttered, "no spring chicken," before realizing he had spoken out loud.

"Pardon me?" she begged.

"Nothing, nothing," he assured her as images of Ali raced through her brain like a National Film Board documentary. Muhammad Ali was an icon, a legend who crossed all boundaries: sports, entertainment, religion, and politics, as handsome as a movie star, as controversial as Castro. The Rumble in the Jungle, the Thrilla in Manila. Float like a butterfly, sting like a bee. Hadn't the Beatles even made a special stop to pose with the Greatest?

"What do you think?" Barney asked.

"Perhaps," Constance allowed.

"It has bothered me since the first time I met Turmoil, and then, when I found out that they had the same birthday,

January 17, it struck me as prophetic." Constance gulped. "Of course, Turmoil is bigger, which is not unusual for offspring. At the same age, Ali was only six-foot-two, one-eighty-five, with a thirty-two-inch waist and a forty-six-inch chest, and he compared himself — rightly so, in my opinion — to a Greek god. He was still Clay then, Cassius Marcellus Clay, and he wore three coats of white polish on his boots and Vaseline on his arms to accentuate his muscles."

"He *was* a handsome man, but I thought Turmoil was from Trinidad."

"Excellent point."

Constance smiled as Turmoil and Fred picked up their gear.

"But Ali travelled the globe," Barney continued. "The most recognizable man on Earth, if you recall. They did a poll and I wish I could remember who came second. Maybe, Joseph Stalin, the pock-faced executioner and brilliant military strategist. I just can't remember, which is the problem with getting old."

"Has anyone talked to Mr. Ali?"

"No, this is pure conjecture. I don't think it would be right to approach him on something like this, not without adequate promulgation."

"What about Turmoil's mother?"

"I understand she's a private lady, very devout. She sings in the church choir, in a beautiful, clear soprano voice that can give you goosebumps. I'm sure you can empathize, a refined lady like yourself."

"Yes, yes, I see."

38

With the news conference about to start, the TV producer affected a jaded air of world-weariness. He wore a watch with six time zones and he was dropping place names like bread-crumbs in the forest. "When I was in Rwanda/Haiti/Davis Inlet . . ."

His cameraman, Carl, had a cellphone stuck in his Domke vest and all of his electronic toys spread out for the others to see. Reluctantly, Carl had left his flak jacket in the truck. It was a BCJ with neck collar and groin protector, six pounds of defence against mortar, grenade fragments, and handgun fire up to a .44 Magnum.

"Did we see him in L.A.?" The producer nodded at Smithers, wearing a Habs jersey.

Carl squinted through loonie-shaped glasses, took a geographical fix, and mouthed the word "Looocal." He made it sound like a disease.

The brewery hall was filling with locals, network jocks, and two chirpy Brits named Lionel and Desmond who'd spent the night in a strip club. Supported by an updraft of gossip and gripes, the media was hovering over sandwiches. A thick man with fire engine red pants sidled up to the producer, the top three buttons of his shirt undone, showing a nest of gold. His mouth hung open like the lower hinge wasn't working.

"What are you guys doing here?" Vance, who wrote a column for a complimentary TV guide, was known as the

Scrumbuster for his uncanny ability to derail a scrum with off-track questions.

"National wants something." The words floated from Carl's mouth like a yawn. "National" was a codeword that set them apart, that gave them status, money, and access. The producer pulled away from Vance like a leech touched with salt, knowing there was a danger here. If you got too close, you might turn into one of Them; you could get lost in a grove of inconsequence and never escape. The producer pulled a sterling silver Tiffany's yo-yo from his pocket, and turned his back on Vance, who was conveniently light-footed in bowling shoes.

"I thought you had an in here," Smithers said petulantly to Scott.

MacKenzie had ordered a two-page spread on the fight, which had generated so much attention that even Boomer, the publisher, had asked for tickets. Smithers had been assigned to help Scott fill the pages.

"I do," said Scott, pissed by the hockey reporter's presence.

"Well, how come there's no beer?" Smithers griped. "This is a brewery."

"Shhh!" Scott nodded toward a weasly man with a bowl haircut, flotsam from a wave of Brits that had crashed ashore in the 1950s, flooding newsrooms. Linden Jones lived below the poverty line selling stories to trade magazines and rags. "STAG ENDS TRAGICALLY WHEN CAR DRIVES INTO LAKE AND GROOM DROWNS WITH BALL AND CHAIN AROUND HIS ANKLE." Deep Throat for a local gossip sheet, he regularly infiltrated news conferences and reported journalistic lapses and overheard conversations.

"Yeah, well he can go fuck himself," Smithers announced, then louder: "Fuck himself!" He stared at Linden, who smoked cheroots and wore ladies 10D pumps on weekends. "And I don't like being watched by some asshole who thinks he's one of Herman's Hermits."

Used to abuse, Linden pretended he didn't hear.

"Whadda they let people like that in for?" Smithers demanded.

"Him?" Scott looked at Linden, sultry in grey eyeshadow.

"Nah," Smithers scoffed. "I can't even look at him. He gives me the creeps, like one of those half-human dancers in *Cats*." He shuddered. "No, her," he said, pointing at Constance, who was wearing leather boots under a flowing cabbage-covered dress. "All that Ali bullshit."

Last week, Scott had seen Constance leaving her South End house, a country cottage with a lattice gazebo and a plaster dog she decorated each season, co-coordinating his bow with the other garnishes. He had heard that she was having an affair with a burnt-out radio producer, an alcoholic who had applauded her analysis of boxing's rebirth ("It's a bit like disco or bowling, platform shoes or Betty Crocker, so out that it's in"). Scott shrugged. "She's harmless."

The news conference had started, the two fighters and their trainers seated at a table in the front of the room.

"He's a much improved fighter." Ownie fielded an early question. "Now he has something besides raw power; he's dropped the wild swings and awkward footwork and added grace and smoothness."

"Uh-huh." A radio reporter nodded.

"I'm not gonna try to fool ya." Ownie squinted from the TV lights and the effort of sounding sincere. "He's still a hitter: Bob Fitzsimmons, Jack Dempsey, Max Baer, Rocky Marciano, with TNT in either fist."

"Do you agree, Turmoil?" Radio man had a Sony slung across his chest like an old newsboy, one finger on the rewind button.

"Yes, mon." Turmoil leaned in to the host mike, which drooped under a dozen heads: metal joy sticks strapped on with black tape. "Ahve learned how to box bettah and get away from punches, where before ahd take one to give one."

Turmoil looked chic, Ownie concluded, in a beige, stretch-knit polo shirt with a dark collar and waistband, a clean, retro look that showed he was the good guy: Pat Boone meets Sugar Ray Robinson. Charcoal dress pants. The clothes worked with his short hair and churchgoing face; it showed his bowling ball biceps without getting ugly. Turmoil was handling himself well, Ownie allowed, glancing sideways at the fighter. He seemed okay.

Ownie had never met anyone, he told himself, who had been helped by a shrink. It was like pouring water on a grease fire. He worked with a guy once named Woof. Woof was all right, a bit gregarious, mind you, but fine, until he saw that shrink. "You have a rare psychiatric disorder," the shrink informed Woof. "It makes you believe that everyone loves you. You misinterpret innocent gestures as overt signs of friendship; you form unnatural bonds with people you barely know. You are living in a delusional state." That ruined Woof, whose delusions had made him the happiest man Ownie knew, giddy from the lust of unsuspecting waitresses and the promise of imminent promotions. How could you have a bad day if you thought that everyone loved you?

"What about you, Calvin, what are your strengths?" asked Smithers.

Calvin Mackey was slumped in his chair, legs spread, widening the gulf between him and the world with wraparounds and a grisly shirt that made strangers stare and then step back in shock. On his chest was a photo of an open grave of black bodies in cotton clothing, nameless victims stacked high as his grievances against the world, cut down by a death squad or a plague. Mackey's head was covered by a skullcap.

"Are you in shape?"

Ownie wondered who had dreamed up Mackey's macabre shirt. Bundini Brown got recognition for taking the bear trap to the Liston weigh-in, but Ownie didn't give that much credit to Mackey's trainer, who seemed wishy-washy, a charcoal drawing that hadn't been fixed.

"You wahn to try me out?"

The room laughed as Smithers flushed.

In the back, Ownie could see two politicians — one was a senior cabinet minister — with their laundry fetchers. One of the fetchers had the same desperate look as the shakos from his childhood in Charlottetown, the guys who drank their four-bottle ration book in two days. Years ago, when they had a gym on Hollis Street, that guy had showed up unannounced and said he needed models "for an art group that meets each Thursday." Archie Dibbs signed up — he was game for anything — and came back laughing. "I almost caught pneumonia, sitting there bare-assed."

The fetcher was trying to distance himself from the Running Joke, who was making small talk while collecting free sandwiches.

The questions drifted until a kid from a weekly paper piped up, a journalism school grad with his own business cards and dreams of a foreign posting. ("I am ready to move at a moment's notice," he promised in a letter to potential employers. "I have a passport, international contacts. My favourite authors are Tim Page and John Kennedy Toole.")

"What about the suggestion that Turmoil may be the son of Muhammad Ali?" The kid stuck out a hand-held recorder. "Is this some cheap publicity stunt?"

As Mackey sniffed in amusement, Constance frantically set her counter at 000. Resting his Evian on the floor, the producer gave Carl the nod to record.

"Turmoil would rather not discuss it," Ownie sighed. "It's too personal."

The kid wanted to be tough, distanced from the faux journalists he had studied with, the timid mice who respected people's space. For four years he had suffered at journalism school, one of only three males in a class of prudes who wrote tortured diary entries and sneered at his lust for the mainstream gig.

"But someone said —"

"Yes, but I think out of respect to Turmoil, we should let it drop."

"You can't just let it drop! I mean, if it's a publicity stunt." The kid was praying that someone from a real paper, someone who offered benefits and full-time employment, someone impressed by his tenacity and his willingness to expose these frauds, might see him and say, "Right on."

"You might be right. I'm just saying it's not important to *this* fight."

"Let's ask Turmoil." The kid shook from his own boldness. "What do you think?"

Here we go, Ownie moaned, wondering how Turmoil was going to respond. Why did I let that woman with the freckly skin into the gym where Barney could feed her bullshit? Ownie asked himself. The same woman who turned around and spent two nights with Fred — professional sparring partner and ladies man — when she already had a husband and an alcoholic boyfriend. Why did I do it?

"Ah dohn know, mon. Ah know ah feel something special when ah watch movies of him fight. Ah feel som'tin comin out in me, som'tin ver-ver powerful."

The kid stopped trembling, and Carl the cameraman clicked.

Tale of the Tape		
Davies		Mackey
23	Age	26
240 lbs	Weight	225 lbs
6 ft. 5 in.	Height	6 ft. 2 in.
83"	Reach	76"
47"	Chest normal	41"
50"	Chest expanded	44"
18"	Biceps	16"
15 ¼"	Forearm	13"
35 ½"	Waist	34"
28"	Thigh	24"
19"	Calf	15"
12"	Ankle	10 ¼"
19"	Neck	17"
10"	Wrist	8"
13 ½"	Fist	12 ¼"

It was just him and Turmoil in the dressing room, an acrid dungeon, a windowless cell filled with sweat, promise, and the sting of liniment. "Now look at me closely," Ownie ordered. "Look in my eyes."

Fiddle music filtered through the ceiling as the crowd left their seats and started to roam the arena like a pack of wild dogs, sniffing the hallways for beer, pretzels, and a place to piss. Some fiddler was playing, Ownie noticed, a dervish who'd cut a record in New York.

"Now I'm going to put you under," Ownie warned as Turmoil filled his chest with air. Ownie tightened the fighter's metallic silver robe. "You don't want to get a chill when you're under. Your body temperature could drop."

Turmoil shivered. Up above, the music mounted. Ownie knew that the dogs were getting restless, scrapping, snapping, hungry for the main event, a bloodthirsty pack waiting for a body. They'd get their fill soon enough, he realized. They always did.

"Are you ready?" Ownie dropped his voice so that he sounded like a movie doctor he had seen on TV. "Ten . . . nine . . . eight . . . seven . . . six. . . ." He snapped his fingers. Turmoil tilted his head back like he was getting a shampoo. Then the door opened.

"Not now." Ownie waved off Tootsy, holding a towel. Then he continued in his low voice. "You will control the fight. You *will* overpower him and beat him."

Last year, in another fight that Ownie had studied, Mackey had opened the artery of a big Mick, who had bled like a stuck pig. Ownie wasn't worried; most of those white guys were walking blood banks. Like Henry Cooper. He was so ridiculous that Ali said he could *hear* him bleeding.

"You've got it all: a left hook like Al Davis or Joe Frazier, the right cross of Tommy Hearns, the uppercut of Marvin Johnson. You've got the style of Leonard and the killer instinct of Chavez. You're as big as Primo Carnera, but you got more moves. Okay." He snapped the trance-inducing fingers. "Come out of it."

Turmoil opened his eyes as though he had just enjoyed a catnap. He yawned and stretched his arms, touching the bare cement behind his head.

"Just remember the strategy. Remember what we worked on."

The wild man had stopped playing his fiddle and Ownie could hear the crowd returning to their seats, the slow, clumping shuffle that signalled it was time. Ownie made the sign of the cross and asked for the blessing of God.

"Let's go."

Ownie shoved Tootsy down the arena aisle, blinded by a psychedelic spotlight, deafened by the roar. "Move up!" he shouted at the second as Turmoil jabbed his way past the swills in the cheap seats. "Up Up Up!" Unattached arms groped the air like ghouls from a grave, touching Turmoil's robe and trying to feed off his power. A bowtied usher shoved them back through the dry-ice mist.

Waaah! Waaah! A bagpiper was piping them toward the ring, clutching his plaid sack, his cheeks distended like a blowfish. The crowd tried to clap in rhythm, and his skunk sporran shook.

"Th-th-th-is o-k-k-k-ay?" Tootsy moved forward, clutching his stopwatch as a man with a video camera teetered on a seat yelling, "Turmoil, Turmoil. Over here! Smile."

Ownie blinked like a hostage first seeing daylight. For this, the big event, he had added a cutman, a dude who called himself Doctor, wore white, and kept a stash of mysterious ingredients in a terry wristband. Doctor stepped over a pile of plastic beer cups. Turmoil's greased face glistened as they moved by ringside, past a woman with a miniature poodle in her lap. Someone shoved a Nova Scotia flag in Tootsy's hands, and he took it without thinking. SAVE THE GAELS! A sign waved. A boy covered his ears.

Mackey's people had already passed, a funeral procession of black armbands and attitude. Ownie rubbed Turmoil's neck as their parade stopped, marchers bumping against one another. A cameraman walking backwards had stumbled on a cord, setting off a chain reaction. An usher moved in as a woman in stonewashed jeans and a shag tried to give Turmoil a rose. When pushed back, she started to cry.

"Okay, okay." They were moving again. Turmoil broke into a trot, nodding at a fan. "Now, man." Ownie pushed Tootsy, who was still holding the flag. He wanted the little second in position, his body just in front of Turmoil, when they mounted the red steps, near the ring girls dressed like step dancers, under an inflatable beer car the size of a car. A guy as short as Tootsy would make Turmoil look ten foot tall. The image might startle Mackey for just long enough to plant the seeds of fear.

The time clock flashed:

MAIN EVENT

HALIFAX EXPLOSION. TAKE TWO.

"From the city that brought you the *Mont Blanc* and the *Imo*, now Turmoil Davies and Calvin Mackey," an announcer roared. "Hold on to your seats and prepare for a towering tidal wave of action."

For a while, until they were banished, the ring was full of TV cameras, microphones, cords, and cellphones, people with notebooks, laminated IDs, and no real reason to be there. The skirl was gone now, displaced by expectancy.

Through the blue haze, Ownie could see Hildred and his son, Pat. His daughter, Millie, wasn't there because she couldn't bear to go to the fights; they always upset her. Lorraine, Turmoil's girlfriend, was sitting next to them, and some guys from the boxing commission. The laundry fetcher was in the good seats, tending to the cabinet minister, whose face looked, on this night, as grey as his hair. Beyond that, everything, including the press box where Scott sat, was a blur.

Ownie did not know that in addition to the regular fight crowd, there were hipsters being camp: filmmakers, artists, and a throat poet. There were colleagues of Lorraine's, friends of the Mi'kmaq professor, and a small group of hairstylists who had come with Malcolm, the effusive makeup artist, who was too nervous to open his eyes.

"Hey, Flanagan, don't go near no microwaves." The heckler zeroed in on Ownie's T-shirt, metallic grey with TURMOIL TIME printed over a tornado.

Ownie blocked the noise and told himself: Never listen to the peanut gallery, never lose your focus. Remember what happened to Butch in New Waterford when a brawl broke out in the audience, with chairs flying through the air and heads cracking? Butch turned to see what was going down, and *boom!* he was it.

Mackey spat jabs at the TV lens. He had a flag draped over his shoulders and a black bandana on his head. Tyson did the black duds best, Ownie thought, with no robe or socks, just boots, black trunks, and chill.

Mackey removed the bandana, showing a quarter-inch gully in his hair. His entire corner, even the wishy-washy trainer, was wearing those T-shirts, the ones with the stacked-up bodies. He's got that look all right, Ownie thought, like he wants to hurt someone, like he wants to work from hate, to get another marker on that tally sheet he calls a heart. Oh, baby. You're a bad one.

"C'mon, girls, whaddya waiting for?"

After two rounds, the crowd was impatient. They didn't know nothin' about timing, Ownie cursed, or strategy, or feeling your opponent out; they didn't know that one shot could turn your ears into doorbells, your piss red for weeks.

"I seen better fights at bingo."

They were the same birds you met in slopshops, he decided, the yahoos who said, "Let's see how tough you are," then cried assault the moment they found out. Ownie sponged Turmoil clean, one eye was puffed as though he had been crying. When two men this big entered a ring, they were bullet trains heading into a tunnel, the impact imminent, along with the wreckage and the fury that guaranteed that nothing would ever be the same.

"Okay, he's fast, just like we expected, slick, a bobber and a weaver." Pulling Turmoil's trunks, Ownie kneaded air into his stomach while the Doctor stood by ready. Ownie squinted through the blue haze like a man looking for a seat in a steam bath as Pat held up fingers, round-by-round scores from the overhead TV screen.

"You've got to take his speed away." Turmoil nodded and sucked in air. "You've got to slow him down."

"You did some damage," said Ownie, arming Turmoil for round eight. "But it's not enough. You've got to want it more." Turmoil was standing, refusing the stool. "It's up to you now." Ownie stretched to rub Turmoil's neck and his winglike shoulders. "You're the Man, you're the One."

Ownie knew Turmoil had muscled Mackey around, slammed him with hooks and uppercuts. He could feel the shift in Mackey's corner. The talk was faster, the messages more shrill, running from the doubt that was creeping in, as insidious and unstoppable as the tide. This was the time to dig, to focus, to summon everything into one eruption of lavalike will.

"Listen to me," Ownie pleaded, a hostage with a gun to his head. It didn't matter what lies he told, because this was life and death, with no one willing to take his place. "This guy's stealin' your dreams from you, man."

Turmoil muttered something.

"He's stealing that big car and that pretty painting by LeRoy Newman." Turmoil flinched as though he had touched a live wire. "They should belong to you, man. You earned it, you are the one with the movie-star face, not that ugly bastard, but it's gonna be him drivin' that car, his Jesus *ugly* face in that Newman painting, not yours."

Another mutter.

"What?"

"Nei-man."

"Yeah, that's right."

As he touched Turmoil's back, Ownie felt the fighter push off like a shot putter, power surging from the soles of his feet straight through to his upper body as it straightened. "Now go out there. Remember the plan."

Mackey unloaded a right uppercut from outside.

BOOM! The counter right.

Sweat shot off Mackey's head like exclamation marks.

Ownie leaned forward, moving his shoulders with the punches, willing them through, straining so hard he almost lifted off. That was it! Just like the tape.

When Mackey threw the right uppercut from outside, he left himself open for the counter right. The uppercut is supposed to come from inside, Ownie told himself, you put your whole body into it. Sugar Ray had such good balance that he threw double uppercuts: right left, right left, with his feet perfect.

"Over here! Over here!" The crowd was shouting so loudly, so hysterically, that Ownie turned. Sweet Jesus, Ownie cursed, not now, not when we've got something going! Ownie needed all of his concentration, he needed to be Uri Geller, bending the outcome of the fight with his mind, twisting the odds like a spoon, driving home punches.

Jesus! He couldn't help but see two paramedics rushing to the good seats, clambering over legs and beer cups, clutching a medical case. Ownie strained to see what was happening, hoping, for Turmoil's sake, that it wasn't a rumble. No, it was the fancy suit, the cabinet minister with his laundry fetcher. Even clutching his chest, in the throes of a heart attack or a seizure, the man had the polished face of money. His mouth was open, showing fine gold work that raised him above the dentured masses.

"Get in there, you muthafucka!" Mackey's corner was hurling bags of trash that scattered in the air. Another right uppercut from Mackey. "You no good . . ."

Another counter right.

Yesss! Turmoil nodded, his plays in place.

"Is it him?" A murmur spread through the crowd like the Wave as the paramedics hovered over the fallen politician, lifting his hand for a pulse and then removing his glasses. "Is he dead?" The crowd demanded, and then in the direction of the stricken man: "How do you like your health system now?"

The panicky fetcher, the same man who had given Archie Dibbs fifty bucks for posing naked, tapped the ring doctor's shoulder.

"No, no, I can't leave now." The doctor pointed at the fight.

"Go, Turmoil!" A hard right sent the Brit down to one knee. "Yeaaah." The hyenas laughed their demented laugh. Nocturnal scavengers waiting to feast on a random kill, oversized wolves with Freddy Krueger claws.

Mackey scampered up. Don't worry, he's hurt more than he's letting on, Ownie reassured himself, just look at his feet, they're slower, he's souped up and he knows it.

"Down in front!" the mob bellowed at the fetcher. "Get out of the fucking way!"

The cabinet minister had been loaded onto a stretcher, a mask on his motionless, ashen face. One manicured hand trailed on the ground, through dust and cigarette butts.

"They gave my father a pacemaker and sent him home thirty minutes later." A hyena standing nearby pointed at the stretcher. "He died the next day, you bastard."

"I paid sixty bucks for this seat."

"Get the fuck out of here!"

Mackey unloaded a right uppercut from outside.

BOOM! The counter right.

Turmoil rushed forward, throwing rights and lefts. Open it up, open it up, Ownie urged. Take whatever strength I have left, drain it from my body, through my eyes, my heart, just take it. Turmoil shoved Mackey to the ropes where he could go to work: upstairs, downstairs, on an open target with no leverage.

A photographer, the same kid who had won a prize for the shot of Louie unconscious, chased the paramedics up the aisle just as Turmoil landed a series of rib-crushing hooks, numbing blows that short-circuited Mackey's brain. *Boom. Boom.* Mackey tried to save himself with a pawing right and a jab that had gone soft as a spring breeze, but down he went.

He's not through, Ownie thought, and Mackey staggered up. Turmoil greeted him with a body hook, then a right that snapped Mackey's head.

"Now! Now! Now!" Ownie shouted.

The photographer was tearing back, holding his flapping cameras to his body, cursing the fallen minister for forcing him out of position. *"Now!"* Turmoil dug the body. Slowly, like a kite that had lost the draft, Mackey collapsed and sank, deflated. This time, he's done, Ownie thought, he's done. Mackey tried to get up, but one leg gave way. He tried again, but it buckled. He lay on the canvas, his eyes clouded by a sorrowful mix of hate and disbelief, as a tattooed dragon stared blindly from his chest to the ceiling.

HALIFAX EXPLOSION. TAKE TWO.

The sign had frozen, and debris rained from above like airborne anchors and shattered hulls.

"When ah saw him stagger, ah knew he was mine," Turmoil's voice cracked over the bedlam. "Ah was going to go all out until he drop or ah drop."

Reporters, shooters, and frenzied fans swarmed the ring, adrenalin junkies on a hallucinogenic rush, jumping, jostling, surging closer to the source, arms, cords, and misplaced dreams convulsing on the canvas. Ownie was hanging from Turmoil's neck, two miles from Earth. "Turmoil, Turmoil, Turmoil." The name was a drumbeat. A maladroit cameraman smashed his elbow in a woman's face as Turmoil raised the ornate belt high, as though it was the head of a vanquished warrior.

"That was the plan, to start slow and then go head to head, toe to toe," Ownie sputtered to the press. "We did it, and it worked."

"Did you know Mackey broke his ankle in there?" asked Scott, holding out a tape recorder.

Blood was dripping from the injured woman's nose; strangers were breaking into the inner circle, surging closer to something they couldn't explain. Someone tried to haul the piper and his skunk sporran into the ring, where he could add to the staggering noise.

"No, ah didden know." Turmoil pushed away the shades offered to him to hide his swollen eyes. "The mon was brave, he fought like a wounded wolf."

"This is definitely the biggest night of our career," Ownie shouted. The tension had left his body, lifting like a fever, rendering him young and weightless. "This moves us into the top-ten ratings, it puts us in position." His eyes were wet with tears. "This man might as well be the son of Muhammad Ali." The tape recorders whirred. "I don't care who hears me say it." Reckless, drunk with success. "He has something special, he has powers that come from someplace else. I know it in my heart."

40

Ownie approached the office building with Turmoil, knowing everything had changed. A bearded bum was camped on the sidewalk, a Tim's coffee cup extended for coins. Ownie slipped him a buck, and the old bum smiled a toothless thank you.

When you had a fighter like *this,* Ownie decided, there was potential that no day job could offer. It was like being in a rock band that could — if the pieces fell into place — tour the world, make millions, and invade the public psyche, leaving reference points for a generation.

"Hey, champ," a courier driver shouted. "You looked good, man. Who you fighting next?"

"Ah dunno yet," Turmoil replied. "Someone big, mon, someone big."

Had it really been two years, Ownie wondered, since Champion had brought Turmoil to Halifax, a stranger in the crowd, as anonymous as the courier, as broke as the bum? Ownie felt as though the months had blurred and melded, the seasons indistinguishable in the ever-present grey.

They rode an elevator to the second floor. The fighter opened a glass door and Ownie spotted a secretary, a woman in her fifties, sitting primly at her desk. She had allowed herself one personal touch, Ownie noticed, a framed photo of three blond children in Irish knit sweaters.

"Ah like your blue dress." Turmoil tossed the compliment over the blond heads directly at the woman, who responded, "Why thank you." Eager for praise, however trite, she instinctively glanced at the flaxen children, her legacy of good genes and manners. She had crow's-feet, Ownie noticed, and tear-damaged eyes.

"That blue remind me of the ocean back home," Turmoil continued. "It was so nice and wahm, we would take our hosses down every Friday and give them a bath, let them splash 'round and 'round. Ahd say, 'Come on, hosses, it's bath day,' and they would smiiile."

"It is a soothing shade, isn't it?" The secretary's hair was cut in an off-centre wedge that matched the crisp decor. "They call it cornflower," she said, inching out from underneath the massive egos that overshadowed her existence, the unexpected divorce that had condemned her to this job.

"It looks good on a han'some woman like yourself."

For the first time, she smiled. The secretary touched her silk scarf, and Turmoil strolled the room, taking inventory of the walls, all cold and mute, a soundproof confessional where you waited with your sins.

"Cahn you tell Douglas that Turmoil Davies is here?" he asked. "Him and his trainah, Mistah Ownie Flan'gan." And then, to Ownie's surprise, he added, "We dohn hab time to fool aroun.'"

"I'll buzz him at once." Her voice was a bone china teacup.

"See, Ownie." Turmoil's voice boomed off the circumspect walls. "Ah tole you 'fore we come up here that this woman is a ver-ver smaht woman. She prolly do all the work and that ole Douglas, he juss play around with his sailboat. Ah dohn know why Champion want nothin to do wit that *locho*. They cahnt get a better lawyer?"

The secretary flushed, shocked but secretly pleased.

Inside the lawyer's office, Turmoil pointed to a painting on one wall. "Is that your sailboat?"

"My yacht," Tobin Douglas corrected him.

Douglas had purchased the oil painting from an artist, who had assured him it was de rigueur in the right social circles. From his desk, he could cast an admiring eye over the *Margarita*'s lines, noting the double-planked mahogany and stainless-steel rigging. The forty-five-foot ketch had a seventy-horsepower Mercedes diesel, a three-kilowatt diesel generator, and the added allure of being from New York State.

"Ah forgot, mon," Turmoil laughed. "You muss be Aris-sotle O-nasis. Maybe ahm Jackee O."

Douglas blushed. At play, in his pink Polo shirt and Ray-Bans, he felt more like a Kennedy than an Onassis, more like a South End scion than a self-made man.

"Would you like to go sailing some day?" Douglas asked disingenuously. On another wall, Douglas had hung the *Margarita*'s framed plans. "She has a marvellous disposition."

"With our luck, we be wit you the day you get 'rested!" Turmoil snapped back. "The day the poleese figure out what you doin with that boat and all them little girls. Ah cahn risk nuthin like that, and neither can mah trainah, who's a vet'rin."

Douglas, who wore a gold scrollwork bracelet and a tan, smiled his patronizing smile, one of many in his repertoire, letting the dig fly by. He believed there was always a point in a conversation where someone tried to take control by being disagreeable. If you smiled through it, acted like you enjoyed it, you were back in charge.

"What about a workout in a mall?" Douglas had already

suggested a bachelor auction and an open-line radio show as ways of promoting Turmoil.

"No." Turmoil sounded bored, with a headache coming on. Right then, before things got worse, before Douglas got smarmy and Turmoil enraged, Ownie moved himself to a neutral corner in his head. "Ah dohn hab time for that. The peeple wahn to see me, they can come to mah gym, charge admishun, show them it worth somethin, not go hangin arown some ole mall."

Douglas smiled, the charming look he'd perfected on nubile eighteen-year-olds as he whispered, as though they had a choice, "Only if you want to."

"You cahn sen someone over to colleck the money," Turmoil added.

"We'll see."

On Douglas's desk, five men in slickers grinned. Ownie looked at the men and then back at Douglas. This guy was as phony as a whitewashed Islander, he decided, one of those poor fools who went to the Boston States, got a job as a maid or a truck driver and came back talking like Ethel Kennedy. "*Cah*," the biddies would snort behind their back. "What is a *cah*?"

"We lost money on the last three fighters we brought in." Douglas sounded sombre, as though he was laying out a client's limited options. He had a wooden dory compass at his elbow, an antique sextant on the wall, nautical aids for sinners who had lost their way.

"Thass too bad." Turmoil knew that it was Douglas who had rented him that room in a crack house when he had been promised an apartment. He had almost frozen to death in that dump, he recalled, with those lynched teddy bears that *had* to be a sign of something evil. "You should be a better bis-nismon."

"I guess I should." Douglas smiled.

"Afta my lass fight, the premier stop all the bisnis in the legislature, juss to mention my name, Turmoil Davies, champeen of the whole Commonwealth."

"Really?" Douglas smirked. "I missed that."

"Oh yes. They talkin 'bout havin a Turmoil Davies Day."

Ownie squinted, knowing that Turmoil was telling the truth and that Douglas was being a smart ass. But then again, every day was Tobin Douglas Day now that he drove a Mercedes convertible purchased with the spoils of bankruptcy law. A guest lecturer at Dalhousie, he had appeared on *As It Happens,* and every morning, after installing his green contact lenses, he gave thanks for casinos and VLTs, the scourge of the poor.

"Those peeple, they aftah me all the time, all the time." Turmoil stared out a floor-length window. He studied Georges Island, the drumlin in the centre of the harbour, but it seemed to make him weary. "From, now on, ah goi to say, 'G'won, you go talk to Douglas.'" He spoke quickly as though he had solved his own problem. "Ahll tell them to phone you and work it out. Ah dohn hab time for all that foolish stuff."

"Sure, I'll talk to them."

"Nebber mind, you cahn talk to nobody. Ah menshun your name and ebbybuddy think ahm a crim'nil. Mah trainah here can take the calls if ahm too bizzy. He got a lot of my stuff on comp't'r."

Ownie, who had never operated a computer in his life, nodded, and Douglas flashed the smile that greased the skids for the young girl's panties, before the interminable row back to shore, ignoring the sight of her high heels soaked in salt.

Turmoil looked at Douglas's cluttered desk, at the dory compass and the stack of files. "No wonder you losin money, with this mess. Dohn you know nothin about comp't'rs?"

"I guess I'm a bit of a Luddite."

"Whass that? A freak or a *teef*?"

Tilting back in his chair, Douglas stroked his highlighted hair, which was thinning on top and too long in the back. Ownie saw a business suit duck into the adjacent office, and realized with a start that it was the bikers' lawyer, the fixer with the prune eyes from the strip club near Tootsy's, the guy who had once run for office.

"We have no guarantee you're going to sign with us again even after all the money we have invested in the last two years." Douglas smiled. "All the work we have done."

"*Pa pa yo!*" Turmoil leaned forward, and Douglas blinked. "You juss hab to wait and see."

41

Smithers had just returned from the college hockey championships in Toronto, an outing he had described to Scott in
excruciating detail. On the plane, he'd had a middle seat, he
said, flanked by two college wrestlers with shaved heads and
bad skin, whom he'd mentally christened Jethro and Jethrine.

"I'm one eighty-one and a half," Jethrine shouted over
Smithers. "Just one pound to go." He had the smallest ears
Smithers had ever seen, the size of fiddleheads.

"Awesome!" Jethro gave his approval. "One fifty-six."

The wrestlers, doubles in hooded sweatshirts, had been
talking through Smithers since takeoff. Unlike hockey players,
wrestlers had no finesse, no style, he decided, tapping the neon
knee brace that he wore.

Already bored, Smithers hoisted his carry-on from the floor
to check on his pucks, add-ons to his collection. These guys
are winners, he grumbled to himself, Jethro pretending to read
Dante and Jethrine playing with a calculator. They reminded
Smithers of the old Red Rose tea ads with chimps in glasses,
banging piano keys with knee-length arms, grinning. He
laughed at the image and wondered how long chimps lived.

"Watch this, dude." Jethrine grabbed his air-sickness bag.

Smithers snuck a covert look at the wrestler, who was, he
believed, probably pulling the goalie, using the bag as cover.
Smithers tilted his chair back wishing he'd flown Business
Class. Maybe the stews would have been better-looking. Ever

since they had started filing age-discrimination suits, the stews were getting older and uglier. What is the point of an ugly stew? he wondered. It's not like they're NASA engineers or supersonic pilots; it's their *job* to look good.

"What the shit!" Smithers snapped up his seat. "*Bluuugh. Bluuuuugh.*" The goalie was still in position, but Jethrine was leaning down, pimply neck bent, ralphing in the bag. "*Bluuugh.*" Another barf. It was too gross even for Smithers.

"Awesome!" Jethro slapped his leg." You'll ace weight now."

Jethrine punched the number one eighty in his calculator, held up the screen, and laughed, showing chimplike gums. Jethro laughed with him.

"You rabid ape!" Smithers fumbled to push the help button, to summon the ancient stew, who would probably, he feared, have a heart attack before she reached him. This cretin was ralphing on purpose, he realized, and he might catch AIDS or hepatitis B or distemper if he didn't get out of here. Reaching over, Jethrine pulled Smithers's air-sickness bag from its designated spot and asked, "Are you going to be using this?"

Scott had shrugged after hearing the story and gone back to work.

"What happened to your eye?" demanded Smithers, pointing to a welt.

"It's a bug bite," said Scott.

"Bullshit."

Scott ignored him. In the newsroom, the memory of Jethrine fresh, Smithers was cranky, taking out his frustration on an intern named Fisher, the nearest twentysomething lifeform, the only person he knew who owned composting worms and pretended to like William S. Burroughs.

"No wonder you people can't get jobs." Smithers lobbed the insult at the intern.

Fisher, who was wearing plum wide wale cords and a cardigan, ignored him. It was Warshick's day off, and the intern had been assigned the sports agate, which took all of his concentration. He was having trouble getting it right, Scott noticed. You needed a precise sequence of computer symbols to make the numbers line up on the page, and if you made one mistake, they ran together like hieroglyphics.

Smithers picked up the phone. "It's for you," he said, nodding at Fisher. "Keep the personal calls down."

Even absent, Scott believed, Warshick was bombarding Smithers's psyche, catapulting hits across his protective moat. Last year, Warshick, who weighed two hundred and seventy pounds, had taken up lawn bowling with his best friend, Roger, an insurance salesman. "Imagine a sport so stupid they can't even make the balls round," Smithers had taunted, and now, one year later, Warshick was going to New Zealand to compete in an international event. "They tell me I'm the Bobby Orr of the greens," he bragged to Smithers. "I'm a natural."

"Ahhh." Fisher looked nervous as he hung up the phone. "That was my landlady. I have to excuse myself for a few minutes."

"Well, forget it; you're not going anywhere."

"There is a problem, really. It's my cat."

"Is it dead?"

"No, but he's fighting off an attack in my living room. The neighbours called and reported the noise. If he's injured, I can't afford vet bills. I leave the window open so Kerouac can have freedom, so he can come and go through the balcony. Another cat must have followed him in."

"No wonder none of these kids can get ahead," Smithers muttered to Scott, who had been in the newsroom more than usual that week.

Smithers let Fisher leave with a warning — "I am timing you" — and then stood up to stretch his legs. Walking by News, Smithers felt a palpable chill, the same one that had been lingering since that flap over the Cheese Club. The orders came in every month, and, according to Smithers, you would swear it was the NHL draft, with people racing around, counting cheese blocks, stashing them until quitting time like they'd never seen cheese before. Well, somehow, one of Squeaky's baby Gouda rounds went missing from the fridge. She launched an investigation and demanded that the thief step forward. She and her henchman formed a posse to track down the missing round and found it, half-eaten, covered with carpet lint, under Warshick's desk. Warshick swore he hadn't touched it — "I have my own cooler" — that it was a set-up by Smithers. Not knowing who to blame, the Cheese Club members were mad at both of them.

Scott believed that Smithers was locked in an eternal battle with Warshick, two halves of the same slovenly self. Smithers had adopted a series of shallow conceits to distance himself from his indolent nemesis. "I only wear cotton shirts," he said, sneering at Warshick's polyester jersey. "I listen to jazz. When I'm drinking beer, I prefer imported." Scott believed that fear stalked Smithers, fear that the genetic vortex would get him, that it would suck him under like leaves in the gutter, joining Warshick in his joyful sloth.

"Jesus Christ." Scott heard Smithers curse. In the hockey reporter's mailbox was a note from MacKenzie assigning him a Where Are They Now? on bicycle messenger boys.

"It's that moron, Fisher. He did this, by bringing his bicycle to work," Smithers fumed. "He caused this; he planted the idea in the Seagull's head."

Unaware of Smithers's outburst, Garth was at that moment watching a government photographer, a wimp who had worked for the paper fifteen years ago, drop off an envelope of prints. One time, Garth recalled, the publisher had sent the shooter to Newfoundland with Frank Mobley. It was just after Frank had been caught selling cab chits for booze, but he was still hot as molten steel. Frank always drove on road trips, that damn cowboy hat on his head and Captain Morgan at his side. It was just after they had opened the Trans-Canada, and you could see parts of Newfoundland you'd never imagined: outports, glacier-stripped fjords, mud flats. It was spectacular, Frank later told colleagues, like visiting parts of Europe.

Things were fine until just outside Gander, the photographer later explained when trying to analyze the trip. Gander — now that was a real town, Garth believed. Built around an airport, a refuelling stop for transatlantic traffic. Back in the 1950s, when they called Gander the Crossroads of the World, it had all of the big airlines.

They'd been listening to Frank's beloved country music on the car stereo. But then, according to the photographer, Frank gave Hank a rest and put on a tape of Joey Smallwood addressing a meeting. Frank, who'd been taping Smallwood speeches since they hit The Rock, claimed that Smallwood was a genius. His eyes narrowed, and he took a swig from his bottle. "After that, Frank lost it," the shooter reported. Apparently he was overcome by the verbal gymnastics, the oratorical grace of the tiny premier. Frank had insisted it was like hearing Patsy Cline sing or seeing the Sistine Chapel.

Joey was in full flight when Frank and the shooter reached the flashing highway light. They hadn't seen a car in hours, and now, in the middle of nowhere, with not a house for miles, was a yellow Pinto, idling. The car, unaccustomed to highways, which were new to Newfoundland, shifted gears and darted like a mouse leaving its hole. "Hey, Frank," the shooter yelled, but Mobley didn't hear him. His eyes were closed and there were tears of awe filling the corners. The Captain shattered when they hit the Pinto, spinning it round and round like a top. When they pulled out the driver from the wreckage, he said his name was Jerry Canary, and he was from Buchans. "Bye, aye t'ot aye was dead."

"Oh, Garth." Carla entered the office, holding two memos from Boomer. "Your wife called three times. She says it's the pigeons."

MEMO TO STAFF:
(Please post on bulletin board)

The auditing firm of Boise Blackburn will be
in the office on Friday. Be prepared to provide
any documentation they may request and to
cross-reference receipts with stories and dates.
Long-distance charges and freelance accounts
will be examined. Department heads may be
required to provide contact lists and numbers.

Garth reread the memo and smiled, believing that auditors were like the tooth fairy, creatures you heard about but never really believed in.

MEMO
(Please post on bulletin board)

Harry Mathers, a twenty-year employee of News,
has decided to take early retirement. Buzz Bailey
has retired from Sports.

42

Ownie was sitting on his front step with Louie, monitoring events across the street. A city truck pulled up to the duck pond, earlier visited by a police cruiser. Someone (according to the radio) had killed one of the geese. Ownie assumed this was the reason for the activity. Two workers in coveralls circled the pond with measuring tapes.

"Did you know that the paper had a story on the goose?" Louie asked.

"Nah," Ownie admitted. "I didn't see it."

Ownie hadn't read the *Standard* yet because Hildred was having their hardwood floors refinished, putting some rooms temporarily off limits. Parked outside the house, Ownie was contemplating the murdered goose, O'Riley's dead cat, and karma.

"I'll go get it," Louie volunteered. "Besides, I've got some new tapes I can lend you." With that, Louie trotted to his parked Jeep and returned with a morning copy of the *Standard* in one hand and *Ring: The Leonard-Hearns Saga* and *Best of the 80s* in the other.

"Here it is." Louie opened the *Standard* to the Dartmouth page. "The headline says, 'VICIOUS SLAYING SHOCKS DARTMOUTH COMMUNITY.'"

Ownie snorted. "The only thing shocking is that someone didn't kill one of the bastards sooner."

"The newspaper is quoting some alderman, who says it is a tragedy."

"Tragedy! Lemme see." Ownie grabbed the *Standard* and read out loud: "'Alderman Gary Schofield said seniors in his ward are shaken by the brutal killing. If teenage punks would murder an innocent goose, can seniors be next?' So now he's comparing seniors with those bastard Rottweiler geese."

Louie shook his head in disbelief.

According to the newspaper, Schofield said that a businessman was planning a funeral for the goose with a blue satin coffin, an honour guard, and a preacher.

"'This goose was a favourite of the seniors,' declared Schofield. 'They named him Gramps.' There he goes with the seniors again," scoffed Ownie, "making it sound like they are all idiots."

"I saw Schofield on TV, and he was crying," said Louie. "He said he wouldn't rest until police found the killers. He said there'd been a tip, pointing to the low rental."

"They always nail the lo-ros," Ownie said, "don't they?"

Louie left, and Ownie went inside, only to hear a knock minutes later on his door. It was O'Riley, the former cop, looking puffy in a creased sweatsuit. He looks pale, Ownie thought, even for a man who spends his days inside with four TVs playing, one in each room, all tuned to a different channel.

"I guess you heard about the geese," O'Riley panted.

"Yeah."

"Well, I was talking to the boys down at the station, and they've cracked the case. You'll *love* this one."

"Lay it on me."

"An old lady from the seniors' home said she saw the whole thing," O'Riley explained, excited to be back on the inside of a crime investigation. "She said she would've spoken up earlier, but she was embarrassed because her husband was nailed once for obscene phone calls."

"Who'd she finger?" Ownie looked into O'Riley's eyes,

which seemed to gel, to momentarily lose the liquidity of retirement. "A Chinese restaurant?"

"Nope." He looks half-alive for a change, Ownie thought, even in slippers, illogically clutching a remote.

"Another goose." O'Riley savoured the irony.

"A *goose?*"

"Two, actually. Agnes says she saw them holding down Gramps and pecking his head till they'd killed him. The boys talked to a biologist, who said this can happen during nesting."

"I guess that's it for the funeral," Ownie scoffed. "I always knew they were vicious."

"Tell me about it, after what they did to my cat." O'Riley raised his brows for emphasis. "My grandson, Simon, can't come into the house any more without crying, 'Where's Taffy, Nanny? Where'd she go?' I think this Gramps or whatever the hell his real name is had something to do with Taffy."

"Don't you know it."

"I should have taken care of him. I still have my service revolver."

"Nah, it's way better this way, and you stay out of it."

A half-hour later, when all of the activity at the pond had abated, Turmoil knocked on Ownie's door. "Ah need to fill up mah water bottle," he announced, stepping inside.

"Why didn't you do it before?" asked Ownie, as they walked down the hall to the kitchen, which was Hildred's domain. Ownie was nervous any time someone entered her work space, which was overflowing with pans and nozzles, half-built cakes and finished products. Today, he noted, there was one particularly large cake under construction, a white *Love Boat* that glistened like ice. The three-storey cake, built for a cruise line, was, in Ownie's estimation, her most ambitious project yet.

Ownie believed that Hildred had a gift, like the British artist he'd seen on PBS, who painted landscapes the size of postage stamps, using strokes as thin as eyelashes. "Some people have special hands," he had told Johnny, who didn't know a lot about life, let alone art. "Musicians, brain surgeons, Gretzky, some fighters too, like Orlando Zulueta, who could slice you up quicker than a Ginsu knife." When fighters got hit by the Cuban lightweight, Ownie recalled, they swore that he had razor blades in his gloves, and some insisted that the refs check them. Ownie read somewhere that the Hatchet Man had been stabbed to death outside a San Francisco bar where he had been working. Two Hells Angels were charged.

"Ah got somethin to talk about," Turmoil mumbled after filling the bottle.

Hildred had laid out her palette, Ownie noticed, which was dominated by cool blues and darker shading. She had made a marzipan propeller, life rafts, and miniature yellow deck chairs. Tennis courts were coming next, she had told him, along with hot tubs.

"Ahm planning . . ."

Why is he talking in such a low voice, Ownie wondered, when most of the time he sounds like he's broadcasting without a microphone? "Don't plan too much till we get this next fight out of the way," he chortled, the dead goose popping into his head. He couldn't help thinking about the old saw "What goes around comes around." Yes, even for geese. And didn't that Alderman Schofield look the fool, he decided, talking about seniors and funerals when those bloody geese had killed their own?

"Ahm planning to leeeave."

"Huh?" Ownie heard a car honk outside.

"Ahm."

Yeah, that's what he was saying. The words hit Ownie like a shot to the neck, and his hearing faded as Turmoil babbled on about Florida, a promoter, and a title attempt next year. Ownie couldn't hear the rest because there was a party line inside his head: Hildred saying she was sorry, Butch telling him he was a sucker, Douglas demanding to know if he couldn't have seen it coming, Johnny promising that they could still get that fight with Hansel Sparks. Holy Mary, Mother of God! After all the time he had spent making something out of this crazy, good-for-nothing bastard, teaching him everything he knew!

"This is what ah worked foh."

"Yeah, all by yourself." Ownie was embarrassed after feeling smug about Gramps with this coming down on his own head. "You lousy —"

"I juss —"

"I heard enough. Just shut up."

That's what he got, Ownie decided, for dreaming, for imagining money and fame, for allowing himself to think that they came without a price. It had never been like this with him and Tommy because they were a team, and the punches hurt him as much as they hurt Tommy. That night in South Africa, Tommy fought with every nerve and fibre in his body, plowing in like a born-again freak driven by will and conviction, facing a sea of non-believers. Ownie patched him up, but it didn't help. Blood stood between Tommy and his reward, not heart. Ownie cried when the ref held up the champ's arm, when Tommy lowered his swollen head and said, "I'm sorry. We'll get another chance."

"God wudden want you to be judgin peeple. Good Christians nebba judge."

"Bullshit!" Ownie's voice returned, drowning out the ones in his head. "The most Christian man I ever met lived next to us on the Island and never said a bad word about nobody. 'Live and let live,' was his schtick. 'Gossip is the devil's language.' Turns out he was a bank robber wanted down in Maine, a regular Jesse James, hiding out for ten years. So whenever I hear somebody talking that way, I wonder how many banks he robbed."

"Ah nebba robbed no banks." Turmoil stuck out his chin.

"I wouldn't put it past you."

"Ah nebba."

"You crazy bastard."

"Ah *neba*!"

"You crazy, bank-robbing bastard!"

Turmoil took an outraged step into Ownie's confusion. "Dohn talk to me that way." Ownie braced himself, thinking about the time Turmoil had sucker-punched Suey, laying out the Tumblebug and hissing "Iccce." You'll sucker me, all right! Ownie picked up a rolling pin stained with fondant and issued a silent challenge: Make one move, just one. C'mon, baby!

"God dohn wahn you to have eeevil in your heart. In Jamaica, long time ago, there wuz a cit-ee full of py-rits and bukc'ners. They call it the moss wicket city on Earth. They wudden change, they wudden lissen to God. They juss keep robbin ships, killin peeple. So one day, there be a big earth-quake and a tidal wave and it bury them all."

"Should've taken you with them."

"Ah wassen even bohn."

"Too bad!"

"Ahll put a spell on your fam'ly." Turmoil arched his brows and let the words hang, knocking the wind out of the room. "All of them."

"You'll what?"

"Ahll put a spell on them all," Turmoil muttered, as though he had reconsidered. Ownie dove across the room, hitting a stool. He lifted the rolling pin over his head and yelled, "You crazy, no-good bastard!"

"You'll be sorry," Turmoil screamed as he bumped into the *Love Boat*, knocking a deck and life raft to the floor with a sickening thump.

43

Light streamed through Tootsy's windows, exposing ghostly spots on the walls, spaces left by Turmoil's ripped-down clippings. Music drifted upstairs, the unmistakable strains of "Let Me Call You Sweetheart."

The music was coming from a new business downstairs. That day, Ownie had peered through its window, which contained a mannequin, a picnic blanket, and a bottle of Spanish wine. In the centre of an unfurnished room was a couple waltzing. One-two, one-two across the floor. The woman looked like a cook Ownie had known in the navy; she had the same skinny hips and pot belly.

BEGINNERS SPECIAL, a sign said. 5 LESSONS: $19.95. BALL-ROOM. LATIN. COUNTRY.

As Ownie watched the middle-aged dancers, a mustachioed man in tight white jeans and an open shirt darted toward him, desperate for business. Ownie was surprised he could move that fast in cowboy boots. Life, Ownie conceded, was tough.

Ownie had made himself come to Tootsy's, but he wasn't in the mood for much. He was determined to ignore Louie, who was talking nonsense to the Runner. Louie informed the Runner in a pleased voice that he was going to Canastota, New York, to visit the International Boxing Hall of Fame.

Take a tape of your fight, Ownie thought, for World's Biggest Bum, and then felt guilty. He shouldn't be so hard on Louie, he admitted, since none of this Davies business was his fault. Besides, the poor fool was doing all right considering what he came from. Louie's father was long gone and his mother was no good. Every three or four months, she would phone him and tell him that she was moving. It was always something: "These neighbours are a bunch of stiff necks. The seagulls are keeping me awake. I know those tight-asses are spying on me."

And each time, Louie had to drop everything, including his job, to haul her stuff. The mother moved more times than Pretty Boy Floyd on the lam and always sent Louie back for the deposit. The worst part was, it was one of her old boyfriends who got Louie on the fire department, so she owned him. "At least Lester was a real man," she'd throw it up, drunk and dirty.

"Rocco Mar . . . uhmmm . . . Mar-chegiano?" Louie was now playing the name game with the Runner.

"Is that a joke?" the Runner asked.

The world is full of crazy bastards, Ownie thought. That morning, he'd seen two shakos shuffling down the street, the same two, always together. Out of the blue, like someone had flipped his remote control to ballistic, one started yelling in the other's face, in an awful, spit-flying attack. On and on, while buddy stood there, blank. Suddenly, the screamer stopped as abruptly as he had started, and off they went, Hope and Crosby on the Road to Nowhere.

Over the drifting music, Ownie heard someone climbing the stairs. It was probably Sandra, that ugly little girlfriend of Louie's. They were back tighter than a jam jar since Louie's fight disaster. Sandra, whom Johnny generously described as a four, had even persuaded Louie to retire his alter ego, the Arabian Knight.

A muscular man with puffy supermodel lips stood in the doorway, dressed like he had a court appearance. Hepped, bouncing on hot metal, it was Roddy Nason. He glanced about and then looked confused, like he didn't know what came next.

"Hey, Roddy." Ownie signalled him over. Roddy crossed the room, hands in the pockets of his dress pants. It was the same spring-toed walk that carried him into amateur fight nights, deaf to everything but the faded cheers and the long-ago chants of "Roddy," guided by phantom arms, inaudible jokes, always too big for the room.

When Roddy reached him, Ownie gave himself a slapstick punch to the head and staggered, suckered by Roddy's invisible left. They laughed.

"Lookin' good, you old bugger." Roddy rubbed Ownie's bald head.

"You still got the hammer, Roddy."

"How ya been, brother?" Roddy's words were as thick as molasses, which made Ownie believe the rumours, the ones about dope.

"Like Little Mary Sunshine," Ownie boasted.

"You sure?" They both knew what he was talking about.

"Yeah. That stuff don't bother me. I don't need guys like Davies; I'm on a full pension."

"Good, good."

"Roddy, this is Louie Fader," said Ownie as the fireman trotted over in sweats.

"Louie got arrested this year for impersonating a fighter."

"Too bad, man." Roddy missed the joke.

"Louie, this is *the* Roddy Nason. He beat Nigel Baxter for the Commonwealth title. The writers said that fighting Roddy was like facing the Amazing Kreskin. He knew your next move before you did. Every block had radar, every counter punch was a Stealth bomber. It's too bad you never saw him fight."

For years, Ownie recalled, Roddy had been something. He had driven around town with a Newfoundland dog, a lovely big animal that rode shotgun. It was black, with webbed feet and a soft, understanding face. The dog weighed one hundred and fifty pounds. "We fight in the same class," Roddy would joke, proud of that dog. "Toby's a hero. He earned a citation in New Brunswick for saving a three-year-old boy who fell off a wharf. He jumped in and swam him ashore, and they ran his picture in the paper."

One night, Toby escaped from Roddy's house and fell into a swimming pool. In a sad twist of irony, the heroic dog swan round and round until he drowned, exhausted, three blocks from home. In denial, Roddy couldn't believe that the dead dog was his. "Toby would've never drowned," he'd argue, pointing to the citation and the newspaper picture from New Brunswick, so he kidnapped another Newf. When the owner found him and the dog, Roddy slugged the man, got charged with assault, and pulled thirty days, which seemed to spell the end of it, really.

"This Ownie here, he's A-1."

Ownie nodded, humouring him.

"You going to that surprise dinner they're holding for Darren?" Ownie walked Roddy to the door. "He'd like to see you there."

"When is it?" Roddy squinted.

"The tenth," Ownie said. "I'll write it down for you."

Roddy pocketed the paper. He'd been in and out of jail a couple of times since Toby died, and then he fell down a flight of stairs, rupturing an eardrum and doing damage to his head.

"Good, good, but don't tell Darren I'm coming."

"It's a *surprise*."

"I know, I know, but don't tell him I'm coming. Me and Darren go way back."

44

A black Mustang rolled by, a mobile boom box of jive.

From the dashboard crown to the chain-link steering wheel, the whole car shook. Ownie was walking down a Halifax drag with attitude: badasses bumping into cars, drug dealers with calculators, big fat mamas pushing strollers. What a joke, he thought, small-time losers going nowhere.

Ownie had gone to Halifax to sign papers for Douglas. The lawyer had given Ownie a tax slip and a pissy look as though it was Ownie's fault that Turmoil had left, as though the lawyer hadn't been the one who put Davies in a crack house. If Douglas was so smart, Ownie thought, why hadn't he written a better contract, one that lasted more than two years?

"Hey, bitch." A boy with FRESH tattooed on his neck jumped in the face of a legal aid lawyer, trailing her past a theatre that had closed with *Jurassic Park*. "I thought you had titties, but you don't have none," FRESH sneered, and the woman fled through a door.

Ownie thought about the street fights he'd had down here with cats a hell of lot tougher than that, all with a built-in crowd. "Go find Butch," he'd yell when the odds started shrinking. Butch was easy to find; he worked in the Outrigger Tavern cracking heads for a living. Butch and Suey's brother, Percy, were a regular attraction on the streets, squaring off more times than Jack Britton and Kid Lewis. Percy was okay when he wasn't rolling sailors, he was good in the clinches, and he had a way with cars. Percy's home base was a dance hall up a side street, a smoky CANEX of soft girls and hard liquor, and that's where they found him with a New Jersey knife still in his gut.

Cutlass, said a car that was the colour of Orange Crush and boldly claimed: IMITATED BUT NOT DUPLICATED. Even the gaudy car, with windows that glittered like sequins, looked dull and insignificant in the fog.

It's this bloody weather that's making me so mad, Ownie decided, not this street, not Turmoil, not cats like FRESH. It's the months of darkness hanging over your head like a bell tent. What's that do to your soul, to never see sunlight, to never feel warmth? Ownie had read about a fogbound village in Hungary where people were lining up to commit suicide. Ownie bet nobody killed themselves like that in sunny Mexico. He'd seen pictures of poor people in Mexico, kicking dusty soccer balls and wearing sombreros, gathered in squares. Here, the poor were scattered like litter on the sides of the road, empty coffee cups that would blow away or dissolve like the mounds of dirty snow that stood each spring in odd corners.

"Hi, Slugger." Ownie had almost missed him. "Heading back to Dartmouth?

"Yes, I'm waiting for the Number Eleven." Slugger was sensibly dressed in a duffel coat and thermal boots.

Winter was longer than a Russian novel, Hildred liked to say, and just as bleak. When spring came, you saw neighbours you thought were dead. When the sun broke through, it felt like the liberation of Holland, with people running into the streets, holding their faces to the sky, buying ice cream cones and patio furniture that would soon turn mouldy and wet.

"How's the swimming? Any problem with them women?"

"No. They've switched to ah, ah, aqua . . . whadya call it?

Aerobics." He looked at Ownie quizzically. "Have you ever seen one of those?"

"No, I don't keep up with that stuff."

"Weeeeell," Slugger started. "They stand in the shallow end and the instructor puts on music. She likes that song about someone named Gloria. It gets them worked up and they wave their hands in the air." He demonstrated, hoping to make himself clear. "It's the strangest thing. There's always one man." He held up a finger. "Every class, and it's never the same one." He looked at Ownie to see if he had an answer.

"Different guy, eh?"

"Twenty, thirty women and always one man!"

"Maybe he reports back to the other guys."

Slugger shrugged, and Ownie noticed the sling. "Hurt your arm?"

"I had a fall off my roof."

"How'd that happen?"

"Well, my blood pressure's down," Slugger explained. "It makes me dizzy sometimes. I find that I weave a bit when I walk."

"What were you doing on the roof?"

"My wife likes things clean, so last week she noticed that the roof was dirty. You can see it, you know, when you're driving up the hill. She got me to run the vacuum hose up through our chimney. Then I had to get up on the roof to vacuum it off."

"How'd that go?"

"Perfect except for the fall. It's very clean now."

Ownie said his goodbyes to Slugger. He passed a cluster of sad schizophrenics on the Sally Ann wall, delusional drifters with sagebrush beards and Thermoses hooked to their belts, guys with thousands of miles and no destination on their tattered shoes. He turned around as a bus arrived and a woman appeared from nowhere. As the door opened, she shoved in front of Slugger like a bridesmaid fighting for the tossed bouquet. The old man stumbled. "What's wrong with people these days?" Ownie muttered. "What's making them so ugly?"

45

Scott felt guilty coming to Tootsy's, as though he was reminding everyone that something was missing. When he entered the gym, Johnny was sitting on a bench.

"Has anyone heard from Turmoil?" Scott asked in a low voice.

"Nah," Johnny scoffed. "We seen one of his fights on TV. That's it."

"Oh well," Scott replied nonsensically.

He was still on the boxing beat, which had been reduced to part-time with Turmoil gone. He rode the desk two shifts per week, and had finally finished MacKenzie's Where Are They Now? on School Boy, who had, he discovered, died three years earlier from congestive heart failure.

Johnny and Scott heard a slow clumping noise on the stairs, a noise that lasted too long. The door finally opened and Johnny's brother, Marcel, hobbled in. Using a metal walker, it had taken him five arduous minutes to navigate the stairs, so when he appeared inside, bent and heaving, Johnny believed the visit must be important.

"What's up, Marcel?" he asked, uneasy.

"I'm going to Norway."

Scott dropped his eyes, pretending he hadn't heard.

"No seriously, man, what's up?"

"I'm leaving on Tuesday." Marcel produced a passport that, when carefully opened, showed him grim-faced, glasses secured with elastic. Johnny studied it and handed it back.

The trip, Marcel explained, had arisen from his work as a grief counsellor. A retired music teacher named Twyla had lost her closest companion, a spectacular Norwegian forest cat named Thor. The orange cat had great tufts of fur between his toes and in his ears, plus two layers of fur that enabled him and others of his breed to survive harsh Nordic winters. He was the kind of cat you couldn't take your eyes off, Marcel explained with an enthusiasm that Johnny had rarely seen. When the sun hit him, he looked like a fireball. "Thor weighed thirty pounds," Marcel added. "And he had eyes the colour of Sultan's gold. They glowed."

As grief counsellor, Marcel had helped Twyla through her loss, accompanying her to the cremation and making a scrap book of Thor. A big cat, he didn't go too far from home, but he did, like all Norwegian forest cats, seek high places: lamp-posts, Christmas trees, and bridges, climbing down head first. Johnny listened, taken aback by his brother's knowledge. One day, after the funeral, Twyla turned to Marcel and said, "Marcel, let's take Thor back where he belongs. Life is too short, let's not waste it."

"We are going to spread his ashes near a fjord," said Marcel, who wanted Johnny to check on his own pets during his absence. "Many of the Norwegian forest cats came over with the Vikings on the longboats. Their job was to protect the food from rats. They're descended from the Siberian cat of Russia and the Turkish angora."

"Really," said Johnny. "And how do you know all that?"

"You'd be surprised," sniffed Marcel, pocketing his passport, "by how much I know."

Johnny looked at Scott and shrugged.

In his parents' spare room, now freshly painted, Scott opened a high-school yearbook, a hard-covered collage of typos, ironed hair, and puerile insights into life.

"Hi and Freak Out!"

"Forget the Glass. Give Me the Bottle."

Scott stared at a groover with wire-rimmed glasses and mutton-chop sideburns that lifted him above the throng. Gary Carson was wearing a Nehru jacket and a smile that celebrated his coolness. *"I bequeath my Hendrix hat to Gus and my Acid Indigestion to Duke."* Scott stared, trying to age the face by twenty years, wondering if Gary was the guy who'd installed his cable last year. He heard the basement door open with a creak.

John Miller had no picture, just a nihilistic space. *"John enjoys reading counter-revolutionary literature. His pet peeve is petty Bourgeois Dilitants. 'Without a people's army, the people have nothing. I bequeth my guns to Quebec Liberation.'"*

Scott scanned the sayings that dated each page like the rings of a tree.

"O Wow How Prime!"

"Smash Capitalism."

"Can You Dig It?"

"The future sees pretty Cindy as a stewardess visiting Hawaii and California. Cindy plans to sleep till noon when a train will come through her bedroom with orange juice and French toast."

Scott rubbed his aching eyes and tried to remember when orange juice tasted good. Beer was his beverage of choice, the fuel his personal mechanic recommended for a race car that idled, stopped and started, gummed up on city miles. After four beers, Scott was on the Autobahn, blasting through carbon.

"I was talking to Bert out back." Upstairs, Scott's father was talking about their neighbour. "He's going in for the triple next week. He's scared to death."

"No wonder," his mother said.

"It's his own fault! He stayed up half the night watching the medical channel on TV. They showed an open-heart surgery, the entire five-hour procedure. Bert watched them saw through the guy's chest and then stop his heart. So now Bert's convinced *his* heart won't restart, that it doesn't have enough juice."

"Madeleine shouldn't have let him watch it."

Scott turned to the General classes, a depository for have-nots plucked from the university stream and forced into a pool of non-academic math and typing. Mickey Church had slicked-back hair and the good sense to know what was happening to him in life.

"Mickey's activities are girls, fighting, and drinking. His pet peeves are Communists, stuck-up girls, and phonies. He plans to join the Army."

Scott remembered seeing Mickey running in the early morning in two-stripe sneakers, driven by red devils and conceited girls like Cindy.

Verna Johnson looked sadly middle-aged, with bleached hair pulled into a cascade of artificial ringlets. *"Verna detests long-haired boys, enjoys working at the Best Boy, going out with a certain Ralph. She plans to be an efficient secretary and to be happily married."*

Scott had no quote, just a picture in back with the retakes. Under his name, an officious editor had inserted the word "Paddler," as if there was nothing more to say.

Scott thought about paddling, about how the pain of failure had been eased by quitting, how it had banished that loss to another life. Gradually, after the thrill of that absolute gesture had faded, the pain returned, a malaise that greeted him each morning with a wave of doubts and what-ifs.

Scott closed the yearbook and dug deeper in the box. He found a birthday card from his parents when he turned twenty-one, a school ring he had never worn, a driver's licence, and a coaster from a strip club that sold Harvey Wall-bangers.

He lifted out a postcard with a crack down the middle and a pinhole near the top where it had been posted on a bulletin board. He studied the picture: a bleak sunset over a snowy field of frozen firs. Everything was blue, from the gelid snow to the sky. There was an intense feeling of cold, emptiness, and isolation; it was the kind of place where you could freeze to death and never be found. Curious, he turned the card over. Where had it come from? Four stamps and a Par Avion Luft-post sticker. Then in the upper left corner:

> *Vinterstemning*
> *Winter in Norway*
> *Winter in Norwegen*
> *L'hiver en Norvège*

Scott thought about Marcel and Thor, and in the frozen firs, he saw double-coated cats, muscular felines with dense undercoats and almond-shaped eyes, *skogkatts*. He saw an old lady and a disabled man celebrating life with a zeal that he envied.

> *Dec. 27, 1972*
> *Dear Scott:*
> *Skiing is great over here by Nova Scotia standards but it is the mildest winter since 1936.*
> *Hope you are staying in shape. I know I am. The food is delightful and the people are cool. See you on the lake this summer. Watch out for those*

crazy shells. Remember, we're like lobsters, always
scurrying backwards.

Your pal, Karen

Karen? He scanned the files in his brain. Was it the rower, the blonde with the crooked smile, the girl who had shared the storm with him one morning on the lake? Had she really gone to Norway to cross-country ski that long ago and sent him a postcard? How could he have filed this away and lost it?

Scott descended the stairs, clutching the cracked postcard from Norway. "Look." He handed it to his mother and waited.

"Karen Burns," she said.

"Yeah?" Scott sounded like he expected more.

"You know, that blonde girl whose parents lived on Rigby. She started cross-country skiing one winter to train for rowing. I saw her mother in the grocery store, and she wasn't very happy about it. She was always afraid of avalanches, she said. It was just something she couldn't get over."

"Uh-huh?"

"I always thought Karen liked you. She moved to Australia, didn't she?"

"I dunno."

"Well, she was *your* friend," his father snapped.

"I don't remember."

"Maybe you were abducted by aliens," Rusty suggested, "and they performed ghastly experiments on your brain. It's on all the talk shows now. If you're having problems, and I guess complete memory loss would qualify as a problem, you may have been abducted. You don't have to blame your poor old parents any more."

Scott sat down and bit into an apple. It tasted good, like real food, like something he should eat more often. He felt the vitamins coursing through his body and wondered, was his take on life this skewed?

"When I was young, I had a best friend named Celine," his mother said. "We were as inseparable as twins. One night, we were at a dance, and a girl walked by, and Celine said, 'She shouldn't wear that dress; she's too short.' And I said, 'What do you mean, Celine? She's taller than you.' And Celine said, 'No she's not. You and I are the same height.' I made her stand in front of a window so she could see our reflections. I was four inches taller, but all that time, she thought of herself as a tall person."

Scott finished his apple.

"Sometimes, it's all in your own mind."

Maybe it wasn't all physiology and fate, Scott allowed in a blasphemous admission. Maybe the chances had been there all along, and he just wasn't man enough to take them. Scott's decision to quit had been his alone. He had not been forced out by injury or money; he was not one of the walking wounded who'd been shafted by a committee or a coach. Scott had not been like Taylor, who had, on a hunch, driven to another lake one day, a secluded spot with a wharf and a motor boat, and seen his coach, the man who had trained him for five years, the man who had written his program and critiqued his style, explaining, stroke by stroke, metre by metre, to a young new star exactly how to beat him.

Maybe, just maybe, there was more to life than going fast.

Riiing. The phone was ringing, but Ownie was not in the mood for conversation. The caller was probably a client ordering a cake, or a telemarketer, or, God forbid, Tanner the promoter nagging him about LeBlanc and a fight that Ownie hoped would never happen. *Riiing.*

Right now, Girlie's boy, Hansel, would take LeBlanc apart like a Lego village, piece by plastic piece. Hansel even had a new name, the Maroon Harpoon, and fresh duds, all in shades of crimson. Even without the threat of Hansel, Tanner was wearing thin for Ownie. Forty years of his crap was plenty, the trainer decided: that drugging story he'd made up, Louie's ring disaster with Verne, and now Tanner saying he's found out he's adopted and expecting people to care.

"What difference does it make at your age?" Ownie had asked him. "Everyone connected to you is dead and you've got one foot in the grave yourself."

"I's got to know, you."

"If you got to know, you got to know."

Tanner headed back to Tancook Island like the Maroons drawn to Sierra Leone, looking for his roots in a compost of sauerkraut and schooners. "There's only two-hundred people on the Island, half of them never been past Halifax," Ownie noted, "so it shouldn't take long."

Riiing. Riiing.

Tanner started going door to door and they stonewalled him, the way those old fishermen do. "No, son, I can't help you." "No. Don't try pullin' my mouth." The truth had been covered up, Tanner said, painted black as a rum-runner slipping through fog. Finally, he found an old woman who said she'd known his father. "He was a Portuguese sailor named Rui, a little fella with hair like a French poodle and one gold tooth. He had eyes like a husky dog: bright blue, which kinda put a spell on the women, with him being so dark. I remember him because I never seen them dog eyes before."

"So what are you going to do now?" Ownie had asked Tanner.

"I's got to live with it, that's all. I got to live with the God's truth."

A week later, Tanner showed up with a guitar that resembled an oversized banjo.

"What do you have there?" Ownie asked.

"It's Portuguese; I'm learning to sing a *fado*."

"A what?"

"It's a sad eerie ballad from the Old Country, you," he explained. "It's the song of Portuguese seamen missing their loved ones."

"I suppose you're the loved one."

Tanner shrugged.

"Hello." Ownie picked up the phone, worried that Hildred might miss a cake order and he would be blamed.

"Hiii, Ownie."

"Who's this?"

"You juss kiddin me." The caller laughed as though Ownie was pulling his leg. "There no way you wudden know mah voice."

Lord dyin' Jesus, strike me dead! Ownie swore he'd never have this conversation, not after how he'd been betrayed, disappointed, and forced to deal with Hildred and her mutilated cake.

"Ah juss wahn to see how you doin, you and your wife."

"After six months, you're wondering how I'm doing?"

"How you like ta come down for a lit'l visit, get sum sun and relax? Ahll pay all your 'spenses, ahll take care of ebbyting. A mon your age should do a lit'l trav'lin."

"I've done plenty of travelling."

Turmoil laughed. "Ah bet you nevah even ben to Flor'da?"

"I've got no need for mobile trailers or Mickey Mouse."

"Iss nice down here." And then without a pause, without giving Ownie time to nurse his grudges or listen to reason, it was done. "Ahll have mah secretary send you a ticket. Dohn you worry 'bout nothin. We got a fight comin up, a big one. You'll see. Iss big."

Ownie was on a stopover in Toronto. A tanned woman in a Club Med T-shirt was handing out tickets to bleary travellers who stumbled through the glass doors, which opened slowly, allowing the wind to dart inside.

Ownie watched a short man in an Aussie outback hat take a timorous step across the salt-stained airport floor. He introduced himself to another lone traveller, who said his name was Bruce. Together, they approached the woman for their tickets.

Both men looked uneasy, but their panic level visibly dropped the more they talked. "No waaay! Garnet Rogers, I looove him!" They marvelled at every inane detail, blowing them up until they formed a collective armour against the social dangers that lay ahead.

"Blue Jays?"

"My mother was born in Toronto!"

Both guys were what Ownie would call debutantes, single dudes in their thirties. Gary, the first guy, was a roofer from the Ottawa Valley, it was revealed during introductions, and Bruce was a postie with environmental illness. Both men were, they admitted awkwardly, making their first trip to Club Med, a hedonistic resort that they believed would change the course of their lives.

"My foreman warned me," said Gary, who was short even in the outback hat. "Don't go on the Wednesday picnic unless you like to strip naked."

"Oh, that's good to know," said Bruce, the postie, who was bald.

Everything was going fine, Ownie noticed, until Gary started asking questions about passports — he didn't have one — and Bruce decided, in the blink of an eye — to cut him loose. "I'm going to try this line," Bruce snapped as though they were no longer friends. "It's shorter."

Gary started to blink, and Ownie felt sorry for the roofer, who wasn't much taller than O'Riley's brother, Larry, who had permanently joined the land of the little people. Nothing good would ever come of Larry's situation, Ownie decided. A while back, Larry had heard about the Anna McGoldrick tour of Ireland from Mrs. Carmichael down at the church. On the spot, Larry decided that he had to go, him being a leprechaun and Anna being a major Irish singer. Mrs. Carmichael, who should've known that Larry had no way of getting his hands on three grand, had talked it up good, with Galway Bay, the Blarney Stone, and the medieval banquet. So Larry robbed the priest, and now, O'Riley, his brother, can't even show his face in church.

Ownie sympathized with O'Riley, knowing what it was like to have a brother who got under your skin. Every few months, Butch got his shit going. "The old man liked you best, and here I was a ten-round fighter and you were nothing!" Or throwing up the fact that Ownie had joined the navy without him, ignoring the fact that he was twelve years old at the time. And now, his latest schtick: "I'd tell that two-faced bastard to kiss my ass before I'd go to Florida with him."

Ownie touched his passport and the one-way ticket that Turmoil had sent him. They had six weeks to go before a twelve-round fight in Vegas with Antonio Stokes, a real talent with a right that could crack cement. At six-three and 235 pounds, Stokes was 30-1-0 with twenty-five KOs, good enough to generate talk of TV rights and a step into the million-dollar circle.

The winner was promised a date with Roy Newton, the WBC champ.

Ownie had seen the tapes of Stokes, a class above Turmoil's last opponent. Even still, he did not know what to expect. With Turmoil, it was all in his head, a place inhabited by a multitude of characters who could change everything.

Ownie knew why Turmoil had called him. In his last fight, he had two Civil War veterans working his corner, and in between rounds, you could hear them on the tape, slow, and confused as slaughterhouse pigs. One kept saying, "Give him watuh, giiive him watuh," but no one was doing a thing. The other mumbled, "Do the same thang, boy, do the same thang."

Nobody was wiping Turmoil's face or giving him hope. In round four, Turmoil returned to his corner, tired and stung, and found one guy asleep. "Whass wrong with you, mon?" Turmoil's screams carried through the corner mike. "You crazeee?"

When you work the corner, Ownie knew, you have to give the fighter thirty seconds to suck in wind, to settle him down, and then give him one thing to concentrate on, one thing only. "Move to your right. Step up the pace." You can't overload it, Ownie had learned, you can't go playing to the mikes. You have to keep it as simple as mopping a floor. Baxter, Ownie mumbled to himself, that was the name of the old corner man on the tape. Ownie had met him twenty years ago when he was already ninety.

Arms crossed, a surly flight attendant guarded the plane's doorway. Down the aisle, Ownie saw a man fumbling with a cardboard box. His hair stood up like it had been dipped in glue and his clothes were Eastern Bloc black. The attendant stormed toward him.

"What's in it?" she demanded.

"A breadmaker," replied the man, as though he always travelled with small appliances. The attendant rolled her eyes and shoved in the box.

All around Ownie, doughy people were stuffing heavy coats into bins, slamming the door on winter, coughing and hacking up bronchial phlegm. Then, strangely mute, they settled into their seats, hope tucked under their tongues like a key, eyes fixed on escape.

"Excuse me." A man climbed over Ownie, then fussed with the overhead light.

"May I have a pillow?" he asked the cranky attendant.

"You'll have to wait," she snapped without a glance in his direction.

Hours later, the man — his name was Paul — pointed to an egg that had fused with his plate. "This was in the microwave too long," he pronounced. "We should write a letter, you know." Some time after takeoff, Paul had appointed himself row spokesman for Ownie and the woman in the middle seat, who never spoke, just shrugged. "It's deregulation." Paul pointed at the threadbare carpets and stained upholstery as evidence.

While Paul fussed, two divorcees across the aisle were drinking margaritas, celebrating US airspace with toasts to Jimmy Buffet and the sun gods. Both were wearing low-cut T-shirts, push-up bras, and tiny gold chains.

Paul had peculiar eyes, Ownie noticed, that made him look as though he was deep in prayer or the middle of a convulsion. Never at a loss for words, he was a lawyer from Bathurst, he explained, a late bloomer admitted to the bar after a few indecisive years.

"Are you going to eat this?" Paul asked, eying the woman's untouched roll.

"No," she mumbled. "You can have it."

Taking a bite of the roll, he washed it down with a sip of his double rum, his third drink, even though he had made it clear that he was far from satisfied with the service. When he'd asked for a beer glass and the attendant told him she didn't have any, he'd sighed in exasperation, "See, deregulation!"

"Are you going to play golf?" Paul asked the woman, who wasn't in the mood for conversation. "Do you have hole-in-one insurance?"

"Pardon me?" She frowned.

"Insurance in case you get a hole in one. In most of these clubs, you have to buy the whole clubhouse a round of drinks if you get one. It could set you back a couple of grand, you know. That's a lot of money."

"I didn't know that."

"You should check it out." Paul sipped his rum again, secure that he had made contact, one of those people who developed lifelong friendships on five-hour flights. Ownie opened his eyes, refreshed from his nap.

"My biggest regret is that my mother died before I could pay her back." After two more rums, Paul was as soppy as a bread pudding.

Ownie had heard the whole story by now: how the father died when Paul was eight, leaving seven kids and a widow's pension. Five became teachers, and Paul, after drifting, had landed in law. Ownie didn't mind listening because it kept his mind off Baxter, the old corner man, whose face kept popping up, confused and sleepy, with hair like cumulus clouds. Ownie wondered if Baxter felt bad about the snooze or if it had all just drifted by like the clouds.

"Seeing how you all turned out was probably good enough for her," said Ownie, alone with Paul while the woman was in the washroom changing into summer clothes.

"I know, but she worked so hard." Paul eased his anguish

with another drink. "She never thought of herself. No, no, all of her energy went to us or to St. Pius. She was a self-taught expert on nun's habits." He raised his brows for emphasis.

"Is that right?"

"Oh yes, she made close to fifty different habits, all to fit on a Barbie doll. They had a display once of all her dolls and habits in the church basement. All of the priests from the diocese were there, and one man came all the way from Shediac."

"That's a fair piece," Ownie conceded. He'd never seen a nun shaped like Barbie, and he'd seen a few nuns in his day. When Ownie was a boy, his school put out a breakfast for the hungriest kids. An old nun would walk into the classroom like a death-camp guard, searching for starvation and signs of rickets. Never once did she pick him. She passed him by like his stomach wasn't growling and his head wasn't aching so bad that he couldn't see the page. Too healthy, she decided. Healthy. Lord jumpin' Jesus! Forgive me for swearing. How can you be healthy when you have no food, when the last thing you ate was a bowl of cabbage soup on Friday? Never once, not until Lucy Miller was home in bed, feet wrapped in fish to bring down the fever that eventually left her deaf. "Okay, Ownie, this morning you will go in Lucy's place." Before the nun could change her mind, Ownie jumped from his chair and joined the line of sickly wretches. Don't change your mind, he tried to get inside the old nun's head. That command drove him all the way to the basement, where the nuns had laid out twenty glasses of milk and three stacks of bread. While the others lined up, humble, Ownie marched to the table and grabbed the first glass. Gulp. Down in one swallow. Then another. Gulp. The nuns were yelling, but he didn't hear them. Beating his back with a wooden ruler as he reached for more, but he didn't stop. He didn't stop until he'd finished five glasses, ending his only trip to the breakfast basement.

"That was probably the proudest day of her life," recalled Paul. "Christmas would be coming, and you'd say, 'What would you like, Mama?' And she would say: 'A Barbie,' like that would make her the happiest woman in the world. And what could you do?" Paul shrugged. "They were her lifework." He wiped a tear. "It had to be a Barbie, that's all she asked. They're made of a thicker, more rubbery vinyl than the cheap dolls, and they're exactly eleven and a half inches tall. Skipper and Skooter, they are no good, they are too small, and Ken, Ken he is one foot. Not that Mama would want a Ken."

Paul closed his eyes, and Ownie thought the lawyer was asleep, dreaming of Ken or Barbie. "I told my . . ." Paul sprang to life, and Ownie jumped in shock. "I told my sister Genevieve that I will find a home for those dolls and their habits where everyone can see them. That will be my homage to Mama. That is the least I can do after all she did for us."

48

Ownie folded his jacket and stood on the curb, soaking up the sun. He watched a porter heaving bags onto a metal cart, her stringy hair drooping under a hat that could have belonged to a 1950s sea captain. On one wrist, she had a skittish tattoo that looked like a panther.

"You have a nice stay." Paul squeezed Ownie's arm.

"Yeah." Ownie was still getting his bearings after the lengthy flight. "And good luck with those dolls. It sounds like they're in the right hands."

"They are." Paul smiled a drunken smile that melted, like old memories, into melancholy. "It is not a big price to pay."

A pink Cadillac, as thick and smooth as a hotel Jacuzzi, stopped to deposit a woman in golf gear, raising the ire of an airport cop, who shouted angrily: "Move, move!" As the car eased away, Ownie saw the bumper sticker, WE DON'T CARE HOW YOU DO IT UP NORTH.

Palm trees lined the hazy, hibiscus-filled parking lot. The air was so dense and fragrant that it felt as if there were a shampooed poodle sitting on his chest, making it difficult to breathe. Ownie tied his raincoat in a knot as a couple with a stroller, a car seat, and two squirming kids tumbled over themselves. The porter was one step behind.

A topless sports car swerved into the curb, driven by a young man in sunglasses, with Turmoil unmistakably, at his side.

"You hab a good trip?" Turmoil asked, one arm outside the car.

"It was all right." Ownie picked up his bag.

"They treat you rite?" Turmoil asked, and Ownie shrugged. "They bedda or they have to deal widt me."

In a plain white T-shirt, Turmoil's chest looked as expansive as a home-movie screen, a memory bank of birthday parties, freak storms, and Christmas mornings. Is he bigger, Ownie wondered, or just sun-darkened and more in tune with his surroundings?

Ownie was not surprised to see that Turmoil, who ate a near-perfect diet of vegetables and low-fat protein, looked fight-ready. Unlike Johnny, who bloated up between fights, Turmoil had no flab to drop. Ownie looked at Turmoil's arm. The bicep was solid, approaching, without weights, without juice, the twenty-inch gold standard that a Mr. America had set decades ago, and that bodybuilders pursued with a regimen of barbell curls, prone curls, and incline curls. And yet, Turmoil's arm, despite its size, looked loose and mobile, with the range of motion of a baseball shortstop and the reflexes to snare a line drive most humans couldn't see. Ownie felt encouraged.

The driver hopped out, running one hand through wavy hair that was brushed back to his shoulders. He was wearing a Hot Tuna T-shirt and a leather anklet beneath baggy shorts.

"This is Greg," said Turmoil, nodding at the driver and ignoring the incensed waves of the airport cop, who seemed intent on moving everyone along. "He goin to drive us to mah place."

Ownie settled in the back seat and folded his hands. Beating down on his pale skin, the sun felt like a poultice that could soak up winter's poisons. He looked around him and saw flowers everywhere: geraniums and tiger lilies that made him feel recharged. "Nice to meet you, Greg," Ownie said. "Are you from here?"

Greg flashed a bright smile amplified by his tan and then lifted his glasses off a pair of kryptonite eyes. On his teeth, Ownie noticed with surprise, were multi-coloured braces, orange, purple, and green. "Yeah, I met Turmoil at the beach, and we've been hangin'."

"Greg, he thinkin of bein a sports trainah someday." Turmoil flipped the information over his shoulder.

"Is that right?" Greg, Ownie noticed in the rear-view mirror, looked surprised.

They cruised down a four-lane highway past budget car rentals, gas stations, and convenience stores that stayed open all night. A preppy in cut-offs was sitting roadside with a sign that said, STRANDED, WILL WORK, while a clock shaped like an orange gave the temperature at ninety-one degrees Fahrenheit.

"Is it cold up there in Nova Scotia?" Greg grinned.

"Not bad." Ownie shrugged his reply. "About ten below when I left."

"I guess that's why everyone plays so much hockey." Greg reminded Ownie of a character in a surfer movie, either that or a pickpocket. Ownie wondered if he had a job or a family.

"Yeah, it probably has some bearing on it."

Ownie squinted; he'd expected his eyes to adapt to the sunlight, to filter out the unfamiliar rays. Instead, everything looked overexposed, as though he was watching a cheap Canadian movie shot on video, one of those films they showed on Friday nights, set in Legion halls or Alberta hockey rinks, like you hadn't had enough of jerkwater joints. The actors had bad hairdos and uncapped teeth; they wore plaid shirts or Mountie uniforms and spoke dialogue you could never believe.

"Ah was profesh'nul hockee player in Can'da," Turmoil

announced. "Ver-ver good player, one of the bess. A poleese-mon, they call me."

"Yeah?" Greg grinned, intrigued.

"Ah spen a lot of time on the ice, breakin up fights, takin away the bad guys. Ah never had no gun or nuthin; iss differen up there. Ah got paid so much money, ah was losin it all to the taxmon." Turmoil shrugged as though the decision had been made for him.

"Wicked." Greg caught Ownie's eye in the mirror and asked, "Did you ever see him play?"

Ownie tried to get a look at Turmoil's eyes in the mirror, but they were now veiled by dark shades and a straight-ahead stare. "Oh, yeah, he was a dandy." Ownie's voice was dry as he wondered what lay ahead. "I've never seen a skater quite like him."

"Yeah?" Greg grinned. "This man slays me."

Ownie never knew when Turmoil was playing with people, forcing them into uncomfortable corners with no escape. Ownie was not a doctor, but Turmoil had seen one in Halifax at Champion's request, a sombre man who had listened to Turmoil's boasts and claims of future greatness, and told him in a grave voice: "Mr. Davies, I see delusions of grandeur." Turmoil had thrown back his head and laughed, "Ahm the smartest man in the world."

The highway ended at an intersection, and Greg turned onto a two-lane road that followed the coast, which felt like it had slipped into beachwear, sporty and bright. It had the mood of a permanent vacation. "Mah place two mile from here," Turmoil said. "Wait till you see it."

MISTEE'S CUSTOM-MADE BIKINIS. They drove by a string of condos, beach cottages, and stucco bungalows the colour of pastel candies. In between were motels filled with sand, pull-out beds, and bargain travellers who had been assured: CANADIAN, AMERICAN, AND BRITISH SPOKEN HERE.

"Do you play golf?" Ownie asked Greg as they drove by a miniature course built around Blackbeard's ship.

"Yeah, a bit."

"Did you ever get a hole-in-one?"

"No, dude, I'm not that good."

"Probably just as well."

The cheap motels were disappearing now, squeezed out by larger houses with wrought-iron fences, tennis courts, and oceanfront lots sliced, with the precision of a diamond cutter, from an old pineapple plantation. It was an area where you never saw trash or chipped paint, never smelled need, sealed off from the slums of America by a Plexiglas wall of money. Was this where Turmoil lived? Ownie wondered. Was he really this rich?

Greg slowed in front of a two-storey stucco house painted the colour of French vanilla ice cream, an expansive concoction with a three-car garage and a Mediterranean feel. He buzzed security and they turned up a driveway lined with flowers and trees that looked like inverted pineapples.

"So, what kind of shape are you in?" asked Ownie, who had already decided that the fighter's body looked ready.

"Good, but not the bes. Ah got to be the bes."

A stained-glass bird soared across the front door of the house.

"How much do you weigh?"

"Two fifty."

"What kind of shape is your head in?" That was the key question.

"Good but not the bes."

Behind the house, Turmoil pointed to a blue pool in the shape of a boxing glove, the kind of indulgence that made buyers believe that America really was the land of opportunity, a land of billionaires and gangsters with electrified walls. In the pool was an inflatable recliner holding an architectural magazine that had managed to stay dry.

"Very nice," shrugged Ownie.

Striped lawn chairs surrounded the pool while blue-and-white recliners shared drinks with the glass-topped tables. The sun was beating through the sweaty glass and the impotent umbrellas that had been set up for shade. Ownie saw two books and a pair of women's sandals, beige and made of leather, stuffed under one chair.

"How you like mah view?" Turmoil pointed past a screen of baked fronds. Ownie saw a bare-chested jogger teasing the tide, running just beyond its reach on compact sand that, when you got close enough, smelled like pickles. The rest of the beach was empty.

"Good." Ownie sounded indifferent.

"Goood?" Turmoil's voice shot up, offended.

A gull squawked like an unoiled swing.

"You know how much a view like this cost?"

"I don't care, man. I'm not here for the view."

"You can still 'preciate it."

"Why?" Ownie demanded as a powerboat churned along the horizon. *Thummm. Thumm. Thummm.* The ocean swished in and out gently; the waves sounded like someone turning the pages of a newspaper. With an ease that Ownie found disturbing, you could walk, with the same number of steps it took most people to collect their mail, to the water's edge, and you could walk back without seeing another person.

"You juss should."

"Man, you sound like I never seen an ocean before."

"This mah kitchen." The room was so big and bare that it felt indecent, with pale wood, rich ceramic tiles, and discreet appliances that blended into the decor.

Ownie nodded, and wondered if, when he spoke, he would hear an echo. "Very nice."

"This room biggah than mah whole place in Halifax."

Ownie glanced around the room, at the glass doors, the pot lights, and the runway counters that looked as though they had never seen food. He counted three spots for eating: a table, a built-in booth, and an island with an overhang of copper cookware.

Turmoil waved his hand through the air, slicing the sun that streamed in floor-to-ceiling windows and pooled on the floor. "Ah buy it foh cash afta mah lass fight. It come with a golf membership and ebbyting. Mah lawyer take care of it all."

In a room that smelled like New World and leisure, Ownie could feel no connection between his surroundings and his soul. To him, it was a hedonistic room that had never felt hunger, cold, or the pain of original sin, unsettling in its shameless celebration of today. It spoke a different language, it worshipped a different God than he did, and it all felt confusing.

"Sit down." Turmoil pointed to a stool.

"Sure." Ownie climbed up, feeling exposed. "Don't you have any real chairs?"

In the hallway, on the way to his room, Ownie stopped before a vivid four-foot painting that controlled the space. Studying the canvas, he saw a man who was, he believed, the biblical Noah. I wonder how he feels in all this emptiness, Ownie wondered, in a space without memory, a space devoid of bogs and ghosts with donkey carts. It was all light, it seemed, with too much air and freedom. Up close, Ownie saw zebras, hippos, and lions being led onboard a boat by Noah, who was, in this tableau, black. The water was ice blue, the trees lush. Ownie leaned over a carved sideboard for a better look, noting the monkeys and giraffes.

"I like that one too."

Ownie knew that Lorraine had joined Turmoil in Florida, but he was startled when he turned to see her face, which looked worn, as though the sun had bleached the good from her. Despite her weariness, she had the same poise he'd noticed when they'd first met in her vibrant house with the white piano.

"We've collected a lot of West Indies art and furniture." Her voice had the rotelike tones of a tour guide. "I've learned a lot about them. Each island has a unique style that developed over the centuries, styles influenced by the ruling country of the day: England, France, Holland." She smiled a wan smile. "In some cases, it changed a lot."

Ownie noticed that the house was neutral, an airy backdrop for the bright art and the dark wood furniture that seemed weighty. It had white marble, eighteen-foot ceilings, and towering windows that opened to the sky.

Everything that Turmoil had predicted: the money, the grand house, the investments, everything that had seemed improbable in the doctor's office in Halifax, had materialized. Did that mean that the doctor was wrong, Ownie asked himself, or could Turmoil still be crazy?

"I like this." Compelled to say something, Ownie pointed down the hall at a panelled screen that seemed to depict several stories unfolding at once, all in the Caribbean. In one corner of the screen, three chiefs were talking to explorers; in another, two men were riding elephants. People were fighting, a man was pulling a tiger by the tail. An awful lot was happening, Ownie decided, as though the artist was trying to express everything he felt, everything he believed in.

"Most of it is from the nineteenth century," Lorraine explained. "It's become quite valuable as people discover it."

"You mean it's dear?"

"Uh-huh. Some beds can cost twenty thousand dollars, some chairs three thousand." She stopped, self-conscious. "I'm not saying we paid that much."

Lorraine led Ownie up the stairs and into a guest bedroom with a balcony facing the swishing ocean. Standing in the doorway, she pointed at the heavy poster bed where Ownie would sleep that night. "Jamaican cabinetmakers often carved pineapple fronds on their headboards." She barely smiled. "This is very typical of their work."

Ownie wondered if Antonio Stokes, Turmoil's next opponent, the badass who had knocked out twenty-five stiffs, was lying in a poster bed and thinking about the ocean.

"Pretty fancy stuff."

49

It was fifteen miles and four tax brackets from Turmoil's beach mansion, in a rough clearing hacked from cypress and swamp. "Who's staying here?" Ownie eyed the corrugated metal trailer. A snarling lion painted in loud strokes stared back, wet teeth bared.

"Jus you 'n' me. Iss mah trainin camp."

The camp, as Turmoil called it, was a thirty-foot-long trailer with four high windows and two doors, all made of metal. Ownie walked to the back of the trailer, where he saw more furry-headed lions, fiercer than the first, big golden beasts with outstretched arms and claws as sharp as razors. "What's with the cats?"

"Ah bought it from a circus wummin." Turmoil pointed at the two-tone trailer, which reminded Ownie of an all-night card game. It was the only thing standing on the road, other than mossy trees and an ominous ALLIGATOR WARNING sign. "They spent wintah near here."

"Yeah?"

"Sum'one got eaten by one of them lions, sum trainah name Carlo." Turmoil stared at Ownie, who refused to react to the story or their isolated lodgings. "The wummin said she cudden stahn to look at this place no mohr. Ah tell her that them lions bring me luck, they cahn hurt me, becuz ahm as pow'ful as them."

Ownie ignored the last comment. Miles from the ocean

and Turmoil's indulgent house, his surroundings felt too hot; the air was funny. Ownie couldn't get it into his gut; it stopped short in his chest like a piece of steak caught in his windpipe. Out here, the past had not been erased for a shiny vision of American affluence; out here you could imagine homesteaders poling through swamps, fighting mosquitoes thick enough to kill cows, living in palmetto shacks without schools or doctors. You could imagine wildcats and homicidal hurricanes. Ownie wondered why he'd felt ambivalent about Turmoil's pleasure-seeking house when this was the other option.

"Ohhh, mon." Turmoil sounded disappointed, as though Ownie was ruining something special. "You prob'ly dohn even like lions."

"Oh, I love them," said Ownie, who was not going to get tricked into a ridiculous argument. "They're my favourite wild animal. When I was in South Africa with Tommy Coogan, we had one staying in our hotel." Ownie paused, picturing the beast. "He was so nice and friendly, he used to deliver newspapers in the morning. He'd take them around to the rooms."

"Yeaaah?"

"Oh, yes. He was a lovely big lion. Kumba, they called him."

As Turmoil climbed the three metal steps, the trailer sagged like a limp handshake. He opened a door and they stepped directly into the kitchen. It was a small room with indoor-outdoor carpet, a two-burner range, and the feeling that someone had left in a hurry. Turmoil cranked open a window — the air was hot enough to melt butter — and dropped his groceries on an orange Arborite counter.

Training camps were a mixed bag, Ownie reminded himself. Marciano, probably the most disciplined heavyweight ever, used to hole up like a Mexican bandit months before a fight, staying clear of everyone, working on his mind, his body, his will. Ali couldn't stand them. The charismatic champ needed people. Joe Frazier was somewhere in between; he did eight weeks in a camp before the Thrilla in Manila.

There was only so much they could do out here, Ownie decided, after a quick look around. Greg had driven them to the camp and left with Turmoil's car, promising to return in a couple of days. They would still have to go to town for sparring and ring work, all essential before a fight. Ownie wondered what kind of sparring partners Turmoil had lined up; he wondered where the gym was located.

"What happened to this trainer, this Carlos?" Ownie tried to sound casual.

"Oh, the lion, it get Carlo by the neck and chew his head rite off. Carlo's wife, she try to stop him but the lion wohn let go. Carlo thought he know all about lions, but he didden know nuthin at all."

Turmoil offered this explanation as he led Ownie down a snug hallway, his vast shoulders brushing the walls. The trailer seemed forlorn, Ownie decided, like a family shattered by divorce, saddled with mixed memories and untrustworthy things. It had a sadness that Ownie found unsettling.

"What happened here?" Ownie asked when the hallway ended abruptly at a wall. The wall had clearly been added, he decided, and it looked artificial, like something that the murderer in a TV cop show had erected to hide a body. What was behind it?

"Only paht of this place is fo peeple." Turmoil tapped the gyprock. "The back half iss for the lions and their stuff."

"What stuff?"

"All kinds of stuff, a tramp'leen and a whole bunch of lion toys with teeth marks. Ahm keeping some of mah gear back there now."

After leaving his bag in the bedroom, Ownie returned to the centre of the trailer. The living room walls were covered with wood panelling painted to look like dark, irregular boulders. Trying to relax, Ownie climbed inside a hanging bamboo chair with a floral seat. He got out, lifted a newspaper from a smoked glass table, and climbed back in. He felt like a go-go dancer.

The news in the paper was depressing, he decided, a labourer had gunned down his pregnant wife because he suspected she was cheating; a senior citizen had shot a burglar dead. Ownie didn't like the idea of so many guns. In the old days, you had a chance in a street fight, but now you were done. Ownie stretched his legs, seeking the floor, and asked: "How many lions lived out back?"

"Ah dunno," Turmoil shouted from the kitchen. "Two, maybe three. They dohn need much room. Lions sleep twenty hours a day."

Ownie never knew when Turmoil was being straight or when he was bluffing. He turned the newspaper page to a story on Florida panthers, which were indigenous to the area. Scientists, who feared that the panthers were endangered, were trying to decide whether to crossbreed them with cougars to strengthen the line.

"You ever see one of those panthers?" Ownie leaned out of the basket and held up a picture of the sleek night predator taken through the bars of a cage. The story said there were only thirty to fifty left in the wilds of southern Florida, which made mating incestuous. As a result, scientists had noticed a crook in the panthers' tail and a cowlick on the back; they were finding heart defects and missing testicles.

"Oh yes, mon. Ah see them many many time. Som time ah see them out here in the nite in the woods. They dohn scare me. No, mon, not at all."

"Well, I wouldn't want to run into one."

"Ah wudden care."

Turmoil entered the living room and sat on a couch. Ownie kept reading, working his way through the story. If the scientists artificially introduced new blood, it said, the panthers might lose the traits that enabled them to survive in the swamps, but if they didn't, the cats might disappear.

"I had a cat once that could throw his voice," Ownie said. "He was a biter, an attack cat with black fur like patent leather. You'd sit on the couch and then you'd hear this *meeeooow* across the room. You'd figure it was safe, so you'd stretch your legs out, and that's when he'd get you. *Yeow!*" Ownie shook his leg wildly. "All the time he'd been hiding under the couch. I'd hate to think them panthers was the same."

"Ha ha," Turmoil scoffed. "Why you talkin 'bout ventri-liquist panthers? They cahnt throw their voice."

"You a cat expert all of a sudden?" Ownie asked. "You told me before you didn't know nothin' about cats."

An hour later, Ownie surveyed his bedroom, which was barely big enough for a cot and a night table. It had one window and a newspaper clipping taped to the wall. Ownie stood close and examined the clipping. It was a story about a trainer named Carlos, who must have been the same Carlo who was killed. The story was one of those stock pieces that small-town papers crank out for no real reason. Carlos was descended from a long line of circus performers, the article said. His family spoke four languages, including Russian, which was the mother tongue of his wife, an aerialist who had trained with the Moscow Circus School.

The story included a photo of Carlos surrounded by animals, some resting, some not. On the top rung of a wooden ladder was a polar bear, a squinty-eyed albino with a narrow head and a sooty nose, a cold-blooded carnivore disguised as a Gund. Underneath were four lions. CIRCUS CATS IN PURR-FECT FORM, said the cutline, which identified the mustachioed trainer in riding boots as Carlos Ramirez.

The lions were his favourites, admitted Carlos in the interview, even if they weren't as smart or as fast as the tigers.

He fed them horsemeat and eggs and never used whips. For a reward, Carlos gave the marmalade-coloured cats kisses. Only one in five could master the hard tricks, but Carlos kept them all because they were family, he said, they belonged.

Ownie studied the lions, naked as though they'd been shaved, everything pooled in the outsized paws and heads: the power, the danger, and the beauty. One animal stood out; her hair was electrified like Don King or a troll doll, giving her an unusual air. The air, Ownie decided, out of nothing more than instinct, of a killer.

Ownie could only imagine the stunned silence that would have followed Carlos's death. He had seen a man die in the ring and he knew the numbness that went with that. He knew what it was like when people would bring it up, people who didn't understand who you were or where you came from, and they would expect you to defend it or explain it, as though it had a logical explanation, as though you could tell them something they didn't already know. It was your world, in the same way that they had their world, it was what you did.

The trainer stripped to his T-shirt and underwear, he put his false teeth in a cup. Kneeling by his bed, he clasped his rosary while Turmoil rattled around in the kitchen. "Dear God, please watch out for me. I know I haven't always done the right thing in my life, but I'm tryin' and that's all I can do. Amen."

God doesn't make it easy, does He? Ownie sighed. He tests your faith every step of the way and sometimes you stumble. No wonder with some of the shots He throws. Imagine being eaten by a lion. Jesus! Ownie shuddered and wondered if Carlos had become overconfident, if he had overestimated his bond with the animals. Had he really, as Turmoil claimed, had his head chewed off?

Ownie suddenly felt tired, worn down by the strange surroundings and the troubles that life hurls at people. He could only imagine how different things might have been if Tommy's son hadn't died at the age of five from an allergic reaction to penicillin. Tommy lost everything that night: his heart, his fear, his reason to live. How do you get over something like that, something so cruel that it couldn't be real? Tommy started taking nerve pills, and his wife, Darlene, fell apart. "Why would God give you someone to love that much and then take him away?" Darlene sobbed. Who had an answer to that?

Ownie tried to talk Tommy out of fighting. There were nights when Ownie thought that Tommy wanted to be killed, walking into a chopper blade of blows, numb and wounded, offering himself up to a God who had already done the unthinkable. Just take me, you bastard, what more can you do? And him, in the corner as helpless as Carlos, patching up cuts that seemed inconsequential in a world that let little boys die.

"Maybe, God, I've wanted the wrong things. Maybe I'm after too much glory, too much fame." Ownie uttered the words, knowing, in his heart, that he and God were on closer terms than that, knowing that God accepted his need to prove himself, to use the skills he'd been given in place of others. God, despite everything else He did, was fair enough for that.

Ownie walked, as quietly as he could, to the bedroom door and inserted two plastic knives into the upper corners, two midway down. At least, he told himself, he would get a warning if a deformed panther broke through.

In the middle of a dream about red fields and Island tractors, the plastic knives shattered like icicles. Ownie sat up in his bed and blinked, not believing it had actually happened. Everything in the bedroom was black, except for a grey zone under the window where a murmur of light had entered.

Swishhh. Through the dark, he could feel something

dangerous, something still and malignant, breathing near his narrow cot. He strained his eyes, trying to break through the blackness, pushing so hard he saw cataract spots.

Creaaak! The floor buckled.

Panthers and lions rumbled in Ownie's brain, muscular thugs with switchblade claws and blackjack paws, low to the ground. Slowly, out of instinct, like a tourist touching his wallet, Ownie reached for a clock by his bed. On TV, he had seen a lion kill a wildebeest, biting the victim's neck until it smothered and then shredding the flesh like overdone pasta. What would it do to an old man with a clock?

I can't see nothin', he cursed as the thugs moved forward, closing in with night vision, cutting off his escapes. He heard his flimsy sheet rustle, his mattress creak, deafening signals that led to him. Were cats like bears, he wondered in his disbelieving state, were you supposed to run or not? He had seen a story about a man who'd been killed by a cougar. Afterwards, experts said he would have lived if he had run, or did they say *didn't* run? Ownie heard a cough. Holy Carlos Monzoon!

It wasn't a lion, it was human, and God knows what kind of lowlife lived in these parts: jammers, freaks, two-bit spiders who'd kill you for a buck, hepped-up kids taking orders from Satan! Maybe it was a hit man sent by Stokes, who didn't want to risk a payday that big.

And then a motion to his left.

I gotta make my move, Ownie told himself, I gotta go for the door. One more step, and they mean trouble. If they block me, I'll drive my head into their guts; I'll use this clock as a weapon. If they've got a gun, I'm dead. If not, I've got a chance.

The lowlife moved into the grey zone under the window, and Ownie could tell, from the form, it was just one person. I can take this sucker.

And then, in light so low that it barely registered, Ownie

saw the eyes: Turmoil's, as dull as a soap-stained car. "You bastard! Get the hell out of my room!"

"Ohhh mon," Turmoil moaned. "Whass wrong?"

"What's wrong?" Ownie shouted. "Turn on the goddamn light." When Turmoil hit the wall switch, Ownie held up the clock that read 3:15 a.m.

"It's the middle of the goddamn night and you're standin' in my room like the Tooth Fairy." Adrenalin shook Ownie's arms, his heart raced, but he tried to look defiant. He thought about all of the suspicions he'd had about Turmoil: the battles over rubdowns, the unprovoked attack on Suey, and then he wondered: how can I feel vindicated — how can I feel smart — when I put myself here? "Now get out!"

The seconds ticked by interminably until Turmoil yawned and announced: "Ah wahn to do sum roadwork."

"Roadwork?"

"My wind not as good as it shuhd be."

"You can run in the morning. It's pitch-black outside."

"No, mon, iss not."

Ownie needed time to figure out his next move. How do I argue, he asked himself, with the room shrinking and Turmoil filling up the doorway, sucking up the oxygen like a hydrogen bomb? "Get out until I get my clothes on." He'd think better with his teeth in.

50

They stood outside in the night. *Cawww*. The screech came from nowhere, and it felt like an aural switchblade ripping Ownie's flesh. "Holy Mary!" He jumped — *cawww* — as a multi-coloured bird emerged from the cover of a palm.

"How ya gonna do roadwork in this?" Ownie waved at the darkness, his heart racing like an overheated clunker with the choke stuck out. *Boom-boom-boom.* Slow it down — *boom-boom* — take it easy, he urged himself.

"You goin drive mah car," replied Turmoil. "You'll turn on the lights so ah can see."

"Car? What car? Greg took it."

Ownie looked at the heavens for guidance, but all that he saw was the moon, a luminous glass eye that unnerved him, an eerie Cyclops in a tie-dye sky. Even with the moon, the night was so dark that he could barely distinguish the trailer and the painted lions.

"Mah new car." Ownie followed Turmoil's finger and then spotted, against all reason, in a flat gravel opening, a hundred-thousand-dollar Jaguar sedan with a leaping cat on the hood. Where the hell did that come from? he wondered. How could it arrive here in the middle of the night without me knowing? The ground shifted beneath his feet.

"You know I haven't driven a car in thirty years," he argued.

"It dohn matter." Turmoil opened a car door.

"You know I've got no licence."

"You dohn neeed no licence. We juss go up this ole country

road." Turmoil gestured into the darkness past the ALLIGATOR WARNING sign. "There nobody on it. You juss put the lights on me and ah run. Underrrstannnd?"

Ownie looked unconvinced.

"Juss dohnt look afraid."

The dash felt foreign, with buttons, knobs, and new-fangled gizmos. The last car Ownie had purchased was a Packard, a broken-down heap that leaked oil and lost its steering just before Ownie crashed into a tree and suffered a concussion. After that, Hildred took the wheel, and Ownie drove a bicycle, which he came to enjoy so much that he never drove again.

"Christ," Ownie muttered. "If I ever get outta here . . ."

Settle down, he told himself, you're as edgy as a rummy on the cure. He turned the ignition and searched the controls for the headlights. *Urrr.* The leather-and-wood steering wheel tilted like a dentist's chair, up and down.

Ownie stared at the path carved by the headlights, trying not to think about Turmoil in his room, trying not to wonder what was happening. Shaking his arms loose, Turmoil started to run. In behind him, Ownie eased the maroon machine, pleased he could still drive after so many years on a bicycle. "Okay, buddy." He smiled despite himself. "This *is* a car."

This might work, he thought, as Turmoil picked up speed, sparring with trees and invisible goblins. If an alligator gets him, Ownie chuckled, then too goddamn bad. Some of those creatures were twelve feet long with armour-coated bodies and lock-cutting jaws. They were so fast that they could dart from a swamp, grab a cow, and vanish before you could say Bugs Bunny. If one got Turmoil, he'd sit here, in the middle of the night, with his shaking nerves and speeding heart, and he wouldn't move! Not a goddamn muscle.

A little extra roadwork never hurt anyone, Ownie decided irrationally, especially when you were fighting someone like Stokes, who was bound to go the distance.

Ownie checked the dash. The engine was so quiet that it didn't feel real, it was virtual reality gliding through the night. You could run the rack-and-pinion steering with a finger, he decided, you could trigger the brakes with a toe.

"Pick it up," he yelled out the window, empowered.

Turmoil turned and ran backwards just like Marciano used to do. For some reason that made Ownie feel better. As long as I don't run the bastard down, Ownie chuckled, as a Firebird appeared from nowhere like a swamp-dwelling alligator, hurtling down the road, spitting stones, all smoked windows and homicidal speed. Turmoil dove for the ditch, screaming as the car brushed his arm. "Pull over! Pull over *now!*"

Ownie hit the brakes with all of his weight and Turmoil charged over, panting. He ripped open the Jaguar door and fumbled for the dash. Ownie wondered what he was doing until he saw the black revolver in his hand. "Did you see the licence plate?" Turmoil demanded. "Did you?"

"Christ! I didn't even see the car."

51

Boomer had hired a new assistant, a substantial woman with wiry hair that threatened to consume her head, voracious hair that had to be set into submission. Garth didn't like her. It was the assistant's birthday and all of the secretaries were gathered around her desk in some sort of celebration.

"You can't be forty-five," one gushed.

"Nooo!" gasped another.

Garth shifted in his chair, impatient. He had been waiting ten minutes to see Boomer. He tried to ignore the assistant, who had just been given a cake and an oversized card, which she had to push back her hair to read.

"You can afford to eat it," he heard Carla say. "I wish I had your metabolism."

Forty-five was nothing, Garth decided. Age was only the enemy, he reasoned, if you let yourself slip. Garth had seen ace reporters lose their bearings with age, analyzing events they'd never been to, adrift on the raft of irrelevance, not even aware. Jock Smith was the best spot man he'd seen next to Mobley. Jock wrote the book on hard news, and when a DC-30 crashed, he stayed on the scene for four days while they pulled out bodies, a human teletype running open. Sledgehammer leads, tear-jerking sidebars so riveting the paper had to order an extra run. Garth's thoughts drifted off.

"My sister, Janine, is two years younger than I am, thirty-five," an accounting clerk named Billy announced. "Last month, on her birthday, someone planted fifty pink flamingos on her lawn with a sign HAPPY FIFTIETH, JANINE."

"Nooo?" A shocked chorus.

"It was probably her husband," someone snickered.

Garth was tired of waiting amid this bunch of cackling hens. Where the hell was Boomer? Here he was — the paper's managing editor — and he was wasting his time, time that could have been spent tracking down office thieves or, failing that, planning his model plane formation, a visual feast of colour and aeronautic history. In the old days, someone would have brought him a coffee.

Hey diddle diddle. Garth checked his watch, which confirmed that he'd been waiting for fifteen minutes. Carla said she'd heard bitching over Where Are They Now? but it was probably Smithers in Sports, since he did such a lousy job on the bike messenger story. He was nothing but a pain in the ass, that Smithers. Yesterday, Garth overheard him asking that reporter named Marcia to pick up a puck when she went to Prague.

"It's my honeymoon," Marcia had groaned.

"So what? Like you haven't done it before."

Garth would find a way to fix Smithers, who could probably, with a little planning, be nailed for sexual harassment. That Books editor, what's her name, was the new shop steward, and, according to Carla, she hated Smithers' guts.

"Good day," snapped Boomer.

"Good day." Finally, twenty minutes late.

Boomer had barely given Garth time to sit down. Garth was still mentally debating what to do with the olive drab British Sopwith Camel. Maybe, he decided, it would have to stay on the landing pad next to the black British Sopwith.

"There are going to be some changes," Boomer announced. Garth froze; he should have seen it coming, but with Boomer, the shrunken eyes were deceptive.

"Katherine Redgrave will be taking over your duties . . ."

For the good news, Garth knew, you went to lunch; for the bad you stayed in the office and took it like a man, and when you walked back into that newsroom, stunned and near tears, no longer worth a lousy twelve-buck lunch, wondering how it had happened, why it had to be you, everyone already knew.

"You will be given the title of senior editor. If that's not acceptable, there is early retirement." Boomer gave him a mean smirk. "That is *your* choice."

52

Ownie pulled the Jaguar into the wake of a Monte Carlo. He had to concentrate, here on this deathtrap, this four-lane freeway dotted with work crews.

In the passenger's seat, Turmoil was singing strange words that Ownie didn't know. Once, when they had met another man from the Islands, Turmoil claimed that they shared an underground language. "When the slaves arrive, they come from all ovah Afreeka speaking diffr'nt languages, so they invent their own, Tower of Babel, mon, eye-land-style."

Eyes fixed on the road, Ownie no longer knew what to believe. It was like looking at life and seeing ghost images, he decided, orange instead of blue, red instead of green. He refused to contemplate the dash, the revolver, or the homicidal Firebird near the camp.

Their maroon car and its alloy wheels drew a covetous stare from the MOTHER OF A CAPASKAT HONOUR STUDENT, who had no idea Ownie swore to himself, no idea. They were going to a restaurant for dinner. Turmoil said he couldn't drive because he had lost his licence for speeding; if caught, he could be deported. "What about me?" Ownie had shouted. "What the hell about me?"

"Pass this jalopy," Turmoil now ordered.

"Yeah, yeah, yeah." Ownie felt the Jaguar, supercharged to go from zero to one hundred in seven seconds, overtake a Jimmy that liked to DIVE NAKED. A spectral wave of heat shimmered from the highway. "I've got to phone my wife."

Turmoil's singing was getting on Ownie's nerves. He was already antsy enough stuck out in the woods, incommunicado, held hostage by Turmoil, the alligators, and a travel bag of doubts. He couldn't stop thinking about Carlos and his fatal betrayal. That morning, Ownie had found a stick outside the trailer, which he had stashed for protection under his bed near a framed picture of Carlos he had found in a drawer. The animal trainer had posed with a sinuous cat draped around his neck like a feather boa. In the newspaper story, Carlos told the reporter that he modelled his act on the masters of the Golden Era. He taught a tiger to ride an elephant — even though they were natural enemies — and he put his head in the mouth of a full-grown Bengal. Lions wore their mood on their faces, he explained with insight earned through the years, unlike poker-faced polar bears that could surprise you with their anger.

"We'll see." Turmoil didn't even shrug

"I haven't talked to her in a week."

Ownie had also promised Scott, the reporter, that he would phone him with periodic reports, but Scott had become, quite frankly, low on his list of priorities. Ownie still felt bad about what had happened to the man, but he had his own problems now. One night, before Turmoil had pulled up stakes and headed south, when things were still upbeat and encouraging, Ownie had arrived at the gym and found Tootsy wide-eyed.

"F-f-f-uckin' Turmoil," Tootsy stuttered. "He knocked out Scott."

"Whadya mean?" asked Ownie, confused.

"He tuh-tuh-told him he wanted to spar, and then he knocked him out."

"That crazy bastard," cursed Ownie.

When the heavyweight arrived back at the gym, Ownie confronted him. "What the hell did you do that for?" demanded Ownie. "That man has been good to us."

"Oh myyy." Turmoil smiled. "He a big strong white boy. He shuhd be able to tek it."

"Who you gonna knock out next?" Ownie demanded. "My wife?"

At least Scott was home in his own bed, Ownie figured, while he had not had a decent sleep in days, not since Turmoil had started chasing demons in the night, rattling the metal walls of the trailer like a windstorm, disturbing the ghost of Carlos. What was he doing? Ownie wondered. How could they be ready for Stokes if the man didn't sleep?

"We'll see." Turmoil stared out the window while conducting himself with swoops of his left arm that cut into Ownie's space.

Poor Carlos, Ownie thought, defending those lions. In the end, it was probably something stupid, a loud noise or a runaway horse, that spooked the cat and broke the bond that Carlos had established. Ownie knew that Carlos wouldn't go around the lions drinking; he was too much of a pro for that, and he certainly wouldn't hurt them on purpose. Carlos had given those animals everything he had, Ownie believed. Was it ever enough?

"No, I want to call her." Ownie tried to sound unshake-able.

"We'll see," Turmoil repeated. "Ah got lot of bisnis to tek care of."

Turmoil threw a Bible-sized hand in front of Ownie's face, just missing his nose.

"What the hell are you doin' that for?"

"Mon, ah got ebbyting." Turmoil was defiant. "Ah got ebbyting and ebbyone fooled. Ah dohn need nuthin." Out went the arm again.

"I am telling you, that is ignorant. Stop it."

THE PROSTATE PROFESSIONALS. RETINA VILLAGE. They were driving down a medical strip, a supermarket of surgeons and

318

quacks competing for business. I Think I'm Having a Heart Attack, a billboard screamed at Ownie. The Pain Is Killing Me, a competitor yelled back.

"You dohn know nuthin, mon. Ah know all about you, but you are mah trainah and you dohn know nuthin."

Ownie stretched his legs for the floor pedals, the twelve-position seat was back too far, and the sun was in his eyes. Distracted, he swung in too close to a Buick, and his heart did a jig. "Make sure you tell me where this turn-off is."

"You dohn know nothin," Turmoil repeated the charge.

"I know all about guys like you." He tried to catch Turmoil's eye to show that he was serious, and when he turned back to the road, he saw two pasty sunbathers, stunned by their surroundings, wading into traffic with a manatee kite. Holy Sweet Jesus! Ownie twisted the leather wheel, avoiding the sunbathers but sending the car into a fishtail.

Bring her back. *Swiiish.*

That damn power steering! *Swiiish.*

"Jumpin' Joey Giardello!"

"What you doin?" Turmoil screamed. "You gohn crazee?"

Men Working. The car skimmed the side of a tar bucket and slammed into an orange pylon. Ownie clung to the wheel as the car grazed the curb, the pylon spiralling through the air, round and round, as though it had been shot from a circus cannon.

Still shaken, Ownie picked a fuchsia chair across from a deeply tanned man and his tiny tanned wife. The man — his name was Chad — was a motorcycle cop, he explained over the noisy restaurant decor, and a third-degree black belt. Bonnie — "She's not athletic" — was a banquet manager who had made their matching shirts. Without explaining the connection, Chad said they were friends of Turmoil.

Turmoil was sitting at the end of the table next to Lorraine and Greg, who had just arrived. All of the fighter's guests, two women and three men, were now seated for a meal that Turmoil had promised would be special.

Ownie studied the couple's matching shirts, which were maroon with a pattern of gold horse's heads. "The place I grew up on, Prince Edward Island, is horse crazy," he said after the introductions. "They have horses everywhere, tucked away like crazy uncles. If you look inside any little barn or shed, some place in the middle of nowhere, you're liable to find a horse."

"Really?" Bonnie smiled.

"Either a horse or a still."

She laughed, tickled by the thought of something so quaint. "We should go there sometime." Bonnie tapped Chad's arm, which seemed tense. Chad smiled a thin smile, as though he was almost tempted, almost weary of the scorching sun, almost tired of silencers and sawed-off guns.

"When cars first came out, they had them banned on the Island, on accounta the horses." Ownie sensed this was a safe topic. "People were afraid they'd replace them or spook them. You could get six months in jail or a five-hundred-dollar fine just for driving a car."

"Oh my!" Bonnie's eyes widened.

Chad, who had a scrub-brush moustache, nodded his approval. Ownie wondered if it was the idea of horses or jail that he liked. "Did you ever own horses, yourself?" asked Chad.

"Nah," Ownie scoffed. "We could barely afford a rabbit."

"Well, you can still love them." Bonnie smiled again, the nervous smile of a woman always trying to make things better.

"I grew up in Charlottetown." Enjoying company for the

first time in days, Ownie glanced at Turmoil, hoping he had noticed. "They call it a city, even though there's ball stadiums down here with more people. The main square was called Dizzy Block because people could go around it so fast that it made them dizzy."

"That's nice for a change," said Bonnie, who was wearing heavy foundation and dark lipstick. The look surprised Ownie, who thought everyone in Florida would look natural, ready for tennis or golf, like people who spent their days lying on the beach, noticing that when the tide crept out, it left the rippled footprint of an orthopedic sandal.

"I had a cousin in the country. Every summer, the old man would take us out there. He had this saucy little pacer named Limerick Lou that would nip at your ankles like a rooster. He liked rolling in the dirt and eating it. He was the sauciest little horse I ever saw."

Chad smiled. "There is nothing like horses."

Ownie studied the menu, which offered a tantalizing selection of stuffed flounder, crab cakes, gumbo, smoked mullet, grouper, pompano amandine, conch chowder, gator tail. Ravioli stuffed with shrimp. There was much to choose from, he decided, there were so many different flavours.

Poor old Limerick Lou — his mind flashed back to the horse — ended up as fox meat. Twenty bucks the farmer gave his cousin, twenty lousy bucks. Back then, he recalled, those bloody foxes were like Aztec gods, and the farmers would do anything to keep them happy even if it meant fertilizing the land with warm blood and lame horses. In those days, the stink of fox was like Chanel No. 5; they both smelled like money.

"My son, Coy, was all-state football," Chad announced abruptly. "A natural athlete." Bonnie turned to a window overlooking a marina scented with salt spray and orange blossoms. "I say that honestly, even if he was my boy."

Ownie glanced at Turmoil and yawned deliberately. You're

not rattling me with your "You don't know me" bullshit, he wanted to say. If you think you are going to shock me with an outrageous revelation, Ownie vowed, then you are wrong, because I have seen all the craziness this world has to offer.

"I worked my guts out with Coy."

Ownie nodded, giving Chad his due.

"I did everything possible and he did too. He had moves, speed, and a heart as big as Texas. In the end, the scouts said he was too short."

"No?" Ownie shook his head.

"He was five-foot-eight and one-ninety with a career total of fifteen one-hundred-yard games and forty-one TDs. He did the forty once in four point seven and I think there was a headwind. No, I *know* there was a headwind. All that, and they said he was too short."

"That's an awful shame."

"He could press four hundred pounds before breakfast. I know that because we did it together. Every time I'd add an extra ten pounds to the bar, he'd look at me and he'd say: 'Okay, Dad-Chad,' and he'd do it! I'd say 'How to beat, Coy-Boy.'" Chad choked up as though Coy-Boy had been sacrificed to the God of Spring, as though he'd been shot through the chest with arrows. "Just like that!"

"He would," Bonnie added as though it made a difference.

"Four hundred pounds ain't shabby," Ownie agreed.

"What can you do?" asked Chad, suggesting the futility of it all.

"Life ain't fair." Ownie looked around for a phone.

"I don't know if you ever noticed it." Chad swallowed his regrets and proceeded. "But all of the top athletes get their height from their mothers. It's her genes that determine it."

"Is that so?" Ownie figured Chad for five-eight tops.

"Oh yeah." Chad squeezed his hand white and blinked. He looks like the kind of cop who would rough you up a bit,

Ownie decided, clip you with a sapstick when your back was turned. His uncle Dew Drop spent three months in a Maine jug after a ram-pasture brawl, but luckily for him, the screws wanted boxing lessons. Some of the others guys weren't so fortunate.

"I've seen a number of NBA players with their mothers," explained Chad. "They are all tall women. Shaq O'Neal's mother is six-foot-one."

"But his father," Bonnie said timidly, "his *real* father, he's tall too. I saw him on TV when he was trying to get in touch with Shaq, but Shaq won't have anything to do with him."

Chad bit his roll with authority. "In *most* cases, it comes from the woman." Bonnie stared at her plate.

"Turmoil." Greg grinned after a few moments silence. "How tall is your mother?"

"Oh she a biiig wummin," said Turmoil, who had been admiring his reflection in a shell-crusted mirror. "She as big as me."

Chad nodded, vindicated.

Greg laughed sarcastically. "Not as big as you."

"Not as heavy!" Turmoil spat the word. "Ah didden say she as heavy as me. She has fine bones . . ." His voice trailed off. "More delikit."

"That's still pretty big."

"Why you arguing widt me? Why you so *basa basa*?"

Greg's head dropped and Ownie thought, now look what he's got going.

"Is she your mooma?" Turmoil demanded, his voice rising. "Maybee you come up on ah banana boat and ah dohn know it. Maybee you mah long loss brutha. Maybe you the mos wanted mon in the eye-lands and you got the M-16 in your car, juss waitin for trubble."

"Yes, sir?" Rescuing Greg, the waiter arrived and everyone became quiet.

323

Ownie examined his menu and decided that just for spite, he was going to order the most expensive items he could find, the conch chowder and the twenty-dollar ravioli. He'd never had conch that he knew of, but he'd earned it after days in that trailer.

Greg started the ordering. "I'll have —"

"White fish." Turmoil cut him off. "Ebbyone hab plain fish. Six. Fish is a healthy food."

Bonnie stared at the window and Chad squeezed his wrist.

53

Garth saw two PR men holding up the Press Club bar: a compulsive kisser who indiscriminately smacked both men and women and an alcoholic named Eric who, at some point every night, toppled off his stool.

They were paying court to the dragons, three fifty-ish women who smoked incessantly and stared down newcomers. Every year, there was a move to bar the PR men and the dragons, to limit Press Club membership to working media, but every year, the motion died as quickly as a moth. Garth moved by the flacks, who were shouting nonsense. For years, Jean had wanted him to leave the paper and get a job in PR, which she believed was glamorous and well-paying, relenting only when Garth became the ME with a salary that bought her dream house.

Eric, the alcoholic, was shouting now. "'It was a woman who drove me to drink. And you know, I never even thanked her.' That's W.C. Fields."

"How about this one?" the kisser countered. "'I have taken more out of alcohol than alcohol has taken out of me.' Winston Churchill."

"Ahhh, good old Winnie." Eric saluted Churchill, and the dragons chuckled.

Garth worked his way past frozen flash points on the Press Club walls — clippings from the Halifax Explosion, D-Day — past a petition to free journalists in South America, his head spinning like he'd stepped off a midway ride. He'd had a great idea for Where Are They Now?, a drummer who'd played with Wilf Carter before Montana Slim thrilled the world with his trademark echo yodel. The drummer had been in Halifax for bypass surgery, but why bother now? As senior editor, he was still on the payroll, but he was a ghost really, with no duties or clout.

"Maaame."

Garth ignored a man sitting at a piano, belting out show tunes not worthy of his attention.

Garth thought instead about Carter, whom he'd seen in 1950, the year the singer set an attendance record at the CNE. Boomer, that Upper Canadian bean-counter, that big-headed freak, wouldn't appreciate the magnitude of the story. He wouldn't know a legend if it bit him on the ass. He wouldn't know that Carter, a native of Hilford, Nova Scotia, had written more than five hundred songs.

He hadn't told Jean about the pay cut.

Garth tried to steady himself, to fight off the nausea that kept coming back. He stared down the length of the bar until his eyes settled on an older man with watery eyes. In his worn tweed jacket, the man looked like someone who'd been shipwrecked on the sea of self-destruction and crawled ashore, exhausted but saved. Protectively, as though she knew what he'd been though, a woman gripped his arm.

Hey diddle diddle. Christ, it was Frank Mobley, Garth realized, but the woman wasn't his wife. Maybe he was divorced from — what was her name — Garth searched his brain. Nancy! That's it, a nurse from New Brunswick. She'd probably had enough of Frank's antics, Garth decided, amazed to see his old colleague after so many years. He recalled, with a nostalgic chuckle, the year that the *Standard* had sent Frank to Providence to cover the New England governors and Eastern premiers, a vacation, since nothing ever happened at those things. Frank rented a black Caddie, stuck a Nova Scotia flag in the hood, and told security he was the lieutenant-governor. All week long, he drove around drinking Coors and waving out the window.

Garth looked at Mobley again. He *knew* it was him. Normally, he would let them approach him, given his former position, but on this day he needed to touch base with a time he understood, a time when the rules may have been harsh and arbitrary, but they were rules they both understood.

Up close now, Garth took a deep breath and exhaled: "Hi, Frank. Garth MacKenzie." Frank steadied himself and gave Garth a look that he could not place, a look that Frank must have acquired somewhere else.

After he left the paper, Frank had gone to the wire service as a lead writer, a gunslinger who handled election night returns. It was fast, pressure-packed work, like being a stock trader or a short-order cook. "Hatfield lost his seat," someone would yell, and Frank would crank out four paragraphs that would fit perfectly onto a typeset page, seamless and filled with facts. With twenty-nine leads in one night, it wasn't writing, it was a mental party trick, like memorizing objects on a plate, a trick that required concentration and the bladder of an elephant. Frank was a master.

Frank put down his Coke — Garth noticed that his hand had a tremor — and stepped forward. "Garth MacKenzie." Garth extended a hand. "Sparky."

He was thinking about wire guys who'd covered big stories, stories that had made their careers, and had no memory of the events, no anecdotes or telling asides. The stories had poured through them with such speed, such velocity, that nothing had time to attach itself to their brains. Mobley really was small, wasn't he, Garth decided, waiting for his response. And he looks so damn old with that grey hair and his nose streaked with blood vessels. Frank's cheekbones were rocky cliffs over washed-away flesh.

Frank took another step — he was too close now — their chests almost touching, the Coke exhaust burning Garth's face. "Don't you open your slimy mouth to me." Mobley poked Garth's chest, pushing him back. "You pathetic snitch, you Benedict Arnold." Garth stumbled, dizzy and defenseless.

"This is the bastard who gave our names to management when we tried to start a union," Mobley told the protective woman. "He got me fired."

The woman looked at Garth with such repulsion that he blinked. Stunned, Garth did not remember what Mobley was accusing him of. What act of betrayal? All of his life, he'd been driven by fear, the fear of losing his job, the fear of disappointing Jean, the fear of growing old. That fear had eaten away at his moral fibre like dry rot and left it flawed. When the chance came to assuage that fear, he simply took it. That's all.

After Garth had been given the news by Boomer, Carla cleared out his office. The following day, she helped move Katherine in. Unlike Garth, the new boss recognized Carla's degree in office administration, her three accounting courses. With Katherine, Carla decided, there would be no overbearing wife, no demeaning errands. There were things that Mr. Boomer should be aware of, Carla explained to Katherine, pulling out a spreadsheet with numbers and dates. "I've kept good records."

Katherine was on the phone now, engaged in a conversation that Carla could hear through the open door. "Yeah, I miss you too," she heard the ME sigh.

Carla adjusted her mail tray in an effort to appear busy. There was no one on the phone, Carla knew. There never had been, had there? No Dmitry, no worldly suitor, no glamorous escape from the daily stress. Maybe you just had to define *real* differently, decided Carla, recalling the catechism lessons of her childhood, the incontrovertible teachings of dour nuns who never asked why but knew that everyone needed *something* to get them through life.

Katherine hung up the phone. There were moments in life that are burned in your memory, moments more vivid than time should allow. Katherine recalled being at the top of a hill on her bicycle. She was ten. In the distance was a cluster of runners with numbers on their chests, organized, but unconcerned with speed, loping, straggling away from a clearing with balloons. As the runners drew closer, Katherine noticed that some were wearing masks of Winston Churchill and Beethoven, some carried signs: RUN FOR MENTAL ILLNESS.

She saw one man trotting up the hill, pulling a child's wagon. Shirt off, he looked exuberant, like someone who had avoided calamity or received unexpected news. Grinning, he seemed free of family obligations, a liberated man in shorts, smiling so hard that his face threatened to eject his dense glasses. A boy stumbled behind him, preternaturally subdued. Katherine recognized the boy as a classmate from her school, a boy she had never spoken to. And then in a moment that stayed with her, a moment that she replayed and analyzed and stored inside her brain, he waved. It was a wave that erased all distance: the wave of an old friend and a kindred spirit. It was as though he knew her and everything about her.

54

Don't Sign till You Get Me on the Line, the billboard screamed from the side of the highway. Martin Jeffers. Attorney at Law. 1-888-SUEFAST.

The road, filled with clamorous signs urging commuters to litigate, reminded Ownie of how far he was from home and how little he understood this place. It's Never Your Fault, Skip Williams, Personal Injury Specialist. 1-888-SKIPLAW. Se Habla Espanol. 24 Hours A Day.

At least, he told himself, Greg was driving, removing the risk of legal troubles of his own. Ownie was sitting in the back seat of the Jaguar, determined to stay calm. From the passenger's seat, Turmoil reached out and fingered Greg's hair, lifting a sun-bleached curl and turning it in the air. "You know ah used to be a hairstylist?" he boasted as Greg twitched in his Hard Rock Café T-shirt.

"Yeah, man?" Greg swallowed, not sure what to say.

"Ahll cut your hair some day," Turmoil declared. "Ahll fix it all up for you."

Ownie looked out the window. The houses were growing shabbier the farther they drove, with front yards yielding to discarded washers and crippled lawn chairs. A one-eared cat sat on an overturned Pepsi machine that had failed the taste test. How much farther? he wondered.

Chinese lanterns, orange and green, decorated the sagging porch of a shack. A man was attempting to drag a Honda 750 with a sissy bar through the front door. The man turned, and he looked, to Ownie, like a Hispanic werewolf in metamorphosis, with coarse hair creeping up his cheeks, gushing from his ears and nose. He had a tuft on his forehead and bestial eyes, blank and untouchable, eyes that could snap the spine of a rabbit or run a blade through your gut. Ownie shuddered.

It was another hot day, Ownie decided, heavy and close as a neoprene wetsuit. He saw a woman shuffle by in slippers followed by a man in a rubber cap. The man banged on the door of a defeated trailer, which had two Dobermans fenced in its yard. In the trailer's cracked driveway, a french fry wagon, once blue, smouldered.

"This the place." Turmoil pointed at the trailer. The grass was scorched, Ownie noticed, as though someone had spilled acid in the yard.

"How long you gonna be?" asked Ownie, anxious.

"Not long." Turmoil shrugged as though it didn't matter.

"Make it snappy." Ownie tried to sound offhand. "I don't like hanging around a dump like this."

Ten minutes later, Turmoil hopped back in the car without explaining the stop. Ownie was not about to ask; they were going to the gym, a place where he could get his bearings, and that was all that mattered.

After five kilometres, Greg parked the Jaguar on a dungy street. The sidewalk was covered with bottles, empty bags, and two bums who had set up housekeeping in a GE refrigerator box. The bums were sleeping. At the end of the block, Ownie saw a discount liquor store named Party Hearty, which offered guns for rent. Outside the store, appearing like an apparition through the squalour and haze, was a sapphire-blue Lincoln Town Car.

None of this matters, Ownie assured himself, knowing that once they reached the gym, he would know the ropes, he would speak the language. As they stepped over garbage, Greg tilted his head. "What's that noise?" he asked. They were almost in front of Party Hearty, which sold shot glasses and Elvis bar towels.

"What noise?" replied Ownie.

And then, he heard it — *thump, thump, thump* — coming from the back of the fully loaded Town Car. *Thump.* Up close, with a new-found interest in cars, he studied the machine, which seemed to have more legroom than a frigate. *Thump, thump.* There was a beat, a rhythm. Swinging a metal bat was a spindly boy who seemed as detached as an hourly labourer. *Thump, thump.* Hammering the car, wearing a T-shirt that said: SKATE OR BE STUPID.

Ownie saw a woman trudge by, observe the automotive carnage, and keep walking. WE'RE SPENDING OUR GRAND-CHILDREN'S INHERITANCE, boasted a sticker on the greedy car, now being punished, it seemed, for its shameless indolence.

Ownie wiped his face as they passed the boy, who didn't seem to care who saw him. It was so hot that Ownie believed his skin was melting. He wondered if the boy, when bored by the Town Car, would move on to the Jaguar. Turmoil didn't seem worried. "Here! This is it!" The fighter stopped at a low stucco structure shaped like a garage. Painted black were two front windows. The steel door was dented by knee-high buckles. There was no sign, Ownie noted, just a street number and a cross. "Here the gym," Turmoil announced, "where we be trainin."

The eyes of the Lord are in every place, beholding the evil and the good. Holy Bible. Proverbs Chap. 15, V. 3.

Inside, Ownie squeezed the heavy bag, lifted it, and took aim. *Pah. Pah.* The overhand left — his bailsman, the punch that got him out of more jams than a smart bribe — still had stuff. *Pah.* Testing the bag was the first thing you did in any new gym, instinctively, it was like bouncing on a motel bed after check-in.

Ownie surveyed the gym, which resembled a whitewashed service bay. Ownie liked to tell Hildred that one imaginary person, a failed set designer he named Barry, had decorated every gym on Earth for sixty years. Barry made everything look like a cliché, cut from cardboard. He had an ageless photo selection: the trainer with the mattress on his gut, Marciano holding his baby girl like Beauty and the Beast, the leopard on a chain. If it was an ethnic gym, he threw in some soul; for the whities, the good old shamrock.

This gym had five heavy bags, two rings, a Stairmaster, and biblical references that located it somewhere in the southern USA. GOD IS IN MY CORNER, one declared hopefully. JESUS IS MY SECOND. Two men with cigars were plopped in theatre seats. Over their heads, which were covered by hats, was an oil painting of a wiry old fighter named Boomerang posing in the crouch.

I HAVE FOUGHT A GOOD FIGHT, I HAVE FINISHED MY COURSE, I HAVE KEPT THE FAITH. HOLY BIBLE. 2 TIMOTHY CHAP. 4, V. 7.

Boomerang must have found religion, Ownie figured, since it was his gym and his likeness up there. His real name was Jackie McCready, but everyone called him the Boomerang because he always came back, through the Dirty Thirties and one hundred fights, the Flinty Flyweight with the granite right. Ownie studied the painting and decided it wasn't bad, except for the eyes.

Boomerang's son, Sonny, sauntered over wearing a Stars and Stripes ballcap and the added pressure of running the gym while his father was in hospital. Ownie sized up Sonny, who appeared oddly out of date, one of those people who'd look better in another decade, stepping off a potato boat or chasing Jimmy Cagney.

Sonny reminded Ownie of his old friend Ronnie Jackson.

When he and Ronnie were kids on the Island, fox farming was bigger than the Gold Rush. Business was so flush that farmers hired armed guards, and the Queen of England wore a silver-fox stole. A pair of breeders could bring in thirty grand, enough to build a mansion, a PEI plantation with a marble fireplace, central heating, and pillars. Fox Homes, they called them. In the spring, the rich farmers came to town, down to the tubercular shacks of the poor folk, and offered to rent your cat if she'd just had kittens. Ronnie decided to go for it, since his old man hadn't worked in months. "I'll bring her back in a week once the pups are fattened up," promised the farmer. After a week, Ronnie was missing his cat, out on that farm by herself. As Ronnie later discovered, one day, when the fox pups' eyes were opened and they were strong enough, the foxes turned on that poor mother cat and ripped her to shreds. The cat wouldn't fight because that wasn't her instinct, her instinct was to nurture. "I should never have let her go," Ronnie cried. "I killed my cat."

Anyway, Sonny reminded Ownie of Ronnie, a hard-luck case who had learned, early on, that people are like silver foxes. Even when you're trying to help, they can turn on you just like that and rip you apart.

With Turmoil in the dressing room, Ownie decided that he would rather talk to Sonny than Greg, who was useless. "Are you a veteran by any chance?" Ownie asked, noting the hat with the inscription: THESE COLORS DON'T RUN.

"Ah yes, sir." When Sonny spoke, he sounded crisp, unlike Ronnie, who was sawny, and said haych for *h*, chimley for chimney, and bodado for potato.

"So am I."

"Oh," said Sonny, softening. "What branch?"

"Navy."

Sonny nodded, which is when Ownie noticed the shiny pink skin, unnaturally smooth in places, like Silly Putty, and bumpy in others, ending with a stump where one thumb should have been.

"I joined up when I was sixteen," Ownie said. "I spent five years on boats. We used to make the run back and forth between Newfoundland and Derry."

"I was air force. Paratrooper."

"No picnic, I guess."

A fan blasted air from the corner and Sonny swallowed. He looked at Ownie, who noticed, with surprise, that his eyes were cock-eyed, just like the painting of Boomerang. Maybe, he told himself, he had sold the portrait artist short.

"No sir, it wasn't."

"Paratroopers got guts though."

A fighter with a flat top turned on a boom box and started dancing next to the preacher curls and presses. Ownie saw two guys arrive together, a featherweight named Julio from Brazil and a lightweight from San Juan, Puerto Rico. They both looked hard. Boomerang used to charge a buck for the show, but the audience was gone now, scared off by stabbings and drive-bys, so now the curious went to a safer part of Florida, to slick gyms with chrome and leather decor.

Sonny swallowed again and his hands clenched tight, as though he was holding something in, a snared mosquito or a heart full of hurt. "I got burned pretty badly." Slowly, he stuck out his arms. "Ahhh." Ownie pretended he hadn't noticed the pink skin, and Sonny choked up as though he couldn't bear to explain any more.

"I had a double-fractured skull," Ownie volunteered.

"Is that right?" Sonny's hands unclenched.

"I was unconscious for fourteen days."

A fighter in a prison-style jacket handed Sonny a key.

"How you doing, Earl?" asked Sonny.

"Everythang is everythang," Earl shrugged. His hair was

an exercise in crop rotation: a shaved fallow strip on the bottom, then a thin strip, followed by a rich, thicker one on top.

"I didn't remember nothin' about it," said Ownie as Earl shuffled off. "Then four years ago, they had a reunion for my ship in Halifax. I walked in and one of the guys looked at me funny and said, 'Tiger! It's Tiger!' I laughed. Nobody calls me that, but that's how he remembered me because of this." Ownie opened his shirt and exposed a droopy, faded tiger that made Sonny smile. He had his own tattoo — GOD IS MY JUMPMASTER — above the pink skin.

"Anyway, as it turns out, this guy was the medic who looked after me in sick bay," Ownie said. "He told me how they brought in a priest and anointed me for death." Ownie paused. "I never knew that."

"That's pretty serious."

"All I remembered was coming to. When I opened my eyes, it was like someone had stuck a knife through my forehead. I had to lie still for weeks; I couldn't move for fear of a blood clot. There was a guy in the bed next to me off a British ship who kept talking about how glad he was to be going home to see his family. Finally, they let him out, and he dropped dead the next day."

BLESSED BE HE THAT COMETH IN THE NAME OF THE LORD. HOLY BIBLE. PSALMS CHAP. 118, V. 26.

Ownie noticed a boy tapping a miniature bag, following step-by-step posters of THE LEFT JAB and THE LEFT HOOK taped to the wall. He was as skinny as a foal, all legs and arms, and he reminded Ownie of little Ricky back at Tootsy's.

"Hey, Peewee," Sonny said. "Come here." Sonny had a few words with the boy, who kept his head down to hide a missing tooth.

"He don't go to school?" Ownie asked.

"No, his mother don't send him. I figure he's not missing

much down here. Last week, some kid put rat poison in his teacher's coffee."

Ownie shook his head, knowing that some kids never got a break. When he was growing up, the Coolens had a little homeboy, a mentally handicapped son who couldn't get a job. Back then, there was nothing for them, no schools or workshops. They called them homeboys because they never left home. One day, this boy — his name was Murray, and he was as gentle as a lamb — wandered onto the railway tracks and got killed. The worst part was, Ownie always thought that the family was relieved he was gone, that the mother knew she wouldn't have to worry about how he'd live when she was dead.

"There he is, Washington." Sonny pointed to the door, which opened for a big man with reservoir eyes and a high forehead. Washington had a fade do with orange dreads on top, and these days he went for thirty bucks a round.

"He used to be good," Sonny confided. "Golden Gloves, the works. Then he got into the yah-yo too heavy. That finished him."

Ownie figured the man ran about six-three, two twenty, close enough to Stokes. "Is he the best we can get?"

"Yeah, he's worked with some good ones."

"Will he go hard?"

"Yeah, deep down he's still got something to prove. And you don't need to worry about him telling Stokes's camp nothing," Sonny added. "He don't have no head for the he-say-she-say. That boy can barely remember his name when he leaves here. You got to flip him a quarter once in a while so he don't forget."

55

"That's me." Ownie pulled out a photo of a young sailor with black hair.

"Great pipes," said Sonny.

Ownie shrugged and picked up a laundry bag. It was one day after the first sparring session with Washington, and they were sorting towels in the locker room, an echo chamber of heat and stink. GANGSTA RAP RULES was scrawled on a buckled door, then amended to GANGSTA RAP AND REEBOK RULE.

"My wife tells the kids that when she met me I was standing on a corner, sleeves rolled up, showing off my arms like Popeye." Ownie chuckled at the vanity of youth. "Look at me now."

"You don't look so bad."

"Compared to what: a corpse?"

Sonny smiled and handed back the picture.

"My wife was only seventeen when she met me. She came to town on a bus and the driver told her — I'm not kidding — whatever you do, don't get mixed up with one of those Flanagan boys. She got a job at a luncheonette and met me one week later."

They laughed, the only sane people in this whole screwy place.

"I had a nurse look after me when I got hurt," Sonny said softly, like a man who wasn't used to having people listen. "Sweet thing from Virginia, she held my head and told me not to look at my arms. When I got real scared, she sang to me, that James Taylor song, 'Sweet Baby James.' I always meant to write her and thank her for being so kind."

"You should," Ownie advised. "You'd never regret it."

Ownie counted a stack of ten towels, then another ten, relieved to be away from Turmoil, who had gone into town with Greg to meet his banker. Ownie put one towel inside a grey locker belonging to Billy (Pit Bull) Tait, who wasn't, he believed, doing the dog any favours, not with a face like a gravel pit. Washington had worked out well, Ownie decided; he was big enough and hard enough, even though they'd only gone four rounds.

"I never saw the medic until that reunion," said Ownie.

"Yeah?"

"I shouldn't tell you this, but . . ." — he thought for a minute — ". . . awww, it's kind of comical." Sonny, he figured, could stand a laugh at someone else's expense. "When I first came to in sick bay, he started talking, telling me how glad he was I'd made it. I appreciated what he'd been doing for me, and after a couple of days, we became good friends."

Sonny nodded.

"See, I still couldn't move my head." Ownie steadied his head with both hands. "I had to stare straight ahead; they were afraid of a hemorrhage. On the fourth day, he brought in pictures of him and his friends in a club in St. John's and held them in front of my face. Close, so no one else would see. They were all as naked as skinned rabbits. I just about died. Then he whispered, 'When you get out of here, Ownie, I'll take you there. We can all have a good time.' And there I was unable to move."

Sonny shook his head and laughed as they headed back into the gym.

"Did Boomerang write that?" Ownie asked, pointing to a framed prayer behind the ring.

The Boxer's Prayer
Oh Lord
Protect us from the low blow of crime, the
   sucker punch of drugs,
        the TKO of jealousy and greed.
Make us fair and honest in everything we do.
Moral heavyweights, true sportsmen, humble
   servants of you, O Lord.
Watch over us as we step into the ring of life.
Guide us through each round.

"Yeah," Sonny nodded. "He thinks he's a bit of a poet."

Ownie looked up, surprised. In the entrance, near the water cooler and a hamper of bloody towels, was a lanky young woman in jeans and a cotton shirt. It was strange to see a woman in here, he decided, especially one who didn't look like a hooker or a mule.

Like a deer waiting to cross the highway, she stood in the doorway and then darted across the gym. Everything about her was vertical, Ownie noted, from her stride to her teeth. She had a mane of shiny black hair that looked like it had just been released from braids, hair you wanted to reach out and squeeze just to feel it spring back. Brushed off her oval face, it was held in place by barrettes. Maybe she's with the government, Ownie thought, a health inspector or someone from the licence board. On the Stairmaster, a dog gawked.

"Are you Ownie Flanagan, sir?" She must be six feet, Ownie figured, but graceful as a wind chime. Her nose led to an explosion of teeth, and her voice was southern like lawn swings and lemonade. "I heard you could help me."

I AM THE ALMIGHTY GOD, WALK BEFORE ME AND BE THOU PERFECT. GENESIS CHAP. 17, V. 1.

All of a sudden Ownie had a funny feeling about the place, something that told him nothing good would ever come from

all of this, one of those feelings. The night before Ray Robinson fought Jimmy Doyle, the story went, he had a dream that he hit Doyle in the ring and Doyle died. It bothered Ray so much he went to the commission and said he couldn't fight because he'd had this dream. Ray said they brought in a priest or a minister who convinced him it was all right, and then he hit Doyle with a left, and Doyle died just the way Ray had seen it.

The woman was a member of the US basketball team, she said, and had met Turmoil in New York. She was studying kinesiology. "He started phoning me from Halifax every couple of months," she explained. "Now, it's every second day, usually at night." She had decided to come to see him, but now she was uncertain. "I'd like you to tell me what kind of person he is before I go any further."

Ownie looked away, trying to hide his surprise, trying to keep the questions from slipping to his tongue. How was Turmoil making calls from the trailer in the middle of nowhere? When? What about Lorraine?

"I'm not going to get into what he's all about or what he's not all about." Ownie wondered if *this* was Turmoil's secret. "But I'm looking at you and you look like an intelligent person." Ownie liked the way she stood her ground; he liked the way her crinkly hair was pulled back. "You're an Olympic athlete and that's nothing to be taken lightly." She squinted as though she was figuring out a difficult play. "I'm only going to say one thing to you. Do you have a return ticket back to where you came from?"

"I certainly do, sir."

"Then turn right around and forget you ever saw the guy."

"I was told you would tell me the truth."

"That is the gospel truth."

"Amen."

56

Garth stood in the doorway of Jean's bedroom, braced like a deckhand stepping into an unforgiving gale. It would be weeks, he figured, before she learned about the pay cut, and in the meantime, he wanted to renegotiate his allowance.

"Why would you bring that up?" Jean spat from her bed. "After all I've been through with those pigeons!"

"I just —" Garth started.

"Any other man would have handled them. But no, I'm left here to worry myself sick while you're at that stupid newspaper being demoted!"

Jean was so stupid, Garth reminded himself, that she did not realize that the demotion meant a salary cut. She arrogantly assumed that her life would stay the same. Garth backed off the oriental carpet, wondering how Jean was connecting pigeons with his meagre allowance, fixed and non-indexed at five bucks a week. Five bucks a week was something back in 1974, Garth reasoned, but now it was as insubstantial as vapour, with beer at twelve bucks a case and a lousy sandwich at three dollars. Five bucks through twenty years of inflation and double-digit interest, twenty years of GST, PST, and clawbacks.

"You know I have an appointment with Dr. Zimmer." Jean dropped her voice, exhausted by an undetected ailment. "God knows what he'll find."

Garth made a sympathetic sniff, which was more for himself than Jean, who, once through with Dr. Zimmer, would visit a tanning salon. To save on cab fare, she often accepted a ride home with Harvey, the real estate agent, whose office was in the same building as the salon. When he wasn't wearing his orange blazer, Harvey favoured yellow golf shirts and shiny beige pants. Garth hadn't bought a new shirt in years; he looked as shabby as Albert Conrad in his white Velcro sneakers. Always short of cash, Garth hid whenever someone in the office collected money for a worker who was pregnant or retiring. What could you do with five bucks when model glue was priced at five-fifty a tube and paint at seven dollars? It was twenty-one dollars alone for his Red Baron series.

"Dr. Zimmer says I am an amazing woman the way I am holding up under the stress. If you worked for a decent company like the one Harvey works for . . ." Each word was a crack of the whip driving Garth back into his sanctum of airplane models and faded formations. "If you had something to show for all of these years, you wouldn't need an allowance."

It wasn't just about money, Garth realized, since they had nothing when they married. For the ceremony at city hall, Jean had borrowed a suit from her cousin; her father had worn a plaid shirt with ketchup stains. No, this was payback for something bigger. Was it all of those years of reporter's wages, out-of-town assignments, night shifts, and card games? His obsession with his job? Jean was an unforgiving woman, and he, on every imaginable level, had somehow fallen short.

Hey diddle diddle. Garth cleared his throat and left her room.

He could tolerate his wife's harangues, but that didn't solve his principal problem. Garth needed disposable income, so little by little, over the years, he had learned how to steal. He had started with false receipts for items that went through the *Standard's* petty cash unchecked: twelve bucks for a meal he'd never shared with a staffer, eight bucks for a taxi ride he had never taken to a meeting with advertisers.

After a while, he could count on fifty bucks a week, enough for beer, food, and gloss cote, money that Jean never saw.

When no one noticed, Garth knew that he could do better. That is when he had thought of Helen Anderson, his mother-in-law, who was in a nursing home, diabetic and delusional. Garth had signing authority for Helen, cashing her paltry cheques and paying her bills. Helen's freelance byline started appearing on a regular basis on the Lifestyles pages, where it blended with reams of innocuous drivel. What to do with a cranky cat? Seventy-five bucks. How to select the best apples for pie? Another fifty.

Garth could produce a Helen Anderson submission in ten minutes by pulling a story off the wire and inserting a local, albeit manufactured, quote from someone in the city. Before long, Helen consumed the freelance budget for Lifestyles, her copy blurring into one forgettable bore, the process becoming so easy that, after a while, Garth stopped writing and simply submitted the bills.

57

"Where y'all from?"

Ownie heard the grocery clerk greet an elderly customer.

"We're from Can-a-da." The matron gave each syllable its due.

"Uh-huh, isn't everyone?" The grocery clerk — whose tag identified her as Jeweline — cackled as she packed canned ham, cocktail crackers, and travel-size shampoo in a bag.

"I guess." The old lady smoothed her polyester pants as her pale green top — nine bucks at Manatee Mall — sparkled with vacationing rhinestones. "Sudbury, On-tar-i-o," she added as though that made a difference.

Ownie was sitting on a bench near the exit, waiting for Turmoil, who was storming the aisles in search of broccoli and brown rice.

"My husband had a family from Sudbury last week," said Jeweline. "He drives the Executive Minibus" — she paused for recognition — "to and from the airport. I bet y'all came in on his bus. It's purple with green dolphins, real nice." The old lady nodded numbly as Jeweline rang in Evian water. "Duke drives four to midnight, then delivers flowers until noon. Ten days on, two days off."

"The flowers down here are lovely."

"Uh-huh, honey."

As she bagged a newspaper, Jeweline glanced at the front page, which was sprinkled, for the benefit of snowbirds, with

Canadian content, such as: QUEBEC TOWN SETS A RECORD FOR WORLD'S BIGGEST SNOWMAN. "I'd like to see one of them snowmen," said Jeweline as she rang in coffee filters. "How long he been blind?" The clerk gestured toward the old man clinging to the matron's elbow in ballast-filled shoes.

The old lady looked startled, as though she had been scalded by a sip of tea. As Jeweline rang up the total and waited for an answer, the customer touched her pants, then decided that Jeweline meant no offence. "It's been a gradual thing," she explained. "The last twenty years. Now he has cataracts."

"Nothing they can do for him?" Frowning, Jeweline handed over change.

"No." The snowbird shook her head, white as unbaked meringue.

"Well, you have a nice stay down here." Jeweline squeezed the man's arm. "Y'hear." He nodded in a jaunty skipper's cap. "Just be glad you didn't bring none of that snow with ya. I swear you two can't be from Canada because you both look like movie stars."

Smiling, the couple wobbled by a pyramid of bedpans and Depends. "Lovely day." Ownie nodded.

"It certainly is," the old lady said brightly, then whispered to her blind husband, "I bet he's from Canada."

"Fresh-cooked chicken in our deli." The manager's voice carried over the PA system, drowning out Ownie's thoughts. "Four dollars for a whole mouth-watering chicken. Save yourself the time and trouble of cooking on a hot day. Take home this delicious meal."

Ownie picked up a newspaper and turned to the obituaries out of habit. Mary Carter, 92. Moved to Paradise in 1970. Hiram Tate, Godfrey Jones. They were all the same: 79, 80, 76, originally from Pittsburgh, New York, or Somewhere Else, which is where he wouldn't mind being right now.

Last night, out in that trailer, miles from the comforts of

habit and place, in the same spot where Carlos had been eaten by a lion, Turmoil had charged across the kitchen and stuck his face in Ownie's. "See see that!" Glaring, he pointed to a quarter-sized spot on his cheek. "Thass frossbite!!"

"Too bad." Ownie had shrugged.

"Thass what ah got livin in your country." Turmoil made it sound as though it was Ownie's fault, as though the trainer had voted for six months of winter, for slush and sleet and mind-numbing cold. "Mon, ahm lucky ah didden die up there. Ebbyone with assma, pneumonia, whooping cough. Ah checked, and the avrej temperture is seven degrees, seven degrees widt fog and rain. You cahnt grow nuthin in that."

"That's where I'm from. I'm used to it."

"You could live ten years moh in this weather."

"The old man lived to ninety-four; that's long enough for me."

"Ah tell you what we do." Turmoil lowered his voice, shifting to a tranquil place of soothing sun and endless beaches, a place without frostbite or fog. "Ahll buy you a nice litt'l house where you cahn see the dolphins; you cahn ride your bicycle all year long. Your wife, she cahn come to visit."

He laughed and Ownie felt a chill, realizing that Turmoil had resented, since the day they had met, anyone near him, anyone who had filled the space between them. He had hit both Suey and Scott; he had laughed when Louie had his lights put out. He had melted down when he found Ownie with Jonathon, the hockey player, and now, he was trying to move Ownie *here*, where he'd be alone and at the big man's mercy.

"You see!" Turmoil promised. "Iss the happiest years of your life."

Ownie heard a commotion at the foot of Jeweline's aisle. "I can do it myself," insisted a leathery woman who was arguing with a man in a paper hat. They were fighting, Ownie realized, over who should push the woman's grocery cart. Caught in the crossfire were two loaves of French bread.

"Nooo." The man sounded like Darth Vader. "I *have* to do it."

Unflappable in blue glasses, Jeweline turned away from her register. "Let him help, honey." When the woman released her grip, Ownie watched the man commandeer the cart out the door, trailed by the unhappy owner. He must be eighty, Ownie figured, and he has one of those things — one of those voice boxes — in his throat. Curious, Ownie scanned all of the checkouts, working his way from Express down to Customer Complaints. Christ! All of the checkout boys were seniors, a paper-hatted army of shrunken men with white hair and the clubby, take-charge air of Rotarians. It reminded Ownie of the time that he had walked into an after-hours bar in Boston and discovered that all of the waiters were dwarfs. He'd be damned if he'd end up like this: spending his final years drifting between discount malls, playing shuffleboard, driving a tricycle, never belonging, never having any sense of purpose or place, like a wise guy on witness-protection.

Aisle three looks like Teddy, Ownie decided as the shock wore off, just fatter. Teddy only ran about one-fifty. He and his wife went to Florida one winter. "You know, Ownie, they've got whole trailer towns down there just for seniors. They've got big signs, No KIDS, and if they catch you bringing one in, they'll string you up. How would they feel if they came back here after six months, after everyone had pulled a hellish winter, and they saw a sign with NO OLD PEOPLE? I wonder, Ownie, how would that sit?"

After Ownie and Teddy joined the navy together, they went to Halifax for basic training. Back then, the city was a blur of hammers and drills and destroyer-grey paint. Guns boomed, and the downtown was like a United Nations of merchant seamen: Greeks, Belgians, Danes, everybody keen until the

348

food ran low and the wounded men started coming home, legless reminders that war was real.

At the start, a Norwegian whaling fleet, stranded when the Huns invaded their home, cut the city up pretty good, strapping blond sailors with nothing to do but smile at the girls and eat fish and chips. They looked like they came from a place with light and sun, with their yellow hair and blue eyes. They looked like they ate good food and never got fat. It was all an illusion, the girls discovered too late, since Norway was cold and barren and far away.

Teddy got tinfished in '44. They ran his picture in the Charlottetown paper along with the names and address of his parents. When he returned, he looked nothing like his picture, not after a year in a POW camp, living on bread, nerves, and the odd bowl of skilly. It was the skilly that did it.

When they were kids, Teddy lived at the race track, helping the grooms sweep stalls and roll bandages. One of the trainers, a guy named Flaherty, would give Teddy a carrot to stick in his pocket for his favourite horse. One day, in a moment that Teddy never forgot, Flaherty let the boy jog Flashfire along the outside rail. He gave Teddy the lines and said, in a voice that seemed to possess all the wisdom of the world, "Feel the rhythm of the gait in your arms and shoulders, feel the wind in your hair. Listen to the shoes cracking on the surface." Well, that day, Teddy was Peter Pan and Jackie Robinson rolled into one.

Teddy was skinny as a rail with sores on his feet when they brought him into New York on a troopship. For years, he swore he'd never drive a German car, not after choking on that horse-meat soup. Nowadays, with more wisdom than Ownie seemed to possess, he stayed at home. Teddy said he'd take the cold before he'd end up somewhere he didn't belong. At least he'd know who he was and what he was eating.

Ownie put down his paper as Turmoil rounded the corner.

58

Ownie walked the beach behind Turmoil's mansion, collecting his thoughts. A girl in a Pocahontas bathing suit was panning for seashells, placing each find in a plastic bucket. "Look, Mommy." She waved an empty casing.

"All right, baby!" The mother was power-walking twenty-foot arcs around the girl, hooked to hand weights, too engaged to notice what the child was holding. "Keep it up."

Ownie figured the girl was about four, maybe five years old. When Butch was that age, his mother put him in dresses: frayed sheets of dying flowers with cracked buttons, raggedy hand-me-downs scrubbed bare with lye. "How come he wore a dress?" Ownie asked years later, figuring it was past the statute of limitations.

"He always wore a dress," said his mother, who made it sound matter of fact, like he always liked licorice or dogs, like something Ownie should've known.

"Right," he nodded. "But why?"

"For protection."

The old lady was cheap with words, as though she was handing out dollar bills or favours. What's she saving for? Ownie would wonder. How could *she* be the daughter of a *shanachie,* a man who went from Irish town to town travelling on stories? She was one of those fair, faraway Irish with high cheekbones and small Slavic eyes, the kind of person who would rather cut peat than talk. Maybe if you'd lived, early on, with blarney and supernatural tales about gentle giants named

350

Finn McCool, headless horsemen, and malicious fairies, you got your fill.

"From what?"

"The fairies; they steal boy children if they aren't dressed like girls."

Or maybe the stories of cluricauns and leprechauns went too deep, to an unspeakable part of the melancholy soul, to the same place that harboured Turmoil's spirits, or *jumbies*, forces with power and import that Ownie could not understand.

Ownie remembered rounding the square and seeing Butch, nose bleeding, ginger hair matted, with a rip in his wretched cotton dress. His eyes were drowning in tears, the quick tears of rage. He'd get so mad that you could barely keep him in his skin. The image stuck with Ownie: a four-year-old boy in a raggedy dress stained with red dirt, taking out all the hurt that a four-year-old heart could hold.

Ownie kept walking on the coarse sand behind Turmoil's house, on trampled shells that crunched like macaroni. His mother's answer only went so far. There were five boys in the family. Why just Butch? Had she received a warning? He would have asked her if she hadn't been so tight with words.

"Sit down, Ownie." Turmoil gestured inside the house. "Sit down."

Ownie placed his cap on a round table made of swirling insets of wood. Staring at the swirls until they blurred, Ownie let himself drift to a land of red roads and horse trailers that glistened like gum wrappers, to a farmer leading his black-and-whites to graze. He let himself return to a simpler, more normal place.

"How you like the beach?" Turmoil asked as a cow fixed her punch-drunk eyes on Ownie and mooed.

"Huh?" Ownie hadn't been listening. He looked at Turmoil, who was lounging in a chair with flat arms that stuck out like a sleepwalker. Turmoil swung his leg over one arm, sticking up a sneaker bleached from the sun. Ownie ignored the ill-mannered shoe. It was too bright and modern in Turmoil's big house, too easy. "Uh good," he offered vaguely.

Ownie remembered, during a trip to the PEI countryside, walking on the road's edge where a coating of dust, fallen from Mars, recorded the nighttime wanderings of dogs and raccoons. On both sides of the road, the fields looked like sample cards in a paint store, rectangles ranging from spinach green to tan. Everything was shadowless. Blemish-free, the sky looked like someone had dipped a brush in cerulean blue and covered a gesso surface.

"I saw some dolphins," he added, then looked around the room. He didn't know how he'd missed it; it was so big and so inescapable. On one wall was a portrait of Turmoil in a silver robe, with a palette of blues, pinks, and reds mixed like ice cream, and signed by LeRoy Neiman. The same LeRoy Neiman who had painted Babe Ruth and Ali and was called by some the premier sports artist in the world.

Across the room, Turmoil's TV was playing a tape of a talk show interview with Roy Newton, the WBC champ. Newton was the man whom either Turmoil or Antonio Stokes would face depending on the outcome in Vegas, depending on how well Ownie did his job. The interview had a testy start, with the host, a man named Tony Tennyson, suggesting that Roy hadn't won his last fight. Tennyson rattled off numbers like an auctioneer. CompuBox computer analysis, he claimed, showed Tyler landing 341 punches to Newton's 264, including 180 jabs to 36. "And, Roy, what were you doing in round two, lying on your back?"

"I know I won the fight," said Newton, a simple, slow-talking man. "The good Lord was with me and I know, in my heart, I was the better man that night."

"Was he throwing any punches?" Tennyson smirked. "The Lord?"

Newton gave him a pained look. "No, he was in my heart and my soul. He wasn't mixing it up none."

"Good, good." Tennyson rolled his eyes. "That might be against the rules."

"They call this a plantah chair." Turmoil tapped the arm. "At the end of a hard day, the plantah sit in the chair and put his feet up on these looong ahms. Then the servan come 'long and pull off his boots. Ah need me a servan."

Ownie ignored the implications.

"Iss time we had a talk." Turmoil stood up and started toward Ownie, a storm cloud blocking the sun, a mass of contradictions. Ownie wished the house wasn't so hard and rootless, a hydroponic building with no history or heart. He wished that he could see the sweet pink face on the Pope plate; he wished he could borrow his wisdom and draw from dumb blind faith. He missed Hildred, his house, and his poor little dog.

All this emptiness, Ownie squinted; it felt like a place without boundaries, a place without a conscience. Turmoil slammed his fist on a table, knocking a book to the floor with a crack that echoed off the white walls.

"Mon, you dohn know nuthin 'bout me!" Turmoil stuck his face in Ownie's, so close that Ownie could see broken blood vessels that looked like water-seeking roots. Don't flinch, he told himself, don't flinch.

"Did you see Madonna ringside?" Tennyson asked Roy on TV. "I hear she was there, along with Jack Nicholson."

"I only know one Madonna," Newton mumbled. "The Holy Virgin Mary."

"Ahhh, correct me if I'm wrong." Tennyson mugged. "I don't think we're talking about the same woman. What do you think, Miguel?" Tennyson turned to the bandleader, who shook his head mournfully.

"I know as much as I *want* to know," said Ownie, who believed that people were too quick to spill their guts. He never wanted to know about the medic and his friends; he never wanted to contemplate Greg, Lorraine, or the basketball player with the crinkly hair. "I don't care nothin' about your personal life *or* your hang-ups."

"Who talkin 'bout hang-ups?"

"You, man!"

"No, ahm not." Turmoil seemed enraged.

"So what are you goin' on about then? What's your beef today?"

"Ah juss wanted to tell you something since you're my trainah and all, and you dohn know nuthin 'bout me. You dohn even know that ah nebba fought in no 'lympics."

"What are you talking about?"

"Ah nebba."

In the background, Tennyson rose like he was ready to announce an amazing, if predictably ridiculous, stunt. One week earlier, the show had challenged a Heisman Trophy winner to throw a football from one office tower to another, hitting an open window, twelve floors above a bustling street of traffic. "Do you think you could teach me how to box?" he asked Newton.

"Sure," shrugged Roy. "If you want to."

"Nebba nebba." Turmoil started to laugh, and Ownie, in a paralyzing realization, knew that the fighter was laughing at him: at his unsolvable fractions, his pathetic stable of fighters, his fears about growing old and leaving nothing real behind. "All you white peeple are crazeee. Your lawyers and your bis-nismon."

Tennyson grinned a gap-toothed grin at the camera; Roy responded with a short right jab as solid as a piston. *Vaaarroom.*

A drum rolled as Tennyson toppled backwards, dazed. Another drum roll, *varroom,* as a tooth pierced his lip.

"They order themselves a fightah, but the mon they wahnt he gohn. So a mon come to me and say, 'How would you like to move to Canada?' And ah say, 'Okay, mon,' ah got no job. Ah been sick for a while from spirits and danjurous demons. But the mon — he a wise mon — he know that ah got som'tin special, some powah you peeple dohn understahnd."

"Don't give me that bullshit." Ownie denied it, but, in his heart, he *knew* that nothing had seemed quite right. Not the mouthpiece, the clumsiness with the speed bag, or the trouble with Donnie in the ring. What power? Ownie wanted to know. What demons? The entire crazy story, as improbable as dullahans, was flashing like a slide show through his brain, and he couldn't keep up.

"Juss think, mon, ahm goin to be the next heavyweight champeen of the world," Turmoil spat. "Ah got powahs that no one understahnd. Ah fooled ebbyone, ebbyone, but that bad Suey Simms. He a *jab jan.*"

"He never cared much for you neither." Ownie took a breath, trying to steady himself. He wanted to say something defiant, but the words wouldn't form. The TV had gone to commercial, and when Tennyson returned, Roy wore a pained, puzzled look.

If all of this was true, Ownie struggled with his thoughts, then Turmoil Davies was his greatest achievement, but who would believe it? Did he want to believe it himself, or did it shift things so drastically that his game plan was flawed? Maybe Turmoil wasn't even from Trinidad. Ownie's brain was rushing now, stopping at random questions, all disconnected and likely to prove nothing of value. "Did you ever meet Yolande Pompey?" he heard himself blurt, as though that would settle something, as though the mystery would be solved if Turmoil could tell him something about Pompey, who had been celebrated in Trinidad even after he was knocked out in the tenth round by Archie Moore. "Did you?"

Turmoil laughed as Ownie stared at him stupidly.

"Oh mon, you were so glad to get yourself a big ole fightah. Mon, you wanted it so bad. You wudda done an'ting, even try to hipmotize me. Mon, ah got to tell you, you are one crazy ole mon." Turmoil leaned close. "But dohn worry, mon, ah got ebbyting under control. Ahm takin care of you now, your mind, your future. Ah took some things from your howse, some socks, that balla-rina, and now, mon, ah got the good voodoo workin on you. Is all for the bess."

59

"What you doin?" Turmoil shrieked.

"I'm doing a ghost." Washington, the sparring partner, kept moving across the ring, lifting the blue rope with one mitt, waving off Turmoil with the other. This is done, he signalled, and Ownie, sitting ringside, nodded.

"No, mon, you not!" Turmoil shrieked.

"I did foh." Sweat dripped into the sparring partner's dead eyes, down his bulky neck, onto a Spiderman singlet that smelled like defeat. "That's it, man."

"You only sparred three!"

Washington climbed out of the ring, unbuckling his headgear. A deep ravine ran above his nose; razor-scarred lids were falling on the outer wings of his eyes, heavy and foreboding, like an early curtain.

"Get back in," Turmoil ordered. "Get, get, get!"

Confusion flooded Washington's face, but he kept moving, driven by something deep and primal, something that told him he couldn't stop now. A half-hearted goatee sputtered on his chin. "Fuck you, mutha!" Washington exploded, the rage of four generations purified and ignited by junk. "I say, Fuck you!"

Outside Boomerang's gym, nature's lights had dimmed, Ownie noted with an uneasiness that had been growing. Sonny had turned on a radio, which was carrying a weather warning: a hurricane was ripping up the coast, closing in. Maybe it will clear the air, Ownie hoped, make it easier to breathe, easier to live with all this craziness and noise. Turmoil turned ringside to Greg who, being an idiot, signalled back three rounds. Ownie cursed.

"No way, man," Washington shook his head, knowing he was right. On one shoulder, above a skull-and-crossbones tattoo, was a scar the colour of ham. "Don't you go making me have to prove my point, muthafuckas."

"Pay the man for four," Ownie instructed Turmoil. "If you're not happy, report him to the Better Business Bureau."

Ownie tried to sound offhand, and Washington nodded, relieved. Despite the dope and his own failed career, Washington had been useful, so why was Turmoil challenging him, pushing a guy who was barely, by a thread of pride and memory, hanging on?

"You gettin threee rounds." Turmoil tapped his glove three times. "And thass it."

"Foh." Washington was stripping.

"Three!" Another tap.

"Foh. And I had enough of your bitch talk. Your mouth is too big, man, and I want what's coming to me! I earned it."

The rain had started, great sheets of water driven sideways by a wind that had come from nowhere, bearing furniture and peril. A lawn chair flew past the gym, then a cardboard box and a road sign. In ten minutes, the ocean had gone from blue-green to angry grey. Whitecaps hurled themselves forward like slam dancers, rabid foam lined the beach. Nature's colour tube had been pulled, leaving only black and white.

WHAT SHALL IT PROFIT A MAN, IF HE GAIN THE WHOLE WORLD AND LOSE HIS OWN SOUL? ST. MARK CHAP. 8, V. 36.

Opening the gym door, Washington pushed his way through the wind to an elongated car with smoked windows and dalmatian seat covers. Inside, Ownie could see the driver rocking back and forth like he had a toothache, a third form huddled in the back. If I get out of this alive, I'll take up golf,

Ownie vowed, just like Joe Louis. I'll keep this whole crazy story to myself and live a quiet life like Dew Drop when he finished roaming. He found a house in the country, a woman, and never once spoke of the past, never felt the desire to spill family secrets that no one needed to hear.

What was truth anyway, Ownie reminded himself, how many versions of life — laundered, censored, or rewritten for survival — existed in people's minds?

"Don't go out there." Sonny pointed at the car.

If you play golf, Ownie decided, you don't have to deal with fools like this, telling you they stole a china ballerina from your house — the house you lived in for thirty years — and put the voodoo on you. How could he, a man who barely understood fairies and sheep-stealing ghosts, deal with voodoo and zombies, with spells and hexes and poisonous secretions?

"This is serious shit," warned Sonny. "Those maggots had a shootout with the cops last month. One guy took a bullet to the hip." Exhilaration was creeping into Sonny's voice. "When they're on the pipe, they don't care about nothing, they got Saturday night specials, they got . . ."

Ownie waited for Sonny to finish, for the part about the gang war and the armour-piercing bullets, the dead grandma, and the howling dog. Ownie waited for Sonny's danger-induced rush to end, then asked, "Could you have told me this a little sooner?"

Bent trees were dusting the sidewalk while sheets of lightning lit the horizon, groundstrokes of one hundred million volts. Water swept the road like a massive carwash, and a bicycle hurtled by, doing spastic cartwheels.

REVELATION 16:16

Just stay cool, Ownie thought, and deal with this situation. So what if Turmoil says he wasn't at the Olympics? He also said he played pro hockey and was a professional hairstylist. But if this is true, it means *you* made him something, *you*

359

made it work, not voodoo or magic. You can still take him into that fight with Stokes, you can still be a part of something great, something that Charley Goldman, if he were alive, might admire.

"He bedda not think he ever gettin 'nuther cent from me." Turmoil cast the warning at the door. "Ahm thru widt fools like that. Ahm thru."

Just shut up, Ownie thought, as Washington's car eased into the storm. Just let me get through this life without seeing another set of dead eyes, another corpse laid out too soon. The war was bad enough, but then he had to be in Montreal when they carried out Cleveland Denny, he had to be on the waterfront when his buddy Aubrey Mills was crushed by a paper bale on his first stevedoring shift.

"Peewee, get down." Sonny pushed the kid under the table.

A piece of siding flew by on wings of sand as a shock wave of thunder boomed. Sonny unhooked a heavy bag and rolled it over, a sandbag for Peewee's makeshift bunker. Oh Jesus, Ownie thought, looking at the kid, he's going to end up like that little homeboy, Murray, dead and barely missed.

"I'm gonna try to get him out of here." Sonny, drawing on his military training, had the manoeuvre planned. "If those guys come back with reinforcements, and I expect they will, he could get it."

THERE IS NONE OTHER THAN THE HOUSE OF GOD, AND THIS IS THE GATE OF HEAVEN. GENESIS CHAP. 28, V. 17.

Sonny had turned up the radio, which was relaying storm updates. Stay off the roads, warned an announcer, who said a bridge had been wiped out and the airport highway closed by forty-mile-per-hour winds. A Japanese tourist videotaping the storm had been killed by the spar of a boat.

"It's too late," said Sonny as the car returned, driver in the gangsta lean.

"You cowards wahn me, you stan up like a mon." Turmoil

charged through the door as thunder roared an ear-splitting clap. The dented door blew off its hinges, inviting the chaos inside. "There no mon down here scarin me; there's no mon ever lived who scare me." Through the wind, Turmoil struggled, arms outstretched, head back like a runner crossing the finish line. A bench flipped at his feet, landing on an advertisement for CARING HANDS, THE MEDICAL CLINIC FOR CANADIANS while Sonny pinned Peewee to the floor.

"Nobody scare me." Turmoil's voice wailed. "Ahm scared of nobody." The wind scrambled Turmoil's words and lightning flashed about him, forked bolts of doom that heated the air to fifty thousand degrees.

"When ah was a boy, a powahful bolt of lightnin strike me down. Ah be standin under the pimento tree holdin mah mongoose. The lightnin kill the mongoose, but the powah go from the lightnin to *me*, and ah know right there, it's a contrack with the Gods, mah mongoose for the powah. So now ah *cahnt* be killed." His voice had reached a mad pitch. "Ah cahnt die, mon, because ahm sign'd up widt God, he own me, lock, stock, and barrel."

60

Smithers shuffled through News brandishing a magazine. "Now someone's onto something here," he read, louder than necessary. "Genetic altering and selective breeding have created turkeys with breasts so *large* that it is almost impossible for them to mate in the traditional way. Imagine the *human* ramifications."

BAM! An angry Gouda round shot through the air, hitting Smithers's libidinous head. "Aaah." The hockey reporter dropped to the carpet, where he felt for blood, checking his hands like a street mime and moaning, "That is assault! There's a dangerous criminal in here!"

Scott didn't care about Smithers or the overdue cheese attack, which may have come from Books. He was sitting at his desk with Ownie, sorting through a pile of Florida pictures, forming a visual timeline to the catastrophic end. Outside, snow was falling from the grey sky, burying hope, light, and the hapless tulips that had reared their heads. Children shivered in spring coats, shut-ins turned up the heat.

"I talked to the state police this morning," said Scott, scanning his notes. "An Officer Petrie says they still don't have a suspect." A collective sigh rose from the street, then fell under the weight of resignation. "They said Washington checked out."

Ownie nodded in his army surplus jacket, hands folded, stilled by truth. When you get into the fast lane, he decided, it was only a matter of time before everything shattered in a wreck of big dreams and easy money. Ownie had not repeated the improbable story Turmoil had told him in Florida, the one about the Olympics. What difference did it make at this point?

"They talked to me for four hours before I left," Ownie explained. "They asked me if I knew anyone who might want to kill him." Ownie smiled a joyless smile. "'Other than me?' I asked."

In the distance, Scott saw MacKenzie approaching Sports, green sweater inside out. His face was flushed and his eyes were uncertain behind his glasses. He's probably looking for Smithers, Scott assured himself; following his outburst, the hockey reporter had waddled to his desk where he now sat, subdued.

MacKenzie was rubbing his thumb and fingers together like he was trying to start a fire. He ignored Smithers and stopped in front of Scott. What does he want? Scott wondered, annoyed, as MacKenzie wobbled, stomach stuck out, butt collapsed like a dented football.

"This is Garth MacKenzie, the paper's senior editor." Scott felt compelled to make the introduction. "This is Ownie Flanagan, the boxing trainer."

"Ownie Flanagan." MacKenzie held out the same hand he had extended to Frank Mobley. "You've been around the fight game for a long time."

Scott hoped that MacKenzie would not, in the midst of something grave, bring up School Boy.

"Sixty years."

"What are you here for today?"

"We're talking about Turmoil Davies," Scott interrupted.

The two men were less than ten years apart in age, Scott realized, but they had nothing in common. MacKenzie, the younger of the two, seemed far older, trapped in a boozy haze of stand-up bars and levees, guys with press hats and cigars.

Retirement parties with Swedish meatballs and fruit salads made with marshmallows. He was one of those people, Scott realized, who had so embodied and so embraced his generation that he could never transcend it.

"I never saw Davies fight." MacKenzie was bombed, Scott realized. "But I'll give you my opinion. He reminds me of a great fighter I once saw, Johnny Jacobs, a super fighter with a dandy left hand. I covered him at the Forum when he faced Ricky Roper."

"Yes, Johnny Jacobs was a good fighter," Ownie agreed flatly. "An 'A' fighter, we'd call him. He fought some of the best in the world."

"How long do you think Davies would have lasted against Jacobs?"

Why get into this now? Ownie thought. What did it matter? He had no time for talk like this, especially from a man with liquor in him. "I couldn't say." Ownie narrowed his eyes.

Turmoil was dead, gunned down outside Boomerang's Gym, which, despite all of its devotion and faith, had not been able save him. The bullet had ripped through his rib cage and landed in a lung. Like the sweet nurse from Virginia, Sonny held Turmoil's head in his bumpy pink arms, telling him not to quit while Peewee phoned for help. As Turmoil struggled, Sonny prayed: "'Even when I walk through a dark valley, I fear no harm for you are at my side,'" over and over again. When the ambulance arrived in a blur of fear and confusion, Peewee was shivering, and Sonny's arms were crimson.

"I don't think Davies would have lasted a round." MacKenzie ignored the unspoken warning.

Ownie twisted his hat in his hands. Ownie had felt the stunned silence after Turmoil's death, the numbness. And then there were the questions from people who did not understand who you were or where you came from, people who expected you to defend it or explain it, as though something like that had a logical explanation.

"That's your opinion."

Ownie kept his head down, wise to birds like this. They'd missed the war by a few years but sucked up all of the rewards: the cushy jobs, the indexed pensions, and thirty-five hour weeks. They never had to wash a man's blood off their clothes; they never had to beg, in the depths of the Depression, for food. They had never stood on a Halifax pier and watched the *Lady Nelson* dock with a cargo of five hundred men, some in wounded stripes, some without arms or legs, young men in hospital blues crowding the rails, waving, men cut down by snipers, land mines, and mortars. They'd never searched the deck of a merchant ship for a boy named Butch with ginger hair.

"Who else did you train?"

Big phony four-flusher! Ownie decided. Like the birds who got rich during the war by gouging military families, the same people who had closed the Ajax Club and put up signs No Dogs or Sailors, and then wondered why the sailors went rabid on V-E Day. Ownie pursed his lips. "Well, Tommy Coogan . . ."

"Kid Coogan." MacKenzie snorted. "I saw him in the Derby twenty years ago and he could barely talk."

"Tommy was a very shy man."

"Shy?" MacKenzie snickered.

"He didn't particularly care for strangers."

"I'd call it punch drunk."

Scott dropped his eyes and wondered why MacKenzie, threatened, and emasculated by his own weak will, was choosing *this* moment to take *this* stand. He looked at the editor, whose eyes were vacant.

Garth had scorned the aged, the infirmed, and the afflicted, fearing, it seemed, to see himself in them. Their obsolescence, their weakness. He hated the nursing home, he despised the armless woman from the library, he mocked Albert Conrad. That indiscriminate loathing made him feel both safe and superior, and now Ownie was in his newsroom — Garth was panicking — this wise guy from the wrong side of town who didn't give a damn about anything Garth thought.

Ownie picked up his coat and started to rise. He was here as a favour to Scott, who had given them good press and had, after all, been knocked out by Turmoil, but he didn't have to tolerate this. Stay calm, he told himself. Don't let this bastard get the best of you.

"I just realized, Scott, I've got an appointment."

Scott nodded. And Ownie felt like he could cry, thinking of Tommy and his little boy and his broken wife and his bad nerves and all those death-dance fights. He didn't want to be reminded, not today, not with everything else he was carrying in his head, not by this drunken bastard!

"Call me if you need something." Ownie waved to Scott.

As MacKenzie clutched the trainer's shoulder and said, as though he had a right, as though his grand house in the South End and his fading position had entitled him — "I'm not finished with you" — Ownie drove his left fist, the one with the dented knuckles, the one that cracked Pinky Parker's jaw in round two, into the editor's slack face. *THUMP!* The force of the blow, which came from down low, sent MacKenzie tumbling backwards. *THUMP!* Straight from the crouch, a good one for Tommy.

MacKenzie's bifocals flew off, hitting a desk, as he crashed onto a swivel chair and slid to the floor. His leg caught a phone cord, toppling the green machine. Someone gasped as blood trickled out to a dial tone.

The senior editor started to move. "You want more?" Ownie held his fist in MacKenzie's face. "Just get up off that floor." Ownie picked up his pictures, nodded at Scott, and

366

walked to the elevator. He pushed the down button without signing out, and nobody tried to stop him.

It was all over, realized Scott, as he watched the elevator door close, as he looked at his quotes from Officer Petrie. Turmoil Davies had possessed the gifts, the God-given qualities that Scott had coveted, the magic, the exquisite, breathtaking *it*, and he was dead. Why, Scott wondered, did I think that life was supposed to be fair? Why did I think that *I* had been cheated?

And then, as an afterthought, he looked at Garth MacKenzie, drunk and bleeding, still on the floor, hours before he would stagger back into the *Standard* and set fire to the Accounting department.

Epilogue

Johnny LeBlanc climbed two flights of creaking stairs. He leaned into a door. Tootsy's still smelled musty, he decided, as though it was shaking off dust and depression. Laminated newspaper clippings were tacked to the wall.

> TURMOIL DAVIES DIES IN FLORIDA
> HEAVYWEIGHT CONTENDER GOT HIS START IN HALIFAX

To the left, displayed with equal prominence, was the prize-winning photo of Louie unconscious in the ring, mouth open, as lifeless as a harpooned tuna.

"Hey," said Louie as soon as Johnny sat down. "Let's work the ball."

Johnny struggled to his feet with a sigh. Turmoil was gone, but the essence was the same, here in this shabby sanctuary built on hope, pain, and the promise of salvation. Johnny had laughed when he heard about Ownie nailing MacKenzie, and somehow that punch, landed in front of an entire newsroom, recorded on a surveillance camera, added an outlandish footnote to Turmoil's tragic tale. It was better, everyone decided, to talk about *that* instead of Turmoil's passing, which had been as abrupt and dreamlike as his arrival in the city.

"Did he go straight down?" Johnny had asked Ownie.

"Like an anchor." Ownie had shrugged.

Thump.

Johnny checked the glove-shaped clock and noticed that Tootsy had added pictures on one wall, all black and white, some the colour of tea stains. He recognized a few from Ownie's basement: Tommy Coogan posing with a lion in South Africa, Thirsty at a restaurant table with Ownie, Butch with golf balls under his eyes.

Thump.

Louie was wearing a T-shirt with Marciano's face silk-screened on his chest.

Thump.

Ownie was working with little Ricky, who had grown five inches. Ricky's body had become confused by the growth spurt, which had left him with gangly limbs, an unfamiliar nose, and adolescent acne. His brother, a wannabe who claimed he'd been shot in one leg, resulting in a badass limp, had been arrested for stealing a car, but the kid was still straight.

Ownie spent ten minutes on balance, getting Ricky's feet properly positioned, the right distance apart. "It's the foundation for everything." Now the trainer was showing him, step by step, how to throw a complete combo to the head. The left jab followed by a right cross and the left hook. One, two, three.

"You'll catch onto it," Ownie assured him. "Just practise." Ricky nodded.

Johnny heard stomping on the stairs. The door swung open.

"Is this the best you can do?" Butch barked accusingly.

"It's better than some of the dumps you trained in." Ownie turned around.

Two steps behind his brother was Suey Simms, who, after catching up and settling into a chair, urged Butch, "Take your coat off, brother, and stay a while." Butch removed a thick knit sweater and a salt-and-pepper cap. He eyed the gym suspiciously.

Louie dropped the ball and moved across the room.

"How would you like to go a round with a senior citizen?" Ownie asked Louie. "That man there is so old that you can hear him dying."

Louie blinked and nodded no.

Slowly, Butch walked over to the heavy bag and instinctively took two shots. *Boom. Boom.* It was the first thing you did in a gym. Some trainers liked their fighters to work on heavier bags, he remembered, some preferred the lighter ones. Butch went into a crouch and threw a barrage of punches, combos to show that his timing was good.

"You can still shoeshine, Butch," Suey decided. "You can shoeshine."

Butch squared himself in front of the speed bag and tapped a little tune. Every tap was a note: a slow march from the poor streets, a jig into the Garden. If he wanted to, he could, after all of these years, hear Lou Stillman yelling insults across his gym, he could see the doorman collecting fifteen cents, and he could feel himself sitting on a bench, face coated with Vaseline, waiting his turn to climb into ring number two. In the air was cigarette smoke, a mist of sweat, and nerves. "Slip and slide baby, slip and slide."

Ownie watched Butch and nodded.

When Butch was eight, Ownie took him into a dressing room where an old sock-peddler, a preacher when he wasn't in the ring, was sitting on a bench reading a Bible. Looking up, the preacher fixed his eyes on Butch and drawled, "My oh my, you're just a little schoolboy. Does your mama know you're here?"

Butch and another schoolboy were supposed to go four rounds before the fights started. The preacher said he'd go in Butch's corner for free. It was cold that night; they must have been out of coal, and a longshoreman was coated with foul-smelling fertilizer that stung Ownie's eyes. There was moonshine, and horse pictures on the walls, and everyone was talking about a ruckus on the waterfront that morning. While hoisting up a steer in a sling, something had shifted and the animal had plunged over the side.

In those days, the kids didn't get paid; the crowd threw change in the ring. "Look busy," the preacher urged Butch. "The better the show, the more they throw."

The room was filled with hawking men on crates and wooden chairs. "Hey, mama's boy," one taunted. "Where's your titty bottle?"

In the first round, Butch danced around, afraid he'd be hurt, and then the preacher told him: "Man, you're as fast as a wingbird. Ain't nobody goin' to hit you," and the words sounded good.

Butch and the other schoolboy split four bucks, maybe five, after they counted the pennies and dimes, enough for some grub, enough to fill them up. When Butch came home that night, Ownie remembered, their mother never said a word.

"You know, Butch," Suey said. "I still think Percy won most of them fights."

Finished with the bag, Butch rolled across the hardwood floor, past the dusty crosses, past a photo of Turmoil triumphant in a Halifax ring. Butch's nose was flat, the area around his eyes looked like an old stuffed sock. It was all the same, Ownie decided, it was all the same.

"That kid there." Butch pointed at Ricky, who stiffened, not knowing what to expect. "He looks like he's made of something. Like he could go somewhere."

"Solid gold, brother." Ownie made it sound as certain as anything in life.

Ricky lowered his head and smiled.

Here are the old names I picked out of the papers. My favourites are Ransom for a man and Fairy for a woman. Ivy Delight had a nice ring, along with Princetta. I didn't find any starting with X or Y, and just one K. I noted that many of the women's names ended with A.

Your father.
Ada, sister of Ida
Adelbert
Adret, mother of Vernetta,
    Raya, and Tahirah
Albina
Alfretta
Alma, sister of Burns
Alonza
Alonzo
Aloysius
Alpha
Alpheus
Althena
Alvil
Ambrose
Amedee
Amilene
Ancil
Annison, father of Enos
Annora
Arabella
Ardeth
Ardis
Arizonia
Artamus
Arvilla
Arzelie
Asa
Aseph
Audley
Auldon, brother of Mercie
    and Lovitt
Avelena
Aveling
Avonne
Avora, sister of Rhea, Lela,
    Phebe, and Willoughby
Azade
Beda
Bent, father of Eudora
Bernetta
Beryl
Beulah
Bowman
Brenna
Bryson
Budia
Burnett
Burnley

Byrnus
Cantley, brother of Arvilla
and Fielding
Chestena
Cloe
Clotilda
Colena
Corrilda
Delle
Delma
Delmer
Delphina, sister of Elta
and Melda
Demmick
Denson
Dimerize
Dimock
Dolena
Donelda, sister of Guilford
Doran, brother of Elva and
Meda
Dorette
Dorina
Drucella
Easterby
Eben, brother of Spurgeon
Eckhardth
Eden
Effie
Egon
Elbridge
Elden
Eldena

Eldibert
Eldora
Electa
Eleda, sister of Nina and
Roxella
Eli
Eliam
Elisha
Eliza
Ellard
Elliwishes
Elmor
Elva
Emelda
Emery
Emiline, mother of Electa
Enos, brother of Amos
Ensley
Erdine
Erema Flo Ella
Ervina
Esau
Estella, daughter of Elisha,
sister of Elta
Ettrick
Euphemia
Evelina
Everine
Ezekiel, husband of Radie
Fairy
Fenwick
Fielding
Firmin

Flavian

Flossy, sister of Daisy and
  Fowness

Ford, husband of Minerva

Garnetta

Gezina

Gideon

Glenola

Gonzo

Grampian Bella

Hance

Handley, husband of
  Melitta, son of Amos and
  Linnie, brother of Mamie
  and Goldie

Harlen Elvert

Harmia

Havelock, husband of
  Orien, predeceased by
  first wife, Gezina

Hennessey

Hezekiah

Hibbutt

Holgar

Horatio

Hulda

Hulga

Idaline

Idella

Ilean

Imogene

Ina

Inez

Iola

Iona, sister of Vergie, wife
  of Orville

Ivor

Ivy Delight, sister of Ancie
  and Opal, wife of
  Cannice

Jacinth

Janetta

Jeromia

Johnena

Jovita

Kelton

Laliah, sister of Alvah

Lavin

Lavinia

Lawney

Leander

Leila

Lemuel

Leontine

Leoro

Leota

Leoutrah

Lermoa

Leta, sister of Laurena

Lexena

Lezin

Liah

Lillias

Locklin

Lomer

Lorena, daughter of
  Beulah

Lorinda

Lottie
Lovitt
Luelle
Lyda
Lylla, daughter of Lyman
Lyman
Mabelle
Mafalda
Maisie
Manetta
Manley
Marcella
Marcellin
Maritta
Marvel
Mayford
Mayola
Meda
Medley
Mehetabel
Melba
Melda
Melitha
Melzena
Mercie
Merdina
Meta
Minna
Moody
Moya
Moyle
Murdena
Murna
Muroye

Myrna
Nedra
Nema, sister of Nonie,
   Ardith, and Nan
Nettie
Neva
Nona
Nuala
Oda Belle
Olena
Ona
Oneita
Ora Generva, sister of
   Kelton
Oran
Orellia
Orien
Orinda
Orlea
Ormal
Orphima
Orris
Parmenas
Parmilla
Pemmiuphy
Perley
Phares
Pharonie
Philson
Princetta
Prior
Proctor
Queenie
Raeburn

Ransom, son of Odessa
Rathbone
Relief
Remegius
Retha
Roblin
Roboam
Rosamond
Rosella, sister of Angel
Roswell
Rowena
Rowlin
Rustin
Sedella
Seretha
Seth
Seward
Silvanus
Spurgeon
Stairs
Stricklen
Suther
Sylvan
Teemis
Thursa
Tressa
Treva
Truth

Tuddyd
Ula
Ulric
Uriah
Vally
Vanetta
Venette
Verner
Vernetta, sister of Hulga,
    Locklin, and Moyle
Verona, daughter of Addie
Vesta
Vida
Vina
Viola, sister of Elva
Volney
Wanetta
Wilda
Willard Bazel
Williamina
Woodbury
Wynn
Zachariah, father of Titus,
    Judson, and Hosea
Zena
Zillah
Zita

Not old, but worth chucking at you:
Pussy, Rango, Chicks, Huck, Skippy, Tootsie, Scruffy, Doll,
Checker, Dooks, Ebb, Duff, Snorky, Dancie, Bun, Goose, and
the brothers Spud, Babe, Sunny, Bub, and Lol.